To the amazing dr ~~~~~ Eva...

Haverca__

Enjoy L ~

Fortune Favours the Brave
Virtutis Fortuna Comes

Steve Ellis

xxx

Published by
Media|Able Ltd
Chairose Dale
Longtye Drive
Chestfield
Kent
CT5 3NG
United Kingdom
mediaable@gmail.com

This book is a work of fiction. Except where historical fact as known during the period of its setting, any resemblance to actual persons, living or dead, is purely coincidental.

A CIP catalogue record for this book is available from the British Library.

ISBN 978-1-326-99565-2

To the generation of Olivia, Leo, Sofia, Luca, Finley and Lucas. *and Eve!*

You can't change history. You can help make it.

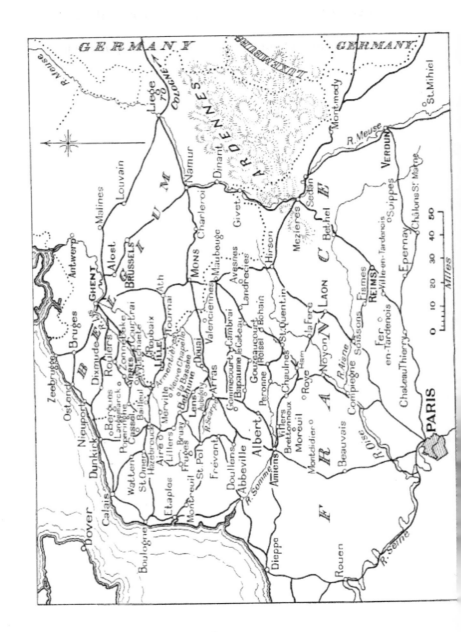

iv

PREFACE

This novel tells of one soldier's struggle for survival during World War I.

Alongside life as a rifleman sent to the front in France, it reveals his innermost feelings about the death of friends, the girl he left behind, battle-field carnage, courage and cowardice. It also captures many of the war's key historic characters, battles and events.

Havercake Lad Samuel Ogden joined the Army three years before Britain entered the conflict on 4th August 1914. Samuel is fictional. But the activities of the 2nd Battalion of The Duke of Wellington's Regiment, in which he serves, are based on official Army records. Many of the names used are those of officers and men who served in the Dukes between 1914 - 1918. They became heroes: ordinary men made exceptional by the circumstances in which they found themselves.

The scale of suffering caused by World War I was immense, almost beyond measure and comprehension, then and now. Over 65 million men mobilized. More than half died or suffered injury. Nearly eight million taken prisoner. Between six and seven million civilians perished. In the British Army, around 36 out of every 100 fighting men suffered a recorded injury; nearly 13 out of 100 died. Front line infantrymen and aircraftmen suffered a higher death rate. Over 250,000 lost limbs. Millions, soldiers and civilians, suffered psychological trauma for many years, often for the rest of their lives.

To many now, over 100 years later, the war seemed a pointless fight between trenches on mud-soaked shell-holed no-man's-land. The major battles of Passchendaele, Somme, Verdun and Ypres are icons of war, alongside the failure of the Allies at Gallipoli and the triumph of Lawrence of Arabia. Monochrome pictures of men with rifles scrambling 'over the top' to be shot dominate our thoughts of the conflict: a cliché image, etched in our consciousness. Through today's lens, we look back and see weak political and military leadership, resulting in death and suffering on a scale hitherto unknown for no discernible gain. But travel back to 1914.

Kaiser Wilhelm II wanted Germany to become a world power, if not *the* world power. His ambition could only be achieved if France and Britain, and their overseas territories, fell under the German Empire's yoke. Since becoming 'Emperor' in 1888, Wilhelm II dramatically expanded his military might. Krupp became the biggest arms manufacturer in the world. Germany's Army grew to the largest in Europe. Its naval fleet developed to rival Britain's Royal Navy, then twice the size of any other.

If World War II was a 'just' war, the right response to stop Adolf Hitler's domination, efforts to stop the Kaiser share the same moral ground. Soldiers, sailors and aircrews did not die in vain. The sacrifices of men, women and children supporting the war effort in Civvy Street were not futile. They had purpose: to stop tyranny, stay safe, maintain independence. Belgium, nor France, nor Russia, nor Britain wanted the Kaiser's Army marching through their territory any more than Hitler's jackboots.

The Great War was the first industrial-scale war and dwarfed all previous conflicts. It set the geopolitical template for the twentieth century. The outcomes it produced remain with us today. Borders changed across Europe. It fuelled revolution in Russia. The Ottoman Empire was defeated encouraging Arab nationalism. It created or reshaped successor states such as Iraq, Jordan, Lebanon and Syria. In 1917 commitment to a Jewish national home in Palestine was made by Britain: the Balfour Declaration formed the basis of the mandate leading to the state of Israel, albeit 31 years later. It facilitated the growth of American militarism and involvement outside its own continent.

Many politicians, economists and historians believe the harsh treatment of post-World War I Germany, the reparations Germans were forced to concede, fuelled resentment that allowed Adolf Hitler's National Socialists to flourish. His many tirades against the 1919 Versailles Peace Settlement, alongside his anti-Semitism and anti-Marxism rants, fell on impoverished Germans like dry seed on damp soil.

***

In fiction, our Samuel Ogden could have fought Adolf Hitler. Both were at Ypres and Passchendaele, one in my imagination, the other in fact. Hitler was twice injured and once, in 1918, temporarily blinded in a mustard-gas attack. With billions of bullets and millions of bombs exchanged, it's tempting to imagine how today's world would be different if one had killed Hitler.

Could a bullet from Private Samuel Ogden's rifle have prevented World War II? Did a young soldier in the Dukes literally miss Hitler's head by a hair's-breadth?

Havercake Lad is the story of one man, and his regiment's war. It also strives to record many of the major events of World War I: history in a novel. Using contemporaneous sources, every effort has been made to describe these accurately. Post-war revelations, revisionism, rationalisation and hindsight have been avoided - as far as it is possible to eliminate 'interference' from all that has since come to light. Imagine yourself reading this book during the war itself, as Samuel recorded his thoughts, feelings and actions. The knowledge, language and attitudes of the time run throughout the storyline. The narrative also reflects his development and increasing understanding of life, love and loss as the war rages and tragedies unfold.

Samuel could not benefit from over 100 years of reflection and remembrance. And, frankly, there is no evidence that contemporary analysis or conflict resolution is any better now than in 1914: witness the wars around the world since 1918. One lesson of history is that we never learn from it. Bombs and bullets remain the basic tools of conflict; borders and barriers the main means of division.

***

It's time to explain the book's title, *Havercake Lad*.

Havercake is a simple oatmeal flatbread. For hundreds of years it was eaten regularly throughout northern England, especially the counties of Cumbria, Durham and Yorkshire.

'Havercake, lads' became the cry of recruiting sergeants during the 1700s enticing men to become soldiers. They impaled havercakes on their swords or bayonets and, with the weapon aloft, roamed through towns and villages inviting men to enjoy a piece. The bread became a banner, a symbol of recruitment. To poor and perhaps hungry lads at that time this basic bread acted as bait. Once attention had been gained, the sergeants coaxed their prey to serve King and Country. If a young man succumbed and accepted the King's Shilling, he committed himself in law to serve in the Army for at least three years 'or the duration', should Britain go to war.

The practice died out long before Samuel Ogden volunteered to join the Army, but the nickname stuck to soldiers of The Duke of Wellington's Regiment. Many 'Dukes of Boots' came from the Yorkshire town of Halifax and its surrounding villages and hamlets on the Pennine Hills.

Steve Ellis
July 2017

CHAPTER 1

1914
FRANCE

Thomas gazed at the empty page, his mind as blank as the paper. He could not think of anything to write after Dear Mother. Well, nothing new. But duty called, a son's obligation. Father said letters to Mother signified the difference between life and death. Their arrival confirmed he had breath in his body, life in his limbs. That's all she needed to know. If a letter failed to drop onto the doormat after a week or so, her chronic concern turned to acute anxiety. The weight of worry grew heavier. Even a simple field-service postcard would bring relief, although all it said was 'I am quite well'. Still, she fretted about the meaning of 'quite'.

He heard the lieutenant say long letters always start with one short word. Just start. Then put one word after another. Thomas started and, as usual, mentioned how many Woodbines he'd smoked. And the rats. Always 'as big as cats' he'd say because everyone said it, although really only kitten-size. He'd grouse about the ever-present lice and, however many chats he squeezed between his filthy fingernails, or whatever powder promised to rid his body of these irritating bugs, their infestation persisted.

Alongside his fellow infantrymen, Thomas became convinced the rum was being watered down as the war went on. Maybe he was growing tolerant to it. More likely, because the nights in northern France grew colder, thick rum's warming qualities failed to be as long-lasting as they had on those sultry summer evenings. To reassure Mother there was not wholesale drunkenness at the front - she supported the chapel's temperance movement - Thomas stressed an officer was always present at stand-down when the rum is issued. This was the procedure laid down in Standing Orders. The ration also had to be drunk immediately after the sergeant poured it into a mug. Your tot couldn't be shared or squirreled away for a swig at your own leisure. Some chaps held out their mess tin tops thinking they'd

1

receive a more generous helping. But sergeants knew all the tricks and poured the same measure whatever the vessel, or so they said.

Thomas never wrote about serious matters. Few of us do, not to our mothers. They worry. Each letter is read by an officer before being sealed and despatched by the Field Post Office. If we mention locations, troop movements, weaponry or casualties, a lieutenant's thick dark blue crayon obliterates the offending word or phrase. Nor did Thomas express his innermost feelings or fears. Few do, to anyone. Such thoughts should not be shared. Those of us with sweethearts, and the married men, can request an Honour Envelope. We are promised these intimate letters are read only by officers in London at the new General Post Office in Regent's Park. But I would never commit all my feelings to paper, especially about Alice, even if the censor lived in Timbuktu.

I'll never understand why Thomas stood stretching his legs and arching his back. Before I could shout 'Get down!' half his head had blown away. He failed to remember the golden rule of trench life: keep below the parapet. As a rifleman, he knew snipers only need an inch of head to place a bullet in the brain. Thomas forgot one rule for one second and was dead for ever.

That night, after they laid my friend's body on an old hay cart and the horse pulled away, I finished Tom's letter. I wrote to Mrs Bailey that Thomas had died bravely for King and Country. It was true. He had. I wiped the splat of blood off the page and hoped his mother, who ran our village bakery, would think it was a smudge of mud. After posting the letter I remembered in horror that, with my colour blindness, I confused reds with browns, especially in poor light. I'd completed the letter in the dim glow of a single candle flickering in a draughty dugout. To my eternal shame, I realised his mother would see the red blood of her son, not the brown earth of some foreign field.

***

It's quiet now, thank... I was going to say God. But you can't thank God for living in Hell. The guns are silent, though there is no peace. When it's quiet, the ringing in my ears gets louder. Our medical orderly calls it something like 'tins', although I couldn't catch the whole word. I don't know how long I'll be able to write my notes. I may have to stop mid-sentence, even mid-word. Nobody tells you when you're going to die. At least the condemned man has an appointment with death. We don't. A bullet or bomb could strike any moment. They do. Day, night, usually in barrages. Occasionally a lone shell bags a few chaps, sometimes a sniper's single shot does for one. Death is to be expected in war, but it still comes as a surprise. Already many of my friends have copped it, lads I've known all my life from the village, such as Thomas Bailey.

Even if I survive tonight I don't know whether I'll be able to carry on writing. My notebook is soaked, pages fall out, my pencil short, the lead stubby. Even a well-honed bayonet can't sharpen a pencil to a fine point. My clasp knife usually does the job. But that's lost in mud somewhere on the road along with the rest of my kit. A shell blew our supply wagon to smithereens. Another two men lost. And three horses needed shooting because too much shrapnel penetrated their flesh. The mare might patch up all right, I heard the veterinary captain say, although her injuries will take weeks to heal. She'll need a lot of care and a regular change of dressings. After a shake of heads, it wasn't long before a fourth shot rang out.

Objects are as easy to replace as men and beasts. I'll find a dead man's clasp knife soon enough. There'll be a whole spare kitbag of a dead man's things should I need one. There are thousands of things lost in the earth. Caps, mugs, tins, forks, razors, spoons, guns, all below our boots. And corpses. Some fresh, some stale. Whole, if hit by a bullet or piece of shrapnel, in pieces if near an exploding shell. Most bodies are buried, in whole or part, laid to rest with prayers and polite words, especially officers' corpses. Some, officers and other ranks, are left down deep where they fell. There they will remain perhaps for all time undiscovered, unrecovered, like sunken ships at sea. Their bodies buried by the bomb that killed them: murderer and gravedigger as one. Many corpses are abandoned in the damaged land between friend and foe, us and them, British and German. We call it no-man's-land. It should be called dead-man's-land. Every time we stand on it, men die.

We pay our respects at gravesides and someone religious commits the bodies to the ground saying earth to earth, ashes to ashes, dust to dust. But many men have been left to become earth, ashes and dust without any ceremony. We have no choice. If we're busy killing, there's no time to bury our kill. If we're the quarry retreating, a delay would be our death. A fox doesn't wait for the hounds. If we took time to bury bodies, we might as well throw ourselves into the hole we've dug.

***

Nothing to worry about chaps, it'll be over by Christmas, an officer said as we sailed from Dublin aboard *HM Gloucester* on 13th August. We looked forward to our foreign adventure. The Germans had become too big for their boots and deserved a good thrashing. For many of us this would be our first real taste of action. Calming the civil unrest caused by the labour unions in Ireland couldn't count as war. By December we should be back at our Regiment's home in the north of England and a week of well-earned leave. If however mobs continue to kick up a fuss in Ireland, we'll be sent back to Dublin to keep the peace. As it now looks certain the Germans whipped up strife about Home Rule amongst the Irish to distract us from the Kaiser's invasion of Belgium, our officers believe the trade union troublemakers will fade away once the Germans are beaten.

It was a calm crossing, the only excitement offered by two French gunboats challenging us approaching Le Havre. For a short while we thought they would open fire. Our war could have ended before we fired a shot. But once the French sailors realised the ship had a cargo of British troops, they waved, cheered and tooted their horns. We returned the waving and cheering, although our ship's captain declined to blast the *Gloucester's* klaxon. A feint red ribbon of light remained behind us on the western horizon as we disembarked on the evening of 16th August.

Night fell, and so did the rain. The arrival of several hundred British troops at the port appeared to come as a surprise. Many voices became raised and a great deal of gesticulation went on between officers and officials of the French army, navy, police, harbour authority and local administrators. The city's mayor joined the gathering too. There was a dispute over where we should stay overnight. Our platoon commander, Second-Lieutenant Simon Harcourt, was asked to interpret the shenanigans for our Brigade's colonel. As the endless discussions went on, the strong wind off the Atlantic turned into a gale. Hundreds of infantrymen, including me, waited in line on the open quayside getting wet. And wetter. The arguments and arm waving continued for an hour before an agreement was found and, at last, we received orders to move. As soaked as sponges we marched four abreast to a warehouse on the quay, our accommodation for the night.

The Battalion's first morning in France commenced at 6 am with a five-mile march to Bleville. French boy scouts directed us to the camp and the locals along the road appeared very friendly. Many offered drinks, bread, fruit and crumbly crescent-shaped puff-pastries. Very buttery. Delicious. Our camp was not as nice. Any hope of improved accommodation for our second night in France soon vanished. A muddy field awaited us where half the tents had been flattened by the gale we endured overnight. Gratefully, by mid-morning, a hot sun and gentle breeze dried our clothes and kit and the field as we re-pitched the fallen tents. A column of horse-drawn wagons arrived loaded with thousands of tinned rations. Each wagon off-loaded a shoulder-high pile of shiny cans: jam, and of only one kind. It seems we plan to fight the Boche on stomachs full of strawberries.

After two nights at camp, already fed up of strawberry jam, we marched at dawn back into Le Havre to catch a train. At the station a colonel from the Royal West Kents told his troops that we'll beat the Boche and have the Kaiser's cowards running backwards through Belgium before they know what's hit 'em! We appreciated his rallying spirit, but few believed it would be so easy. Our colonel was more measured. The Germans, he said, have been building up to this war for years. They have a large well-trained Army and in recent years have developed a formidable Navy. It would be folly to underestimate the enemy.

As the train belched smoke and spat steam pulling out of the station, two French soldiers ran alongside the track desperate to board. They threw their kitbags to the outstretched arms of our troops before being hauled on board themselves. Once they caught their breath, Corporal Boutard and Private Guérin explained they had been sent as our Battalion's interpreters from the 133rd Regiment of the French Infantry. 2nd Lt Harcourt was greatly relieved the burden of translation would be shared.

Our journey took us through Rouen to Amiens, where two companies from our Regiment joined us. They had travelled sixty miles north from a railway station called *Gare du Nord* in Paris. This I'd spelt 'Garder Nor'. It wasn't my first mistake spelling French words, nor my last. Mother told me to spell words as they are pronounced. It was bad advice. But I can't blame her. She'd had little schooling and went into service aged thirteen. That spelling rule doesn't work for many English words. It certainly doesn't work with French, *any* French word I suspect. Seems to me half the letters they use in writing are never pronounced when speaking. I once spelt *oui* 'we' because that's what the Frenchies seem to say for 'yes'. It just didn't make sense to say 'we' then write *oui*.

2nd Lt Harcourt corrected many of my misspellings, and not only the French words. He asked one day if he could see what I'd written in my diary. It was definitely not an order, although I didn't feel in a position to refuse. Good officers have the knack of giving a firm order that sound like a friendly request. He thought I wrote poetry. He 'dabbled' himself in poetry and would like the 'perspective' of a private. I was reluctant to hand over my notes, largely out of embarrassment. I knew my writing was full of mistakes and my handwriting childlike, not at all like his tidy script. My jottings told of this adventure in France. They also contained private thoughts about my sweetheart, family, friends and comrades-in-arms. He laughed when he started reading, not in a nasty way, just amused, although I hadn't written anything light-hearted. Said it was full of errors of grammar and spelling, which deepened my embarrassment. Nevertheless, he encouraged me to keep writing and not worry about 'technicalities'.

I was never much good at school with writing, although my words were better than my numbers. On the other hand, at sport I was usually one of the first to be chosen for rugby, football and cricket. The classroom became a prison, outdoors my freedom. The desk, pen, ink pot, pencil and paper turned into instruments of torture. Woods, rivers, moors and fields became places of pleasure and adventure.

The lieutenant corrected some of my work with a long sharp pencil before handing back my notes. His handwriting put mine to shame. He warned me not to write anything that could be of use to the enemy. No locations, dates, weaponry, troop numbers, names of officers *et cetera*, just in case it was lost in the field and found by a Boche. Unauthorised notebooks have no place near the front, he added. That's a Standing Order. He had however corrected my spelling to *Gare du Nord*, a location. But I'm sure the Germans already know about the major railway stations in France. And the good thing about *et cetera* is that I'm not exactly sure what it means. As 2nd Lt Harcourt was about to return the pencil to his pocket, he handed it to me, noting mine had nearly worn out.

We stayed overnight in Amiens, sleeping in and around the railway station. It was warm and dry, so no hardship. Some chaps asked permission to look around the town. There must be shops, a museum and old churches, they said. Secretly they wanted to see if French girls proved to be as beautiful as rumoured. Bolder men wished to find women who would offer more than a peck on the cheek, although not one of them had any French money to pay for jig-a-jig. But requests to go 'sight-seeing' were denied: we had to be ready at a moment's notice to board a train towards the front.

Our transport delay was said to be caused by the French. One officer loudly complained that, unlike the British, the French couldn't run a train service for toffee. Pull your bloody finger out, he shouted at a French railwayman, possibly the station master, who seemed not to understand English. And if he did, he chose to ignore the officer. But trains left, packed with French troops, some so overcrowded that chaps clung hazardously to the outside of carriages and horse wagons. They looked as keen as Colman's to get to the Belgium border to halt the Kaiser's invasion.

Thousands of Belgian and French forces had already engaged the enemy near somewhere called Brussels. For some of us the name meant only one thing: sprouts. And I don't mind admitting that, until

I looked at the station's railway route map, I had little idea of its location. Bertie, my best pal and fellow private, said he thought sprouts were named after the man who developed them from cabbages, a Mr Brussels. Some of us wondered whether he was joking. It was hard to tell with Bertie. Then Corporal Bottomley claimed it was the other way around. Cabbages were grown by cross-breeding from ever-larger sprouts, thanks to a Mr Cabbage. He smiled. We laughed. It seemed funny then.

Our Battalion of thirty officers and nearly a thousand men in four companies roused at 4.30 am. We had to board the Frontline Express at 5.30 am and march four abreast to the platform. The train would depart at 6 am precisely. It was light and most of us already awake. We managed to shave using enamel bowls on trestle tables French railway staff set up, although no glass mirrors to guide our blades. Some of us carried a steel mirror which provided at best a bent, scratched or distorted image. A few chaps used the new American 'safety razors', Gillettes. Having tried one, they did not provide as close a shave as a Sheffield-steel cut-throat. Every man had to shave every day. A clean chin was essential. It was in Standing Orders. Moustaches must also be trimmed and combed, although I was one of the growing number of men who didn't sport one. With queues to the lavatories too long and time short before entraining, we were compelled to relieve ourselves in quiet corners. Many had already used nearby nooks and crannies around the station, so had to tread carefully.

People in the fields waved and children skipped alongside the train as it chugged and rattled through mainly flat countryside. It was anything but the promised Express: it stopped often. Some joked we could walk faster, although no-one took up the sergeant's offer to get out and march. Sgt Harry Pratt is not very tall. He is however as wide as a barn door and harder than one made of oak. If ever you've heard a sergeant shout commands on a parade ground and thought them loud, then our Sgt Pratt makes those sergeants sound like choir boys with sore throats.

Our Regiment's 2nd Battalion had served in Ireland on two previous postings. We kept an eye on those rebels wanting Home Rule. For some reason they wished to be independent of Britain and the Empire. They want an Irish Republic and seem determined to cause trouble to get it, although we heard many Irish wish to stay with us. To be in France was quite a different adventure to Ireland. My first overseas posting should have been India with our 1st Battalion. But the Kaiser has put a stop to that. For now, I'll have to make do with France.

When the Prime Minister Mr Herbert Asquith declared war on the Germans for invading Belgium on 4th August, it seemed likely we full-time regulars garrisoned in Britain, or close by in Ireland, would be in the fray pretty fast. It's hard to believe so much can change so quickly and we're already here in France on our way to fight the German Army, however slowly the train moves. We are to stop the Kaiser's troops coming into France. The blighters had already invaded Belgium and doubtless fancy within a few days they can parade as large as life down the *Champs-Elysees*. (Sharneleesy, until corrected.) But we'll put a stop to that. Fritz can trample over little Belgium. Catching them unawares is one thing. Facing seventy thousand trained regulars from Britain and all the Frenchies is quite another.

Our train from Amiens rattled eastwards and eventually arrived at the railhead in Landrecies, a town twenty or so miles south of the Belgium border. We detrained early evening and marched two miles to our billets in a lovely village called Marouilles. French villagers again made us very welcome. Next morning we discovered their curved flaky pastries were called *croissant*. As usual, the spelling didn't match the spoken word. Our translator, Pte Guérin, insisted we pronounced the word like 'cross on'.

'What is wrong with you English?' Guérin asked a group of us, jokingly. He stretched his arms skywards as if to catch the answer. 'You cannot pronounce correctly the simplest words of the magnificent French language. And when you do manage a word, you still put on your accents from the England in the north!'

'Yorkshire!' several chaps shouted.

Guérin, enjoying the banter, said, 'Well, from wherever you are, French must be spoken properly. Your mouth must work hard to make the sound. See.'

He demonstrated by moving his mouth in all directions. We mimicked.

'Ah, you may be doing the joking,' he persisted. 'But I hear from the Londoners that you men from the north can't even speak the English properly!'

This caused much mock outrage before the evening ended with Guérin giving all the men advice on how to woo French girls. 'It is incredible how carefully you listen and how quickly you learn when it comes to, what's the phrase you use? Ah, *oui*, "sweet talking" the ladies.'

All of us slept soundly on that warm evening in the tranquil village of Marouilles on the night of 18th August. By morning everything changed. Peace became pandemonium. The village high street turned into Piccadilly Circus, not that I'd ever been to London. But to imagine the scene became easy when dozens of London motor omnibuses went by. Between these buses came motor automobiles and tradesmen's motor vans. We had been told our Battalion had become part of the 13th Brigade, but that's all. Superstitious chaps didn't appreciate being part of what they considered the unlucky number. Our second night in Marouilles was not as peaceful. Comings and goings by foot, horse and motor vehicle disturbed us every hour.

Reveille sounded at 5.30 am, an hour before expected. We all jumped to it thinking the Germans are about to attack. But no. The early call was prompted by our Brigade officers being told the Divisional Commander, Major-General Sir Charles Fergusson, was to visit. As always when top brass dropped by, many officers became tetchy. They stood on their toes, became nit-picky, wanted the camp spotless, neat and tidy. Our weapons and kit cleaned and inspected, then cleaned and inspected again. Boots and buttons polished and uniforms dusted down. We had to be washed and shaved like cattle prepared for the county show. Hair had to be combed too - even though we'd be wearing caps. Generals can see underneath caps, don't you know, some joker always said. And down your trousers, was the usual retort.

After all the early rush and fuss, the General did not arrive until mid-afternoon. The bugle could have blown at 10 am! Instructions had also come through that the General didn't want any 'pomp and ceremony'. He simply wanted to address the officers and men with the latest information. All our spit and polish and parade rehearsal turned out to be an unnecessary fatigue, if not a waste of time. Our last visit by the General came a year ago in Dublin. Sir Charles had been General Officer Commanding 5th Division in Ireland until this new position. Unfortunately even our generals seemed not fully informed as to the position of our enemy. Were the Germans ten miles away? Twenty? To the north? To the east? In what numbers and weapon strength? The General didn't or couldn't tell us. This 'fog of war', as the officers called it, was as thick as ever.

On August 19th we set out to Maubeuge, where many of the forces of II Corps were to assemble and, perhaps with the French, move northwards to Belgium. We should give the Boche a good beating before they scuttle off back to Germany, otherwise they'll try invading again in a couple of years. It's thought that once we've beaten the Kaiser's troops in Belgium we'll go on to Berlin. Germany could even become part of the British Empire. Then we should take Vienna and teach the Austro-Hungarians a lesson too. They've taken a liberty and invaded Serbia. They blame Serbians for shooting Archduke Franz Ferdinand on 28th June in Sarajevo, Bosnia, sparking this whole show.

I enjoy marching, whatever the weather, although I hope we don't have to walk all the way to Berlin. If we do, I'll need another pair of boots. Breaking in new boots is very painful, as some are discovering. Blisters wider than a penny a few lads are suffering, not having had time to break in the leather. I've advised a couple of chaps to put a handful of alder leaves in their boots to prevent blisters, a tip from my father. One fellow found walking barefoot was less painful. A cavalry captain riding by was having none of that 'indiscipline'. The officer ordered him to don his boots and break in his blisters. Keep a closer eye on your men, he told Cpl Bottomley, before trotting on. What would 'e knows about blisters, the soldier grumbled, cavalry captains go everywhere on bleedin' 'orseback! If we regulars are finding boots tough, how will the new pals' volunteers we hear about cope? Lots of these chaps are from cushy Civvy Street jobs. The likes of clerks, book-keepers, librarians and teachers will find Army life rough. They'll be getting blisters on their feet from Army socks, never mind boots.

Locals along the roadside again showed friendly generosity. At many cottages and farms residents offered tea and cider, known as apple juice to the sergeant, who pretends to believe us. We heard the French often drink coffee, but they believe we British don't. We offered to pay with a few pennies and the odd sixpence for our refreshment. But locals refused, shaking their heads and hands saying *non, non, non*. It seems they can't spend English coins in France, as we cannot use theirs in England. The French don't have pounds, shillings and pence. And where we have twelve pence for every shilling, and twenty shillings to every pound, the French have a simpler system. Their pound, so to speak, is called a *franc*. One *franc* is divided into one hundred smaller coins, *centimes*. A shop keeper explained, in broken English I must say, that our penny was worth about six *centimes*. How he calculates this I have no idea. So each *centime* is worth even less than our farthing. I couldn't make head nor tail of it. I wasn't much good with numbers at school, although I did learn all my times-tables by heart. But this foreign money flummoxed me.

Being harvest time, locals handed over armfuls of freshly picked apples and pears. So much so that fruit was spilling over the road to be later crushed under many an infantry boot. We stuffed every spare pocket and space in our kit, as well as eating as we marched. Eat as much as you can when you can, is every infantryman's motto, because you never know when you'll next have food, or time to eat it. And you can't eat when you're dead, someone always added. That night a lot of men spent a lot of time rushing to the privy.

We stayed in a once-quiet village that became a busy thoroughfare. Thousands of II Corp soldiers, horses, motor vehicles, supplies of every kind went through on their route to Maubeuge. Early evening a local band struck up and played many a jolly tune. Later, as the sun sank into the horizon, the band's snare-drummer struck a long roll to call attention: our National Anthem filled the air. Work stopped. Talking ceased. Everyone stood, backs straight, heads proud, eyes distant, hearts stirred. The band sounded similar to our local Salvation Army players - with a few flutes and piccolos and suchlike joining in. Immediately after our anthem came another drum-roll: their own stirring anthem played, *La Marseillaise*. (The lieutenant wrote it for me after crossing out 'Ler-mar-c-ays'. I'll never understand French.) Out of respect we stayed standing and silent for our ally's anthem. A much better tune than our own, I thought, a thought best kept to myself. Anthems over, the band returned to a mixture of tunes. It belted out several marches with the big bass drum beating marching time: one hundred and twenty steps a minute. As darkness descended the players packed away their instruments and slowly drifted home. The music, however, didn't end. Two accordionists struck up and played for a while, and very good they were too. I started to like these Frenchies, despite what some people said about them.

CHAPTER 2

IF I DIE...

If I die in the days to come, Mother and Father should know how thankful I am for all they have done for me, my sisters and brother. It has not been an easy life for either of them. We know Mother had to scrimp and save every farthing. She took in extra washing and ironing and went off cleaning to make ends meet, especially when Father was away risking life and limb for Queen and Country, as I'm doing now, although today it's King George V.

Thanks to their hard work, they kept our heads above water, always paid the rent on time, and avoided the workhouse or accepting charity. When times became extra tough we managed on bread and dripping. If hungry, we filled our bellies with water. I know Uncle Harold helped bringing eggs from his hens and spare vegetables from his garden, especially when Father was away. And I'm sure the meat on many Sundays came from Uncle Selwyn at the butcher's stall, even if it was scrag-end of mutton or offal. Monday's cold cuts tasted good, as Tuesday's stew. Wednesday's soup with fresh bread we enjoyed too.

It was sad when our sister Patricia died, especially for Mother, who spent so much time at her side. Pat suffered more than any of us youngsters yet seemed the happiest, always cheery, never complaining. As she wisely said, as young as she was, 'It's better to count your blessings than your problems'.

Although tomorrow I'll try to be a hero like Father, I will have failed if I don't return to kith and kin. I trust my dear brother Stuart turns out to be like Father; a good man, kind and strong, who knows the difference between right and wrong. Likewise, my sisters could be like Mother; joyful, hard-working and caring. I hope they have healthy and happy families of their own. I know they'll all take great care of Mother and Father when they become frail, although I will have failed in this duty.

I should have told Alice that my love for her is deeper than any ocean, higher than any mountain, beyond words can say. Not marrying her will be my greatest regret. Oh, for the life of love we would have enjoyed. But, if I die, it will not be. I trust she'll feel free to find a fine husband, a better man he'll doubtless be. I hope she won't be too sad, at least not for too long, when she hears of my end. Alice will perhaps never know that if I have a few moments to think before I die, however painful my wounds, my final thought will be of her, for her. That thought will be my reward for defying death of its instant blow, a bonus for a slow death.

***

These notes belonged to me, Private Samuel Ogden, born 1st December 1895. I'm from a village near Halifax in the West Riding of Yorkshire. The town's mills make the best carpets in the world, and don't let anyone tell you different. Some folk call Halifax 'Toffee Town', because Mackintosh's make Celebrated Toffee at their factory on Queens Road. My village is Haworth. It's quite famous, so people say. That's because three sisters who wrote books lived there until they died, fifty or sixty years back. They were called Charlotte, Emily and Anne Brontë. A few old folks remember their father, Patrick, who out-lived all his children, including a no-good drunk son, Branwell. They lived atop of Main Street at the Rectory, although some call it the Parsonage. I think it was Emily (sorry, I get the sisters mixed up) who wrote a book called *Wuthering Heights*, which has become well known. People come to our village from all over the world to look around the Rectory and walk across the surrounding moorland. I'm not sure I'd travel half way around the world because of a book.

When I was about eight, a tall Yank approached me outside the Baptist Chapel. He asked the way to Wuthering Heights. I told him there weren't any. We've Dick Delf Hill beyond Haworth Moor and, a bit further on, Wadsworth Moor. But there are no Wuthering Heights. It was all in her mind, mister, I said, just made up. The American took a shiny silver coin from his pocket, held it between his thumb and forefinger, and towered over me like a leaning tree. He said it was one whole big dollar and held it right in front of my nose. Now boy, just tell me, he said slowly, as if I didn't understand

English, where are Wuthering Heights? We'd heard a lot about dollars and I thought it was a lot of money, even more than a pound note. So I said, very slowly, as he spoke American, all right mister, cross the road, go past the Sun Hotel and keep walking up West Lane and you'll see a sign to the cemetery. Keep going on the footpath to Middle Intake Farm and all the way to the Withins. That's Wuthering Heights. Thank you, son, he said, giving me the silver dollar and going on his way. Remember, I shouted after him, it's the Withins that's Wuthering Heights. Well, that's what we were told to tell strangers, if they asked.

I've been a foot-soldier since the age of seventeen and enjoy the life. Father thinks I should have been made a corporal by now, even sergeant. He says this war with the Kaiser will help my advancement. 'You'll be made up to corporal quick with a lot of them reservists called up,' he said. 'And some NCOs in your Battalion are bound to catch a bullet.' Father was made sergeant when fighting the Boers at Mafeking, a town in Africa. I was a nipper and can't remember exactly when he was away. Father, Herbert, is considered something of a hero because he was one of the British soldiers who survived a siege for nearly nine months. His picture appeared in the *Halifax Courier* when he returned home. Front page too. That page is now framed and displayed in our front room. We generally only see it on Sundays or when folk visit, because that's when the room is used. Like our 'Sunday best' clothes, Mother likes to keep our front room for special occasions, and Sundays, when the coal-fire is lit wintertime. Father works as a boiler-man now at Dean Clough Carpet Mills, shovelling coke into huge steam-generating furnaces and maintaining the correct pressure to drive spinning and weaving machines.

Often when I was a lad some grown-up would tell me to be a hero like my father. I joined the Duke of Wellington's Regiment to be like him, follow his footsteps. But I'm not. How can I be? You must do brave acts to become a hero. You need to face an enemy. If it's true what some of the lads say, that the Germans are cowards and will turn back before we get to Belgium, I won't be able to fight the enemy man to man, face to face. If he's on the run, you're not a hero if you shoot a man in the back.

Since leaving school aged thirteen in 1908 I worked at Stone Booth Farm with my pal, Bertie Dale. I was known as the skinny one, with legs like matchsticks; Bertie, the tubby one, although he wasn't fat like Eddie Pickles at the butchers. We started on the same day as general labourers for the tenant farmer Mr Booth on land owned by Mr Lister, but we rarely saw him. He lived down in London. When Mr or Mrs Booth mentioned his name, they took on the same respectful tone as the reverend talking about God. This custom was followed even more worshipfully by our foreman, Mr Cragg, who, on hearing or speaking Mr Lister's name, touched his forelock. Mr Lister won't stand for that. Mr Lister insists it's done this way. By 'eck, Mr Lister will be most displeased. It was clear that if Mr Cragg disapproved of something, Mr Lister disapproved too.

It was a mixed farm, but largely stock. Pennine land with its steep hills and shallow soil isn't good for crops, except grass for pasture, silage and hay. Although in the valley Mr Booth set a few acres of barley, kale and potatoes. He kept two acres of rhubarb too, at the back of the farmhouse, which Mrs Booth looked after. For our first two years Bertie and I, as the junior hands, had the job of muck-spreading around the crowns during the first week of February, even those being 'forced' under buckets for the early sticks she twisted off in March. We got a severe telling-off if we didn't put everything back as we found it, or failed to spread the manure deep enough. You'd think we were growing stalks of gold.

I preferred working livestock, especially cattle. We had eighty fine Ayrshires for milk and a well-bred herd of Aberdeens for meat, the best reared in Yorkshire's West Riding. Aberdeens can be a bit troublesome but, if you talk to them quietly, they'll usually cooperate. Even Aberdeen Angus calves will try pushing you around until you show 'em who's boss. If you like animals, they usually like you. Farmer Booth once kept Shorthorns, but he says the Ayrshires do better on the higher moors. We debudded them early otherwise their curly horns would take your eye out or give you a nasty stab. I should mention the sheep, as we ran about a thousand. I rarely worked them except helping at shearing and during lambing, when everyone got involved.

Every spring Mr Booth purchased fifty piglets at market. Depending on what he considered best value that year, he'd bring back Middle Whites or Berkshires. By mid-November the pigs would be meaty enough to slaughter, primarily for Christmas hams and bacon. The pig man stuck the animal and Mr Booth would quickly tie its back legs and suspend the carcass from one of the ceiling hooks. After cutting the jugular Mrs Booth or another local housewife caught the blood in an enamelled bowl or glazed earthenware pot. The organs and innards were scraped out and the head removed before the corpse was split and left to cool. Not a drop of blood nor scrap of sinew was wasted. The following day was almost the busiest of the year when the carcasses were scalded, scraped and butchered. Mr Booth was always very particular about when the pigs were slaughtered. He would wait a few days after the full moon to help the pigs put on an extra pound or so by moonlight grazing. He claimed pigs to be the most intelligent animals on the farm. 'And that includes most of t' humans,' he always added.

Mother, Florence, keeps our little terrace cottage on Sun Street spick and span. She constantly clears, cleans, mends, washes and wipes from five in the morning to nine at night. They produced four of us children before Father was sent to Africa; three girls, Dorothy, Muriel and Sheila, and me. Then, after he returned to the hero's welcome, two more; my only brother, Stuart, eleven, and Patricia, who died last year aged ten. Doctor said Pat had a hole in her heart. I don't know how he knew without looking inside, although she was often fighting for breath and couldn't walk far, or run any distance at all. Our Pat was brave, knowing she would die young, and suddenly, although she was always happy and smiled more than any of us. She put us to shame when we complained or felt hard done by. Pat would simply say something like it's not important or it's no matter, cock her head to one side like a puppy and smile. Every day could have been her last. She knew life was too valuable to waste with silly squabbles or worrying about daft things. Patricia's strength was her spirit. Her weakness, her own heart.

Talking of hearts brings me to my sweetheart, Alice. I know all lads say their girl is the best, but mine really is. I know when the moon is out she'll be looking at it and thinking of me. She knows I'll be doing the same and thinking of her. She's the perfect height for me with the tip of her head just level with my nose. When she looks up with those large bright green eyes into mine, she could ask me to do anything, and I would. At least I'd try, be it swim across the widest ocean, climb the highest mountain, or reach the South Pole like Ernest Shackleton tried to do four or five years back. The only thing I couldn't do is love someone else. Alice is the lass for me. Heaven help any bloke who messes with her while I'm away, although I trust her utterly to be faithful. I'll be the only one, she whispered.

We are to be married when we've won the war, early next year, if many of the generals are right. April 1915 sounds a good time to be wed. Any month of any year would be the right month to marry Alice. The most terrifying thing I ever had to do was ask Alice's father for her hand. That was two months ago in June while on leave from Dublin. I set out from our terrace house in Sun Street up the steep cobbled Main Street to Woolcombers' Cottage, where the Illingworth's live. I donned my Sunday best suit, even though it was Friday. I polished my shoes so hard the toe-caps became as good as a mirror: a sergeant major from the guards wouldn't find a speck o' dust. Alice said the best time to call would be about seven-thirty. Father's tea will have settled and, weather permitting, he'd be sat in the back yard overlooking the valley smoking his weekend pipe. He might be potting-up some chrysanthemums or dahlias, she said, but I was not to be put off if he appeared distracted. It was just his way.

Even though it was a warm mid-summer evening, I was trembling like a new-born lamb on a frosty February night. I knocked on the door. What if he said no? What if he said Alice could find someone better than me? I couldn't disagree, she could. As a regular soldier my prospects didn't look good, even if I became a sergeant. And if this war with Germany hadn't started, I was soon due for an Empire posting: Singapore, or India, or both more than likely, over the next few years. And what father wants his daughter and perhaps grandchildren away in the back and beyond in some mosquito-infested jungle or scorpion-ridden desert? A few old folks still remember '57 when Indian troops of the East India Company rebelled because pig grease and cow fat was used on paper gun cartridges. Many innocent British women and children were horribly massacred. I was ready nevertheless to tell Alice's father I'm hard working and, even though I say it myself, honest, and with a happy disposition. Mr Illingworth should also realise I would move the world to make sure Alice was cared for. I drink very modestly, only a couple of tankards of ale at the Fleece or Black Bull once or twice a week when on leave. Like all parents, the man their daughter marries will never meet their expectations for her. They always want better. And that's how it should be.

To my relief, Mr Illingworth approved our marriage. After all, Alice and I had an eye for each other at school and walked out together for nearly a year. People in the village said we were suited and made a handsome couple, especially when I was in uniform. Mr Illingworth, who owned the village Post Office and general stores, shook my hand and said I was not to let him or Mrs Illingworth down. Mother had given me a plain nine-carat gold ring to present to Alice at our engagement. The stone was not a diamond. Mother said it was an opal, which her aunt had brought back from Australia. Alice insisted it didn't matter that it wasn't a diamond. It could be a piece of brick, she said, and would be just as happy. After announcing our engagement, Alice allowed me to touch her more intimately, squeeze her closer. Sometimes I could hardly breathe and my heart pounded like a blacksmith's hammer, dizzy with excitement, happiness, feelings I'd never experienced before.

Alice's mother, however, wasn't too impressed with me or my opal. A friend overheard Mrs Illingworth at the Post Office say that her daughter deserved better and should have waited until someone more suitable came along. Mrs Illingworth had remained polite towards me, but I sensed her disappointment in me as a prospective son-in-law. Alice is marrying below herself, I admit. The problem is that no man in the world is good enough for her. She is so beautiful with her happy eyes, ivory-smooth skin, trim figure and friendly smile. She could have her pick from any bunch of chaps.

Mrs Illingworth had hoped that Alice would become friendlier with Peter Little, a solicitor's clerk at the Town Hall in Halifax. He went to the grammar school and, one day, will become a solicitor. He's tall with a slight stoop and a long sad face, pale enough to walk behind coffins for a living. Alice said the only time she'd talked to him, apart from a well-mannered 'good day' in the street, was at the Charity Dance in the Village Hall last year. Mrs Illingworth's hopes of their match raised when they danced together. Alice, I was delighted to hear, took a different view.

'He was all tongue-tied,' Alice said. 'Trod on my toes - twice! His hands were all hot and sweaty. Even worse, his breath stank!' I wanted her list of his faults to go on. The more she condemned him, the better I felt. 'I'd rather have you, Samuel, for my husband than a clumsy matchstick of a man with skin like wet fish.'

If I was being compared with that, perhaps I shouldn't feel too good.

CHAPTER 3

BEFORE BATTLE

Uncertain about the exact whereabouts of the Germans, we moved in the general direction of the enemy. From Marouilles, on 21st August, our columns of khaki commenced their march north towards the Belgium border, ten or so miles distant. Whether the enemy had crossed the border into France was not known. They could be in wait around the next bend in the road. They could be curving around our flanks like the claws of a crab ready to grab us. At a moment's notice we must be ready to break ranks and spread to form an outpost line and face them. Britain's war, my war, will begin soon.

It had been an uneasy night, deep in thought, not sleep. When reveille sounded at 4.30 am it came as a relief. We could move. Make noise. Stop waiting. We had something to do instead of being still with our notions and worries of what the day might bring. The air was full of expectation. Everyone stirred with more vigour, a sharper eye. Not one man lingered for an extra minute's kip, even the chaps who normally steal extra seconds of sleep.

By 7 am our advance began. The British Expeditionary Force marched to war, although our gait was not as strict as the parade ground. Sgt Pratt's happy if we keep in step, although it is customary for sergeants never to be content with anything men do. It's never good enough for a sergeant! Fault can always be found. It's hot and humid, our kit and rifle seem heavier than usual. Our stride is often interrupted as we step aside to allow cavalry or artillery to pass with their 18-pounders and wagons of 3.3" calibre shells. They don't notice or care about the dust they kick up in our faces. There are plenty of new petrol-engine vehicles too. Many break down regularly. Horses, even donkeys and mules, are more reliable it seems to me. And a good animal can reach places these mechanical things can't. My pal Bertie thinks motor vehicles will take over from horses completely one day.

We're told our I Army Corps, 1st and 2nd Divisions, and the Cavalry, under Lieutenant-General Sir Douglas Haig, plan to hold a line eastward from a town called Mons. Our BEF will link with the French Fifth Army covering a twenty-seven-mile line west to east from Charleroi to Namur. To their left stands our II Army Corps, 3rd and 5th Divisions, which includes our Dukes. II Corps is under General Sir Horace Smith-Dorrien, and we are to spread along the line of the Mons-Condé Canal.

The sun was soon on our backs, my neck sunburnt before I realised. A few villagers along the way again offered water and tea, apples and pears. Others seemed eagerly engrossed in loading horse-drawn and hand carts to the brim with bedding, tables, chairs, pots and pans. Off to visit relatives in Paris, we were told, as if they didn't trust us to beat back the Germans. The villagers appeared not to panic, but neither did they look happy at going on holiday. Two of our officers, who spoke some French, tried to reassure residents that it was safe to stay. Boutard and Guérin, our French translators, did not even attempt to change their fellow citizens' minds. If they wish to go, let them go, they said. Locals along the way kindly offered us yet more fruit. But because most of us had made regular trips to the privy through the night, yesterday's appetite for fruit had waned. We looked forward to a night of unbroken sleep.

After the miles of marching along cobbled streets and dusty lanes in sweltering heat, sleep should have come easy that night. It didn't. Instead of the village band rallying our courage, we heard the irregular beating boom of artillery in the distance. The rumbling tested our resolve. These were big guns. Very big guns. Hun guns despatching shells of death and destruction. None of us had heard such heavy deep-sounding weapons before. Sgt Pratt, who'd fought Dervishes, said it was thunder, to be expected after this spell of humid weather. The sergeant didn't fool any of us, nor himself. It was indeed a storm, but thunder and lightning made by man.

We settled into camp for the night, some in tents and others, including me, in farm outbuildings to the south of Mons in a village called Bavai. We bedded down to get as much sleep as possible, for early tomorrow we will be stood to arms. Most of us became excited by this news. Action at last. Time to smell the enemy, get 'em on the run, put a silly-looking *Pickelhaube* in the u of our iron sights and shoot the head off underneath. We light-heartedly argued who would

23

be the first to shoot a Fritz, knowing our Lee-Enfield .303 rifles and Vickers machine-guns performed better than German small arms. Or so the officers said.

In the depths of night sounds of shellfire seem closer, louder, more threatening. Darkness feeds fear. Occasionally I felt the ground shake, distant explosions moving the earth where I stood. I said nothing. No-one mentioned it. We shared our trepidation in silence. To the north-east we could sometimes see an arc of red in the sky and the glow would fade before suddenly flaring again. Seconds later we heard a muffled thud and the earth moved again. This red sky at night caused more soldiers' fright than any shepherds' delight.

Most chaps fell asleep, tiredness overcoming excitement, apprehension - or downright fear. For those of us remaining awake the atmosphere in the camp changed. The mood mellowed in the billets and tents. Voices spoke softer, not out of respect for those sleeping, as if they were new-born babies, but because our thoughts turned to tomorrow. Those with experience of fighting - against Boers in Africa or Pashtuns on the North-West Frontier - doubtless remembered their experiences, or recalled their nightmares. They know what tomorrow will bring: dead men, maimed men, missing men. Those of us who have never faced the enemy can only imagine what it will be like, and that's frightening enough. Looking on the bright side, perhaps events won't be as horrible as my imaginings, especially if the Kaiser's lads turn-tail back to Germany when our artillery shells start dropping on them.

I went to find a lungful of fresh air before turning in. The heady fug of cigarette smoke, gun oil and cleaning spirit in our sleeping quarters, a long low-roofed barn, clogged my thoughts. A clear head would help me sleep. Wanted some time to myself too. It's odd being a 'private': privacy is hard to find in the Army, especially as the lowest ranked infantryman. Most of the time I like the company of my chums, the camaraderie, the fun we share. But we all crave time alone. Writing for me provides a reason, perhaps an excuse, to spend time with my own thoughts, even if others are milling around. Jotting things down is also important because we forget so much. Even after a few days it's hard to recall what you've done, where you've been, who you've seen, especially with so much going on.

These ramblings, with all my mistakes and funny French spellings, are just for me: today's notes for tomorrow's memories. My old schoolmaster, Mr Tinkler, won't be marking them and giving me my usual five or six out of ten. Even after my schooling, I'm still unsure when to write 'me' instead or 'I', or 'less' instead of 'fewer', or 'who' instead of 'whom'. Does that make me a bad pupil, or him a poor teacher? Truth is, I'm to blame. I thought more about the adventures we'd planned after school than the rules of English, my eyes spent more time looking outside the classroom window than at the blackboard.

I found fresh air walking through the camp to the horse lines, greeting friends and wishing each other good fortune for the day to come. Around a thousand horses, donkeys and mules are in the lines ready for battle. Some are very fine beasts, private hunters and thoroughbreds, brought over by officers, and perhaps too sensitive to face the dangers of war. Army horses are good enough for their tasks. The cavalry's charges will be up front. Or, more likely, waiting at the flanks for when we break through on foot after our artillery disrupt the Hun's formations. The remaining animals, the heavier horses and mules, will transport field guns, food, supplies and men. Officers report that our force is seriously short of artillery and motor transport. We're told our government has requisitioned more vans and wagons, even from posh shops in London such as Harrods and Maples. Can't wait to tell Alice if I ever cadged a ride in a Harrods motor van! Hopefully they'll have better engines than the Army's vehicles. More horse-wagons, some from nearby farms, have been hastily converted into ambulances with red crosses painted on the panels and, if they have them, canvas tops. I suppose the officers believe our Corps' two motorised ambulances will not be enough to deal with casualties, especially if we pick up the enemy's too. Medical orderlies folded and stacked piles of dressings alongside their stretchers and splints. Surely they won't all be needed.

Tension mounted across the encampment throughout the night. Junior officers rode hither and thither with ever greater urgency. Senior officers, even a general or two, drove through the camp - one in a Rolls Royce! Everyone, including a colonel, stood to attention and saluted as he drove by, though I had no idea who was inside. I heard NCOs reprimanding soldiers for petty uniform infringements, details which had been ignored over the past few days. The jokers amongst us still joked, but somehow seemed less funny than yesterday. Their quips hid fears as much as raise smiles, their own and ours, including mine. Our laughter not as loud or lasting as yesterday's. Men who rarely put pen to paper wrote letters this night.

When I returned to the billet many chaps continued checking and re-checking, cleaning and re-cleaning their 'smelly', as we call our rifles, their full name being Short Magazine Lee-Enfield, a SMLE. It's the Army's reliable bolt-action weapon and comes with a seventeen-inch sword-shaped bayonet. The rifle has a ten-round magazine firing .303 inch cartridges, which come in five-round clips. Our rifle's sights can be set from two hundred to two thousand yards in notches of one hundred yards. Folk might think we're obsessive about our gun cleaning. Some soldiers are, especially the snipers, who treat their rifles with reverence. But to the infantryman this tool can make the difference between life and death. Rifles to us are more important than a hammer to a blacksmith, a plough to a farmer, a needle to a dressmaker. For full-time regulars, our rifles spend far more time at our side than our wives and sweethearts. One or two married chaps claim they prefer their guns to their wives! One thing I'm certain about, I'll never say that about Alice. Joe Thwaites, our section Lance Corporal, made many laugh when he said he'd kissed his rifle more times than Mrs Thwaites. 'And I prefer sleeping with it as well,' he said, although I didn't think that was a nice thing to say. We are constantly aware of where our weapons and cartridges are. It's a serious offence to lose them: serious enough that we could be shot now war has been declared! Besides, each 'smelly' costs over three pounds fifteen shillings to make - seventy-five day's pay at a shilling a day for the lads on basic rate. Thankfully I get paid more after serving three years and as a top-grade marksman. Once married my pay will increase by a couple of shillings and, when our first child is born, an extra three shillings. No wife or child of mine will ever go hungry. That's another - nay, the best - reason to give the Boche a good hiding tomorrow.

Perhaps driven by boredom, or tension, I joined in the gun cleaning, even though my rifle was spotless. Checked the bolt action and lightly oiled it. (Too much oil in the barrel can make your first few bullets go skewwhiff.) Made certain the barrel was clear of any blockage. Mounted the gun aiming at some mythical target in the distance. Squeezed the trigger with more determination knowing that next time, with a bullet in the breach, my sights will have a man in them. I leathered my bayonet again too, though I hadn't used it since its last honing. I also checked my webbing and ammunition pouches, called 'clips' or 'chargers'. I'll need to grab everything fast, without hesitation, with no time to waste fiddling to find bits and pieces. I'll need to keep my all-important eye looking down the barrel of my faithful friend, 'smelly'.

One of the four Vickers machine-gun teams in our Battalion also went through its cleaning and dry firing routine. The lads had practiced this procedure thousands of times. But tomorrow would be different: the targets real men, not wooden cut-outs. And real men return fire. It was heavy work for the six-man team. The mounting tripod, or 'sledge', the gun itself and its water-cooler weighed over seventy pounds. Ammunition added to the burden. Each two hundred and fifty-round belt weighed twenty-two pounds. If the fighting becomes heavy, nearly two belts a minute could be used. Even with my poor arithmetic I can work out that, in an hour's heavy battle, two thousand six hundred and forty pounds of ammunition needs to be carried. Far more than a ton! Heavier than Mr Booth's heaviest draft horse on the farm, Toby, who weighed two thousand four hundred pounds. But the racket the machine-gunners made going through the motions disturbed chaps trying to sleep and Sgt Pratt told them to pipe down. Tension was indeed in the air.

Whatever I write, mistakes and all, neat or untidy, these notes will be left with my kit tomorrow away from the fighting. I won't have time to write and, more important, Standing Orders say notes are not allowed at the front in case they fall into enemy hands. (Not that I've mentioned anything of use to the Hun.) Perhaps in the evening, if it all quietens down, I'll find time to record the day's events. Who knows what tomorrow will bring? Let's hope we're chasing Fritz back to Germany.

***

If you are reading this, you will know I am dead, severely injured or a prisoner. Please post these notes to my parents, alongside my cigarette case and lighter. I don't smoke, but I keep reserves if friends run out. Please take the cigs, a very small reward for your help. As you can see, the lighter was made from a bullet case. Father made it during the siege in Mafeking. It explains why the initials HO are inscribed and not mine, he being Herbert Ogden. It was his lucky charm fighting the Boers. He 'knows' it will bring me luck too, he said. Sadly, its return will shatter his certainty. It would appear I needed a different trinket. Nearly all the men have something from home to bring luck. Cyril Meadows believes his talisman to be the oily rag he uses to clean his rifle, the one and only cloth he has used on 'smelly' since joining the Dukes. It's never been washed.

But if charms worked, war would have few casualties. I can't see what difference a hare's foot, a polished stone, a twig of ash or yew would make. One chap carries an item of underwear from his wife, folded neatly in a pocket. A lucky charm of a different kind, he winks.

CHAPTER 4

MONS, BELGIUM

Belgian and French forces have resisted the invaders for nearly three weeks, since German boots barged into Belgium on 4th August on route to France. Little Luxembourg had already been squashed underfoot in a few hours on 2nd August. It's said up to forty thousand French soldiers have died in the past few days alone. The figure is so large I find it hard to believe, and gossips usually exaggerate. Despite their efforts, the Belgians and French have failed to repel Kaiser Wilhelm II's troops, some say up to nearly one and a half million of them between Belgium and the Swiss border. Now it's our turn to help.

It was early morning on Saturday 22nd August when the British first faced the enemy, three miles north of the Mons-Condé canal. C squadron of the 4th Royal Irish Dragoon Guards came across a German lancer patrol. Their officer was smoking a cigar, don't you know! Our chaps charged and the Kaiser's lads took flight. After catching their tails the dragoons took five prisoners. During this skirmish the first British bullet of the war was fired. The shot came from Cpl Ted Thomas's rifle, and a German rolled off his horse stone dead. Squadron Captain Charles Hornby also drew enemy blood in the confrontation, but not with a bullet: his sword stabbed a German's heart.

The Duke of Wellington's crossed into Belgium that same Saturday. We outspanned in fields allotted to the 13th Brigade three miles west of Mons at St Ghislain. Nearby stood our main rivals in peace, the King's Own Yorkshire Light Infantry. Now, in war, our closest friends. Like us Havercakes, most of the KOYLIs were born and bred in Yorkshire, although chaps joined from all over Britain. Good soldiers to a man, but I would never tell them. It wouldn't be doing to swell their heads! It was good to have them at our side ready for the fight. We Dukes received details to work in support and relief of the 1st Battalion of the Royal West Kents. They, in turn, supported the Divisional Cycling Company. We later learnt this Company was overwhelmed by the German advance. Like minnows swimming into the mouth of a pike, the jaw snapped tight. The handful who escaped reported that most of the cyclists had been suddenly surrounded and slaughtered, those wounded left to die or, if they could walk, taken prisoner. Our escapees became convinced the Germans would treat our chaps badly, such was the enemy's bloodlust. Major Hastings, in charge of the Cycling Company - who had earlier served with the Dukes in Rangoon - was one who had died bravely. Their courage, venturing so far forward to discover the enemy's position, resulted in their deaths. Bravery is never enough to stop a bullet.

Belgian citizens and their troops, gathering in large numbers at the border, welcomed us as warmly as the French. Thank you, *merci beaucoup*, thank you for coming to rid us of Germans, they said, some clasping our hands and speaking English. Others cried at their relief of our arrival. They forced chocolates, fruit and cigarettes into our hands and pockets. Most chaps particularly welcomed the gift of boxes of matches. Belgium ones, smokers said, struck far easier than French matches.

That night we hoped to gain a good night's rest inside billets at Hornu, a village a mile south-east of St Ghislain. It was not to be. At 8.30 pm four companies, around eight hundred men, including me, were ordered back to the front. As night fell my company settled in and around fields and farm sheds on the northern side of the Mons-Conde canal. Some chaps dug shallow scrapes in readiness for the fight. Our platoon was instructed to take cover behind a hedge. A few chaps used corn stooks for cover. I was not convinced the sheaves were thick enough to stop the penetration of bullets. We still had no idea as to the position of the enemy. Two certainties stood out among the uncertainty: the Hun were out there, somewhere, and would strike, sometime.

Our position was not good. We had no forward observation posts. If scouts had been deployed to detect enemy location and movement, we had not been told. The Germans, even if just half-clever about it, could easily creep to within three or four hundred yards before attacking. Shelter for them was provided by the curve of the fields, ditches, hedges, walls, copses and a few outbuildings. It was also a moonless night: darkness always gives advantage to aggressors on the move. Behind us, too, the canal. This had only two possible crossing points nearby, a narrow track across the lock and a railway bridge. Men questioned amongst themselves the wisdom of our forward line. Surely it would be better to use the canal as a defence barrier to our front?

My hunch was that our officers had prepared to advance, not merely hold the line. If so the canal in front would be a hindrance. Several thousand men would be squeezed into a bottleneck at the two crossing points preventing our speedy advance. However, if *we* had to withdraw, the canal would be a major obstacle preventing many of us retiring. We'd have to run the gauntlet of concentrated fire on the two crossings - or risk a bullet in the back swimming across the canal.

After sentries from each company had been posted for the first guard duty of the night, the rest of us rested as much as possible. A hedgerow provided the best shelter, once we'd trodden down the stinging nettles. Sleep was beyond most of us. But Bertie was one of those fortunate fellows who could nod off instantly, seemingly without a care in the world. I had to work hard to find sleep, even at the best of times. I forced my eyes closed. But I couldn't clear my head of thoughts of what tomorrow might bring. My chest tight, breathing shallow, stomach knotted, ears alert to every sound, I realised fear had found me. I was as frightened as a child amid a nightmare. I felt ashamed, scared before I'd even faced the enemy. Told myself there was nothing to worry about, stop being stupid. Surrounded by the finest soldiers in the British Empire, how could I be as afraid as some weedy schoolboy cornered by big bullies? The Germans, realising our strength, will surely turn tail. I'll be all right. A bullet won't catch me. Our artillery will have 'em on the run. I'll keep my head down, stick to our oft-practiced fighting formations. And I have Father's lighter as my lucky charm…

But fools fool themselves. It was time to face my fear, acknowledge the coward inside. Anyway, there was no turning back, for me, for any soldier. I was one of thousands of British troops that night waiting to attack, or be attacked. In a strange way, accepting fear reduces it, although it doesn't dispel it completely. Perhaps I managed a few minutes' sleep in the hedgerow after all.

At first light, around 4.15 am, I could just make out a hundred yards ahead Captain Ozanne leading about a dozen of his men across the steel girder bridge spanning the canal. In charge of the machine gunners, the Captain positioned two teams to either side of the rail track. As the positions dug in and the MGs set up, beyond the bridge a group of cyclists fast approached our lines wishing to cross at the canal lock. The gunners readied their Vickers to fire until Captain Ozanne, looking through his field glasses, identified them as women and children. It was clear by their agitated movements and anxious glances they had fled in great distress. Their pointing back along the road was a clear sign Germans were not far behind. The cyclists couldn't wait a moment longer to get away. And who could blame them?

Word soon came along the lines to prepare for an attack, probably within the hour. Tea was served behind the huts and I enjoyed two mugs. The machine gunners had worked hard to conceal their positions. Capt Ozanne had sited the guns well, each covering the fields at either side of the rail track for a good thousand yards. There was light scrub skirting both sides of the low railway embankment, although not dense enough to cover the movement of men. A good sniper might use it to his advantage. Sensibly, chaps behind corn stooks now started to dig into the ground, and those in shallow scrapes dug deeper. The order arrived to keep down and as still as possible for maximum concealment. My eyes watched for the slightest movement. Never had I concentrated so intensely in my life. I swear I could detect an ant move half a mile away! Every time a bird flew up from a hedge or copse I expected a bunch of Boche to break cover. But they didn't. Not for the next hour, nor the one after that.

At 10 am I witnessed the most extraordinary event. Capt Ozanne, alone, started walking up the left embankment. He was checking how well the machine guns were concealed from the approaching enemy's viewpoint, especially as the angle of light had changed since dawn. Such bravery to be out there all alone! Suddenly a solitary German cavalryman appeared, as if from nowhere. He'd emerged from where the railway embankment levelled and moved into a cutting. Capt Ozanne looked up at the horseman and he, equally surprised, looked down at our officer. After staring at each other for what seemed an age, but probably only two seconds, the Uhlan turned his horse as on a sixpence and galloped away head down and heels kicking. The Captain raced back to our lines, 'as fast as my legs would carry me', he was later heard to say. We then saw a party of lancers racing away towards thick woodland about five hundred yards ahead and into which the railway track ran. The Captain immediately ordered his machine gun on the right to open fire. As far as I could tell not one Uhlan caught a bullet. And if a cavalryman took some lead, he remained in the saddle. The Duke of Wellington's were at war. The first shots in our Battle of Mons had been fired. And we didn't have long to wait before shots rang out in their millions. German infantry attacked in disciplined waves and we picked off hundreds with our rifles. The Vickers machine guns performed well too. Both MG teams cut many down, line after line, as you would expect firing nearly five hundred rounds a minute. But the Germans just kept coming. Hun followed Hun, thousands of them. And when they took up shooting positions they returned fire. But it was Fritz's artillery that started killing more of us than we them.

Platoon-sergeant Greenhalge became the first injured and Pte Shellabear killed close to me. More fell wounded, dead, or dying. Too many to name. Orders were given to retire and we gradually crossed the canal back into St Ghislain. It was exceedingly hot and humid and we became exhausted. But no respite was in sight and we were fighting for our lives. My platoon and one other, reduced to around sixty able men, received orders to climb a slag heap overlooking the canal. Struggling up the slag we became covered in coal dust. Our faces became as black as miners and the whites of our eyes shone like limelight in darkness. At the crest of the heap I thought my number was up. A German shell struck one of the overhead trolleys used to convey the waste slag from the pithead to the heap. The wire snapped and several trolleys crashed down landing just feet away from some of us. But this was no time to reflect on our miraculous escape. The fighting become heavier, and it seemed a miracle that anyone was left alive at all.

We remained on the slag most of the afternoon. Nine chaps in our platoon took shots to the head, two just skinned. A shell did for four more. The height of the heap allowed us a good position to fire down onto the never-ending swarm of Germans, and we needed constant supplies of ammunition. I lost count of my hits, most of them straight kills to the head or heart. To kill a man was a strange feeling - at first. But after several, and losing count, I thought no more of it. I don't believe any of us did. We just drew the bolt, took aim, fired. Repeatedly. There was no time to think. It was them or us, him or me.

The Mons-Condé canal proved not to be a barrier. Because our troops became stretched so thinly, the Germans soon found plenty of crossing points. We got beaten back by overwhelming numbers and a constant barrage of artillery fire. Experienced soldiers hadn't experienced war like this. Fighting the Boer, Dervishes or Pathan tribesmen had been largely small-arms affairs with revolver, rifle and musket, lance, sword and bayonet, not a blitz from heavy howitzers or light field-guns. We also mistakenly thought we killed more of their troops than we had. It seems many Hun fell to ground taking cover behind truly dead men. They would then creep very slowly forward, hoping, correctly, that being four or five hundred yards away, our riflemen wouldn't detect their movement. And while many men still came forward making easier targets, our bullets went to them.

If a man is injured, no longer a danger to us, we are told to leave him, don't waste a second round. Injured men are a burden to an army, especially when retreating. Casualties slow armies down and take resources away from the fighting. Dead men can wait to be collected and buried. Frontline officers don't wish to have fighting men handling the injured. That's a job for the stretcher bearers. Few men wish to be abandoned on the battlefield. There are some brave chaps who, knowing they are soon to die, urge their would-be rescuers to leave them and find another who has a chance of survival. If that choice came for me, I don't know if I'd be brave enough to say abandon me and save someone else. Few people want to die alone.

34

As the day developed at Mons it became clear the Germans had gained the upper hand. Their numbers, their artillery and the way their guns deployed outdid ours. Where our chaps survived, battalion after company after platoon received orders to fall back. I was bemused that we British 'retire', 'withdraw', 'fall back' and always 'in an orderly manner'. I bet the Germans said, 'on the run' or 'fleeing like lambs from a fox'.

I'm quickly learning that in war it's hard if not impossible to get facts or the full picture. There's so much confusion. One man sees this, another sees that. No two people it seems can see the same event and report what's happened in the same way. Troop units get fragmented, not only by death and injury and enemy attack, but by disorientation, especially in the dark when we disperse in every direction. True or not true, we heard nearly two thousand men of ours were lost today around Mons, dead or captured. The 2nd Royal Irish and the 4th Middlesex suffered most, almost wiped out apparently. But who really knows? There are so many rumours and much speculation. It's too early to tell. And will anyone ever know what really happened? Some events seem exaggerated and others played down. All I hope is that our chaps taken prisoner will be treated as well as we treat theirs, which is pretty decently. We hear the Hun torture captives terribly for the sheer hell of it. But some say such gossip is spread so we fight harder and resist surrender. The German prisoners I've seen might have been given the odd poke with a bayonet to get 'em up and moving, but that's all.

One truth we know, at nightfall the Germans controlled Mons and everything north of the canal, including St Ghislain. The French, it was said, would perform poorly as fighters. The same accusation was levelled against the Germans. They were wrong. Very wrong. Those of us who fought at Mons against the Germans, or alongside the French, learnt very quickly the Germans are man-for-man a match for us and far from cowardly. The Hun fought as cleverly and as bravely as our men. Our colonel's words echoed in my head: never underestimate the enemy. The French too are brave and ingenious fighters. Frenchies may *look* less organised than us, but that doesn't mean they are less effective.

As we retired south news arrived that, while the British Expeditionary Force fought around Mons, the French and Germans had become engaged in a far bigger battle in an area called Ardennes, to the east of our position. It's said many more thousands of men have been killed and injured than in our battle at Mons. There must be depths deeper than hell.

CHAPTER 5

Monday 25th August
THE OLD MILL

The early morning mist could not lift quickly enough. A clear view of the enemy approaching would provide fair warning of an attack. The Germans had continued their southerly incursion determined to push on to Paris, regardless of whether we stood in their way. After Mons, perhaps they hoped the British Army would capitulate, leave France to the French, go home. If they thought that, they don't understand British pluck.

Two aircraft of the Royal Flying Corps heading north roused anyone still sleeping. We hoped these flying chaps could discover the enemy's current position and strength. It was the first time I had seen these contraptions on the wing in France. It still seems strange that something with a heavy metal engine carrying a man or two can get off the ground at all. I suppose once air is under the wings, like a paper kite or hovering bird, they keep afloat on a sea of air. Not all aeroplanes get off the ground however. Engines stall, 'conk-out', the pilots call it. Wings collapse as aircraft gather speed to take off. At least these pilots survive. Some aeroplanes have conked-out or broken up mid-flight resulting in pilots plunging to their deaths: terrifying falling from such heights knowing of your certain end. On bumpy landings some aeroplanes have ended up 'arsey-tarsy', that's upside-down in RFC language.

If the RFC chaps return safely our commanders will know where to deploy our remaining forces to best effect. I say 'if' they return because, like us, the Boche have started shooting at aircraft. Flying is already a hazardous job, now made more so by troops on the ground taking pot-shots. Nobody in my unit has yet had the opportunity to fire at a German flyer. We can't wait. What sport that will be! A shotgun would of course be a better weapon to use than a rifle if the aeroplane is flying low: the spread of pellets would improve the chances of a hit over those of a single bullet. They say it's harder to hit an aircraft than it looks, far trickier than crumpling pheasants, but surely not as hard as fast-flying grouse.

Le Cateau resembled a busy ants' nest before a thunder storm. The main square and surrounding roads became packed with motorised vehicles, horse-drawn or hand-pulled wagons and carts. Belgians carrying cases had fled from the fighting to the north. Military and civilians criss-crossed each other in the narrow streets. Movement wasn't panic, but it was urgent. Fresh battalions marched through the town and mixed with those of us who had withdrawn from Mons. Hundreds of men, me included, felt exhausted and peckish. Some chaps looked dazed, particularly hard hit by our defeat at Mons. Besides our infantry losses, news arrived that several cavalry and artillery regiments were missing, which was very worrying. How on earth, we asked each other, can you lose hundreds of horses and artillery pieces?

Everyone speculated about what the Germans would do next. Would they go around us and move directly on Paris or face us here at Le Cateau? No-one knew with any more certainty than naming the next Derby winner. I'm not a betting man, because odds are never even. They are set in favour of losing more than winning and everyone knows bookmakers win in the end. I trust we can hold the line here because being forced backwards is demoralising. It seems more dangerous too. Like climbing rocks, coming down is more hazardous than going up. But if we stay and get surrounded, it will be the end of the British Expeditionary Force. We would need lots of chaps from home and Empire to rescue us from Fritz's clutches, if anyone of us is left alive to release.

After we withdrew and the civilians departed, Le Cateau became a ghost town. Our Company, back to around two hundred and fifty strong, received orders to occupy forward rifle-pits. Our section of seven was ordered onto the roof of a nearby mill, given this task because we had the best riflemen in the Regiment. (Our squad had won The Duke of Wellington's shooting trophy for the past two years.) The three-story mill stood out as the highest building in the area, providing the best opportunity to take long range shots at the first sign of Fritz. We'd be able to pick-off many from this vantage point. But the mill stood out from the surrounding countryside which spelt danger for us as the prime target for their rifle fire and, far worse, artillery cannon. We accepted the likelihood that this mill, alongside cottages nearby, would be reduced to rubble by the day's end.

The day dragged on with not a shot fired. Waiting. Sometimes it's all we seem to do. By mid-evening the feverish activity had stopped. Nobody was marching or running or riding or driving hither and thither, apart from the occasional lone horseman or vehicle either going to or coming from II Corps HQ at Bertry, eight miles to the south-west. There was some movement along the road to my right, the key route south to 5 Division HQ two miles away in the small town of Reumont. No civilians had been seen since early afternoon. If they hadn't fled, locals would be sheltering indoors, probably in their cellars, 2nd Lt Harcourt said, which, by the way, are perfect for storing their excellent cheese and wine.

As the day gradually closed the soft smell of hay filled the still air. Blackbirds and thrushes sang as if in competition to find the sweetest song. Sparrows chirped and quibbled over spilt grain around the mill. A flock of goldfinch settled on the ground for a minute taking their share of seed before flying off together creating a streak of yellow stripes in the sky. Martins, swifts and swallows soared and swooped catching the evening's bounty of insects on the wing. A wren was chit-chitting away, the smallest bird with the biggest voice, but I couldn't spot it. Day became dusk. Twilight turned to night. It was dark enough for war, but too peaceful for it.

The stillness became unnatural, unnerving. Thousands of men lay all around, but not a whisper could be heard. The loudest sound came from my heartbeat. It had been pounding all day, despite my efforts to breathe deeply and keep calm. My stomach was knot-tight, palms wet, mouth dry. Those of us on the mill roof fell silent, the banter stopped. Suddenly, it changed. What's that down there? Hearts beat faster. Nothing, just a machine-gun crew finding a better emplacement, someone would whisper reassuringly. And we would start to breathe once more. Look! Top of the field. Two o'clock. Did you see something? Pulse up. No. Nobody saw anything. Pulse down. But that doesn't mean there was nothing. My finger had stayed so long lightly curled around the trigger it had become stiff. I had to shake my arm to loosen it. I recalled the sergeant's words from my very first day on the rifle range: 'You can't fire straight if you're all fired up, and, if you want to hit the man, you've got to want to kill him.'

Cpl Bottomley suggested we took a ten-minute break, one at a time. 2nd Lt Harcourt had given Cpl Bottomley field glasses to help detect any enemy movement. The rest of us constantly strained our eyes watching for the slightest activity across the downs or on the abandoned streets of Le Cateau. When the last band of light left the sky, a half-moon became our only illumination. La Cateau gradually faded from view, black into black. Only the tops of distant hills could be distinguished against the night sky.

Cyril Meadow's whisper broke the silence. What time do you make it, corporal? Just before eleven. Hell's bells, is that all, Bertie said. Look lads, said Bottomley, there's no point in us all staying awake. We can hardly see a damn thing anyway. Why don't three of you try and get a couple of hours' kip? We'll know soon enough when the show starts, by George we will. So, who wants the privilege and pleasure of keeping the first watch with me? Far from sleepy, I volunteered. Joe, Cyril and Bertie all settled down for a bit of shuteye. The corporal ordered me to go below and instruct Nugent and Smith to take a nap too. I was glad of the little exercise it provided. On my return the corporal whispered he'd rouse a couple of them to take over the watch at one o'clock.

I had no trouble staying awake, alert to every sound of the night. Gravel crunched underfoot when someone moved along the track below. I could even hear whispering, although not the exact words. And Bertie snored. A gentle snore, fortunately, not loud enough to tip off the German Army. Below me a barn owl took flight on its ghostly-white wings from its nest in the mill wall. It would find a perch and swoop on its prey at the slightest movement of whisker or tail. If only I had the owl's eyesight. Any Fritz crawling in the field within half a mile would have a bullet in his head. Another owl, a tawny this time, started its haunting hoot from woodland some distance away. Then someone, someone very clumsy, dropped a metal object making an almighty clang. It jangled everyone's nerves and caused Joe and Cyril to stir. Bertie, as I'd expect, remained

40

undisturbed. The clumsy culprit received a string of shushes and plenty abuse! Silence returned. Our pulses settled a little. Where the swifts and swallows had hunted by day, the bats had taken over, sweeping the sky for insects. Their hunting was welcome, because the fewer mosquitoes and midges biting me and everyone else, the better. The white-winged hunter-owl returned with a tasty rodent clenched in its talons. Judging the shape of the silhouette, the owl's prey was a large rat.

It was impossible to concentrate on any single thought for long. The slightest noise or movement grabbed my attention. I tried hard to think of Alice, naturally, recalling every feature of her face, her smile, infectious laugh and neat figure. How wonderful it would be to hold her now. Warm, reassuring, safe, comforting. But Alice isn't here. It's stupid to have such thoughts. This place, with one army facing another, with men about to kill others, is not the place for kind, loving and gentle people. Alice must be cast out of my thoughts, away from this place, away from this time. Before I would see her again I had to face the dark of tonight, and the darkness of the day to come. For tomorrow, even if the sun is shining without a cloud in the sky, dark deeds will be done. And the light will go out forever for many.

Many still say this war will all be over by Christmas, except Field Marshal Kitchener and those of us who felt the force of the Germans at Mons. Kitchener says we need a much bigger Army and the war will go on for longer. Some said war wouldn't happen at all. The Kaiser's ultimatum to Serbia was a bluff after the Archduke's assassination last June. They said we'd beat the Boche back at Mons. But we got beaten back. The generals say we'll hold the line here at Le Cateau. We'll wait for the French Fifth and our own reinforcements with more reservists, and then start pushing the Boche back to Berlin. We'll see. Generals can't appear downhearted. We all know officers must chivvy us along, stay cheerful and hopeful. After all, if we don't have the confidence to win the war, we will surely lose it.

Fighting Fritz is the right thing to do. We cannot let Germans think they can dominate Europe and take over civilised lands. Belgians and French are not colonies in far off places. They are civilized people. If Germany takes France and Belgium, they will come for us next. We all agree on that. I don't know any British man or woman who wants to become a subject of the Kaiser. We must stop the Hun landing on British shores, otherwise all our women and girls will be in danger of horrible assaults. It is well known what Hun soldiers get up to, as they have already with Belgium women. Hun soldiers will be told to impregnate as many British women as possible to start turning us into Germans. And, as in Belgium, men and boys will be mercilessly shot. The thought of Alice being man-handled by a gang of Fritz is enough to make me shoot straight at every German I see. And that horrible thought of our girls and ladies being molested is what I shall keep in mind when I push my bayonet into a Hun's stomach.

Footsteps could be heard ascending, each step louder, closer. Cpl Bottomley and I glanced at each other. Afraid, we both quickly turned our rifles to the opening trapdoor. Surely the Boche hadn't sneaked round the back? But when Sgt Pratt appeared through the hatch with a canister of tea, our fears turned to delight.

'Thought you'd like to get this inside you,' he whispered, respecting the night rather than any thought of waking Germans. 'We've a brew on in the cellar. Suppose you've haven't seen anything, Corporal? Light in the village? Movement on the fields?'

'Not a thing, Sergeant,' Bottomley said.

The sergeant surveyed the skyline, 'Too bloody quiet for my liking.'

'Aye, Sergeant, you're right there. If there's going to be a scrap, I just want to get going.'

'There'll be a fight, all right, there's no doubt about that. But don't be too hasty, Bottomley, because once it starts we'll all be praying it hadn't.'

'Right enough, Sergeant, right enough.'

'How are you, Ogden?'

'It's the waiting, Sergeant, it gets to you,' I said. 'All sorts of stuff go through your head. It's just like Father always told me, "the waiting's the worst thing in war".'

'He was at Mafeking, wasn't he?'

'Yes, Sergeant.'

'I can tell you now, lad, this fight is going to make Mafeking look like the vicar's tea party. Not that I'm doing your father down, mind, far from it. They were brave fellows in Africa all right, stuck out there in the middle of nowhere with those tribes everywhere, some of 'em cannibals, thy knows. It must 'ave been as scary as hell. But these Boche 'ave got some bloody big guns, an' a lot of 'em, which weren't the case with them Boer or them cannibals.'

We supped our tea. And, like me, I'm sure Bottomley was thinking of those big guns facing us. As if Sgt Pratt heard our thoughts, he said, 'We'll learn soon enough what they can do.'

Bottomley asked, 'Any idea what time they'll start, Sergeant?'

'Best guess is daybreak,' he replied with a shrug of his broad shoulders. 'Scouts say they're moving into town and lying low over the horizon. Watch out at first light in case some of their snipers have crept forward, although you should be all right up here.'

'There's only one area they can get a clear shot at us, from that tree line,' Bottomley said, pointing to their silhouette in the moonlight. 'We'll keep a close eye on them come dawn and pick off any Fritz who dares go up 'em.'

'Good man,' the sergeant said as he stood up. 'Well, I'm Pratt the Tea Boy tonight, and I expect a few more chaps want a brew.'

'Many thanks, Sergeant,' I said, 'best brew I've had for ages.'

'Let us know the second you see anything,' Sgt Pratt said as he took his leave. 'See you later.'

'I bloody-well hope so,' Bottomley said, 'because the alternative wouldn't be good.'

CHAPTER 6

Tuesday 26ᵗʰ August

At 3 am Pte Joe Thwaites took watch from Pte Bertie Dale and Pte Cyril Meadows. Ian Bottomley, taking his responsibility as corporal seriously, served a second shift. Bertie instantly put his head down and started to snore loud enough to wake Fritz a mile away. The corporal kicked his boot to stop him. Bertie snorted, rolled over and continued sleeping, quietly. For years I'd been dumbfounded at Bertie's capacity to fall asleep quickly and deeply, anywhere, anytime. He could sleep on the head of a nail, seemingly in comfort. An hour later I remained awake, any hope of sleep driven out by fear. It was still dark, but felt darker. Folk say it is darkest just before dawn.

Anxiety rose with the rising sun within the hearts of thousands of men for miles around. An officer from 5 Division HQ at Reumont, galloping hard on a fine-looking black thoroughbred of a good sixteen hands, more suited to the Epson Downs than Le Cateau, rode along the lines delivering the latest intelligence of the enemy and new orders. At least a suffragette didn't throw herself in front of his horse, as at last year's Derby. I could see officers briefing their juniors who, in turn, dashed to their platoons spreading the orders. Platoon commanders rallied their men with heartening words, each hoping fortitude would replace fear. Men braced themselves, encouraged each other. They joked saying please leave the first Fritz for me or I'll bag a Hun before you. Several chaps quickly stepped aside from their posts to relieve themselves, a sure sign action was afoot. The five of us on the roof took another sip of water, and I suspect we all wondered if it would be our last.

'Right, men,' said Cpl Bottomley, 'let's get ready. And that includes you Dale.' Bertie was ready for action within two seconds of being kicked up the backside by Bottomley's boot.

'By God, where are the buggers?' Bertie quizzed mounting the rifle looking for a Fritz.

'They've not started yet,' said the corporal, 'but they could any minute, so get sorted and...'

'Look out!' Bertie yelled.

A shot rang out. Then another. The second from Bertie. I felt its draft go past my ear. We turned following the direction of Bertie's bullet. A grey bundle of dead German tumbled from his perch in a distant elm and crashed to the ground.

'By God in Heaven and Mary the Mother of Jesus Christ and all the frigging saints,' Thwaites shouted as we dropped to the floor aiming our rifles at the trees. And the strangest thought went through my head: Thwaites was Catholic, we'd been in the same platoon for two years and I hadn't twigged.

'Everyone all right up there?' Sgt Pratt shouted.

We all looked at each other to confirm that was the case.

'Yes, Sergeant, we're all fine,' replied Bottomley.

'Who shot Fritz?' asked 2nd Lt Harcourt.

'Dale.'

'Damn good shot, Dale.'

'Thank you, Sir.' Bertie beamed and kissed the stock of his rifle.

It was indeed a brilliant shot from a very difficult free-standing position. Any true rifleman would have admired it, even our dead Fritz. More amazing, which others wouldn't know, Bertie had been fast asleep ten seconds earlier. But, as you'd expect, we all ribbed him saying it was a lucky bullet!

'That Fritz couldn't shoot for toffee,' Joe said. 'His bullet missed you by a foot, Corporal.'

'Close enough, thank you very much, Thwaites,' said Bottomley, ballooning his cheeks. 'Close enough.'

'Let's hope they're all as bad as him,' Cyril said.

'And our shots as lucky as Private Dale's,' Joe smiled.

Yet again we took up our firing positions and waited. Watching and waiting; waiting and watching. The order was to stand fast, hold position, stop Fritz marching further forward. The Boche had to make the first move. They are attacking; we are defending. They are France's foe; we its friend. At around six o'clock that morning, as at Mons a few days earlier, life for thousands of men and their families changed for the rest of time. Life would never be the same again. For many, that's where life ended.

German howitzers opened the battle. At first the shells landed harmlessly off target, the nearest to us fell two hundred yards short. But soon they found their range. Death and destruction followed. Exploding shells shook the earth, sucked the air. Volley followed volley. No pause. No mercy. No respite.

Half a mile to our right the Suffolks, Cornwalls and East Surreys started to take a heavy battering. Explosions ripped through their lines. Fireballs engulfed men in flashes of flame and sheets of smoke and shrapnel. Flat fields became pitted. Green grass churned into brown earth. Strong stone walls blasted to rubble. Majestic trees broken as easily as matchsticks, their foliage stripped to bare branch and twig, left to stand like aged cripples. It rained dirt and dust and debris. Shouts and screams of pain could be heard, even across the barrage of shell blasts. Our men, some my friends, lay dead and dying. We could see our riflemen and machine-gunners firing furiously, but bullets are no match against howitzer shells.

Bottomley, using field glasses, reported the Germans flooding through Le Cateau and up the road towards us at the crossroads a mile away. With the naked eye, we could see hundreds - thousands - more of the blighters across the horizon and striding across the fields.

They'll kill me if I don't kill them, I thought. This was beyond German against British, army against army, soldier against soldier. This was men hunting men. Animal versus animal. Them against me. My heart pounded, stomach tightened, breathing fast, short and shallow. Bile stuck in my throat. Legs shook like aspen leaves. I gripped my rifle - a simple tool of metal and wood - to steady my shaking hands. Grip too tight. Bad. Wrong. Curse. Order myself to remember my training, my experience. Breathe naturally, slowly, steadily, establish target, focus only on point of aim, pause breathing, hold still, squeeze trigger, kill. Repeat action.

Our men in forward positions stood no chance against the attackers. They put up a good fight with superb rapid fire and held the enemy back a good while. Too many Hun proved too much. Hundreds of men died in front of my eyes. Of those retreating, many took bullets in the back. Others who raised their arms in surrender were gunned down. Some suffered the bayonet. 'To save a bloody penny bullet, I'll wager,' Bottomley roared in fury.

It was our turn next. The Hun's howitzers, pitched two or so miles north and north-east from our front line and out of sight, launched shells at us and the Norfolks. These guns had not turned on us away from the Suffolks and Cornwalls to our right, as we first thought, but additional guns in the enemy's line. Big Hun guns, far out-numbering and much more powerful than our light field artillery. The first shells landed halfway between our now frail front line and my squad in the mill. Within minutes their gunners found the right trajectory. We, the rooftop five, could do nothing as shells ranged in on our chaps at the front. Five, ten, sometimes more men blasted to dust or cut to pieces by shards of sizzling shrapnel as each shell landed beside or burst above them. We looked hard to find a Fritz artilleryman to shoot to help stop the carnage. But their guns hid out of sight, range and harm's way. Artillery shells not infantry rounds caused most of our casualties.

The fighting raged for two hours. Stuck on the rooftop, with the enemy still out of range or behind cover, we riflemen became inactive observers. We couldn't go forward or backward. We couldn't shoot. We couldn't help our comrades with cover fire. We couldn't move to rescue fallen men. We couldn't kill. But we could be killed - the moment a shell struck. We had to wait on the mill rooftop for the war to reach us. Wait for the hit. Wait to die, quickly or slowly, with pain or without pain, knowing of our death, or not knowing we had died. Wait was all we could do, even as shells exploded all around and crept closer, minute by minute. Waiting without being able to fight is the hardest wait of all in war.

Idleness allows the mind to wonder and worry. Questions and thoughts, serious and silly, enter the head. Will I die today or be injured? If my face is scarred by shrapnel or flame and I can't face my own face, how can I expect Alice or anyone else to look at it? Is it better to lose a leg or an arm? If an arm, being right handed, I hoped it would be my left. If a leg was lost I could still get around on crutches, providing I had the use of both arms. I could sit at a workbench and make things, perhaps turn wood. I would be able to hold Alice. If I lost one arm or two, but had both legs, I could still get around. But losing a leg and an arm would make life very difficult, perhaps intolerable. And what if an injury stops me having children? Rumour has it the Boche deliberately aim bullets at our manhood. Alice so wants children, she said. If I returned home, why would a beautiful young woman take up with a broken war-aged man unable to father a child?

***

The waiting ended. I could fire my gun. Hundreds of Hun emerged from the fields to reach the crossroads and in range of our rifles. And we in range of theirs. Bullets began striking the low wall in front of us. Some found their target in our men on the ground around the mill. We heard their cries of anguish, screams of pain and calls for help.

Rapid fire from our Vickers kept many invaders pinned down. But it wasn't long before Huns started rushing forward once more, seemingly fearless of our machine guns. Through my loophole I could see the legs of a German lying behind a wall. I regretted my first shot at Le Cateau wouldn't kill, only cripple. I took aim and fired into the back of his knee. In agony he turned and bent forward to nurse the wound. By which time I'd drawn the bolt ready to fire again. And I did, right into the back of his head which he'd foolishly exposed. Two bullets for one death: I could almost hear the sergeant complaining at the waste of a round. Immediately after my second shot a German machine gun raked the top of the low wall in front of me. It scattered pieces of brick and mortar over my head and down my neck. One brick was shot out, and I worried the wall wouldn't hold fast for much longer, even against rifle fire.

'That bloody MG crew,' Cyril Meadows shouted. 'They're in that copse mid-field. Can you see?'

'Thanks,' I said, 'looks like five of 'em.'

Cyril fired.

'You can't count, my friend,' he said. 'There's four.'

I fired.

'Three,' Cyril reported, 'the rest have ducked for cover.'

The Hun machine gun didn't stay silent for long. It started spitting bullets again within seconds. Every man we shot was quickly replaced by another, each body cast aside like a sack of potatoes by the next keen gunman - knowing his turn for death and disposal would soon follow.

Lines of Boche continued across the fields. Like an incoming tide, wave followed wave creeping ever closer. They made easy targets. My barrel had never been as hot. Boche fell like ninepins, although every man down seemed replaced by another two or three. Nothing prevented them moving towards us - except a bullet. Even then, some casualties crawled forward. The prospect of certain death didn't deter them. And not one Fritz stopped to help a man down, their eyes fixed ahead, sparing not a glance to the side when neighbours fell. They followed orders to the letter. It was remarkable to witness. In a moment of weakness, I started to admire this display of courage, be it misplaced or mad. But sympathy for your enemy is not good when you're trying to kill them. Few of them returned fire until they found shelter behind a wall or hedgerow, copse or corpse.

Our building shook as a shell shot through the mill's lower floor. It failed to explode. But it took lumps of masonry away tearing through to ignite somewhere behind. We had been spared, but it destroyed a horse-drawn ambulance and did for the men being conveyed to a casualty clearing station. Germans took control of the crossroads, all our chaps there dead, injured or withdrawn. Every minute or so, under orders, a squad of Germans rushed forwards. Often there was little or no cover to find and we quickly picked them off, as easy as shooting roosting woodies. I'd been firing constantly for I don't know how long, having lost all track of time. I'd also lost count of the men I'd killed: a hundred, two hundred? Besides the sure-kills, I'd wounded others. I fired at any bit of exposed body, even a hand resting carelessly on top of a wall. Perhaps these casualties felt grateful to me! I had caused injury to relieve them of frontline duties, but not fatally. Thanks to my bullet, they might be sent home to their loved ones, permanently, or at least until they recovered. My victims may walk with a limp, or live without a leg or arm, but I'd saved their life. And I truly hope the man whose hand I shot is not a piano player, because I admire all those who can tickle the ivories.

Hundreds of Hun found firing positions in ditches and behind walls along the road opposite. More machine guns opened fire on us. It became clear one of these was worth two-dozen rifles. At first we held the Germans back. But their accurate artillery fire caused severe damage. Our artillery fired 13-pounder field guns with 2.95" calibre shells. These disrupted some infantry moving forward a few hundred yards away. But our field guns had little if any impact on the German's distant howitzers. To my right, in fields and around farm buildings, remnants of the Surreys, Cornwalls and East Surreys joined us. Whole companies had been wiped out.

Confusion spread along our front. Some units received orders to retreat, others to stand fast. Several messengers died before they could deliver orders. Some chaps believed they heard buglers sounding cease fire and stopped firing, even when they could see Germans advancing. They discovered German buglers deceived them and many died as they stood to surrender. Others fought on because they had not received any counter-order to the stand fast. These men, brave beyond words, stayed put knowing this would be their time and place of death.

Bewildered chaps, isolated from comrades, fought on alone, driven by fear or bravery - or bravery driven by fear. Terror spurs sensible chaps to commit acts they would never do if they had time to think about the consequences. Some surged forward to take out teams of German machine gunners without a chance of survival. None that I could see succeeded in his mission. Others, stranded behind enemy lines, attempted to run back to us, ducking and weaving in a bid to avoid the bullets. Most didn't make it.

Cpl Bottomley died first in our squad. The back of his skull shattered as a bullet found its way through the loophole. L/Cpl Joe Thwaites copped it a few minutes later. He had seen enemy machine gunners setting up to his left. Frustrated at being unable to get the angle through the loophole, he made the fatal error of shooting over the wall. Within seconds of resting his rifle on the edge, a bullet smashed into his head. His beloved rifle was left swinging like a see-saw on the top of the wall as his body jolted backwards. I'll never forget Joe's heroism, nor the sickening sight of his skull and brains spray out behind him. Three of us remained alive on the mill roof. We asked each other if we were all right. We replied 'yes'. That wasn't the truth. Cyril shouted down to Smith and Nugent on the floor below asking if they were all right. Only Nugent replied.

Le Cateau was clearly lost. Mid-morning and the enemy's pincer movement began to bite. Germans now commanded the road ahead and their artillery continued to destroy our ranks. To the east the Suffolks, Cornwalls and East Surreys had been completely ousted. Westward, to our left, the Norfolks had scattered like hens with a fox in the run. It was our turn next. We knew we were done for. The three of us remaining on the roof checked to see what ammo we had left. I had four clips, twenty rounds; Cyril Meadow three, fifteen bullets; Bertie Dale one, five. But we might as well down as many Hun as possible to help our men who survive.

The three of us picked off all we could, counting down every precious bullet. But this fight had become a battle of big guns, not small rifles. Rapid-fire artillery sent storms of shells killing and injuring groups of infantry, ours and theirs. Bullets killed hundreds, shells thousands. Rifle against howitzer is not a fair fight, mouse against cat. Corpses littered the landscape. Bodies, if recognisable as such, strewn in grotesque positions like fallen puppets, their strings severed. Heads, limbs and torsos, useless and lifeless, spread over fields and roads, as breathless as abandoned caps, spiked *pickelhaubes* and rifles at their side. If not dead, the injured lay as still as the dead.

Farmland had become war land, green fields stained blood red. Fertile earth that had for centuries grown food for life was now rich with the harvest of war - a crop of dead men. Across this land gentle villagers' folksongs had been replaced by the violent noise of war. Then, be it the draining heat of mid-afternoon, or men on both sides spontaneously deciding it was time for a breather, there was a lull in the fighting. Not a total ceasefire, rifle shots and artillery shells continued, but nothing like the intensity we'd suffered for the last seven hours. I'm not sure the pause was welcome. I just wanted to get things over with. Bertie, Cyril and I knew how this day was to end, and that tomorrow was a day beyond our reach.

We could have made a run for it, gone south. There was still time. But we stayed. We all knew what each other was thinking, for we thought the same. After all, Bertie, Cyril and I had known each other all our lives. We lived in the same village, played in the same streets, went to the same school. Bertie and I even joined the Army as Havercake Lads together on the same day. But no-one suggested we make a run for it. We could feign injury, or give ourselves one. We could say we got lost, confused, our officers and company went off somewhere. Nobody would blame us abandoning this post, sticking to an order that no longer made sense, even if anyone found out in this chaos. Surely it would be sensible to survive today to fight tomorrow, get away while we could. But none of us said a word. I thought our stubbornness bordered on stupidity. But our last orders were to hold this position, and we would stay until we heard otherwise.

This was the end, or very close to it. We couldn't hold out much longer. Behind their firing line, to the front, to our left and right, masses of German grey uniforms started forming attack squads. To order, they fixed bayonets. We decided, without orders, it was time to fix ours 'in the spirit of the bayonet', as we say. Fixing a bayonet somehow makes you feel braver, though in this situation it was a futile act. Alone on the roof, it felt like the three of us were up against three thousand, even thirty thousand. It reminded me of Father's oft-told tale of how a few British soldiers in Africa held out against thousands of Zulus in the defence of Rorke's Drift in '79.

Keeping his body below the parapet, Bertie crawled towards Cyril and held out his hand. The handshake was a gesture of friendship, of good times, of goodbye. I copied Bertie and scrambled near enough to extend my hand to both friends. I shook Cyril's hand and then stretched over to reach Bertie's. No words were spoken. Nothing needed to be said. We looked at each other, pursed our lips, raised our eyebrows, and nodded in understanding of what we faced. Then Bertie and I scampered back to our corner positions and poked our rifles through the wall in readiness for our final fight. A few more minutes and it would be over. We'd be killed, perhaps captured. Either way we would know soon enough. But it was already clear the

Hun were more interested in pushing on to Paris than be inconvenienced by prisoners.

Again, the waiting and watching started. This time was different, strangely different. For I knew this was the last wait, the last watch, the last act of my life. Any moment the Germans would advance, and with only a handful of bullets, they'd be on us in a minute.

I thought of Alice, my family, friends and people in the village. I searched for happy memories to help bring my life to a happy end. The time of your death should not be the time of regret. I felt content: at peace, in war.

***

A direct hit. The mill exploded. Bricks and mortar and metal and oak beams flew in every direction. Parts of Cyril spun sky high along with the wreckage. My head throbbed as if punched by a bare-knuckled streetfighter. A mouthful of warm salty blood confirmed my injury. Through a falling cloud of choking dust, I could see Bertie crying out to me. I couldn't hear anything except a distorted muffle through the high-pitched hum in my ears. He held out both arms appealing for help as an infant desperate to be picked up by his mother. I crawled towards him, surprised I could even move. Debris still fell all about. Not one yard ahead of me, the roof collapsed and crashed to the floor below. The gap was now too wide to cross. One second later, one yard further forward, and I'd have fallen with it.

Another shell struck. The roof on both sides collapsed forming a v-shaped ravine through the length of the mill, front to back. Bertie and I couldn't prevent ourselves slithering down either side and tumbling together in a heap. His right leg was slashed across the knee by a bayonet-length shard of wood. Bright red blood gushed from an artery. I'd never seen Bertie's face so white, even on a January night rescuing sheep on the moors in waist-deep snow. As if our suffering wasn't enough, the Germans continued firing. Bullets hissed past our heads and danced at all angles around the ruins.

As the cloud of dust cleared I could see 2nd Lt Harcourt outside furiously defending our position with his revolver. At his side Sgt Pratt fired his rifle rapidly, round after round. I was pleased to see them, I thought they'd died or retreated. Others too, around twenty in all, perhaps all that remained of our Battalion, maintained the fight against the fast-approaching enemy. In the far corner of what remained of the mill an ambulance orderly had set up a first aid post and struggled to care for several wounded. Across the roads and fields, near and far, bodies littered the ground. Dead men on top of dead men, contorted in every conceivable angle. Dozens of horses, fine thoroughbreds to farm cobs, lay dead or injured. One, just outside the mill, writhed in pain and panic, its eyes rolling in manic confusion. If I had a rifle, I'd have shot it. But my rifle was as shattered as Bertie's leg and lost in the debris. Everything everywhere was damaged or destroyed. Men, machines and animals, broken to bits.

Bertie faded. I called the orderly. Can't you see, he yelled, I've got ten men to patch up and one pair of these! He held up both arms. My friend's dying, I shouted back. Just pack the wound, he said. Stop it bleeding. Apply a tourniquet at the top of his leg. Shall I pull the splinter out? No, you bloody fool, he screamed, that'll kill him. Let the surgeons do that. Fat chance of getting to hospital, I shouted. Look, stop arguing and get on with it, he said. So I did as I was told and, amazingly, the flow of blood curbed almost immediately. The lower half of Bertie's leg was hanging on by a single ligament. His ankle was completely twisted and his calf so crushed that, had it been fully attached, would have been useless anyway. Bertie was writhing in agony saying Oh God Oh Jesus over and over again. Then he calmed, his eyes opened wide and he expired. Or so I thought, but he'd fainted, which brought some relief from pain. If Bertie had been a dog or horse, any animal suffering so much, I'd have put a bullet in his head. No hesitation. No second thought. To kill would have been kind, the right thing to do.

'It's no use,' Bertie groaned when he came around. 'I'm done for.'

'Nonsense,' I said, 'you'll be up and around in no time.' Bertie knew I lied.

'My innings is over. I'm out for a duck.'

'Don't be daft. You can still hit sixes on the green against Hebden Bridge next summer.'

Bertie closed his eyes imagining such cricketing glory and then, slowly, opened them again. 'My running days are over, Samuel, and you know it. Is it done for?'

I couldn't lie about his leg. Bertie, true to Yorkshire bluntness, always called a spade a spade and wanted the news without a sugar coating. 'I'm no sawbones, but I think it must come off.'

'Aye, thought as much.'

Bertie took a deep breath, grimacing in pain. 'You do it.'

'Do what?'

'Cut it off.'

'Don't be bloody...'

'Look,' Bertie cut in, 'how many sheep and pig tails have you docked? How many lambs you castrated? Hundreds! It can't be any more difficult than that.'

'Hardly the same.'

'Just get your bleedin' knife out and do it. Or I'll do it with...'

Machine gun fire raked the wall inches above our heads. Debris scattered over both of us. I spat out blood and bits of brick. I turned and saw the medic clutching the guts German bullets had just ripped out of him. He looked at me with a strange expression, half-smile half-scowl, as if he didn't know whether to laugh or cry at his fate. He slumped forward crushing the patient he'd been treating. It was time to leave the mill, or die. I stumbled across the rubble to the back of the ruins hoping against hope to find transport for Bertie heading away. There was nothing. No wagon, van, cart. Horses, mules and ponies had stampeded to safety hours earlier.

Something caught my eye in the hedge across the track. I feared a German and that I was a goner, to be shot, unarmed, unable to defend myself. But instead of the barrel of a rifle, the white face of a goat poked out. It had been tethered to a post and it came with a bonus: a cart, the size of a baby's pram, was harnessed to it. A goat-cart for Bertie!

While my back was turned, Bertie, screaming in agony, yanked out the splinter. As the orderly predicted, the wound gushed blood. I tightened the tourniquet to stem the flow. Pulling Bertie onto his good leg, I feared he might refuse to move, insist on leaving him or, worse, ask me to finish him off. But despite the damaged leg, dangling squashed and useless from the knee, Bertie hobbled outside with an arm around my shoulder. Bullets, shells and shrapnel whistled and criss-crossed through the air as Bertie collapsed into the cart.

'Is this… the best… transport… you could find?' Bertie wheezed, breathless.

'Oh, I'm so sorry m'lord,' I mocked, 'I gave your chauffeur the day off with the Roll's.'

Bertie squeezed out a smile. 'It's a bloody goat, not even a bleedin' mule.'

'That's right, Bertie. But I reckon a goat's cart with four wheels is better than you with one leg.'

'Eee by' gum,' he said, speaking Yorkshire, 'this will 'ave to do then. But next time I want…'

Bertie slipped into sleep…perhaps the longest sleep of all.

CHAPTER 7

ESCAPE SOUTH

Choice is not always welcome. Standing Orders in the Army make life easy. Just do what you're told. I had followed orders for three years. Now I had decisions to make. No officer, sergeant, even a one-stripe lance corporal stood nearby telling me what to do. I had to think for myself, and Bertie. Do I withdraw, as many had done? Find a rifle and fight on, as some are doing? Surrender?

Throwing my arms up might get Bertie treatment sooner. The Germans can't be more than half an hour from victory. And I'm sure German doctors can saw off legs as good as British ones. But from what we witnessed on the battlefield, Fritz was in no mood to take prisoners, certainly not casualties. A half-dead Englishman might as well be completely dead. They would let Bertie bleed away or use his body to blood their bayonets. They might shoot him, although that would cost a penny. And if they wouldn't care for Bertie, I doubt they'd spare me. There was, then, no choice.

With Bertie sprawled in the cart, I took the halter and walked the goat along the shell-scarred road south to Reumont and our Divisional HQ and medical attention. A proper surgeon could remove the lower half of his leg, still hanging by a single ligament at the knee, and repair the damage. Although Bertie remained weak, having lost a lot of blood, he regained consciousness. We weaved our way along the road littered with bomb pits, broken vehicles, smashed field guns, debris and corpses. Dead men lay scattered everywhere, their spirits seeping into the soil as sure as their blood. The old saying that waiting for war was worse than war turned out to be untrue. Waiting for war is far, far better than fighting it.

Bodies, human and horse, littered the road. The gagging smell of excrement, spilled innards, burning and decaying flesh was horrible. Most of the animals suffered shrapnel injuries too severe to patch up. Many had been put out of their misery with a bullet, a kind bullet. Reumont was only two miles away. But given the state of the road and with Bertie in tow, I reckoned it would take an hour to reach.

The goat would normally pull fruit and vegetables in its cart, so Bertie made heavy cargo. At least the animal was a strong Saanen and seemed willing to help: a rare quality in a goat!

Away from the fighting, still raging in the background, it became eerie when we found ourselves on the road alone. Or so I thought - until a bullet chipped the ground one step ahead of my boot. A German rifleman, about two hundred yards away in a field of stubble to our left, had spotted us. Damn the man. He fired again, missed, but was closer. The roadside ditch was our only hope and I dragged Bertie, the goat and cart down into it. Bertie groaned in pain. The goat, unconcerned, chewed fresh grass in the gully. I hoped the gunman would give up and go away, re-join his company in Le Cateau. I suspected he was an ordinary soldier who had lost his unit, not a sniper. If he had been a half-decent rifleman, I would be dead, or at least wounded. A good infantryman could not miss at that distance, unless his gun had been damaged.

What could I do but wait and hope that Fritz would leave us alone? Then, for the first time in days, a bit of good luck. Six feet away stood a trusted Lee-Enfield propped against the ditch wall. Its keeper, a corporal, had not shared such fortune, although I couldn't see what had killed him. Goats being escape artists, worse than pigs, I tied the Saanen's rein firmly around my leg before I edged forward to grab the gun. It looked in perfect condition, almost clean enough to pass inspection, and with a full clip of five rounds. A bullet struck the road above my head, then another. If I wanted to get on and find a doctor for Bertie, who was getting weaker by the minute, there was no alternative but to have a go at this Fritz. I risked, very slowly, looking over the edge of the ditch. At first I couldn't spot the gunman. Then I saw him walking openly across the field, confident I was unarmed. He went down on one knee and fired. I ducked. The round thudded into the earth inches behind me. I cocked the bolt and waited. That's what he should have done, but he fired again. The ground swallowed another bullet. There was no point in waiting, just time to do it - kill or be killed, do or die.

It seemed a strange moment to think of the only three words of Latin I knew: *Virtutis Fortuna Comes.* Our Regiment's motto means 'Fortune Favours the Brave'. So, without hesitation, hoping the

German hadn't moved, I placed my rifle on the ditch edge, put his body in the sights, squeezed the trigger. Fritz crumpled backwards as my round ripped through his chest.

It was the most vital shot of my life and nobody was there to witness it. When I tell Bertie later, he won't believe me, especially the first shot with a rifle I'd never fired before. (Rifles, like people, behave differently, sometimes slightly, sometimes markedly, and riflemen quickly learn each weapon's peculiarities.) I kept my head down for a full minute before checking the coast was clear. The shots could have attracted the attention of others. I was now certain Fritz wasn't a sniper. No self-respecting sniper would be so careless and exposed, and would rarely miss even small targets at twice that range. Snipers also usually work in pairs, a spotter and a shooter, and you would rarely see them. I couldn't see any movement in the rolling fields above us. But I feared the Germans would be marching down this road within minutes. Hence, with renewed urgency, I heaved Bertie back into the goat-cart to continue our journey.

It wasn't long before another danger presented itself, this time to our right. About ten men with rifles emerged from behind a hedge in the distance. This time no chance of escape. No ditch to hide in. Nothing to hide behind. They'd seen us and they would have Bertie and me. And the goat - perhaps for supper! I raised my arms while keeping hold of the goat's rein and stood still facing our end.

After these days of hell, I accepted my fate. I was done for. It was time, as they say, to meet my Maker. But any faith in God had gone, blasted to bits as sure as thousands of men had over these past few days. There could be no Maker who enjoyed destruction so much. An all-powerful God would not allow such carnage. Preachers say God understands pain because he allowed his son to suffer on the cross at Golgotha. But no loving father would allow such suffering if he had the power to stop it. Believers can't have it both ways: God can't be all powerful who allows war *and* be a lover of peace. If that's God's love, it's no better than the Devil's hate.

I could no longer flee or fight, just freeze. Any moment now my life will go black. These fields and the distant woods would be the last landscape I would see. I regretted not dying in the hills and dales of Yorkshire. And, in this turmoil, I doubted my remains would be transported home to my family. Yorkshire born and bred, but died in France. My body would remain forever here in a foreign land. I thought of Alice and saw her face...

'Put your hands down, silly fool.'

'Eh?'

The voice speaking English repeated the order, louder.

'You're not German,' I cried, immediately thinking what a stupid thing to say.

'I'm afraid we're awfully British, old chap,' the Captain said. 'I suppose you've come from there?' He pointed towards Le Cateau.

'Yes, Sir,' I sighed heavily with relief.

'And what news?'

'I doubt if anyone else will make it out, Sir. They'll be over-run soon.'

'You were with the Yorkshires, my man, if I detect your accent correctly?'

'Yes, Sir. Duke of Wellington's Regiment, 2nd Battalion.'

'Who else was up there with you?'

'County battalions, Sir,' I said, 'the Cornwalls, East Surreys and Suffolks east of us and the Norfolks to our left. I think we're all but done in, Sir.'

'What happened?'

'There were orders to retreat in an orderly fashion, Sir, so some got out. But it looked like some companies didn't get the order at all. There was so much noise and confusion, Sir. Others stayed to give covering fire. Not that it did much good. Most of the casualties were caused by artillery shells.'

'What happened to you?'

'Seven of us were on the roof of an old mill. We shot hundreds of Germans. But they just kept coming. Then we got hit by shells, the building caved in, and before we knew it we were on the ground in a pile of rubble.'

'Bloody awful mess, I'm afraid,' he said.

'And you, Sir, you are...?'

'Royal Irish Rifles,' he said. 'We've had a rum day of it too, five or six miles up the road from you.'

60

Thirty or forty more men emerged from behind the hedgerow. Judging by their cap badges, they were strays and stragglers from the Middlesex, Gordon Highlanders and Royal Scots. One chap was a Norfolk; their cap insignia shows Britannia sat holding a trident with a Union Jack shield at her side. The Captain was the only officer amongst us apart from a young second lieutenant, whose face was heavily bandaged. He'd taken a bullet through the jaw and seemed all at sea.

The Captain turned and addressed his makeshift platoon, 'Jump to it one or two of you and bury this man.' The trail of corpses had finished about half a mile back and I couldn't see a body to bury.

'He is dead I presume?' The Captain looked at Bertie.

I spun around fearing the worst. But Bertie was still breathing - just. I shook him gently to reassure myself. 'No, Sir, Bertie's still with us.'

As if to prove it, Bertie stirred and tried sitting up. 'Water,' he mumbled, 'water.' I gave him a sip from the flask I'd taken from the dead corporal.

'That'll have to come off pretty soon and the stump cauterizing, or the gangrene will set in,' the Captain said pointing to Bertie's leg. 'How long's the tourniquet been on?'

'Must be an hour, Sir,' I replied.

'Have you loosened it now and then? You know, to let the blood flow a bit.'

'It was bleeding so much, Sir, the orderly told me to tie it tight.'

'Well my man, let's just try.'

The officer carefully untied the cotton puttees I'd used as a bandage. 'With a bit of luck,' he said, 'the blood might have congealed enough to stem the flow.'

Bertie was denied a bit of luck. The blood-soaked bandage become bloodier and we realised the tourniquet had to stay. It was, for Bertie, either bleed to death now, or live now with the risk of gangrene later. The Captain squeezed Bertie's shoulder saying he was a good chap and was sure to pull through. Even in his poor state, I could tell what Bertie thought: that's what they tell men before they die.

Just then all shelling and gunfire from the direction of Le Cateau stopped. Silence. The first for hours. We feared what the sound of silence signalled. The Captain addressed the men resting at the roadside.

'Listen up, chaps,' the Captain said, and the men slowly stood gathering their rifles and adjusting their war-torn uniforms. 'We all know what this lull means. I'm afraid it tells us all our units north of here are finished. Let's hope our chaps who've survived, whether injured or able-bodied, are treated well by the Germans.'

'They're butchers, Sir, worse than animals,' a smooth-faced youngster shouted.

'That's right, Sir, we never saw no-one take any prisoners, even the blokes who'd thrown down their rifles and 'eld their 'ands up,' voiced a lance corporal, whose arm rested in a bloodstained sling.

'They just shot 'em down like we shot rabid dogs in India and...'

'Well,' the Captain interrupted firmly to cut the despondent comments, 'we can only hope the Germans do the decent thing now the heat of battle is over...'

'Aye, let's hope so.'

'I wouldn't put much money on it...'

'But what it means,' the Captain persisted, 'is that just two miles back the Germans will be reforming and heading down this road chasing our tails. It's three-thirty and we need to meet up with our main force and...'

'If there's one left,' someone muttered before adding, 'Sir.'

'Well, we won't find what's left of us standing here. The last order I received was that, if we became divided, we would regroup at St Quentin. So, my motley army, I suggest we hard-march that-a-way for about eighteen miles.' He outstretched his arm pointing the way. It inspired the men to start walking with a skip in their step, even the injured and downhearted.

'What's your name, Private?' he asked me.

'Ogden, Sir,' I said as confidently as I could.

'You and you,' he pointed at two young-looking privates, 'give Ogden here a break from pulling that goat and Bertie, er, whatever his name is, and help him along.'

'Yes, Sir,' they replied together, and jumped to it.

'Thank you, Sir. He's Dale, Bertie Dale. And you're Captain...?' He probably thought I was being rude. It's not the done thing for ORs, other ranks, to ask officers their name, unless it's to pass on or confirm an order. But already I admired him enormously and wanted to know out of respect.

'Allen, Royal Irish Rifles, Arnold Allen. And by the way, Ogden, you'd better get your head sorted. It's bleeding, don't you know. Needs a bandage for now. Maybe a few stitches later.'

I'd completely forgotten about my injury, which turned out to be nothing more than a four-inch cut above my left ear. But a little blood can look a lot and spread a long way. A nurse once told me you could paint one side of a door with a thimble of blood. She must have been exaggerating. But my injury appeared more dramatic than it really was. Compared with the injuries I'd seen today my gash was too trivial to consider. My head rested on my shoulders. I still counted two arms and two legs. I felt sane. I hadn't gone raving mad like some poor chaps. And I can honestly say, after Mons and this day at Le Cateau, having all my limbs and my mind intact seemed a bonus. Bottomley, Thwaites, Meadows, Smith and many others had lost their lives. The lieutenant and sergeant have almost certainly copped it. Bertie will lose a leg and maybe his life, if gangrene sets in. I was alive when far better men are not. Who lives? Who dies? Nobody knows. Some cop it. Some don't.

If I'd have died today my family would be saddened. But, as the saying goes, life goes on. They'd labour even harder to ease the pain. Mother will clean and wash and iron with extra vigour, the sandstone doorstep scrubbed with extra elbow-grease. Father will shovel coal into the boiler furnaces with tighter muscles and a firmer grip. Over years the pain of my loss will ease, although never go away, as with their youngest, my lovely little sister, Patricia. Every day, in some way, a passing memory brings a tear to their eyes.

I've only delayed my family's grief. It is just a matter of time before they hear the knock on the door from two soldiers. Before a word is spoken they'll know what is going to be said: *'Mr and Mrs Ogden, I am afraid to inform you that your son, Samuel, private, number 51850, 2*nd* Battalion, Duke of Wellington's Regiment, has died in action for King and Country. His loss is a loss to us all.'*

They will add I died quickly without pain and bravely. Whether true or not remains to be seen. But they'll receive these kind lies, even if I die a slow painful death following a cowardly act scared witless. The news will cover the village as quickly as clouds fall from the moors. Nippers will have marched behind the Army news-bearers, watched on whose door they knocked, and spread the word. *'Aye, missus, they called at Ogden's place on Sun Street.'* Neighbour will call in on neighbour and my demise will be talked about in all the shops, including the Post Office where Alice may be helping her father serve customers. Will she believe the news? Think it a mistake? Will she rip away her pinafore, don her hat and her coat and rush down cobbled Main Street to Sun Street to confirm the sad tidings? Will she see the curtains drawn in daytime, a sure sign of death in the home, before she knocks the door?

I'm pleased the prospect of war didn't rush us into marriage. There are too many widows already. I sincerely hope Alice finds another. It would be wrong for such a kind and beautiful woman to remain unloved. She will, of course, have many admirers and proposals. If not killed, but injured severely, I will not want Alice near me. My proposal will be withdrawn. I could not abide the thought of her married to me, a scarred cripple. The pity in her eyes would be more painful than any pain in my body. When I'm gone, in life, or from her life, I trust it won't be long before Alice consigns me to a watery memory that time will dilute completely.

I hope my family and friends will be proud of me, at least for trying my best, however inadequate my best has been. Getting killed in war is failure. I shall have failed to survive, failed my sworn duty to King, Country and Empire, and failed to fight to stop the enemy fighting. I will have let down my comrades. Death will burden them with my body. My failure means those remaining have more fighting to face.

Yet most chaps here and at Mons could not prevent their own deaths, nor protect their comrades from death or injury. Many, on both sides, took unnecessary risks. Standing up when they should have stayed low. Failing to gauge the time required to dash from one safe cover to the next. Foolish chaps moved into a line of heavy fire when they didn't need to move at that moment, sometimes under orders from over-ambitious officers. Others risked firing over the parapet instead of through a slit or cover, like Joe Thwaites in his enthusiasm to stop the machine gunners. When I die, or if seriously injured, I hope it's not because of my foolishness. In truth, most men died because they were, as every soldier says, in the wrong place at the wrong time.

***

Our ragbag platoon under Captain Allen's command continued its slog towards St Quentin. Retreat does not mean defeat, Captain Allen said, boosting our morale. We remain soldiers, the British Army, the British Expeditionary Force, and we'll fight another day. We caught up with stragglers, weary with injuries to both body and soul, who believed they could not take another step. Most, however, after rest and encouraging words, continued the journey. Just keep putting one foot in front of the other and you'll make it, the Captain said. More chaps appeared from fields, limping, bandaged, dishevelled, in pain and exhausted. Gradually the road filled with a column of troops, mainly British, but also French and Belgians. They too had become separated from their units or, more likely, their units had been destroyed like ours.

Driven by fear, hundreds of civilians from nearby villages and farms joined us. For some it was their second or third move on the run from the Hun. Some had fled south from Belgium staying with people kind enough to harbour them. But the fighting had again moved too close for comfort. Locals, observing soldiers retreating, decided to evacuate their homes and join the trek south.

Belgians told of the atrocities the Germans perpetrated during the invasion. Stories too terrible to be true, too sickening for the stomach to handle. Men, women and even children crucified. Heads of babies cut off and used as footballs. Women and girls violated in front of their families, Hun after Hun. Some said that nuns and nurses and children especially became victims of their bestiality. Surely no honourable man could bayonet women days away from giving birth or stab helpless patients in hospital beds? But they did. And if that wasn't savage enough, the Kaiser's killers burnt whole towns and villages and slaughtered unarmed men, women and children in the street. Even if half true, a quarter true, these barbarities strengthen our resolve to stop even one Fritz stepping onto our soil. We cannot be ruled by men worse than animals.

As Great Britain is a far greater threat to Germany than little Belgium, the Germans will want us to suffer even more. They'll aim to destroy our Empire, demoralise our nation across the globe. They'll defile our women, break the backs of our men and turn us all, including our children, into slaves. I feel ill just thinking about our beautiful country being trampled on by Boche boots. The orchards of Sussex and hop fields of Kent, the Houses of Parliament and Buckingham Palace, Westminster Abbey and St Paul's Cathedral, and the green hills and dales of Yorkshire should remain untainted. But, today, it is hard to see how we can stop Germany's march across France. Our tail is between our legs. We must catch our breath, regain our strength, renew our spirit, review our fighting plans. Let's hope reinforcements will replace our tired bodies and sad spirits on this road. And instead of trudging slowly south to St Quentin with our heads down as now, we must believe our replacements will march strongly northwards soon.

The road to St Quentin, hardly wide enough to accommodate two vehicles side by side, became crowded with civilians. Several motorcars and wagons had broken down or ran out of fuel. Carts of every shape and size, pulled by people, mules, donkeys, horses and, yes, a few more goat-carts, edged around the abandoned vehicles. Every means of transport seemed crammed with items tied on with twine or rope: mattresses, blankets, chairs, tables, pots, pans, tools. Every cart appeared to have a clock, as if time was important. Small children looked frightened or confused, feeling the fear in the air, although a few young lads treated the evacuation as an adventure and started to lark around, until parents admonished them. This was not a time for play.

Chaps suffering leg injuries found support from the able-bodied taking turns as human crutches. We managed to cadge lifts for some, but space on wagons was tight. Captain Allen's young second lieutenant, whose face remained wrapped in a bloody mud-stained bandage, suffered terrible nerves. Occasionally he fell on his knees sobbing. He'd be gently helped to his feet and, for a while, appeared to return to his senses to continue the journey. It was whispered the lad's father was 'something' in the House of Lords, an Earl or Viscount, and a family friend of Field Marshall Sir John French no less, commander of the whole British Expeditionary Force. When we Dukes arrived on the Western Front mid-August the BEF had around one hundred and ten thousand men. After Mons and Le Cateau, it's clearly much diminished.

Bertie drifted in and out of consciousness in his 'pram'. After some light-hearted banter, we decided to adopt the goat as mascot of The Captain Allen Corps and called it Heracles, in recognition of her strength and stamina. Some Smart Alec observed that Heracles was a man and suggested 'Heracalisa' instead. Another pointed out that, as a goat, *she* wouldn't be offended! Such frivolity helped pass the time.

Our jollity didn't last long. A threatening drone of engines could be heard drawing closer. But the sound was from the south. Had Fritz found a route around us? If so, nothing now would prevent German progress to Paris. Our worry was short lived. As the vehicles came in sight we could see they were ours. We cheered. Rescue at last. Even those in despair rallied back to life, their dull eyes finding light. But it wasn't to be. Our hopes dashed. The convoy forced us into the side of the road, soldiers and civilians. These troops were heading north in a hurry. Their plan, grandly announced, was to stop the Hun in their tracks.

To those of us who had faced the Germans, we knew far more men would be needed than in this convoy to cause anything more than a hiccough to the enemy's advance. This one Cavalry Squadron, with around one hundred and fifty men, and a Field Artillery Battery of two hundred with six 18-pounders, would be no match for the Germans. They will be rolled over as easily as small stones in a raging river. They were driving to their deaths. Captain Allen did his best to explain the strength of the enemy force, but the Squadron Leader's confidence remained solid.

Even though we cheered our cavalry on, they unceremoniously pushed aside many civilian carts into ditches along the roadside. Cargoes of piled-high household wares toppled over and a few vehicles suffered damage, some beyond any road-side repair. This lack of consideration annoyed many of the civilians - and embarrassed us, as we felt responsible for them. One old man waved both fists in the air at the passing troops and was clearly blaspheming. As he was not shouting in English, I didn't know the exact insults. But I can guess.

Unexpectedly, thirty minutes later, the Cavalry Squadron returned and again pushed many of us aside. The story had changed. Chaps in the convoy now claimed they'd been ordered to go north simply to establish the position and strength of the Germans, not engage with them. We suspected their scouts had realised the strength of the Germans and decided 'an orderly retreat' before any engagement was the wisest course of action. Their decision was the right one, and I don't blame them for turning back. It would have been suicidal to engage in a scrap with the German First Army.

We tried to persuade the cavalry to take our more seriously injured to St Quentin. It would relieve the casualties of so much pain and could well save a few lives. The convoy had sufficient space to accommodate some of the injured, including Bertie. But they had been given strict orders not to pick up anyone, healthy or injured, soldier or civilian, as speed was of the essence. Transport would be sent to pick us up shortly, they said: a promise not kept. Better to not have the lie than given false hope. The convoy's officer commanding, a major whose name I didn't catch, informed Capt Allen that we would probably have to keep moving beyond St Quentin.

'We're going to form a new front line, don't you know, to the south and east of St Quentin,' he called from the car while instructing his driver to kept moving. 'I see many of your chaps are perfectly able-bodied. Make sure they report in soonest. It's been a pretty rum do so far and we need every man we've got to get back in the saddle pretty damn quick. Yes, let's get 'em all back in the saddle. No dawdling.'

'Yes, of course, Sir. "Back in the saddle",' echoed Capt Allen.

'Toodlepip.' The OC threw a casual salute and his open-top car sped to the front of the convoy, horn blaring and his aide de camp shouting and waving at people to get out of the way.

Capt Allen turned and threw a smile and raised eyebrow to us. He knew we knew better than the major about the 'pretty rum do'. We'd been in the thick of it. We'd lost friends, limbs and blood. The major's pristine uniform, stiff-brimmed dress cap and polished Sam Browne belt and holster, clearly demonstrate he hadn't!

Capt Allen looked at Bertie in the goat-cart and asked, 'Did you hear that, Private Dale? According to the major you'll be firing at Fritz again tomorrow. You're to be in the saddle on the back of a horse. What do you say to that?'

Bertie grimaced, 'That'll be fine by me, Sir, if you give me a two-legged mule!' It was good to know Bertie hadn't lost his wit, even though he would lose a leg.

'Good man. That's the ticket.'

Fear heightened once the cavalry had gone. If their scouts had spied the German vanguard, it could only mean they were close behind. On horseback, even considering the condition of the road, a well-bred German cavalry horse could comfortably reach us in fifteen or so minutes at a steady canter from Le Cateau. Had our scouts seen the fearsome Uhlan cavalry on fine chargers with their 10-foot lances and razor-sharp swords? Had they kept quiet so as not to alarm us? Even though such knowledge would allow some of us to mount an ambush. We could not, of course, beat a Uhlan division. They are, we're told, the best-trained and most disciplined unit in the whole German army. But we could have despatched quite a few before they overwhelmed us with their lances. We would lose the battle, but it would help win the war. One less Fritz now means one less Fritz to fire at fellow soldiers later, one less to invade Britain contaminating our land and darkening our door.

Uhlans are notorious for their lack of mercy. Some say they never take prisoners. With this in mind, those of us who could walk faster did so. We hoped to reach the protection of our new front line at St Quentin, now only five miles away. We encouraged everyone to get a move on without alarming them about the possible attack. But it was no use. Many were exhausted, dispirited and hungry. Some were beyond caring.

A handful of old folks had already surrendered to their tiredness. Those with families told their children and grandchildren to walk on without them, kissed them goodbye, and lied: we'll catch up with you later after a little rest. They spoke a foreign language, but we understood what they said. The warmth of each embrace affirmed it would be their last. Tears fell when their faces turned away from their departing families. They sat at the side of the road, head in hands, going nowhere. They faced their future: hunger, fatigue, collapse, German sword.

CHAPTER 8

ST QUENTIN

The sun slipped below the horizon as our bedraggled column approached St Quentin. The air stood still and humid, a thunderstorm waiting to break, foretold by a blanket of dark cloud. Our convoy arrived safely, but we felt far from safe. It was only a question of time before the Kaiser's army came rolling down the same road we had trudged.

Newly arrived British forces, largely reservists, formed a defence line on the outskirts of the town. Some looked out of fighting condition after their time in Civvy Street. Most reservists had however served at least seven years with the colours as regulars. They knew soldiering: the regulations and routines, drill and discipline, weapons and warfare. One guard had grown distinctly portly since his service days. But if he survives the next few weeks he'll be lean and fit again: shipshape, we say, even though we're not the Royal Navy. With the barrel of his rifle he indicated the direction of Division HQ to where we should report and be reassigned new units. I asked if any Dukes had arrived, but he knew of none, although he'd only been on sentry an hour.

Capt Allen called us together. 'Well, we've made it. It's sad we've left friends and colleagues behind. We'll sorely miss 'em. But now it's time to split up and see if we can find our own units. The sergeant back there has given me a bit of good news - some Irish Rifles are in town.'

The dozen Irish Rifles gave a cheer and smiled at each other.

'It's good to know we're not the only ones left, Sir,' one of them said.

'Quite, Mullingar. We'll go and find them in a minute.'

'They'll be a-proppin' up the local bar, Sir,' another said. 'We'll hear 'em a mile off, so we will.'

We all laughed.

'Before we join them, hopefully for a beer,' the Captain continued, 'I must say you've been a great bunch of men today. It's been wonderful to see you all helping each other, offering a shoulder to lean on and, let's not forget, giving Heracles a helping hand pulling Dale along. I think his pram is all but done in. And you, Ogden, need to get him to the surgeons as quick as possible.'

'Yes, Sir.'

'Thanks to you all and good luck,' Capt Allen said. 'Let's hope we can all meet again in happier circumstances. And if anyone can't find a new regiment, you're welcome to join the Irish Rifles!'

'Aye!' an Irishman shouted. 'You don't have to be Irish. But it helps if you are - to misunderstand the officers!'

Bertie needed treatment, and fast. Each time he woke he was weaker and only held consciousness for a few seconds. As Capt Allen rightly observed, the goat-cart was falling apart, the handle had worked loose and the wheel axle bent to breaking-point. Heracles, thankfully, never seemed to tire and lived up to her name. Even the real Heracles, if he had existed, would have admired the goat's strength and stamina.

With Bertie slumped in the cart, and the desperation on my face, it was obvious to all what I was looking for. People pointed me in the direction of the hospital. The old stone building, with tall stained-glass windows, looked like a church. It had changed over recent days from a school to our clearing hospital. Approaching, I could see a long line of injured men, as many as three hundred, waiting for treatment outside the school's church-like heavy oak doors. I suspected that most of these chaps would be back in their battalions before too long. For in the Army, if you can stand, you can fight.

The line of casualties wasn't my only surprise. To the side, across the school's extensive garden and grounds, a field of stretchers. Men rested recovering after what orderlies called minor operations, although I wouldn't describe the amputation of a hand or foot as 'minor'. 'Serious' cases remained inside the school; classrooms of desks transformed to wards of beds; a place of learning to place of healing. Most of the men on stretchers slept, a few sat smoking and chatting to fellow patients. Where blankets covered the casualty's head, I assumed the occupant was sleeping. But it became clear these bodies awaited collection for burial. In the humid night air the stench of faeces, urine, pus, rotting flesh and vomit became overwhelming.

British nurses and French nurse-nuns, rushed off their feet, provided care for patients, changing blood-soaked dressings, giving comfort to the distressed, sips of water to the thirsty. The stretchers, packed close together, provided little room for the carers to step between. Not surprisingly, a nun lost her balance and accidentally tumbled on top of a patient. It caused amusement to those watching, but not to the man who screamed in agony. The nun, a kindly woman as you'd expect, was rather hefty. She became tearfully upset at the additional pain she'd caused her patient and, to herself, embarrassment. A few stretchers away, an injured soldier became delirious and had to be held down by fellow patients until two orderlies arrived. Several chaps had no obvious physical injuries. They simply sat and stared into space, their eyes wide open, but they could see nothing. Nothing except, perhaps, ghosts. Or worse, the vision of slaughter they'd somehow survived.

I steered Heracles and Bertie in the goat-cart towards the hospital entrance. Chaps kept blocking our way, telling me to get to the back of the queue. He needs urgent attention, I said. We all need urgent attention, they protested. If he doesn't have this leg off soon, I said, he'll die. That goes for a lot of us here, someone whined. Wait your turn like the rest of us. My mate here will have his arm chopped off, I'm sure. We're all going to die anyway when Fritz gets here, another moaned, we're done for. Heracles was having none of it. As if she understood, as if she cared for Bertie, the goat pushed her way through the picket to the door dragging me along. The goat-cart hit two stone stairs at the doorway and Bertie's 'pram' crumpled in a broken heap. Bertie yelled in pain as he tumbled forward onto the tiled floor. He was left prostrate face down in front of the reception desk manned by two nurses. Heracles galloped on into the school scraping the wheel-less remnants of her cart across the black and white tiles. It caused such a commotion that two more nurses and a medical officer rushed to the scene from behind a screen. The doctor, a major, in a blood-stained brown smock holding a scalpel, took one look at Bertie and summoned two orderlies to carry him inside immediately.

'And get that bloody goat out of my hospital - this instant!' the doctor shouted and scowled at me.

'Yes, Sir, right away.'

Heracles stood at the back of the entrance hall looking as innocent as a sleeping baby. Honestly, I really believed she looked smug, genuinely pleased with herself. 'Come on, Heracles, let's find an apple.' I talked to the goat as if it understood every word I said. Stupid, I know, but nevertheless I did. 'There's bound to be stacks of juicy ones somewhere in this town and you deserve a barrel of 'em.'

I unhitched the cart and walked the goat away leaving it for someone else to clear away. A nurse approached asking about Bertie. I told her his number, name, unit and where he was from, and that he'd received his wounds at Le Cateau about twelve hours earlier. And your details? She completed the form on her clipboard. I asked her about Bertie's prospects. She flipped her eyes upwards to the star-filled night sky, tired I suppose of being asked that question. The leg will go, she said in a matter-of-fact way, which came as no surprise. But she didn't give anything else away with words or expression. I asked if I could visit Bertie later.

'Don't leave it too long,' she said, which told me more about his prospects. 'He's very poorly.'

'Thank you, I won't.'

Despondent, I left with Heracles in tow down the row of disgruntled casualties still awaiting treatment. I must eat and sleep, I thought.

'Can your goat have a word with the major to get me treated quickly?' a corporal asked.

'Well I never,' one of the pickets moaned, 'the bloody cheek of it.'

'We've been waiting three hours and you swan along and get in straight away,' another complained. 'It ain't bloody right, not right at all.'

'It wasn't me,' I said, shrugging my shoulders. 'The goat ran off.' I looked at Heracles and, this time, I swear she winked. It was time to move away quickly.

St Quentin's clock tower bell in the town square struck nine times. But the town was so busy it could have been nine o'clock morning on cattle-market day in Halifax. Squads of soldiers marched by, others gathered around officers giving information and instruction. Clusters of men desperately searched for survivors from their company or battalion: joy at success, sadness with news of their demise. Vehicles of all descriptions drove in all directions, some in convoy, some separately. Wagons refuelled, others repaired. Horses refuelled too, with water and hay. And still more civilian evacuees arrived, trudging their way through the town with carts, bicycles, and, the less fortunate, on foot carrying their few precious possessions, some laden like pack animals.

Walking towards headquarters in the mansion house, I noticed a contrast between men who had been in battle and the newly arrived, a difference as distinct as midday from midnight. It wasn't just their clean uniforms, polished kit and dirt-free rifles that divided them from us, but their whole attitude appeared in stark contrast. New fellows displayed bravado and cheery optimism, eager for front-line action. No man who experienced Mons or Le Cateau shared that ambition. Perhaps if these new chaps had seen the casualties at the clearing station, their enthusiasm may have been curbed. I'd been at the heart of war for only a few days. But there was now a lifetime of understanding between me and the men who hadn't killed or witnessed their pals being slaughtered. These fresh troops had yet to suffer scenes of horror. Until they had lived through its dreadfulness, they could not understand the reality of battle.

Words can describe war, but they can't experience it. Whatever words are chosen, whatever order they are placed, they cannot penetrate the flesh like a bullet and rip through your heart. Words can't smell like burnt flesh. They can't taste blood in your mouth, as if your tongue had turned to rust. Words can't shake your body as the blast of a shell, or leave your ears ringing for hours, if not for always. Even if words could convey the full horror of war, perhaps they shouldn't be written.

I needed sleep and food, but couldn't decide which need to serve first. Heracles too should rest and eat. Locals no longer generously gave armfuls of fruit, bread and juice. With war on its way, they sensibly hoarded provisions. Invading armies are hungry. They seize food and drink, and hostile troops won't pay for it. Between the hospital and the mansion, now II Corps HQ, stood an old church set far back from the road. Through iron gates, at the end of a straight stone-paved path, its doors stood open. In candlelight locals prayed at the altar or sat in pews reading Bibles and prayer books. Occasionally a worshipper moved to light a candle, offer a short prayer, and cross themselves. Others had eyes fixed on a large painting of Jesus on the cross. His mother, Mary, was portrayed weeping over her son's bloody feet nailed to the beam.

The smell of incense drifted to the edge of the graveyard where I stood with Heracles. A priest administered bread and wine to those kneeling at the altar. Not understanding Roman Catholic rules or rituals I felt unable to step inside, although I had an urge to light a candle for Joe Thwaites, denied his last rights. Every man who died at Mons or Le Cateau deserved a candle to be lit in his honour, whatever his religion, or none. It's the least I could do for Joe. Not that he would know. Not that he would care. Not that one small candle's flickering flame would make any difference in this new world of darkness. And I couldn't offer a prayer, because they say the first sign of madness is when you talk to yourself.

Plenty of leafy shrubs and trees grew in the graveyard, which Heracles preferred to plain old grass. Avoiding the deadly yews traditionally planted in cemeteries, even in France it seems, I tied her to a small tree allowing sufficient rope length to forage. While Heracles gorged herself, before foraging for my own food, I decided to rest a few minutes.

In that limbo between sleep and wakefulness, I was being kicked, or dreaming so. I could hear voices, familiar voices, calling my name. Ogden. Ogden. Wake up. Get a move on. They're coming. We're going. Even after opening my eyes I believed I was dreaming. Towering above me stood 2nd Lt Simon Harcourt and Sgt Harry Pratt, both kicking the soles of my boots. And they were very much alive, not dead! I jumped to my feet and saluted.

'How on earth did you make it out of Le Cateau?' I asked, astonished to see them, before adding 'Sir'.

'Never mind about that now, Ogden,' Sgt Pratt said. 'We're all in a new unit and instructed to fall back in an orderly fashion. We'll be on the road in thirty minutes.'

'Glad you made it, Ogden,' 2nd Lt Harcourt said. 'Damn bad luck for the rest of your squad. You chaps on the roof fought magnificently. Must have accounted for hundreds of Huns. And I heard you saved Private Dale.'

'How did you know that, Sir?'

'Bumped into an old chum. Told me the tale. Said you shot a sniper or two as well and recruited a goat into Army service. That goat.' He pointed at Heracles.

He paused and waited for my reaction. But I just stood there, open-mouthed, waiting for him to reveal more. I must have looked as stupid as I felt.

'Arnold Allen, captain in the Royal Irish Rifles.'

'Ah yes, Sir, a good man,' I said. 'He helped a lot of people on the way here. Kept everyone's chin up. But how did he know about the sniper? I'd dealt with him well before I met the captain's party. I didn't tell him, or anyone, and Bertie...Dale...was too far gone to know what was going on.'

'That sniper, Ogden, accounted for two of his men and kept the rest pinned down for quite some time before you came along. He saw the whole incident from the field behind. Allen told me you must have found a rifle, because the next thing he saw was you firing at Fritz about five hundred yards away. Best shot he'd ever seen, he said.'

'I was pretty pleased, Sir, but it wasn't five hundred yards away, more like three.'

'Perhaps he meant five hundred yards from where he was watching,' the lieutenant said.

Sgt Pratt, clearing his throat to interrupt, said we'd better be off to the square and get ready to move out.

'Dale!' I cried. 'Bertie, Sergeant, I promised I'd visit him before they sent him home.'

'No time I'm afraid, Ogden.'

'Sergeant,' 2nd Lt Harcourt said, 'perhaps we can make a small exception.' The lieutenant turned to me. 'Ogden, if you're quick about it, go and say your goodbyes to Dale. But be in the main square in fifteen minutes, no later mind. And the goat we can leave - he can take his chances like the rest of us.'

'It's a "she", Sir.'

'Well, male or female, you have fifteen minutes.'

I grabbed my kitbag and gun, the dead corporal's rifle I felt wasn't truly mine, and ran to the hospital. 51891, Private, Dale, B, Ward Two, said the nurse looking at her list. I skipped between beds down four rows of injured men. He wasn't there. I feared the worst. Another nurse, reading my worried face, said she believed he'd transferred to Ward One and pointed the way. I found him among a batch of casualties soon to be evacuated by train to Blighty. The nursing sister told me this was not a good time for visitors. Sensing my determination however she stepped aside, not before issuing a strict instruction: five minutes and not a minute more. That's all the time I had anyway.

Even from the end of the crowded room I could see Bertie looked despondent, very unlike the cheery chap he'd always been. His eyes, fixed on the dark high-beams of what had been the school's assembly hall, appeared lifeless. When he saw me, he braved a smile, although it didn't disguise his deep sadness. Eyes tell the truth.

'Samuel, how are you?' He offered me his hand.

'Surely it's me who should be asking you that question.' I shook it.

'I told you I wouldn't be running between wickets anymore. They've chopped most of my leg off, you know.'

'Yes, I couldn't see any alternative. Your....' It was better to avoid details. In the pause Bertie's smile dropped away and he returned to his reverie.

'There was an alternative,' he said, slowly, sadly, looking in the distance. 'You could have left me. You *should* have left me. I'd have been all right now but for you.'

He grew angrier. 'I'd have been out of this hell, away from this madness. And now I'm left like this, a bloody....' Bertie's head bent down to look at where his leg should have been.

'Hey, come on Bertie old pal.' I tried to keep it light. But it was easy for me, I hadn't lost a leg. 'Look, silly sod, you're alive. That's what matters.'

'Yes, you played the great hero rescuing me with the help of a bloody goat. But alive for what?'

'You'd have done the same for me,' I protested, 'I know you would. You would never have left me behind for the Germans to finish off. And I wasn't going to abandon you.'

'But what's the bloody point, Samuel? What am I going to do? I'm buggered. Useless! Crippled! Crippled forever and a day! And you know what? I can still feel the bloody leg – the leg that's not there!'

Bertie cried. I'd never seen him weep before. I'd never seen him more than mildly upset, ever, and then only for a minute. Bertie had always been cheerful, the optimist, the one who'd push me to do silly things such as run down scree on hillside escarpments, climb higher in a tree than I knew was sensible. Once, in the Yorkshire Dales, he even cajoled me into going deep down a pothole with him with no hat, no rope, no boots and one lamp. One lamp! What if the paraffin had run out? Died a death in darkness, pitch black darkness, that's what! And now my best friend blamed me for saving his life. His despondency took me by surprise. I didn't think anything could knock Bertie off his happy perch.

'Come on, Bertie, this isn't like you.'

'It's like me now, with a bloody peg-leg to come. You should have let me die, Samuel, I'd have slipped away, bled to death. I wouldn't have known anything about it. What's the point of being alive, living with all this pain? I wouldn't have to face all those looks of pity, of embarrassment. And who's going to wed me now? Nobody! You're all right, you've got Alice. I've got no girl waiting for me. And when I get back there won't be a girl who'll look at me. Who wants a man with a stick for a leg?'

At the end of the ward the sister looked at her watch pinned to her apron. She gave me the narrow eye indicating my time was up. And I'd clearly upset her patient. I had five minutes before joining the ranks in the town square, a five-minute dash away.

'Look, Bertie, I have to go,' I sighed. 'We're moving further south before we start pushing the Hun back. My new unit's due to leave any minute. But just think, in a day or two you'll be back in Blighty.'

'You go,' he said flatly. 'Don't you worry about me, just forget about me.'

'You know I can't do that. I'll see you in the village soon enough. You'll find plenty of things to do. Old Booth will have you back on the farm, you'll see. And in cricket, when you hit the ball, if it's not a six or four, someone will run between the wickets for you.'

'Maybe. But my Army days are over.'

'Well, yes....'

'You'd better be off, Samuel.' He offered his hand and I shook it. 'Good luck. You'll need it.'

'Life won't be the same for any of us after all this mess. Things will be better when we've beaten the bloody Boche.'

'*If* we beat them,' Bertie sighed.

'We will. We must. Look, I really should dash, otherwise they'll want to shoot me for desertion. See you in The Fleece at Christmas for a victory drink.'

This was a pipedream. But, even knowing they won't come true, we need dreams. Even the most optimistic generals and politicians back in Blighty must now accept the Germans are much better equipped and organised than first thought. There would be no victory by Christmas, no pint of ale at the village pub.

Reluctantly I stepped away from Bertie's bedside, caught between loyalty to a friend and a promise to 2nd Lt Harcourt that I'd be in the town square on time. I turned for one last look, perhaps a cheery smile and final wave, but Bertie had already shut the door on the world. His eyes, dull, sunken, returned to gaze at the ceiling, or something beyond. I left the ward under the steely eye of the sister. I could read her mind as clear as a bold advertisement: well, that visit was a fine waste of everybody's time. She was right. I had done no good whatsoever.

Running towards the town square I remembered Heracles. I couldn't abandon her, Bertie's lifesaver. I turned and bolted breathlessly into the graveyard. She remained tethered to the fence. I had feared a local might have taken her: a butchered Saanen would provide plenty of tasty meals. I fell on my knees and hugged her. I may have kissed her on the head. For a moment I thought that's exactly what I should have done with Bertie. But any such soppy sign of affection with him would have resulted in a fist in the face.

Maybe I should have hugged Bertie, as father to son. It might have done the trick and snapped him back into his chirpy self.

I removed the goat's halter. She had her much-deserved freedom. Thanks for saving Bertie's life, I whispered in her ear, now you go and save your own skin - I'd go to the woods if I were you. How strange, perhaps silly, I felt almost as sad saying goodbye to a goat as I did my life-long friend. The bomb blasts and blow to my head must have loosened my brain.

In the pandemonium of St Quentin's main square at midnight my lateness was not noticed. The place was packed, men darting around like sheep in a pen surrounded by foxes. It seemed ten thousand officers and other ranks occupied a space built to accommodate a hundred villagers. British soldiers rushed here and there where French locals would once sit and stare. Everyone seemed to be looking for someone. Heads were turning left and right, necks stretched to see over the crowds. Calls of 'over here' or 'this way' or 'over there' echoed everywhere. Those of us whose units had been devastated in the fighting looked for our new formations, officers and other ranks alike. The Norfolks, Cheshires, Royal Fusiliers, Middlesex, West Kents, Royal Irish, Royal Scots, Warwickshires, Yorkshires and ourselves, the Duke of Wellington's - 3, 4 and 5 Divisions of II Corps - had been hard hit. War-weary men mingled with thousands of new arrivals. Some of these new chaps were, in their blissful ignorance, disappointed they would not see immediate action, as keen as Colman's to fight. But they arrived to find our retirement south had been ordered.

2nd Lt Harcourt and Sgt Pratt remained in charge of my platoon, made up to around forty by chaps from our reorganised 2nd Battalion. We now had to make good and pull together, and we would, because that's what soldiers do. Order returned to the streets of St Quentin once the new battalions organised themselves and prepared to move out. The cavalry, artillery and engineers, fortunate enough to have motorcars, buses, horses or horse-drawn transport, moved out first. The last of the field ambulances followed with the remainder of the casualties. The hastily set up hospital disbanded with equal speed. Bertie must already be on the medical evacuation train to the coast and will soon be on a ship home.

Most of us PBIs, poor bloody infantry, found ourselves once again in columns marching. To men who grumbled about legwork, the bark of infantry sergeants was traditional: 'You should have joined the bleedin' cavalry if you wanted to ride.'

'We tried, but they wouldn't bleedin' 'ave us!' was the standard jovial response.

St Quentin's Town Hall bell struck one as our evacuation started. Within thirty minutes the town emptied of British troops. Citizens who decided to stay would soon discover their fate. Resistance would be futile: a few shotguns, hunting rifles and pitchforks no match for German weaponry. I hoped that one day the old men would again sit in the town's square, smoke and drink coffee washed down with their strange aniseed liqueur. But I feared such peaceful days of gentle gossip and old tales had come to an end. Hun scouts will have watched British troops leave St Quentin, and signalled theirs to roll right in.

Having not eaten for two days, I tried to forget my hunger. Chaps said they smoked to stop feeling famished, at least for a little while, and I was tempted. Smoke keeps mosquitoes and midges away too, they added, pushing home their argument. But I'd been put off smoking. Like all lads at eight or nine, I'd stolen one of my father's Wild Woodbines or Capstans and sneaked off with my gang to be all grown up and smoke. The guilt of theft and grown-up smoking weighed heavy. It felt as if we had set light to a barrel of gunpowder under Parliament like Guy Fawkes, rather than lit a few stolen fags. But, like Fawkes' plot, it ended in failure: I nearly choked to death. Since then I've resisted all temptation, despite most chaps smoking. I also want to avoid the persistent little cough many get, and some chaps become quite breathless.

CHAPTER 9

31st August - 1st September
NÉRY

Storm clouds gathered. Brooding black clusters threatened thunder, lightning, and a soaking. But a greater danger weighed heavily on us: the ever-present threat of a Hun attack. It gnawed nerves, shortened tempers, frayed our humour. Five full days we walked, and much of the night. We dragged our sore feet step after blister-making step, leg after heavy leg. Food was scarce, restricted to a daily ration of one tin of bully and a handful of tooth-breakers - corned beef and rock-hard biscuits. No hot food, water only. Not even a warming cup of tea. How we longed for 'ek cup chai', as the chaps who'd served in India called a cup of tea.

So tired was one officer that he fell asleep and rolled off his horse. On a training exercise, this would have caused much hilarity. Any gaffe by an officer is a source of amusement and ridicule, unless he is a well-liked officer who laughs openly alongside you at their blunder. But a stumble now didn't cause amusement. Minutes earlier the very same captain, from the Northumberland Fusiliers, had himself been driving men back to the marching ranks and encouraging them to keep going. Most of us fell asleep on our feet while walking, which I didn't think was possible. But the lessons of war continue: the impossible becomes possible, the unbelievable becomes believable, the exception becomes routine.

Civilians once again joined us on their flight from the invading Germans. Several decided to stay and rest at the Oise riverbank promising they'd catch up after a rest. They didn't, and I suspect they gave up the struggle or the Germans caught them. We'll probably never discover what happened to the hundreds of soldier and civilian left-behinds since Mons. Some thoughts are best not to dwell on. Perhaps most found refuge and survive. For those resting on the roadside I hoped the advancing Hun simply passed by, ignoring their plight. Being old, ill, injured or infirm, they posed no threat. But if the stories from Belgium are true, the Hun would have cared not a jot. These poor souls would have been used for bayonet practice as if their bodies mere bags of sand. Absurd as it seems, we're told the Germans fear every civilian, young and old, women as well as men, as a potential assassin. They eliminate any risk from one - by killing all.

Since Mons many of the men who perished provided for wives, children and elderly parents. Dependents may fall to the breadline, besides the sadness of losing their loved one. We've heard of families that have already suffered the loss of two sons. How terrible for them. To lose one son or husband is tragic. But to have two or more members of your family lost must be devastating, utterly awful. Every son had a mother, but that mother no longer has her son. I too will die in this war or suffer serious injury. It will be impossible to survive unscathed. They say a cat is lucky because it has nine lives. I must have a hundred, but I don't feel lucky. In this my first week of war I've already been within a whisker of death several times. Any one of a thousand bullets or a hundred bombs could have had me. The tree sniper. The shells striking the mill. The machine-gun strafe where I could feel the air the bullets pushed aside. The lone rifleman on the road from Le Cateau. And the war has only just begun. I cannot escape so many shells and bullets in future. One is bound to find me.

I feel such relief I didn't rush to marry Alice before the war. It brings comfort facing my death or disablement knowing she is not burdened with me or my child. I have no doubt her caring parents would have provided for them both more than adequately. My loving family too would have helped in any way they could, even though we Ogdens are quite poor compared with the Illingworths. The child would have wanted for nothing, apart from a father. There will be many fatherless children before this war ends. No soldier who witnessed action at Mons or Le Cateau believes any more the Hun are a pushover, or cowardly, or unskilled. Frankly, they out-manned, out-gunned and out-manoeuvred us in both places. Our disciplined musketry certainly held the Germans back despite their overwhelming superiority in numbers. But eventually we retreated, the Boche advanced.

Being bright and kind, Alice would have cared for our child perfectly and made a fine mother. She is also, in a quiet way, quite independent in spirit, a supporter of the suffragettes. I like that lively spirit and proud of her for taking strong views. Alice disagrees with some of their actions, such as the woman who disrupted Ascot last year, but firmly believes women should be allowed to vote. Alice argues, as women deliver children into the world and nurture them, they can and should take more responsibility for the world into which those children are born. I found myself persuaded by her, although her father believes most women should not have the vote. Women, he said one evening when I'd been invited to supper, cannot understand politics. And, if allowed to vote, they should be at least thirty years of age to understand the world. Well I can't understand the world or politics either. Alice has more of an idea about what's going on than I do. And if this carnage in Belgium and France is a result of men understanding politics, then their knowledge isn't up to much. Maybe with more women helping to run things we would have more talk and less war, although we're told Boadicea and Joan of Arc wielded the sword as good as any man.

**

Oh, the relief and joy at removing boots, pulling off socks, unwinding puttees. The first time for a week my feet - and my poor wrinkled boots - can breathe. Who would believe that cool air drifting across bare feet and between toes could bring such pleasure? Fear kept our boots on, of course, in the ever-ready state to fight or take flight. And, either way, a soldier needs his boots.

I'm resting on a soft bed of sweet-smelling straw in a large fruit barn to the south of Néry, a small town. Our new company is quartered alongside a battery of the Royal Horse Artillery. Their lads claim they are the oldest regiment in the Army and, because of that, some of them think they are better than us infantry.

We've been told we may rest until six o'clock in the morning. Nearly six hours of unbroken sleep to enjoy. Bliss, unless we are disturbed by Uhlan cavalry, who made several raids on us in retreat. As there are hundreds of troops billeted here and well defended, the

85

Uhlan's would however be foolish to try. But shock and surprise, a swift attack in and a speedy retreat, is their key tactic.

It's midnight and I have one important task to complete before I dare close my eyes: write a letter to Alice. Among other things, I can give her the news that Harcourt has been promoted to 1st Lieutenant, and deservedly so. He, Sgt Pratt, Pt Keith Nugent and I are the only members of our original platoon left. The rest are dead, injured, lost or prisoner. The new platoon has however some old friends in it. Percy Jones, whose company was also devastated at Le Cateau, is back. He's a former milkman from Peterborough, Lincolnshire, so clearly not a Yorkshireman, but he'll do, and Lincolnshire is a neighbouring county. At six-foot one inch and as strong as an ox, he's good to have by your side in any fight.

We've also been joined by four pleasant chaps from Essex, the Hanslow brothers: Danny, Ernest, Alan and Davy. Brothers in life, brothers in arms, a squad within a squad, they boast. They've just arrived and haven't yet faced Fritz. All four are privates but Danny, being the eldest, claims to be the family-squad's captain; Alan, sergeant-major; Ernest corporal; Davy, the youngest, private. Davy describes himself as the brothers' dogsbody, but the brother with all the brains. They're all good chaps and, to stop confusion, they are the only soldiers I know addressed by the Christian name. They'd heard that some officers disliked them serving together, even in the same battalion, and certainly in the same platoon. The decision allowing them to serve together went to Brigade for the brigadier-general. He decided that if the brothers wanted to fight together, as we're all brothers-in-arms, they should be allowed to stay together. We joked the Dukes should only be for Tykes, men born and bred in Yorkshire, like players for our county cricket team. But then we took it as a compliment that outsiders wanted to join the best regiment in the British Army. We even have a few Scots, Irish and Welsh in our ranks. And they have, of course, been converted to believing Yorkshire beer is the best in Britain. (Well, until they return to their home brews.)

It's time to share my thoughts with Alice. But where to start? I know what I want to say, but not how to say it. It could be, and probably will be, my last chance to write. She deserves the truth. Sgt

Pratt said there's a Field Post Office here and, if we hand letters to our platoon leader before eight in the morning, they will be delivered in Blighty the day after tomorrow. I can't say all I would like to say to Alice because an officer will read it. All letters are checked. We have orders not to reveal any details about locations, troop movements or casualties. If we do write something to the displeasure of the reading officer, the letter will be handed back to us or, if it is a small error, a thick crayon will cover the offending words.

***

1 September 1914
My Dearest Alice,

It is midnight after the most dreadful week of my life. I am exhausted having not slept for more than the occasional hour. But I must write to you now for I may not get another chance.

Friends and colleagues have died or are severely injured. I shall not name them because the Army must inform their families first and I don't know how long the procedure takes. A long shadow of sadness will befall many families. Tears will fill an ocean.

Some casualties you know. They are from our village or nearby, and from Keighley and Halifax. Please don't try guessing who they are and keep this distressing news under your hat until it is generally known. It is possible some of the men are not dead, but captured. This gives hope they may one day return home. And hope is all their families may have left.

It is hard choosing the right words to say what now must be said. And no words will take away the pain of saying the following.

Alice, my darling, it is almost certain I will die here in France. No, let me be completely honest, I have no doubt that I shall die. It is a miracle I'm still alive, so close have I been to destruction, and this is only the first week of war. As an infantryman in the front line it will be impossible to survive more than a few weeks of this attrition. If luck exists, it will end.

However much I long for you, I cannot imagine returning to you or England. It would be against all the odds, all reason. It is thus only right and proper that I disengage from you. This will allow you freedom to marry another who can bring you love, joy and security.

To live the remaining days of my life, knowing you will never be my beloved wife, will be more painful than anything I will endure here. Yet knowing you are free from me will make my dying easier. Find happiness now, Alice. Don't wait for my return, for you shall be waiting forever.

*If you cannot forget me completely, reduce your memories to one or two of the many happy moments we shared, perhaps walking on the moors '...*where the wild wind blows on the mountain side'*, as you told me one of the Brontë sisters wrote. Over time, and when you have your own wonderful children, all your memories of me will have vanished like footprints in the sand washed by waves.*

Our plans to wed are as dead as the broken bodies I've witnessed this past week. There is nothing more I would have wanted than to love and cherish you in a life together. But that cannot be. This war has killed my hopes and dreams, as it has those of many. This war will dispose of my being and my body. But it should not destroy yours. I will die gladly fighting for your freedom and happiness as well as for King, Country and Empire.

Go, Alice, leave me and memories of me behind. Feel as free as the skylarks we saw soaring in the sky. Seek happiness in the arms of another, and I wish you well together. Shed no tears, for your sadness is my pain. But smile, for that angelic vision is my heaven.

Goodbye and enjoy your life for me,
Samuel
PS: Father was right. War speeds promotion. I have been made full corporal. Platoon Commander Lt Harcourt said I had acquired the necessary experience and demonstrated leadership under fire.

CHAPTER 10

5.40 am
NÉRY

The ground trembled. And again. I was on my feet. Within a heartbeat my sleep turned to scenes of slaughter, peace to war, dream to disaster. Shells landed in and around the orchard. Screams of agony and shouts of anguish filled the air. Men dashed in all directions. Those knowing their duty had firm tasks to complete, others stood injured or aimless amid the mayhem. Fifteen to twenty men already slumped dead in front of me. And for those unlucky enough to have lived through the blasts, their bodies were so severed by shrapnel that any hope of survival was hopeless.

Artillery horse teams, already limbered ready to pull field guns, reared in panic. Dozens bolted at full gallop to get far away from the shower of shells. A stampeding four-horse team bowled over two men like nine-pins. But the pair didn't have to endure pain for long: a shell landed square on them straight afterwards breaking their bodies into pieces. Half the barn's roof collapsed and the front wall looked ready to fall. Of all the things I should have done - running like hell away from this death-trap would have been the best idea - I propped myself against the barn door struggling to pull on my boots. I wasn't going anywhere in bare feet: hot metal, burning debris and smoking flesh littered the ground. And no infantryman wants to die without his boots on.

Those who could hurriedly donned uniforms and gathered kit and rifles. Some had, wisely it turns out, slept in their boots. I couldn't see Sgt Pratt or Lt Harcourt. For the first time since my promotion to corporal, the nine men in my section crouched around me seeking orders, some wide-eyed and open-mouthed. Of all things in this turmoil, the expression 'baptism of fire' came to mind. Surrounded by flames and smoke, this was my introduction to leadership.

What to do? What would Cpl Bottomley have done? What would Sgt Pratt or Lt Harcourt order? Could fire at the enemy's artillery? No, they were hidden and high above us out of effective range. Bullets still kill when their trajectory falls off. But at that distance it would be impossible to aim with certainty, even if we could see a Fritz. My squad, down on one knee with their rifles at the ready, looked to me for orders.

'We can't fight from here.' I felt embarrassed stating the obvious. What did the men think of me? Not up to the task? But my squad nodded firmly their agreement, boosting my confidence. 'We could try climbing out of the valley to get sight of their guns. But until we reach the top we wouldn't be able to get a shot in.' I pointed to a likely route up through scrub of clothes-ripping gorse and hawthorn.

'And as soon as we put our heads over the top their machine-gunners will try shaving 'em off,' Pt Nugent said. As the only other old hand in my section, he was right.

'We can't just stay here, either, Corporal,' Danny Hanslow said. 'We're sitting ducks.'

'Agreed. The quicker we get out of here the better. Let's take as many injured as we can and make our way to the village. We should find some cover and be all right unless we take a direct hit.'

'We won't be able to take all the injured,' Alan Hanslow said, surveying the casualties scattered around the orchard.

'Help those we think stand a chance of being patched up.' What else could I say?

'How will we know?' asked Percy Jones.

'We don't. We're not doctors. But let's take the conscious first who can manage on their own two feet with a bit of help and...'

A shell struck a trailer loaded with cider barrels not fifty feet in front of us. We all ducked fearful of being struck by shrapnel and splinters. The blast's force pushed some of us over. Debris and dust rained on us from a hundred yards in the sky.

'Is everyone all right?' I shouted, counteracting our bomb-deafness.

'I think so, Corporal, except for a mouthful of dirt and bells in my ear,' replied Ernest.

'You'll get used to it.' Sometimes it's best to lie.

'You were saying, Corporal, before Fritz rudely interrupted you.' Davy smiled. Good chaps conjure up humour in the direst situations, a real tonic.

'Yes, as I was saying, let's take those who are awake and can walk.'

'What if they're conscious but stand no chance?' asked Nugent. Like me, he'd seen men with their bowels shot through or chunks of flesh blown away and bleeding badly. For a while these casualties often remain wide awake, but destined to die. As soon as they're moved, they collapse when their remaining drop of life-blood drains away.

'Say we'll be back for them.' Another lie, one which they'd appreciate. Such deception, compared with all this carnage, was an insignificant sin. Even so I disliked myself for saying it. But we either give a little help and comfort, or none.

'The ambulance orderlies will be on their way soon,' I said.

'By which time they'll be dead,' Nugent observed.

'More than likely,' I agreed. 'But those who might live must take priority over those who will definitely die.'

'It's the right thing to do,' Nugent said.

'Thanks.'

Explosion not only followed explosion but shells detonated simultaneously. Bombs packed with metal balls blasted overhead shooting thousands of pellets in every direction to kill, blind and maim. High explosive shells detonated as they hit the ground, their splintered casings propelling shards of sizzling shrapnel through the air cutting down man and horse. So random the onslaught, it was impossible to predict where the next blast would occur. The farmhouse, barn and outbuildings became burning wrecks.

My section set about their task admirably. We found a deep field-drainage ditch about fifty yards behind the farmhouse. It provided the nearest shelter outside the village, which was coming under increasing fire. We dragged old doors and corrugated iron sheeting over parts of the dyke to offer protection from falling debris. A direct hit would prove fatal, but a little protection was better than no protection. Working in pairs, Keith Nugent and Percy Jones, Danny and Ernest, Alan and Davy, Gavin Peters, a Scot from the Southern Upland, and I, collected nearly thirty incapacitated men in about twenty minutes. We packed wounds, gave water, and made them as comfortable as possible in the ditch. At times our rescue missions had to pause, pinned down by intense bombardment. We also had several narrow escapes: shells landed in spots where we'd been not half-a-minute before.

Our good fortune ran out. We knew it would. We had gathered in all the nearby casualties when Alan and Davy decided to make one last search for survivors. Is that all right with you, Corporal? I replied yes. I wish I'd said no. They returned carrying a large chap peppered with shrapnel down his back, from head to ankle. While the brothers lowered him into the ditch the barn took another hit. An oak beam spun through the air as easily as a matchstick and struck Davy in the back. His spine snapped and Davy folded into the ditch as easily as a rag doll. The beam tumbled on into the field behind. We scrambled to Davy's side. But there was nothing we could do. The displacement of his back told us all he would never walk again, even if his insides hadn't been pulped. Keith, Peter, Percy and I drew back knowing it was only right that Davy's brothers be closest. Danny cradled his brother's head in his arms and Alan and Ernest held one hand each, although he had lost all feeling and movement from the neck down.

'It'll be all right, you'll see,' said Danny as tears washed through the dirt on his face.

Davy attempted the slightest of smiles. 'No,' he mumbled, 'I don't think it will be.'

'We should've been a bit quicker, mate, we must be getting old,' joked Alan, trying not to cry.

'I'm the youngest, remember, and quicker than you old 'ens - well, I was.' Davy's mouth was dry and he struggled to speak. Ernest gave him a sip of water. 'Thanks, Ernie, make the next a whisky.'

'We'll get you out of here as soon as these Germans bugger off and all this stops,' said Danny. Three bombs exploded two seconds apart as if to say, 'all this' wasn't going to stop soon. The shells destroyed what remained of the farmhouse.

'You'll be back home in no time with mum's cooking and a mug of jellied eels Friday nights.'

'And we'll still be stuck here in France in some god-forsaken hole,' said Alan.

'I can't feel a thing.' Davy looked deep into Danny's eyes. 'Have my legs been blown off?'

'Don't worry about that...'

'Have they?' Davy pleaded. 'Have they, Danny?'

'Your legs are there, Davy. I think it's your backbone. You got hit by a bloody big beam.'

'I can see my arms, but I can't feel them either, not a damn thing.'

'You'll get the feelings back, I'm sure,' Alan said reassuringly.

'Thanks, Al. I might be the youngest but...but...remember I'm the smartest.' Davy spoke more slowly and his breathing became laboured. 'You don't fool me. These legs ain't going walking again.'

'We know you're the clever one, Davy, but you're not a doctor. After some rest, you'll get the feelings back in your...'

Davy coughed violently and a cascade of blood erupted from his mouth. The brothers threw a worried glance at each other. Davy swallowed hard, gulping then gasping for breath, struggling to stop himself drowning in his own blood. Ernest was so upset he couldn't speak, but clasped his brother's limp hand between both of his as if warming it. Alan looked at Danny, his face spotted with his brother's blood, and shook his head slowly from side to side.

Davy's eyes closed slowly. The three brothers believed this was the end. But his eyes reopened as sluggishly as they had closed. Davy looked at each of his brothers, in turn, deliberately.

'Danny, I'm all right, really I am. I'm not in pain.' A short shallow cough this time before Davy fixed his eyes on Alan. 'You'll be the baby brother in a few minutes after I've gone...'

'You ain't gone, you dope, and you ain't going to,' said Alan, sounding as confident as he could. 'You're still here and you've got to keep fighting. How can we win this war without your brains, eh?'

'A good try.' Davy struggled to find air. 'But you'll manage without me. It just might take a few days longer.' The half-smile froze and Davy's face became a pale mask. 'Danny, thanks for being a great big brother. I couldn't have wished for a better one.'

Speaking became hard now. He paused between most words as each took more effort. 'Tell...tell Mum... I love her.'

Danny could no longer keep up the pretence to Davy, Ernest or Alan. The game was over. He accepted his kid brother was on the brink of death. To not acknowledge this would be a cruel deception.

'I'll tell her, Davy, I'll tell her. Promise. I'm going to tell everyone how you rescued all these men and how brave you were.'

Ernest let out a cry, but held his tears back to listen to Davy.

'But...I didn't kill...a German. I wanted...to...kill a German.'

'No, Davy, but you rescued loads who will kill the bastards,' Alan said.

Then, for the first time since the beam struck Davy, Ernest composed himself sufficiently well to speak. 'I'll kill a load of Germans just for you, Davy, and I'll say, "take that for Davy" every time one of 'em drops.'

'I didn't...didn't...let you down then?'

'We're all very proud of you, Davy, always have been, always will be,' wept Alan.

'We'll remember you every single day, Davy, every single day,' Danny said.

'Then...I'll die...happy. Can...can you...die... "happy"?'

Danny lifted Davy's head closer to his own. 'You can die any way you damn-well like, kid, my best baby brother.'

Davy smiled, coughed a gentle cough, and love looked out of his eyes. 'Then...I'll...I'll die happy.'

With blood leaking from his mouth, dribbling down his neck, all Davy's dying strength went into forming a broad smile, a smile without pain.

Davy, true to his wish, died happy.

But left his brothers distraught.

Ernest turned on me and screamed, 'This is your fucking fault. We should have saved our own skins. Got out of here instead of rescuing all these blokes, most of 'em will die anyway.' He stood up and lunged towards me.

Danny grabbed his brother. 'Steady on, Ernest, it's not Samuel's fault.'

'Whose fault is it then?'

'It's war. It's the bloody war's fault,' said Alan, standing to help hold Ernest back. Percy too jumped up ready to restrain Ernest and protect me.

But the tension drained from Ernest as fast as it had mounted. He turned to the body of his brother and fell over him weeping uncontrollably, his head resting on his brother's chest.

'Sorry, Corporal,' Danny said. 'Ernest knows it's not your fault, it's just…'

'Danny,' I stopped him, 'there's no need to apologise, really. He's upset. We all are.'

Perhaps I am to blame, I thought. Perhaps we should have fallen back, or at least stayed in this ditch under shelter. Nobody would have blamed us. And Ernest was right, some of the chaps we've rescued will die.

'It was bloody bad luck, aye, bad luck,' Gavin Peters said bitterly, his Scottish accent sounding strangely stronger. 'It was the last round of rescuing folk and he was half a second away from getting down the ditch. Half a bloody second more and that beam wouldn't have smacked his back. Aye, that's bad luck right enough.'

'There's going to be a lot of "bad luck" in this war,' Percy Jones whispered.

'Och aye, more bad than good, that's for certain,' said Peters.

Engrossed in Davy's injury, I'd momentarily forgotten the war and the storm of shells landing all about us. It seemed the German artillery wanted to drop a bomb on every square yard of land they could from their hilltop position, a thousand yards away. We couldn't see a single German from our ditch. Nevertheless, we fired our rifles towards them, in hope rather than expectation. We knew our bullets couldn't penetrate artillery guns' thick iron shields. If a Fritz caught a bullet, it would have been a genuine lucky shot, resulting from a ricochet or falling lead, which still has the power to kill.

Our artillery teams, the few left standing, kept their discipline and tried to turn our field guns on the Germans. But men and horses continued to fall from shrapnel. An officer emerged through the smoke of burning debris and rallied several men into action. They mustered three 13-pounders, but two took direct hits before they fired a single shot. The speed and accuracy of German artillery was devastating and, it cannot be denied, impressive. Throughout the onslaught the remaining gun kept firing, but man after man fell until

95

only the officer and two sergeants remained standing to operate the cannon. Then disaster struck. The officer's right leg was blown clean away when retrieving ammunition from one of the smashed guns. That should have been the instant end of him. It would have finished most of us, losing the will to live and accepting death. But this remarkable man, a true officer in leadership, and gentleman in manner towards his men, crawled towards the sergeants and continued to give the 'fire!' order before his life-blood drained away.

The German pounding seemed endless. But after around two hours our fortunes reversed. How quickly in battle the balance of power can change. On the ridge behind us our Hussars set up machine-guns. When they opened fire across the valley, it brought welcome relief for those of us who had been under the German cosh. The enemy's easy open season on us, all but defenceless sitting ducks, came to an end. Fritz had been content to dish out the shells, but not willing to take them. They hitched up their field guns and moved off as fast as their horses would take them. Next, joy on joy, our infantry, fusiliers, Dragoon Guards and Royal Horse Artillery started to encircle the enemy. So desperate was Fritz to flee, he abandoned many of his guns.

Néry and much of the surrounding land was left in ruins. Medical orderlies and stretcher bearers attended the injured and removed the dead. Casualties were to be taken to a hospital thirty miles away. Despite the pain, perhaps because of it - humour eases pain - men joked that it was better to have received a leg injury than one to the arm. If you could walk, you might not get a ride. The seriously injured occupied about a hundred stretchers lined up in the orchard. The doctors called these patients 'borderline cases'. Not a word was spoken amongst the men, it was simply understood these casualties may or may not be taken to hospital. Their fate would be determined by time and their condition. If alive when transport arrived, they would be taken to hospital. If dead, they would be taken to the nearest trench-grave.

Lt Harcourt and Sgt Pratt arrived amidst the flurry of vehicles. They had been at the far end of Néry at briefings when the attack began. I reported the death of our section's youngest member, Davy Hanslow. While Lt Harcourt was commiserating with Davy's brothers, two stretcher bearers approached and, on seeing the body, one asked, 'Shall I take 'im away?'

Ernest's anger rose again. He screamed, 'He's not a lump of meat, you know. He's flesh and blood.'

'We know, pal, keep yer shirt on,' the other bearer said. 'But 'e is dead and we can't leave bodies hanging about.'

Ernest, who had remained at his dead brother's side, leapt out of the ditch as if to throttle the bearer. Sgt Pratt stepped forward to prevent the attack.

'Now, now, chaps,' Lt Harcourt intervened, 'let's have none of this. Our enemy's the Germans, not each other.'

'Sir, we've got orders to gather all the dead and…'

'Yes, of course you have, private,' Lt Harcourt said, addressing the bearer.

'You're not going to take my brother and throw him on a cart like a dead horse for the knackers,' Ernest shouted, restrained by the far superior muscle-power of the sergeant.

'Oh, I'm sorry, chum, I didn't realise. I just thought he…'

'Was just another dead 'un,' cut in Ernest.

'How was we to know he were yer brother?'

'And mine,' said Alan.

'And mine,' said Danny.

Both stretcher bearers looked stunned. Their attitude changed immediately. 'Oh, I'm so sorry for your loss,' one said, and the other echoed his companion.

'Where are the bodies to be taken?' asked our officer.

'There's a site, Sir, about five miles down the road. A grave 'as been dug and a reverend was going to do prayers and a service and everything.' The bearer turned to the brothers and added, 'proper like'.

'May the three brothers accompany you, private?' asked Lt Harcourt.

'Well, I suppose…'

'If I order the three brothers to go with you, that'll be all right, won't it? And if I order you to take them?'

'Yes, Sir, of course.' The stretcher bearer immediately got the drift and I thought he was going to give our lieutenant a wink. 'Who shall I say gave the order, Sir?'

'Harcourt,' he said, 'Lieutenant Simon Harcourt, 2nd Battalion, Duke of Wellington's Regiment. 'And if there's any truck, refer your officer to the Battalion commander, because I'm going to square it with him right now.'

Davy's three brothers carried his body to a hay cart, commandeered from a local farm, although the two supply mules were British Army, not local cobs. To make space for their brother's body, Alan and Ernest respectfully moved two limp corpses and placed them across others further along the boards. Stretcher bearers, watching the brothers' slow deliberate movement, clearly thought they would rarely have the luxury of time to treat bodies with such care, especially under fire. We've a job to do. Must get on with it. Can't dilly-dally like grieving relatives. Bodies must be piled on top of bodies if needs be. Soldiers understand. Better thrown onto the wagon quickly than left to Germans - or scavenging dogs, foxes and badgers, not to mention crows and rats. No, to get on, best to think your shifting a bag of turnips than a dead person.

Davy's three brothers squatted around him on the blood-soaked cart waiting for the convoy to move off. Danny placed Davy's cap over his face, already set hard, his skin pearly white. I wondered why we close the eyelids, cover the face. Is it that the living can't face the face of death?

The remnants of my section, Keith Nugent, Percy Jones, Gavin Peters and I, an unworthy corporal, stood in silence as the cortege of carts slowly weaved its way through the debris and around shell holes. Lt Harcourt and Sgt Pratt joined us. We removed our caps and bowed our heads as the cart carrying Davy's body passed by. My head remained lower and for longer than the others, perhaps because Ernest's accusation that I had caused his brother's death still played on my mind.

CHAPTER 11

NÉRY, AFTERMATH

In the north of England September's sun provides mellow warmth. Here in France by mid-morning the sun's heat was as strong as England's mid-summer. On Yorkshire's Pennine Hills, westerlies would have already carried rain clouds from the Atlantic, refreshing June-cropped hayfields causing sufficient pasture growth for autumn forage. French fields remained brown, the grass brittle, tracks dusty and heat-haze distorted the horizon. The land looked as weary as we felt, and as damaged as many of our brothers-in-arms. The large barn that sheltered our company of nearly two hundred and thirty men overnight had been demolished by the German attack. Sections of its stone walls remained, resembling the decayed foundations of some ancient abbey. The terracotta roof had collapsed and smashed into a million fragments. Wooden beams lay randomly at all angles, as matches spilled from their box, including the beam which broke Davy's back. Many apple, pear and cherry trees had been uprooted, stripped of their fruit and foliage by blasts and burning: a landscape cared for by generations deformed in an instant by the uncaring bombs of war.

A foul-smelling sticky stench of fermenting horse entrails lingered over the land. A hundred or more dead animals cooked in the sun with no breeze to bring fresh air. Most of the injured stock had been used to transport field guns and supplies. But officers' riding horses, usually very fine mounts, suffered injury too. They had come from grand houses and estates across Britain, where they had enjoyed fox-hunting to hounds and cross-country events. Several officers stood over or knelt by the bodies of their beloved animals mourning their passing, and we felt sorry for man and beast. An officer may have ridden his horse since childhood. He would have formed that special bond between child and animal, sometimes closer than with another human. A young man's horse would have shared his secrets, known his adventures and often provided them. The animal may have helped overcome the lad's fears and transported him to places he would not have ventured alone, perhaps deep into dark woods at dusk.

Veterinaries and animal orderlies carried out a sterling job patching up injured stock, cleaning their wounds, stitching and bandaging where necessary. But, following a shake of the vet's head, a report would soon ring out and the injured animal mercifully put out of its misery with a bullet. No decent person enjoys putting down a horse, even a stubborn old mule that's deliberately kicked and bitten you in the past. But it is the duty of all those responsible for stock to end the misery of an injured animal if it can't be healed. It is an act of kindness. And in this cruel war any kindness - to man or beast - should surely be welcomed.

From our platoon of fifty-four men who lodged overnight in the barn or in a bivouac nearby, Lt Harcourt announced that nine had perished. Sgt Pratt, in his deepest voice, read their names, pausing respectfully between each one. With caps removed and heads bowed, most of us stood gazing down at the burnt and blood-soaked earth. Some closed their eyes. In my mind's eye, I could see some faces of the men on the list, especially Davy's waxen smile as he died. Of the six platoon members severely injured, perhaps only two would make it, if they were lucky, the sergeant added. After what Bertie told me from his hospital bed, I was no longer certain living was lucky.

Two young privates new to our platoon could not be accounted for. No-one could recall seeing them during the attack. Had they fled to seek shelter? If so, they should be back by now. Do they lay injured, perhaps buried under rubble, yet unfound? Had they been blasted to bits? And then those pieces blasted again, and again, and again, until nothing but mangled meat and broken bone remained? Although all the bodies had been cleared away, it was impossible to avoid seeing body parts partially buried and scattered around. A working party will shortly be given the grisly task of going over the area looking for anything recognisable - identity disc, pay book, holdall, mess tin, good luck charm, a New Testament - anything with a name to send home with the sad news.

I'd come to think the time for remembering the dead is when the fighting is over. In battle you must concentrate on the living and staying alive, not the dead, or even the dying, or you'll end up a corpse beside them. In the scramble for survival there is no time for sentiment. Perhaps, when this war ends, those who survive will remember those of us who perished. But I wouldn't blame them if they wanted to forget.

Percy Jones, Gavin Peters, Keith Nugent and I awaited the return of the three remaining Hanslow brothers to make up our section. The sun had reached its midday peak and we all felt hot and bothered. I was especially uncomfortable, dreading the reunion with Davy's brothers after his burial. We would on their return be obliged to offer our condolences and tread sensitively as on thin ice. Our usual infantry-humour would have to be curbed and laughter suppressed, at least while nerves remained raw. We'd have to wait until the brothers started to smile again, thereby granting us permission to do likewise. Perhaps the officer who suggested the four brothers should serve in separate regiments was right after all. And what if Ernest continues blaming me for allowing that final fatal rescue attempt of the casualties? Or worse. What if Danny and Alan come around to Ernest's belief and agree I was to blame for Davy's death? How could I be in the same platoon, and certainly not is the same squad? How could I order any one of them to do anything remotely hazardous? How could I trust them to cover my back? And would they trust me to cover theirs?

Our scouts had assured us that all enemy forces had abandoned the area and under no immediate threat of attack. The Germans had moved to fighting French forces at our flanks. Even more welcome than the scouts' intelligence was the appearance of a kitchen wagon. It provided a much-needed hearty meal of stew, delicious fresh French bread and, just as important, gallons of hot sweet tea: the best meal and tea since Blighty. The meat was horse, but it was fresh and fine to eat. Cook had been given a basket of herbs by a generous farmer and used them in the stew. Everyone said they wanted the recipe to send back to mothers and wives. Two of the herbs tasted very familiar to us, rosemary and thyme, but cook had no idea about the others. We started devouring the food like pigs at the swill. Many-a-mother would have slapped their son around the head for eating in such a slovenly manner. And, as you'd expect eating horse stew, it wasn't long before some wit warned us to watch our teeth - to make sure we didn't break them on shrapnel.

Lt Harcourt, returning from an officers' briefing, rode a new horse, a chestnut bay, at a good two hands smaller than his handsome black mare. It was clear from his disposition that Queenie had perished. Famished as we were, especially as second helpings had just been called, out of respect we placed our plates of stew aside and stood, even though the lieutenant signalled stay easy. We offered our sympathy for his loss. We knew, of course, the loss of a horse isn't quite the same as the loss of a family member. But we accepted Queenie meant more to him than any of us. Saying he had no authority to request such activity, the lieutenant politely asked for volunteers to help bury his horse, otherwise the mare would be butchered for meat or left to rot. Without hesitation, we offered our services, but he insisted we finished our meal and mugs of tea first. Arriving at Queenie's body, it was hard to see what had killed her. Some horses died of fright, we were told. Horses are nervous beasts, although it's hard to believe that fear alone can kill. The shock of a bomb blast can make their heart stop, the veterinarians said. Lt Harcourt removed Queenie's bridle and we roped her four limp legs to his new mount, who then dragged the body about fifty yards to an empty bomb crater. Some craters had already been filled with mangled carcasses unfit for butchering. We took shovels, including the lieutenant, and covered her with a good depth of soil. After we men walked away I believe the lieutenant, who stood holding his cap with both hands, said a prayer for his fallen companion. If he kept faith in God, and it made him feel better, why not?

'Thanks, men, that was very good of you, especially as you're all exhausted,' the lieutenant said on his return to the kitchen area. 'The thought of her rotting away or being butchered like an old nag at the knackers would have given me sleepless nights.'

'We'd all agree to that, wouldn't we lads?' said Sgt Pratt.

'Aye,' our united reply.

'Well, thanks again. I'd been riding Queenie for near-enough ten years and, as you could see, she was a handsome gal and a smooth ride.'

'Aye, she was that, Sir,' said Sgt Pratt.

'Oh well, onwards and upwards, as they say,' Lt Harcourt said cheerily. Like many of us over recent weeks - if we remained alive at all - the lieutenant had outgrown his youth. 'But before we can put our feet up for a well-earned rest, we've received orders to move south to a river called the Aisne. The whole Expeditionary Force is heading that way. The good news is that we're to be joined by many more reserves, additional artillery and better supplies.'

'Three cheers to that, Sir.'

'Yes, Peters, absolutely. These Germans are going to take a bit more bashing than we first thought.'

CHAPTER 12

6th – 10th September 1914
MARNE

I can record facts, as best I know them, but no longer feelings. Talking about terrible events makes them feel worse: the horrors still happened. It is a dubious claim to say a burden shared is a burden halved. Most who say that want to meddle in your affairs more than help mend your mind, or use you to heal themselves. For many, a burden shared is a burden doubled. It's selfish to load your worries onto another. We must deal with our own dark thoughts, rid ourselves of them, put them out of mind.

Suffice to say, after Mons, Le Cateau and Néry, I could not believe I would survive another day. I'm shocked to be alive, surprised to be still breathing, bewildered that I have both my arms and legs, and not one scrap of Hun metal in my body. A short scar above my right ear is all I have to show, and that's hidden by hair and cap.

From Néry we continued southwards, forced by the Germans further down than expected. The British Expeditionary Force, under the leadership of Field Marshal Sir John French, eventually regrouped and spanned a line between fifteen and thirty miles south-east of Paris. In early September, it seemed even Paris might fall. The French Government moved from Paris to Bordeaux in case the city was overwhelmed. In a little over a month German armies had penetrated France as a sharp knife in warm butter. Fritz moved to within twenty-five miles of Paris. Most British troops fought south of the River Aubetin, which runs north-westward into the River Marne, which then flows into Paris's famous River Seine. The Boche, using over nine hundred thousand men, trooped south in columns resembling busy wood ants before thunder. However, the men who caused most of the casualties, the artillery firing hundreds of field guns and howitzers, generally stayed out of sight. An infantryman at least looks at his prey in his rifle sights and watches him fold: an artillery gunner is a distant killer who rarely sees his victims fall.

Had the Germans taken Paris, many believed the blow would have knocked the fight out of the French. It would have bruised their spirit, and ours. But the French are resilient. Stubborn and obstinate, are the words our officers use. I, for one, have come to admire the French, although we laugh about some of their funny ways. They are canny fighters, make moves not normally expected. They certainly don't display British discipline and appear quite casual. Their attitude to officers seems, if not rude, surly. We in the British Army would be on a charge as quick as you like if we acted in that manner to our seniors.

On 5th September, at Tournan, we received orders and they were clear: stand fast, no more retreating. Our fire line, with smaller support lines behind and to our flanks, would not be allowed to fall back. This line was the line the Germans would not cross - unless it was over our dead bodies. The order had come from the very top, the Field Marshal, and even Corps or Division generals could not countermand the stand fast order. Furthermore, no fire-unit commander would be allowed to abandon an advancing role to become a detachment for covering fire. After the opening volleys on the advancing enemy, we had ourselves to advance and meet the Hun head on. Attack and keep attacking, go forward and engage in close quarter fighting as quickly as possible.

After being beaten back over the last few weeks, here on the Marne is where we would die as individuals or be defeated as an army. Or, we hoped without much hope, advance. We had reconnoitred our positions well for maximum firing range and surprise. Our frontline platoons, including mine, had dug good earthworks with plenty of loopholes through which to fire. They looked quite natural features in the landscape, so hopefully the Boche would walk openly towards us without suspicion. We would fire when they became fully exposed and get a good start in this fight to the death.

The scouts had reported a huge German force. And, despite their attempts at hiding their expressions, officers looked worried about our prospects. Win or lose, it would be the last for many of us. Or all of us. Within hours our destiny would be decided. We would be killed or captured, victor or vanquished. The German First Army, under the leadership of a General Kluck, who had chased the British Army from Mons, was ready to cross the River Aubetin just five miles north of where we had dug in. From what the scouts said, we believed the Germans viewed this fight as their final push before turning west to Paris. The Boche had placed three cavalry units to the fore, so today we would see the steel of a sword and length of a German lance.

Over the next few days I watched acts of breath-taking bravery well. Every man in my platoon certainly gave a good account of himself and we suffered no casualties. We turned the Germans or, to be truthful, it was often the case they themselves decided to move back without engagement. In view of their superior numbers and weaponry we thought this peculiar behaviour. We wondered if their withdrawal was some sort of tactical trap and half-expected a cavalry attack from the side. We stayed vigilant watching our flanks, but no attack came. Another rumour spread along our lines: Fritz had decided to turn and make a dash to Paris without engaging British Forces.

This turnabout at Marne taught me that advancing is preferable to retreating, where you're constantly glancing over your shoulder expecting an attack, like a stab in the back. Advancing, regaining territory, provides extra energy, strengthens morale, puts a spring in one's step - despite the torrential rain and lack of sleep.

Not all men demonstrated bravery. My platoon came across a few chaps skulking in the shadows and hiding in hedges and thickets. They made every excuse in the book to delay moving forward. Oh, corporal, I think I've broken my ankle, one told me, although there was no swelling. One claimed he'd seen a Fritz hiding in a nearby copse and was waiting for him to show his head. Their lies fooled no-one and an officer would put a flea in their ear and tell them to catch up double-time.

Those malingerers received the benefit of the doubt, their names taken, and a stern warning not to be caught dilly-dallying again. But one man made the mistake of stealing then wearing civilian clothes, providing clear evidence of his desertion. He was caught in a shed hiding his uniform behind a stack of fruit boxes. The absconder, a private in the Royal West Kents, was apprehended by an English gamekeeper working for a wealthy landowner, at first thinking he was German. The keeper was carrying his shotgun at the time and held the runaway at the end of both barrels while he sent a lad to summon assistance. My section was assigned to arrest the deserter and bring him back to our GHQ at Coulommiers. The old gamekeeper told the chap in no uncertain terms that he was a disgrace to the British Army. 'Had he moved an inch,' the gamekeeper told us, 'I'd have blown his kneecaps off. A quick death is too good for a coward.'

But a quick death is what the deserter received the very next day on 8th September. Outraged at the growing number of 'stragglers' and 'malingerers', our corps commander, General Sir Horace Smith-Dorrien, ordered this man be executed as publicly as possible as a deterrent to any would-be deserters. The man faced the firing squad watched by two companies of his comrades, and many others ordered to witness the execution. News of it spread rapidly through the ranks, doubtless as the General desired. It became clear over those days during the Marne battle that officers would no longer tolerate men who, unless severely injured, failed to move forward.

Some chaps talked openly about such cowardly deserters and condemned them. Yet, in our hearts, most of us who had faced carnage realised we had ourselves been on the brink of malingering. We secretly remember times when we delayed an extra few seconds before moving from cover. We might linger in a safe spot to survive another minute, take an extra breath, put off the prospect of pain and death. Like an animal, if a man can't fight or flee, he freezes. That short delay before rushing forward into a barrage of bullets or shower of shells helped us stay alive. Cowardice, or common sense?

Several men accused of cowardice I believe became confused, their minds bruised by battle. In the flash and fire, chaos and confusion, blood and gore of war, these chaps became overwhelmed, stunned, as if bashed by a brick. Unless they were great actors, it looked to me they didn't know where they were, what time of day it was, or whether they were walking towards or away from the enemy. Some stumbled as if blind. Others looked like lost little child searching for a familiar face in a sea of strangers.

Every man facing the fight here is afraid, or should be, unless he is insane. To fight without fear is foolish. It helps keep you alert, your head down, your body low. Most of all, fear helps you kill. When those Huns charged towards us at Le Cateau with bayonets as firmly fixed as their eyes, so thick in number they rubbed shoulders with each other, it was fright that forced me to fight. Fear of *my* death drove me to cause *their* death.

Kill or be killed is often said, and it's true. I must shoot someone I don't know, whose language I can't speak, whose country I've never set foot in, whose mother or wife or children I never think about. For if you think such thoughts when an object is in your rifle's sights, that moment's hesitation will result in your own death, or that of a comrade. The goal of every infantryman in war is to kill with bullets or bayonet as many men as fast as he can. We are not forced to squeeze the trigger. We can choose between life and death. But, at that moment in battle, the decision will determine the death of yourself or that of another.

From 6th September to the 10th we advanced at least thirty miles north from Coulommiers through St Cyr, Rougerville, le Lemon and Crezy. Some officers called Coulommiers 'Cheese Town', we supposed the place was famous for its cheese. Over these days, the French launched a major counter-offensive around the Marne. And, praise where praise is due, French infantrymen, called *les poilus*, put up a magnificent show. Their Sixth Army pushed out from Paris in every kind of vehicle, including six hundred of the city's taxicabs packed with men. This magnificent offensive put Fritz on the run.

We did our bit, of course, fighting between the French Sixth Army to our left and the French Fifth and Ninth to our right. It was wonderful for a change to see the backs of Germans, thousands of them, although they put up quite stiff rear-guard resistance and we suffered casualties. We still had to be cautious and fight our way forward with discipline. Once again, however, some officers and men became too casual in thinking the fighting was all but done. They suffered consequences for their misplaced confidence. I watched one captain talking openly on a street while bullets cracked into the wall behind. A colonel, from the East Lancashires, walked over to join him with equal swagger. Both were killed outright two seconds apart by Hun bullets, one through the colonel's ear, the other through the captain's neck. As a corporal, I cannot criticise senior officers, and most have my respect. Even the young lieutenants do their best. But the bullish behaviour of these two officers invited the bullets that killed them. A strutting officer in open view acts as a magnet to any infantryman's bullet.

As we moved northwards the biggest surprise was that bridges over the River Marne had been left intact, as they had earlier on the River Petit Morin. Likewise, after the Marne, at smaller rivers called Clingnon and Ourcq, their bridges too remained standing. We had expected to be using rafts, wading or even swimming to get across these rivers. We wouldn't wait for the Royal Engineers to reconnoitre the best site for throwing a bridge or repairing blown ones. Rivers, streams and swamps are the bane of all infantrymen. Crossing them always causes delays and inconvenience. No soldier on the move likes getting soaked, whatever the temperature of the water: weight of kit doubles, skin chafes, especially between the legs, boots squelch for the next mile, and when it's cold you get colder. Whatever efforts are made to keep yourself and kit dry, if you wade you get wet. And all the rivers had swollen after days of thunderstorms.

It seemed a blunder not blowing the bridges. Likewise, the Germans had abandoned hundreds of weapons and pieces of equipment. Even more surprising, most remained in working order. They had not even bothered to remove rifle bolts, a quick and simple way of rendering the weapons useless. Different engineering and calibres made our Lee-Enfield bolts unusable inside the German Mauser. But it was negligent of the Germans to leave rifles intact, even with a handful of bullets to use in them. The most peculiar items the fleeing troops abandoned were found in a motor wagon, so claimed a platoon we met a few days later when bivouacked at Serches, south of the River Aisne, on 12th September. The wagon, they said, was packed full of ladies' underclothes! Speculation was rife. Gifts to lure lovely French ladies? Had they raided shops to send these fancy lacy things back home for wives and sweethearts? The answer was simple, Pte Peters joked: Fritzes like wearing frilly things!

109

Chasing the Boche continued and our spirits remained high, despite the heavy rain. We advanced north, reversing our fortunes of the past month. Perhaps the war would be over by Christmas, after all. Then, to our great surprise, I Corps and II Corps, having crossed the Marne with relative ease, received orders to halt. Not even ordered to advance slowly, cautiously, but to stop. Field Marshal Sir John French required both corps to wait until reinforcements arrived from England, a new III Corps. He believed that for the next push the three units should work together. But some officers bemoaned this delay. They thought we should push home our advantage. When the enemy is on the run, keep 'em on the run, was a widespread belief.

CHAPTER 13

14th September onwards
AISNE

When we stopped going forward, the Germans stopped going backward. They dug in their heels on high ground north of the River Aisne valley, north-west of Rheims. Not only did this position provide commanding views but also forced us to attack uphill under fire. It took several days to get sufficient men across the river, suffering heavy losses while doing so. Our company, with around two hundred and fifty men, fared better than most, with only six dead and eleven wounded, two seriously. One chap fell down the embankment breaking his leg caught in the exposed root of a willow. It snapped the two bones in the bottom half of his leg, both stuck out through his skin. My platoon, now with forty chaps, suffered no casualties at all. Supply columns had been delayed and many of us hadn't enjoyed a decent meal for three days. Worse than feeling a little hungry was being constantly soaked to the skin because of heavy rain. Besides being famished and wet, after constantly pressing forward over recent days, we needed sleep. With no advance planned our battalion and others arranged bivouacs or made branch shelters on the edge of woodland. But could we sleep soundly?

Speculation circulated amongst us that, in the middle of the night, Germans would sneak down from their ridge with fixed bayonets, knives and garrotting wire. Whispers turned to open talk. Grown men, even experienced sensible soldiers, firmly declared the Hun had launched such night attacks against the French. Rumour turned to fact. Germans *had* murdered French soldiers in their sleep, stabbed in the heart, slashed across the throat or strangled with wire. And the Germans didn't use small raiding parties, but attacked stealthily in strength: a battalion of silent midnight murderers.

Officers soon heard the rumblings among the men. To reassure our safe sleep the number of night guards to the encampment doubled. Wire and string alarm traps were set between trees to forewarn of any advance. But with woods rich in wildlife, even traps strung high enough to catch a man would be low enough to be tripped by deer, especially male fallow deer sporting antlers. These precautions fanned the rumour fire. Men took this doubling of the night guard and trap setting as firm evidence the Germans did indeed indulge in such 'ungentlemanly' conduct. Few slept soundly that night, or any night for the next month during the Battle of the Ainse. Honestly, being murdered in your sleep by a throat-slashing assassin, unaware of your end, was as good a way as any to cop it.

We arose and nobody had been stabbed, cut or throttled. Our scouts reported the enemy appeared well dug in above us where the woods opened to farmland. It will be tough to oust them. Once again, after Mons, Le Cateau and Néry, I did not believe our suffering could get worse. But it did, at the Ladies' Path, *Chemin des Dames*, on a twenty or so mile ridge between the valleys of two rivers, the Ainse and Ailette. This struggle was as if the previous three battles had rolled into one and lasted, not a day or two, but more than a month. Every new day brought new atrocities and more molten metal to maim and murder.

It would take a lifetime to describe the events I witnessed, and I haven't much of a lifetime left. The images of suffering will stick like scars from a bath of boiling oil. The horrors would be even more horrific to write about than previous horrors, more unbelievable to read, more sickening to remember. It just gets worse. The scale of suffering increases by the day. The horror is beyond understanding. We fought for a field in the morning, a hedgerow in the afternoon, only to be beaten back in the evening. We would fight for hours - sometimes days - over one unimportant position: a wall, a bombed barn, a ruined cow shed, a stand of trees, a drainage ditch. Countless millions of bullets released, hundreds killed, thousands injured, all for a few yards. Bodies fell on fallen bodies, the dead with the injured. Blood flowed so freely it formed veins in the soil.

Rain fell for much of the time, and shelter was hard to find. Persistent rain prayed on the nerves as much as German mortars and howitzers persistently firing 'Jack Johnson' and 'Black Maria' exploding shells. Constant showers of rain and shells affected some men badly. 'The rain is a message from God telling us to stop fighting,' a grenadier, at the end of his tether, suddenly stood and screamed. 'God had sent it to drown our anger.' Then, like Tom and many others, he immediately received a deadly message - from man. A German sniper had him.

The Coldstream and Scots Guards joined the front nearby and within days their losses mounted substantially. Grenadiers also arrived and, in one skirmish at least, appeared to be firing accidentally on Ireland's Connaught Rangers. Local fighting took place in pockets along the ridge, piecemeal battles for piecemeal positions. We occasionally wondered if any senior officer was in charge. Some companies commenced actions independently of others, even in the same battalion.

Pessimism in war is more truthful than optimism: bad rather than good things are more likely to happen. If you think things are getting better, you're usually wrong. When the road ahead looks safe, assume trouble awaits around the next bend. When a situation is bad, you stay safer assuming it will get worse. If a miracle occurred and I found myself strolling down Haworth's Main Street on a summer's evening, I could not feel as safe as I did before this wretched war. Even if my body survives, my disposition will suffer for a long time, probably for ever. I can't un-see what I've seen. I can't forget what I've remembered. Even away from the fighting, I find myself looking over my shoulder, suspicious, wary. I react to the most innocent of movements, picked up in the corner of my eye, as if it's hostile. A sudden sound can cause me to hit the ground and raise my rifle. An unexpected noise starts my heart racing and squeezes my stomach. Should the war end tomorrow, it would take a long time for me to break the habit of constant vigilance. I can't ever again see myself high on the Pennine Hills, looking at clouds crossing the sky, listening to skylarks and curlews, chewing a stem of sweet vernal or purple moor grass and feeling free from danger.

Death occurred almost every minute of every day during our time near the Aisne. Death has no prejudice, no discrimination. Officers and men, rich and poor, experienced soldiers and raw recruits, died at Aisne and continue to do so. The upper-class chaps have no privileges at the fighting front. They have no more protection from bomb or bullet than the rest of us. And, from what I've seen at Aisne and elsewhere, these chaps get stuck into the fight as much as the rest of us. Many of the junior officers give a good account of themselves. Some of them are a little hasty, foolhardy to experienced eyes, but their bravery cannot be denied.

We heard that two aristocrats, a Lord Hay and a Lord Guernsey, fell to one German sniper. I know not whether they were young or old, new volunteers or regulars. Either way, I'm sure their families will feel the pain of their loss just like any ordinary family. But, as in life, officers in death are treated differently too. Most officers are taken to be buried in local churches and usually placed in their own plot, whereas the rest of us ORs, other ranks, are laid to rest in long pits. We generally get a quick Lord's Prayer and a short reading. The vicars do their best to disguise their boredom. But it must be difficult keeping enthusiasm for burying the daily dead delivering the same funeral service. The officers, especially the senior ones or those well placed in society, often have tributes paid to their achievements. But field marshal or private, we're equal when dead. It won't matter to me what the vicar says when I'm below his shoes. I'd prefer he said nothing, and I'm sure the worms and beetles will find my flesh as good as any officer's.

The Germans dug in. We dug in. Spades became as important as rifles. In the wasteland between our positions hundreds lay dead, stinking and rotting, and nobody seemed keen to do anything about it for days on end. Even under cover of darkness, neither side risked retrieval of the corpses. We believed the bodies were, for the most part, German, and so rightly assumed collection was their responsibility. But perhaps the Germans thought many of the bodies were ours and we should clear up our own. Ours or theirs, corpses remained all around - human, horse and cattle - some bloated to twice their size in life.

Reports came from along the *Chemin des Dames* of terrible losses, on both sides. Over three days at Troyon around five hundred men and nine officers of the Loyal North Lancashires died. The French, fighting to the east, suffered frightening numbers of casualties. Talk had it that over two thousand died each day, although some claimed the figures had been exaggerated. It's impossible to tell: a soldier can only see the fight in front of him, not the battle, not the war. One day perhaps the true number of deaths will be known, when sons, husbands and brothers don't return home.

Fighting at the Aisne rarely paused, certainly during daylight hours. After the first two weeks, however, by which time both sides had dug in, we enjoyed periods of calm at night. No artillery, no gunshot. Peace for an hour, sometimes two. Then a rifle crack. And before you could open an eyelid, dozens of rounds had been discharged by those on guard. Calm and common sense was sometimes restored quickly, and men not on duty could return to sleep. At other times one midnight bullet resulted in two hours of all-out war. Resting troops would be mustered and ordered into defensive positions. On investigation in the morning light the 'attacking Hun' turned out to be, on one occasion, an escaped donkey. I'm proud to say that whenever my section was on night sentry, all my men kept a calm head and steady trigger-finger. None of them panicked at movement in the darkness. We found that most of the spooked sentries were town chaps, not used to the sounds of the countryside at night. Most of my section grew up in the countryside and could tell the movement of a fox, rabbit, stoat or vole from an invading German Army. Woods come alive at night with all sorts of noises, and we knew this. Unlike one embarrassed private from the Bedfords, who confused a badger's head with that of a Fritz – his single shot resulted in three hours of gun, mortar and shell fire.

It was here at Aisne we started to excavate longer and deeper trenches. They became elaborate and complex warrens, far from the shallow scrapes we dug in preparation for previous battles. Officers were sent specific instructions with illustrations on how to construct various trenches, redoubts and gun emplacements. Field Engineers supervised our work. They were very strict and precise in what we had to do. My platoon was first assigned to construct several redoubts, small firing fortifications often situated for maximum surprise in unexpected places. The engineers measured to the last inch. Heated discussions sometimes arose between the engineers and infantry because we could see a better way of constructing the trench to aid our firing position. But that's not in the Manual of Field Engineering, they would say. We would reply that we're the men who use the damn things. One way or another, usually with compromise and humour, such disputes became resolved. In any case, as soon as the engineers' backs were turned, we would amend the loopholes and so on to suit us.

Despite the British Army's instinct for attack, the longer we stayed in the Aisne, it seemed defence was taking over from attack. Big artillery guns at the back became set to fight this war more than small infantry rifles at the front. Although, to secure victory, only a bayonet forces a man out of a hole. In October French troops appeared in dribs and drabs and they took over our positions. Most of my Battalion, indeed the whole of the much-depleted British Expeditionary Force, left the area in the middle of October. We were glad to go. All of us left friends and comrades dead at *Chemin des Dames*.

After a day on the Aisne, men who faced fighting for the first time had already grown into old warriors. They had killed. And someone they failed to kill shot the man next to them; a brother, cousin, friend, or some stranger attached to your platoon that very morning. Strangers become close friends very quickly in war, when minutes of life become valued in years. Smart clean uniforms of last month had become as dog-eared as mine. That eagerness to get into the fray had changed into a dull routine. We simply follow orders. We go where we are told to go. We do what we are told to do. We do what soldiers are trained to do: kill. Perhaps, after a break from the front, we'll all think differently and our spirits will rise again. We might actually think. We might actually feel. We might do something independently from the man to our left and right. We might again become human.

Of all my terrible times on the Aisne one memory repeats itself: a military band playing God Save the King. A German band! It was a quiet evening, no fighting, no rain, no wind. Some chaps became angry thinking Fritz was taking the piss. They wanted the artillery to launch an attack to stop the insulting behaviour and teach them a lesson. I told them not to get upset because the tune was a traditional German folksong. They threw me suspicious looks, as if they'd discovered a Germany spy! How could I possibly know that? I explained. Haworth, my village, has a good brass band. In summer, and at Christmas, the band performs a fund-raising concert at the top of Main Street between the Black Bull and King's Arms, just outside the Post Office store ran by Alice's father. (My heart ached at the thought of her.) At the end of the performance, before our National Anthem was played, the Haworth Public Band's conductor, Handel Parker, explained the origins of the tune. Lt Harcourt, overhearing our chat, added that our anthem was indeed the same as the Kaiser's. Well I never, was the general reaction. Those of us at the front didn't fall for Fritz's trick. However much we respect our King, if we'd have stood to respect the anthem, our heads would have been sniped. We felt certain our sovereign would pardon us!

A new army has been formed, the Northern Army Group. It is comprised of the British Expeditionary Force, the French Second and Tenth Armies. To our surprise a Frenchman has been put in charge - in command of British troops! An officer said the dukes of Marlborough and Wellington, not to mention Drake, Nelson and Clive of India, would 'turn in their graves' on hearing this news. The Frenchman is General Ferdinand Foch. And with that name, it takes no imagination to work out what most soldiers call him. By all accounts Foch seems to know what he's doing. He'll need to.

CHAPTER 14

25th December 1914
LOCRE, YPRES

Christmas Day is as it should be, peaceful. No firing from any gun, large or small. We've received no orders to attack or retreat. The war takes a holiday. Every day should be a holiday. If it's wrong to fight on Christmas Day, it must be wrong to fight on any day. Or is war work just like any other trade? Monday to Saturday we fight, kill or be killed. Sundays and special days we're allowed time off. Strangely, the so-called 'day of rest' has usually been the busiest day for fighting, perhaps because both sides believe God is on their side.

We often lose track of what day it is here. It's not important to know the day you die. What's important is that today is Christmas Day, although we agree today is Friday. We're looking forward to a hearty lunch with pudding and, if the rumours are right, extra rum. Then alongside our letters we hope to receive parcels with a present or two from home. We expect at least a big slice of mother-made Christmas cake, but hopefully a whole cake in a tin.

Since *Chemin des Dames* I've suffered several days of darkness. Black thoughts left me with sadness so heavy it felt impossible to carry on. Anguish of one kind or another affects us all, especially with no end in sight to this bloody war. But feelings must be hidden. I was unable to commit my dark thoughts to paper. Too sad to share. Events occurred so despicable that I did not wish to think of them ever again. But I will. Can't be prevented. They stick in the mind worse than dog dirt on boots. It's hard to forget horror, however hard you try, unless you turn to face the wall and find the madness of an empty mind. You can clean dog dirt off your boots, even with your own tongue, but horror is a glue that becomes part of you.

Normal people, people who haven't experienced war, could not image how dreadful some events are. They would not want to imagine them. Even if they could create such vile images in their minds, they would not believe they could happen outside a deprived mind and troubled soul. If I told the truth, people would think my stories had come from a lunatic, a mind so sadistic, perverse and barbaric that the writer himself should be confined to a mad house. Such things should not be written, but outlawed and banned. When truth is so terrible, deceit or silence is kinder. I could see no point in carrying on. A diary recording days of distress in mind, drudgery in body, despair in heart, is a record that should never be opened. It serves no purpose other than to bring more pain and suffering.

Besides despondency, a more sinister feeling overtook me some days: numbness, nothingness. No feeling, no thought, an ocean of emptiness, a dull, blank mind alongside a heart empty of love and compassion. This condition crippled me to where nothing mattered anymore: live or die, eat or starve, kill or be killed, I cared not one jot. I fired my rifle at many a man's head without conscience, concern or malice. My target could have already been as dead as a tin can on a wall. Killing was simply something I did, my duty, my job. I'm sure all of us in the platoon felt this, some more than others, some days more than others, but we disguised it well. We just go through the motions mindlessly until something snaps us out of our malaise, often a good sleep. We wake up to a new dawn even though it's the same old war.

Perhaps I should tell the whole truth and nothing but the truth. But the truth of war is unbelievable - to those fortunate enough not to have been in the thick of it. Through the centuries all men who faced battle must have suffered the same. Whether killed or maimed by club, arrow, lance, sword, bayonet, bullet or bomb, the pain is the same. Death is death. It's no better or worse for a soldier now than when the Romans invaded Britain. A lost leg is a lost leg, however and whenever severed, be you a Roman or Bertie.

Politicians say this war will bring peace once and for all: a war to end wars. But what value can be placed on the promises of politicians? War turns life into death. War is about destruction: of people, of property, of hope.

Educated people, such as historians, will make a better fist of recording the events of this tragic war. I can only talk about my experience and those of the men around me. Rumour chases rumour. Facts change to fiction overnight. Rumours turn out to be true. We're told one thing, then another. The French are here, then there, so too the Germans. One day we're undeniably winning the war, but then we find ourselves fleeing another German advance. In a hundred years from now, if we haven't blown each other to bits, perhaps all the facts will come to light and war will be understood. But I doubt it. If we can't fathom what's going on today, I can't see how history will uncover new truths. However, perhaps it is only after one hundred years that people will understand what happened today, and why.

The Hanslow brothers re-joined us and, after a few days, our platoon seemed at one. Right or wrong, Davy was never mentioned, certainly not outside the three brothers. The day after Davy was buried (and Queenie) and nearly two hundred more men, Lt Harcourt asked me to explain the circumstances of Davy's death. At first I worried he was accusing me of doing wrong, or at least suggesting I could have done better. Nothing could be further from the truth. He praised me and my section for rescuing so many injured men under fire. He regretted that he and Sgt Pratt had been cut off in the village and we had been left to fend for ourselves. Unknown to me, a cavalry officer had observed several of our rescues, before he himself was injured, and described us as exceptionally brave. You did your best in the circumstances, said Lt Harcourt, and our lads saved many lives. He wished to know the final moments of Davy's life because he planned to write to his mother, Olive, a widow. Most officers, we're told, write almost the same letter to relatives of the deceased. There are only a few ways to say your son or husband has died. Lt Harcourt tries to tell as much truth as possible, naturally avoiding further distress. Most officers tell relatives their son had died bravely, quickly without pain, fighting for King and Country. If they had uttered dying words, those words told of how they loved their family. In Davy's case, the truth was told: he had been exceptionally brave saving the lives of others, died without pain, loving his family and sending love to his mother.

***

I came face to face with a German today and didn't kill him. I didn't try to kill him, nor he me. More extraordinary, we shook hands.

Along our front line we removed gloves to share this act of enemy friendship. Most of my platoon met Germans, smiled, laughed and exchanged cigarettes. We could communicate although we couldn't converse. We had been taught a few words of German for when we attack their positions. But 'hands up', 'come out' and 'surrender' didn't seem suitable to use in the circumstances. I'm also sure we wouldn't say 'hände hoch' and 'rauskommen' and 'übergabe' in the correct way. And they could no more speak English than we could German.

Yesterday this man tried to kill me, and I him. Tomorrow these men will try to kill us, and we them. The war will restart. Today's unofficial truce, to which several officers objected, was to me the first day of sanity in five months.

Holding the hand of my enemy was one of the strangest feelings I have ever experienced. Whether warm or cold, all were rough and filthy with damaged nails, cuts and abrasions, like mine. It was a hand, not a hoof, paw or claw. Foe had become friend. It was strangely reassuring to see them as human, not animal. But it was equally disquieting to discover they were human, not animal. They even looked like us and many of them could pass as British if they'd have been dressed in our khaki. Fritz was Wolfgang. Fritz was Otto. Fritz was Gustave. Fritz was Herbert, my father's name. One man as mud-stained and shabby as me, Wilhelm, showed me a ragged torn-edged photograph of his wife, Ulrike, and his two-year-old, Frederick. It struck me, painfully, that in addition to all the men I had killed and maimed, I had murdered much more: hope, happiness, families.

To pull my thoughts and feelings back round, I forced myself to remember that once you join the Army and raise a rifle, it is your duty to fight and fire it. My oath was to serve King and Country. And, after all, it was the Kaiser and his war-mongering generals who started this conflict by invading civilised countries. If we don't stop Wolfgang, Otto, Gustave and Herbert they and every Fritz will take over Europe, then invade Britain. We are slaves to nobody, and won't be.

The war drew to its temporary close last night, Christmas Eve, as more snow fell on the ice-hard ground. Throughout yesterday the gunfire gradually waned to the occasional shot and strafing. Then silence. Until midnight. Across the barren land between ourselves and the enemy then drifted the most beautiful sound. Voices, in perfect pitch, sang *Silent Night*, my favourite carol. Some men cried. I wanted to, but couldn't find the tears. The German Army had changed from killers to a four-part harmony choir.

From holes and trenches, bivouacs and wagons, many officers and men, a massed military chorus filled the night air. We sang the words in English, the Germans in German, sharing the language of music. We tried to get the Germans singing *See Amid the Winter's Snow* and *The First Nowell*. They didn't know either of them. But when we struck up *Good King Wenceslas* both lines again sang in joyful harmony. The Germans struck up *In Dulci Jubilo* and *Personent Hodie*. We knew both tunes but not the foreign words, so we hummed or sang along with la-la's. What a pleasing evening, singing with heart as much as voice.

We thought the night's concert had come to an end until a tenor started to sing, softly at first, *Annie Laurie*. He sang, in English, from the German line, as clear as a nightingale. *Annie* became Alice. When the soloist came to the final verse of this traditional Scottish balled, I cried. I didn't want to, but the tears found me. Tears of sadness for soldiers, friend and foe, dead or alive. Selfish tears fell also for the situation I find myself in. I should be happy that I can weep: dead men can't cry.

Like dew on the gowan lying is the fall of her fairy feet,
And like winds in summer sighing, her voice is low and sweet
Her voice is low and sweet, and she's all the world to me,
And for bonny Annie Laurie – Alice *– I'd lay me down and dee.*

When the singer stopped, silence descended as gently as the snowflakes. I could not hear a breath, perhaps because the world around me had stopped breathing. Then a burst of applause, cheering, banging of metal and calls for another song cracked the peace. The angel did not sing again that night, and perhaps never again, nor the choirs. Most of us settled down to enjoy the quietest night's sleep for many months. I suspect, feeling safe that night, some of the sentries slept too. Fear had been removed, and courage renewed, by song.

Dawn cast a dim light on clusters of German infantry sitting casually on the edge of their hideouts, dugouts and trenches. It looked as if rifles had been left in the trench. Hesitantly, many of our lads perched on the parapet too. I did not join my brave colleagues, suspicious the Boche could be cooking up a trick, and ordered the eight in my section to keep their heads down. In the distance three British officers talked with their German counterparts in full view of everyone. It seemed they had agreed a short truce. We heard later many senior officers on both sides objected to such 'fraternizing with the enemy'. But it was Christmas Day and Germans are supposed to be Christians too. And no soldier I heard complained about a period of peace.

When the officers returned to their own lines, men on both sides opened the barbed wire entanglements and entered the wasteland. Corpses lay everywhere. We searched for our own fallen, the Germans theirs. At least three hundred dead lay scattered a hundred yards to either side of me. Because of the fighting's intensity - when killing the living becomes more important than collecting the dead - bodies could not be gathered. Sometimes at the front more men lay dead than we had men alive to bury them.

The corpses had set stone hard, facial expressions preserved by the icy wind: pain, fear, shock and surprise captured on tissue-thin skin over skulls. Men in their dying had formed grotesque figures, alien shapes and sharp angles, now dusted with snow. Alongside fellow soldiers, British and German, I searched for Dukes, hoping I would recognise them. Whether in my Battalion or not, we carried away those in khaki, the Germans took theirs in grey. Pickaxes, crowbars and augers cracked open the frozen earth to find softer ground for our spades to dig a trench grave. We helped Germans bury their dead, they helped us. Fighting men divided by war now united in death - when the battlefield turned into a burial ground.

Death no longer held mystery. Death was routine, expected, familiar. Bodies became part of battle landscape, corpses as natural a feature of war as ruins, shell craters and twisted metal. I didn't fear death. But I did fear a slow painful end. That's why I hoped, and many prayed, that our death would be painless and its arrival unknown.

I came across the bodies of two men who died fighting each other. They looked as if they had frozen instantly mid-action. Enemies in life. Enemies in death. If they thawed back to life, I could imagine their combat continuing. They had bayoneted each other, died like stags having locked antlers, unable to escape the entanglement. By killing, they had been killed. A lanky German came to help me separate the bodies. Respectfully, he pulled the British blade from his colleague's heart, and I drew the German spike from my compatriot's stomach. Their bodies frozen as solid as the steel that killed them, we could not prevent breaking ice-brittle bones as we prised them apart.

The corpses cleared and buried, we returned in lighter mood to meet our enemies as friends on what had become known as no-man's-land. I welcomed their friendship, if only in passing. We swapped our rum for their *schnapps*. Chatting afterwards, we British agreed rum tasted better. I bet our German 'friends' said they preferred their *schnapps*.

Today we exchanged smiles, cigarettes and rum, tomorrow we will resume exchanging screams, bullets and bombs. We are happy and safe this evening, or so we believe until midnight. But when the clock ticks a second into another day our day-long friends will become our life-long foes. Wolfgang, Otto, Gustave and even Herbert will again become Fritz, Boche, Hun, the Kaiser's....! Wilhelm, his wife and small son must again become my enemies - because they are German.

Men love. Men kill. Kind men. Cruel men. All the same man.

The parliamentarians and generals who said the war would be over by Christmas Day would have been correct if they had said *on* Christmas Day. Still, a day of peace is better than a day of war. The day wasn't however entirely peaceful. Shots were fired - with a football! A cycle messenger from the Bedfordshires told the tale that three miles down the line a football was thrown onto no-man's-land. This was immediately viewed as a challenge. Two teams hastily formed, wooden goalposts driven into the ground and planks fixed as crossbars. Britain versus Germany, the King's men against the Kaiser's, commenced. But the battalion commander put the dampers on it, issuing an order that the match should last only thirty minutes each half. (He told the sergeant he didn't want his troops exhausting themselves because he wanted them fighting fit for the morrow.) The game was quite a spectacle, the messenger said excitedly, with cheering and jeering on both sides. A German officer refereed the first half, a British sergeant the second. The Bedfordshire reported that England triumphed five goals to one. I bet Germans not present at the match heard a different score. Our battalion, looking across the land to the German lines, could not believe a football game could be played at all. Where could they find a patch of reasonably level ground without dug-outs, old trenches and bomb craters? Not to mention the ice and snow covering the surface. And was it right to play football on ground where just hours before hundreds of corpses had lain, frozen, abandoned? As a lad I always felt uneasy playing in the grave yard at St Michael & All Angels and at the cemetery. Although now it could be said I work in one.

***

After Aisne, when the French took over our positions, the British Expeditionary Force quickly expanded with Territorial Army reserves and new volunteers. It needed to. We had been sorely depleted, suffering thousands of deaths and injuries. We haven't been told the exact number of losses. And I doubt if all the bodies have been, or could be, counted. Many men will have been churned into craters by howitzer shells like worms under the plough. Others became lost behind enemy lines, now a corpse or captive. Chaps got shot crossing French rivers. Despite our best efforts to retrieve them, their bodies floated downstream. Most, like lost fishing rods, would have washed up on the bank. Some, if they didn't sink into riverbed silt, would have drifted to sea. Many battalions have been all but wiped out. Within the enlarged BEF, III Corps was formed and led by Major General Sir William Pulteney with two divisions, the 4th and 6th. A provisional IV Corps was also created with the 7th and 3rd Cavalry Division under Lieutenant General Sir Henry Rawlinson.

Nearly one million men across Britain have volunteered to join us. Thirty-three thousand chaps on one day signed up to serve King and Country. New arrivals tell us that back home recruiting posters are everywhere, many with Field Marshall Lord Kitchener on them. He's pointing straight out saying *'Briton wants you'* or *'Your country needs you'*. This recruitment campaign has encouraged groups of men to join from the same town or factory. They're called Pals' Battalions. A whole football team has volunteered for military service. (If they'd have played in the Christmas Day match, perhaps the score would have been 10 − 1!) A bank had to close because all the chaps walked out one lunchtime to sign up. But some bank chaps are a bit weedy, so I can't imagine the Army will accept them all. Former regulars who joined understood Army discipline, how to dress, salute, march correctly, form lines and columns, marksmanship, weapon maintenance, proper use of the bayonet, and the principles of field battle. But they have not experienced this type of warfare. No-one in the history of mankind has. This is a new war with a new kind of fighting.

Raw recruits undergo training in England, but they are still 'green' in the field. All the same, we're jolly glad to welcome back our Reserves and appreciate the Territorials - 'Saturday night soldiers' - than have no reinforcements at all. We need every man we can get. And they'll soon get knocked into shape. The ones who usually take longest to adapt to Army life and fighting will be the chaps who've worked in soft pen-pushing paper-shuffling jobs indoors. They're often easy to pick out: they're the first to grouse about something, the food, the cold, the wet, 'uncivilised' conditions. But not all. A few tell me they like this new life as an infantryman.

***

When the light faded on Christmas Day infantrymen on both sides returned to the trenches. We turned our backs on each other in peace and trust, only to twist and face each other moments later ready for war. Barriers of wire entanglements closed and we started watching for suspicious movement over the bags with our periscopes. Tonight there will be no carol singing, the spirit of Christmas gone as sure as the sun will not shine at midnight. Darkness fell on no-man's-land, and on our spirits. We're now on full alert believing the Germans used today's spontaneous truce to replenish ammunition, reposition and reinforce artillery. While Otto and the rest exchanged cigarettes, rum and *schnapps*, our scouts report their artillery lined up more guns. Our artillery did likewise.

The cold has become as much an enemy as the Germans. One chap said that, as we are further south than England and nearer the equator, the winter here should be milder. But, if anything, the cold is as bad as northern England. We're all wearing extra socks, pullovers and scarves, but the constant cold still makes life uncomfortable. There's no shortage of blankets to wrap around at night, but the wind finds a way of sneaking through. When we fall back into reserve camp we rush to find a brazier or open fire. Turning ourselves like toast, we warm our front, back, and front again until nicely cooked.

We've fought for weeks over the same patch of land, tit for tat. Both sides are well dug inside even longer and more complex trenches and neither side seems to be making much progress.

CHAPTER 15

April 1915
HILL 60

Winter caused lulls in the fighting. Be it short days, long nights, frozen fingers or men and machines stuck in snow or mud, hours would pass without a gun fired. Not a howitzer crump or pistol crack could be heard. Elsewhere along the Western Front battles took place occasionally. But on our patch of war the harsh weather dampened the fight, although hostilities did not cease completely. Had that been the case I would willingly trade spring, summer and autumn for a permanent winter. The war wasn't cancelled owing to bad weather. Winter simply became another enemy.

Following a period of calm, for no reason anyone understood, an artillery attack would be launched. Then, if one side started firing, the other felt obliged to respond in kind. Perhaps intelligence from air reconnaissance reported men and machinery exposed on the move. Maybe a senior general visited the front and action needed to take place: generals like 'a good show'. Or a senior officer had simply woken in a bad mood and wanted to 'hate' the enemy. Perhaps causing death and destruction returned him to a good mood. Often, when a new batch of shells arrived, artillery officers wanted to test their accuracy and reliability. They would order a round of firing to see how the new consignment performed and count any duds in the batch. (Faulty shells are regularly blamed for landing off target and, at times, had fallen short injuring our own men.)

After Christmas at Locre our Battalion marched through Dranoutre, Neuve Eglise and Bailleul to Wulverghem. Much time was then spent digging new or improving existing trenches. Based on sloping land on the Wulverghem-Messines Road, conditions proved terrible. Our backs and spades worked hard cutting through cold clay. As across the whole of 5th Division during January and February 1915, our Battalion was replenished with much-needed reinforcements: five lieutenants and three hundred and thirteen other ranks. Many of the new chaps, eager to 'get stuck in', groused at being in routine working parties. When old hands told new arrivals they would welcome a day of digging to a day of fighting, the greenhorns refused to believe them. Anything's better than digging, many said. Anything isn't. Months if not days later I wagered many of these eager fellas will be dead, limbless, burnt or not right in the head.

On 19th February our Battalion moved to Vlamertinge, two miles west of a small ancient market town called Ypres. If Coulommiers was famous for its cheese, Ypres was once the centre of the linen trade with a big Cloth Hall. Because most chaps couldn't speak French, Ypres soon became 'Wipers'. It makes life easier than trying to get these funny French pronunciations right. Whatever we say, however we say it, the locals always correct us. As our first French interpreters Cpl Boutard and Pte Guérin predicted, the British will never speak French properly. We've given up trying. But, to make the town's name even more confusing, many locals don't call it Ypres either. To them it's Ieper or Yper. And, although we're in Belgium, many of the residents call themselves Flemish. Ypres, Yper, Ieper or 'Wipers' - Belgium, Flemish or soldiers' English - is about eighty miles in a straight line from Dover. But another world.

We lodged in huts just south of Vlamertinge. Our hopes of several days' rest became dashed the next morning. Orders instructed A and C Companies to move into dug-outs near Zillebeke in support of the West Kents. This village lies halfway between Ypres and a key German stronghold, Hill 60, a mile south. B Company and mine, D, marched back to Ypres and billeted in a convent - with nuns in residence. The nuns had provided shelter and nursing care to soldiers; first Belgium, some French, then Germans, and now British casualties. It was said that some of their order had been violated by invading Germans. And not once, but twice, first when the Boche invaded in August 1914, and again as we and the French pushed them back to their current line late last year. The nuns' courage to stay in the convent is remarkable, as brave as any soldier, if not braver: nuns don't carry guns to inspire boldness. Their work tending casualties, especially enemy soldiers, is truly admirable. Then to share their convent with two companies of British infantry is kindness and hospitality beyond any reasonable expectation. Perhaps angels do exist - on earth. Out of respect for the nuns, I was pleased we Dukes conducted ourselves well. Soldiers spoke quietly and refrained from swearing, at least when nuns were nearby. Some men can hardly speak a sentence without a swear word, or several. Keeping their language clean was very hard for them, but such was the respect for the nuns they curbed their curses.

Although often tired ourselves following hours of labour, the chaps helped the nuns in any way we could. We fetched and carried, rebuilt bomb-damaged walls, fixed the roof. My squad volunteered to dig the convent's garden in readiness for their spring planting of vegetables. The Mother Superior was particularly pleased with one chap who discovered a tin of dried beans in a shed, which he sowed in long rows. No gardener in the north of England or Scotland would risk planting these seeds in open ground in February, frosts would kill any growth unless protected by cloches. But the nuns insisted the bean shoots would survive. 'Have faith,' Sister Therese told us in perfect English, 'the crop will be ready to pick in June, even May, if God believes we are worthy.' By that measure, they should be ready in April!

Over the next few weeks our companies took turns in and out of the trenches, especially with the 1st Battalion of the Bedfords. March 13th was a special day. General Officer Commanding II Corps, Sir Horace Smith-Dorrien, visited and thanked our Regiment for its 'splendid services' since the beginning of the war. 'The Duke of Wellington's could always be depended upon to do whatever they were asked,' he added. I'm sure he delivers the same speech to most regiments. Nevertheless, it's still heart-warming to hear, and we stood two inches taller. And the GOC told the truth: we Dukes had been in the thick of things from the start at Mons.

From mid-March it became clear winter's peace and Christmas Day's 'truce' had come to an end. Fighting increased along the line, although our sector near Zillebeke remained quiet enough. It was so quiet that on Easter Day our Battalion attended a church service at Ypres. The Lord Bishop of London, visiting the front, led the worship. He called on God to keep us safe. If God heard, he did not heed.

***

Hill 60 isn't a hill at all, not really. To someone from the Yorkshire Dales or Scottish Highlands, it's hardly a bump on the landscape. Hill 60 is little more than a gentle sloping heap barely fifty feet above the surrounding ground. It must have been named by a man from the flatland of the Fens, where a resting cow is considered a mountain. The ridge was formed by the spoil from a cutting on the eight miles of railway line from Ypres south-east to Comines. Nevertheless, on the level lands of Flanders, little Hill 60 gave a large advantage to the occupying Germans. It afforded our enemy excellent artillery observation and sniper opportunity to the west and north-west towards Ypres. We had known for two weeks Sir John French had decided this position was to be taken. That's why much of our time in and around Ypres thus far in April had been supplying working parties constructing dugouts near Zillebeke from which to launch our attack.

The Duke of Wellington's would not be alone in this major attack. The 2nd Battalion King's Own Scottish Borderers, 1st Battalion the Queen's Own Royal West Kent Regiment, and the 2nd Battalion of our 'sisters', the King's Own Yorkshire Light Infantry, would be at our side as part of 13th Brigade, 5th Division, under the command of Sir Charles Fergusson. All the Battalions had taken turns going in and out of the area preparing the trenches, although none of us knew the exact time of the assault. But the more we dug towards the enemy, the closer we came to kill or being killed.

That moment came at 7 pm on Saturday April 17th. Three of our mines detonated immediately in front of the German trenches near Hill 60. We Dukes were enjoying a hearty hot supper at our billets in Ypres. Although a mile and a half away, the ground quaked, as if the earth itself felt afraid. Our plates jumped an inch off the heavy wooden tables. Water trembled in our tumblers. Puffs of dust blew in from the masonry. Two large windows cracked and crashed to the ground. Before any debris blown sky high had time to fall back to earth, artillery on both sides started pounding. My thoughts went to the poor devils in the thick of it, the Kents and the Borderers. They would now be pouring into the craters and what was left of German trenches. The big push was on. This supper could be our last hot meal for a while. For some it would be the last meal for all time. Although I was as likely to die as the next man, the thought didn't stop me eating every morsel on my plate. And quickly. Most chaps gobbled their food and, wisely, stuffed uneaten pieces of bread in their pockets for later. For a few, battle-scarred and first-timers, knowing they would soon be at the front curbed their appetite. They gazed at uneaten food as if covered in rat droppings and slowly put down their cutlery. We all know that feeling when our insides turn to jelly.

Within the hour our Battalion received orders to be ready to advance at a moment's notice. Meanwhile we snatched as much rest as possible. Most chaps sent a last-minute field-service postcard, ticking or circling 'I am quite well' and 'Letter follows at first opportunity'. (Apart from the date and signature, nothing else may be added to what was already printed, otherwise our postcards are destroyed.) At 3 am A Company started making their way forward. The rest of us, B, C and D, didn't have long to wait: our orders arrived at 6 am.

Overnight the Kents and Borderers successfully occupied the craters and what was left of the German trenches. Although the blasts rocked the enemy, they remained standing. That evening the Boche came back and engaged in close-quarter combat. Both our battalions suffered high casualties and the Royal Army Medical Corps had their hands full. Additional working parties quickly formed to help carry the injured to casualty clearing stations. It's unnerving for us going to the front to see all the dead and injured being brought back from it. As stretchers pass by the same thought crosses all our minds: very soon that could be me.

The storm of shells, grenades and bullets never ended as we advanced. The Germans fired like madmen, crazy to kill. Behind us Ypres too was taking a pounding, especially the Cathedral and old Cloth Hall. My company suffered several casualties along the way, shallow communication trenches providing little protection. In places trenches also became partially blocked with the dead, dying and wounded. It was a struggle not to step on bodies. Chaps who climbed out of the trench to avoid doing so often found themselves joining the casualties. I kept my head down, choosing to crawl over bloody bodies than gamble becoming one.

By 9 am nearly seven hundred men of B, C and D companies stood two hundred yards from the German front. Our chums in A Company stood even closer, so close that hand grenades could be thrown from trench to trench both ways. Many casualties resulted, including A Company's Commander, Captain Milbank. I saw the state of him as the stretcher-bearers carried him by and held no hope for his survival. Until we received the order to go over the top, all we could do was keep our heads down and hope a shell didn't land in the trench and do us in. Our attack looked to be approaching when, mid-morning, our Commanding Officer and the Adjutant visited the advance trenches. At times both men appeared in full view of the enemy but, somehow, they survived their reconnaissance. An hour later one platoon from each of B and C companies, and mine, D, received orders to advance and reinforce the remnants of A Company. They had held their ground valiantly but were done for. Captain T M Ellis was to lead the advance and my platoon was amongst those chosen.

Capt Ellis enjoyed something of a reputation in the Regiment. During our retreat in late August last year from Mons and Le Cateau, he became stranded behind enemy lines alongside around fifty men. They took cover in woods. Some became lost in the dark and others when scattered by close encounters with Germans infantry. Their fate is unknown. After nights of hiding in open woodland, an old hut and a disused lime-kiln, the Captain met a Belgian priest. He in turn introduced the officer to another Belgian who offered to help him escape through German lines and north to the coastline. But this would only be possible if Capt Ellis donned civilian clothes. This would entail the risk if caught of being shot as a spy rather than treated as a soldier. Over several days they walked over one hundred miles north. Much of the time Capt Ellis stayed thirty or forty yards behind the guide, particularly through villages where German soldiers might suddenly appear. Along the way they picked up two privates from the Manchesters. They rested and hid in ditches, hedges, copses, or behind walls in fields away from roads and tracks. At one stage during their escape all three had to hide bolt upright squeezed between an opened barn door and a stone wall as German troops tramped by - for five seemingly endless hours. Had one Fritz decided to relieve himself against the barn wall they would have been discovered, questioned under torture, then shot. But eventually they reached Ostend and found passage across the English Channel. Astonishingly, the very first action Capt Ellis took on arrival in Blighty was to report for duty at the War Office. Capt Ellis told fellow officers that he had two main concerns. First, his carrot-red hair might attract too much attention on the journey. Second, if captured, the Regimental crest tattooed on his arm would confirm his military status and condemn him as a spy.

At noon our advance commenced towards the three mine craters formed from last evening's blasts. We replaced the handful of remaining men from A company in the dugouts just beyond the craters. Hun machine guns set upon us straight away and men fell. Capt Ellis, small in stature but tall in leadership, was cut down not ten yards from me. Five of us rushed to his side hoping we could pull him to safe cover until an orderly could treat him. But he'd taken a line of bullets across the chest and as dead as dead can be. The Hun gunner started up again and we fanned out moving forward. Men fell. And then more.

I zig-zagged through the fallen and the potholes expecting bullets to catch me too. I'll be as dead as quickly as the captain and probably won't know a thing about it. I'll never understand how I avoided a bullet. It was as if I'd walked through a thunderstorm without being touched by a drop of rain. Eventually, exhausted having struggled the two or so hundred yards over the pockmarked terrain, I fell into the foremost trench. It looked like a mass grave. It *was* a mass grave. For every man alive there was one dead and one injured. Looking left, looking right, it was a trench of blood and gore - bloodier and grislier than anything I'd seen at the abattoir when taking animals from Stone Booth Farm. The Boche threw grenades from their trench, most falling short. The gap between their trench and ours at this point must be about thirty yards, out of range for all but the best throwers. Our grenadiers started hurling grenades in return. But they too fell short. Further down the trench towards a railway line, the gap between opposing trenches was shorter. Most grenades landed in the trench causing mayhem. I decided to keep my remaining Mills grenade until close enough for it to do damage. Mercifully we hadn't been long in the trench before the deluge of grenades stopped. I know we had exhausted our supplies, and we assumed the Germans too waited for more to be brought forward.

The two opposing front lines being so close, we trusted that neither artillery would risk firing shells. 'Accidental fire' occurred injuring our own, but only twice over the next few hours. Rifles and machine guns fired at the slightest movement above the parapet, including at fallen casualties who showed signs of life. Both sides stayed ready to attack or defend, but neither knew what would come first. As we launched the assault on Hill 60, it was likely we would be the aggressor. And so it was. At 4.30 pm Brigade Headquarters issued the order to attack. B Company under Captain C E B Hanson was allocated the right section of the attack, Captain B J Barton, in charge of C Company, the centre. In charge of my company, D, covering the left, Captain Ernie Taylor declared: 'We are to attack and dislodge the Germans from that portion of the hill they regained during last night's counter-attacks.' Behind us assembled the 2nd Battalion King's Own Yorkshire Light Infantry. Our 'sisters' or 'poor relations', as we light-heartedly called them, prepared to occupy our trenches and support the attack as a second wave. In all honesty we could not have wished for a better Battalion in support.

With bayonets fixed, clubs and knives to hand, we went over the top. It was the most violent hand-to-hand fighting I had yet witnessed. I'm ashamed to say what men did to other men that evening. No man present will ever forget that fight until the day they die, although they'll try hard to. Few, if any, will ever wish to speak about it. I will never see my fellow humans, nor myself, in the same light ever again. Savagery. Barbarity. Mindlessness. I would not believe men could do such things to other men. My respect for animals doubled: in comparison, the way animals hunt for survival and settle disputes made man the true uncivilised beast on earth.

But war generates violence as violence generates war. And decent men find themselves forced to commit horrible deeds to survive, to save others, to protect the weak, for good to triumph over evil.

My company had the greatest distance to charge, seventy-five yards. There was not a stump or shrub or tussock of grass for cover. Many brave and skilled officers became casualties at Hill 60. Capt. Ernie Taylor, from Halifax, Lt Thackeray, born in India, and 2nd Lt Croft cut down. No man's body could take so much metal and live. 2nd Lt Crisp fell next to me with a leg wound, but he did not allow me to help him seek refuge. He unselfishly urged me and others on without delay. B Company had the least ground to cover and quickly overwhelmed the Boche. But they suffered losses, including Lt Rowland Owen as he courageously approached the enemy leading his men. Lt Owen, from Huddersfield, was a popular officer amongst all the officers and men. C Company had to cover about fifty yards and, from what I could tell, suffered as badly if not worse than us. They fought fiercely in the trench under what looked like the command of two privates - Behan and Dryden - who seemed to have taken charge in the absence of any officer, sergeant, or even a corporal.

The close-quarter violence in the trenches lasted perhaps fifteen minutes: killing-fever dulls all sense of time. Nearly sixty Germans were finally captured and escorted away. Hundreds of men nursed their injuries. Among the dead the dying waited to die. Most cuts and bruises and grazes, which most of us sustain, are never reported. They are too trivial to bother the orderlies with, and no-one likes been thought a sissy. Private Smith suffered two fingers fully bent back in the fight. After finishing off a Fritz, he simply snapped his fingers back and continued wielding his club along the trench. Most of us licked our wounds, so to speak, and carried on. Sometimes we don't realise we're injured until the fighting has died down. It's hard to explain why, but pain often starts when the fighting stops.

The commanding officer said it was vital to consolidate our hard-won position immediately. This meant blocking the German communication trenches then digging new ditches back to our former lines. Before we could catch breath, we achieved these tasks. But nightfall didn't bring peace. The Germans received fresh supplies of grenades, and they made sure we knew it. They lobbed dozens, but few reached us. Perhaps it was the madness that comes with a full moon at midnight, but one Fritz made a suicidal run brandishing a stick grenade. Our chaps on stag duty shot him before he could throw the bomb. He fell over the stick and blew himself in half. German snipers, bursts of machine gun and heavy shelling continued throughout the night. But the Boche did not launch a counter-attack.

I somehow survived the two and a half days at Hill 60, April 17th to 19th, until relieved by the East Surreys and Bedfords of the 15th Brigade. But four hundred and twenty-one companions from the Duke of Wellington's Regiment suffered death or severe injury. The fate of forty-three chaps is unknown, more likely killed than captured. (I did not see the Germans take anyone.) Our Commanding Officer, Lt-Col P A Turner, was wounded while directing the attack at the front. He took a bullet in his right leg, although managed to keep moving despite the pain. But minutes later the Colonel took another bullet to his left leg, which rendered him a casualty. His presence in the thick of the fight had lifted the troops' morale and we admired him all the more. Our second in command, Major W E M Tyndall, also received wounds, more serious. None who saw his injuries believed he would survive.

The patch of land we fought over was smaller than the lambing field we used at Stone Booth Farm: about two hundred and fifty yards long by around two hundred yards wide. To my eye the area looked between ten and eleven acres. On that space the enemy cracked tons of shrapnel and discharged thousands of bullets. We too added a considerable amount of metal to the land. If shrapnel were seed, the crop would indeed provide a rich harvest. Why did we stay? Why did we fight? Why didn't all of us, German and British, stand up and scream 'Stop! This is madness'? There must be a better way of settling grievances between nations. But we don't protest. Each man, educated and ignorant, rich and poor, general and private, is somehow dragged as powerless as a fallen leaf into a whirlpool of war.

After the battle the British Army's Commander-in-Chief no less, Sir John French, addressed the Dukes and Bedfords:

'I have come here today to say a few words to you in acknowledgment of the splendid work you have done throughout the last week in the capture of that very important position Hill 60 which was held in strength by the enemy.

'The enemy's counter-attacks with bombs and other means of attack which they employed so well were all to no purpose through the bravery shown by all concerned. The British soldier never seems to know what defeat is.

'Officers, NCOs and men, I tell you from the bottom of my heart, that I am grateful to you for the work which has been done.

'The capture of that hill is of the utmost importance to us as it is one of the main positions round Ypres. Thank you. And thank you again.'

CHAPTER 16

22nd April 1915
2nd BATTLE OF YPRES

The Hun are more loathsome than the rats infesting our trenches. Fritz has stooped to the most despicable behaviour, lower than low. They have brought dishonour to any soldier worthy of the name. King Arthur's knights with their Code of Chivalry would be outraged. Wellington and Nelson, even Napoléon, would have considered it below contempt. But the Boche, making no headway in a fair fight, have employed a terrible new weapon, a silent method of mass murder.

As if we didn't have enough weapons and ways to kill and maim, the Boche have added chlorine gas to their arsenal. War, I foolishly believed, could not become more brutal. But it has. Gas is a coward's weapon. No officer or gentleman - I'm sure no British soldier - would resort to such unsporting methods. Those who use it are as despicable as men who murder children or violate women. Man against man, fist against fist, sword against sword, gun against gun are acceptable if fights must be fought. But to poison the very air we breathe is below being human. To create a soundless cloud to suffocate your enemy while they sleep is evil even the devil wouldn't devise.

It had been rumoured for months that Fritz considered using poisonous gas as a weapon. The French had thought of employing it during their defence of Paris, as a last resort. But we had been reassured by our senior officers that in 1907 most nations agreed not to use gas, owing to a treaty called The Hague Convention. Our officers said that if the Hun planned to deploy it, they would have done so by now - especially last September on the brink of their breakthrough to Paris. But Fritz, we are quickly learning, is not a gentleman and completely untrustworthy. Germans will sign agreements in elegant palaces and renege on them before the ink dries. I very much doubt, come Christmas this year, we will share a second day of peace. If they feel no guilt about using gas, they will have no scruples about poisoning the *schnapps*.

Firm evidence of Fritz's fox-like cunning came last week. Not that any more proof was required to have them hung for murder, certainly the generals who issued the orders. French forces on a section of La Bassée Canal, a few miles north from where we are near Hill 60, came under attack from a cloud of chlorine. When the thunder-rumble of artillery kicks off you know what you're up against. When the crack of a rifle or rat-a-tat of a machine gun starts, you can duck for cover. You may hear a bullet's whistle cutting the air, see it embed in or ricochet off the ground. But gas is a quiet assassin. Shortly after the cowardly gas attack on the French, the Germans opened more gas canisters to form a deadly drift across the 1st Division of the Canadian Expeditionary Force. These chaps are entrenched even closer to us and had just come all the way from Canada to help us. But before a shot was fired, a killer cloud of chlorine spread over them.

It was simply a matter of time before this invisible evil crept under our door. We didn't have long to wait. That evening our platoon moved to the fire line as sunset arrived, although the sky still held plenty of light. Soon after taking over the watch we saw what resembled a mist that lingers over dips in fields or dells in woods on icy-cold days in England. But this was a warm spring evening in Belgium. This was not a cloud created by nature. It was a slow-moving man-made mist of murder and mayhem. It looked harmless, but we knew it was harmful. We turned to each other and spread the feared word: gas. It was spoken calmly at first. Then voices along the line became louder, as if every time the word was spoken it multiplied the threat. For 'gas' didn't just mean gas, as poisonous as it is. Gas meant an all-out assault from the Hun soon to press home their advantage. We quickly rummaged in our haversacks for handkerchiefs, cloth pads or flannel belts and soaked them in water before tying them round our noses and mouths. Some chaps hastily urinated onto their makeshift masks before covering their faces. It was rumoured that urine was more protective than water to breathe through, but we didn't really know. It couldn't do any more harm than the gas itself. One lad was so nervous, he couldn't pee! Then, all faces covered, we did the only thing we could do: wait, watch, get ready to shoot the first Fritz we see. Eased along by a gentle breeze, the cloud drifted closer at walking pace. The venomous vapour, about ten feet high and seventy-five yards or so to my right, started to spread over our fire line before tumbling into our trench. A stillness settled over us, as if the gas blanket smothered all sound and stopped all movement.

Shrieks and screams and scrambling started as the chlorine cloud spread as slowly as cold treacle over its first victims. The doors of Devil's madhouse burst open from the darkest hole in hell. Man after mad-looking man rushed behind us in their flight to find fresh air. Whatever face-covering employed it had failed to filter the fumes penetrating their lungs. The cloud drifted to within fifty yards from my section, and more men fled from where the gas encroached. We stood firm. Fume-filled men clawed at their throats in pain, ripping open their tunics gasping for air. A lance corporal grabbed a blinded lieutenant's revolver and blew his own brains out. In this madhouse, nobody thought it unusual. Maybe it made perfect sense to die quickly at your own hand than have your body burnt away from the inside by chlorine. In his distress, the young officer seemed totally unaware that his revolver had one less bullet in his six-round magazine.

Men fell to the ground rolling and writhing in agony. Screaming. Crying. Shouting. Gurgling. More stumbled over the choking men, body on top of flailing body. The cloud crept closer and, within seconds, we too would be reduced to this gas-induced madness. Our trench was packed with men fighting and clawing their way out. Some, completely disoriented or desperate to get away, climbed over the parapet and immediately sniped. One man collapsed at my feet and his body shuddered, arched, and died. Men behaved like rats in a pipe trap, all desperate to escape. Those blinded outstretched their arms feeling the side of the trench seeking their escape. Those who could still see, and remained sane, guided the blind through the trench. But others rushed passed them in their own desperate quest for freedom.

When the chlorine cloud poured into our firebay, I tightened the cloth around my nose and mouth and half-closed my eyes. With the gas feet away, Sgt Pratt rushed in and ordered a retreat. I've never been so relieved to hear an order in my years as a soldier! Without hesitation my squad joined the rat run out of the toxic trench. A new private, so desperate to escape, left his rifle behind. I ordered him to retrieve it. He hesitated, seeing the cloud had covered it, but he bravely grabbed his weapon. Even though we'd escaped the thick of the killer cloud in the nick of time, I could taste the chlorine's acrid poison in my mouth and slither down my throat and lungs. I coughed and spat and was desperately thirsty. But escape was the priority. I gasped for breath like everyone else as we weaved our way into the communications trench and away from the gas, which had started to disperse. Some of the cloud drifted back towards the enemy's own lines because the draught changed direction. Let Fritz taste a bit of his own medicine, said someone who could speak. We knew however the Germans would be far better prepared with proper gas masks.

As we coughed and spluttered our recovery from the gas, the Hun's artillery opened fire and we faced a downpour of howitzer shells. Men kept hurrying to the cover trench in the hope of finding space in a deep dugout. The blind and disoriented wondered everywhere, although medical orderlies arrived to help them. Others walked off never to be seen again. Chaps who received a full dose of chlorine gas stumbled to the ground and died an agonising death. There was absolutely nothing we nor the orderlies could do to ease their suffering. Death delivered their only comfort.

After emptying my canteen of water and taking a minute to catch breath, I recovered sufficiently to think properly. I was pleased to see my squad of nine appeared well, apart from the lad I'd ordered to retrieve his rifle. He suffered badly, struggling for every breath. What a fool I'd been. I should have realised his life was more valuable than a rifle, although it is a serious matter to leave your weapon behind. Even so, I deeply regretted sending him back for his gun - and what could be a deadly dose of chlorine gas.

No space could be found for my section in the deep dugouts. The only shelter to be had out of the chaos of the main trench was the latrine. It was two feet deeper than the main communication trench in a small corridor. It had a strong plank roof and an earth covering that would withstand light shrapnel. It would be as safe as anywhere under the Hun's bombs, unless we took a direct hit.

'Not the nicest spot to rest, Corporal, can't you find a decent hotel?' It always pleased me to hear humour in the middle of madness and mayhem.

I played to his cue. 'I'd actually reserved sea view rooms at the best hotel in Scarborough for you all tonight, but Lord Kitchener told me you'd enjoy here much more.'

The lads smiled. We agreed the latrine was not the sweetest smelling section of the trenches. Indeed, especially with many un-emptied 'honey buckets', the latrines stank pretty foul. The worst hotel in England had to be better than this. Many of the latrine and urine buckets - mostly used biscuit tins with simple wire handles - were overflowing. The ill had also used them for their vomit. The buckets are evacuated nightly, but tonight's gas attack prevented the sanitation party. Accepting this was our resting place, we sat with our backs to the wall gathering our wits. I considered sending a man to find Sgt Pratt or Lt Harcourt for orders, but thought it best to wait a while. Sgt Pratt had seen us heading this way. He'd find us when needed. Most chaps nodded off, despite the coughing some still suffered from the gas. Men using the latrine throughout the night reported there had been no infantry activity at the front. But artillery, our own and German, continued to fire.

I stayed awake, comforting the lad I'd sent into the gas. He coughed up blood and became delirious for a minute. He then slipped into unconsciousness. Finally, in the throes of death, he experienced a violent coughing fit before life left him. I won't record his name, for I caused his death by stupidly following a standing order. Rifles are in short supply, I reminded myself as to why I gave the order. New chaps had told us they trained with wooden dummy rifles, even broom sticks. But after all the casualties, we had far more rifles than men. His rifle should have been abandoned: metal and wood would have survived chlorine gas. Later, reporting to Lt Harcourt for the boy's letter home about the circumstances of his death, I suggested that his parents be told he had braved the gas to retrieve his rifle. It was the act of a gallant soldier, I said. That was the truth, but not the whole truth.

Around midnight Lt Harcourt and Sgt Pratt came into the latrine. I roused my squad and we all stood. The officer told us to make our way forward to the positions we had abandoned earlier in the FT, the fire or firing trench. We would be joined largely by new reservists from Britain. A German counter-attack was expected shortly. Lt Harcourt ordered that under no circumstances should we stop on our way forward to assist casualties. It's hard to ignore the injured, he acknowledged, but our job in the front line was to protect those behind. Medical orderlies are gathering casualties for treatment at the dressing station, he said, and then serious cases sent on to a field hospital near Calais. Corpses are being gathered for burial.

With a dim moon our only light, returning to the fire trench it was impossible to tell if men remained alive unless they sighed, cried or groaned in pain waiting for attention. Unmistakably dead was one poor fellow who, in the madness caused by gas, had slit his own throat with a clasp knife. Another had fallen on his bayonet, its bloody tip penetrating the back of his coat, as well as his heart. It would be wrong to call their acts suicide. Their minds had been poisoned by gas and were not in control of their faculties. Many died clutching their own throats in a desperate struggle to breathe. To an observer not knowing about the gas, it looked like they had throttled themselves. Gas hadn't been the only killer. About twenty had perished when a howitzer shell scored a direct hit in the trench. Those who hadn't died in the blast suffocated in soil, when the eight-foot earth walls and sandbags collapsed burying them alive.

At first I couldn't believe it. Now I don't want to. We heard at daybreak that, over the past six weeks here near Ypres, we British had lost around sixty thousand men. It was said the Germans lost just as many. I doubt it. They had dug in deep. They conducted far fewer assaults. And that's when men cop it, exposed to machine guns and shrapnel shells, which explode firing hundreds of lead balls to kill, maim and blind men nearby. Some officers blamed the French for not providing more support, one claiming because we were in Belgium. But the terrain around Ypres advantaged defenders, not attackers. And we attacked more than the Boche.

CHAPTER 17

Early September 1915
LOOS

Letters from home say many people are frustrated at being unable to fight, young chaps especially. They want the opportunity to kill a Hun, forgetting their presence also provides a chance for a Hun to kill them. Would-be fighters are prevented however from joining us because they are too young, too old, too infirm. Boys wish to accompany their father, uncle or older brother. Fathers, as mine, want to come with their sons. Some chaps are just not fit enough, even in their twenties. Others, and many women it must be said, hold jobs so vital they are far more useful at home than here. We need farmers, fishermen, bakers, factory workers, ship builders, gun, bomb and bullet makers and the like. Life at home must go on, not despite the war, but because of it. Every soldier with any sense knows we can't fight on the fire line without support from the lines behind, lines that go all the way back to our homes.

Fighting-fit men have been denied their time at the front. Most tragic was the troop train disaster of 22nd May on the Caledonian line, a mile north of Gretna Green. The packed southbound train collided with a local passenger train from Carlisle. To make matters worse, before any warning could be given to change the signals, the Scottish express from Euston crashed into the wreckage at high speed. One hundred and twenty-two people died, nearly all soldiers, and over two hundred injured. The collision itself would have been terrible enough, but fire broke out engulfing the troops. Many had broken limbs or were trapped and powerless to escape the inferno. The soldiers died because of the war, but not in it.

After Ypres, 'Wipers', and Hill 60, my Battalion moved twenty-five miles south to a small coal-mining town called Loos. The officers pronounced it 'loss', although the men spoke it as it looked. Many moaned again about the spelling. 'If Loos is spoken "loss", Sir, why do they spell it L...o...o...s?' the chaps persistently quizzed a new subaltern. 'I don't know, you just do when pronouncing

French,' came his best reply. I stepped in to relieve the young officer from the questioning and diverted the men to more important tasks. This subaltern, as many new recruits, was aged about eighteen. Many, frankly, wet behind the ears. These lads - 'men' seems the wrong word to describe some of the weedy ones - had just arrived from Britain. They formed part of the New Army, partly thanks to those Lord Kitchener posters. Two of its Divisions, the 21st and 24th, stationed here as reserves. Most of the new chaps however looked fit enough and had undergone basic training. But bayoneting a German in battle is not the same as stabbing a sandbag on the parade ground. They will undoubtedly learn the key difference the hard way: Fritz fights back! We full-time regulars from the original British Expeditionary Force, old timers, are becoming few and far between, and I was promoted to Sergeant and Section Leader.

During September thousands of mainly British troops moved into the region around Loos, Artois. Brigades of the French Tenth Army occupied territory to the north and south of us to broaden the front. We were joined by our First Army's I Corps, under Lieutenant General Hubert Gough, and IV Corps, led by Lieutenant General Henry Rawlinson. II and III Corps stood ready to provide diversionary attacks and IX Corps in reserve.

For the first time since arriving in France, my Battalion didn't have to march from one place to the next. A convoy of petrol engine lorries carried us from Ypres to Vermelles, a little town three miles north west of Loos. Each week we see more of these motor wagons and cars, which are becoming more reliable, although I still prefer horse-drawn transport. I understand living creatures. You can talk to them. They have their own character. Last winter especially I always grinned when horses rescued petrol vehicles from the mud. We joked that we never saw an engine vehicle pull a horse out of a rut. The jape backfired. It wasn't long before petrol wagons pulled horses stuck belly-deep in mud and bomb-crater pools.

***

I experienced a disturbing dream, one I never forget.

Two soldiers stood facing each other, the last two men in the whole world, one British, one German. The war had not ended. Each pointed their rifle at the other. They agreed that when they fired, these would be the final shots and the war would end. Out of a swirling silver mist emerged hundreds of women who encircled the soldiers. They told the two infantrymen that all the boys and baby boys had been killed fighting themselves. If you kill each other, the women said, human life on earth will end when we die.

Noticing several pregnant women, one of the soldiers said they'd give birth to boys and the world would in time get back to normal. But one woman, tall and slim, said that since gas had been used in the fighting no boys had been born. Another, slightly hesitant and embarrassed, revealed some boys had been born - stillborn. And with terrible disfigurements, another lady chipped in.

But the war isn't over, insisted one soldier. My country has not won. We haven't received orders to withdraw, the other protested. My country has not lost. You are the King now, the women shouted. And you can be the Kaiser, others called. You can declare a truce. A victory. Defeat.

Only one of us can be the King or the Kaiser, one soldier said. There must be a winner. The other soldier laid down his weapon. You have won the war, he told his opponent, conceding defeat. To consolidate his victory, the triumphant soldier pulled the rifle's bolt to lodge a round in the breach and aimed at his rival's head. The women jumped him and the bullet discharged harmlessly into the air. They tore the rifle from his hands, beat him to the ground, left him for dead.

The soldier who had surrendered was surrounded and smothered in kisses and adoration. The female throng, from girls to grandmothers, carried him away on extended arms in a jubilant procession. The sun melted the mist along the path as they departed singing and dancing and celebrating the end of the war. But I lost the war, he cried, I don't deserve this adulation. But they joyously shouted, you won the peace, you won the peace.

My dream should have enjoyed that happy ending. It didn't.

Night returned. Fields, hills, woodland, animals and buildings all shades of black. Nothing existed in the world that was grey, except *the soldier left for dead. After shaking his head to return his senses, he hastily picked up his rifle, angrily rammed home a fresh clip of cartridges, squared his jaw, crouched forward and strode out in search of war.*

***

A bullet brought my dream to an end. Fantasy blown away by reality, as if the dream's war-monger had broken into my life. His or someone's bullet struck my head. It found its way through a loophole no bigger than a cigarette packet. I admired the sniper for his good shot, unless it was a stray bullet, and there are plenty of them. Head throbbed. Blood flowed down to my cheek and neck. My brain must be blown away, my skull split. But I could see, although distorted, like looking through broken glass. I could hear, yet every sound hollow, echoing, distant. I could think but... *Dizzy*...Alice. *Dying*...Alice. *Darkness*...Alice...*Fear*...Mother.

I discovered death is nothingness, nothing at all.

His breath stank of stale food and rotting teeth. A toilet mouth, as obnoxious as smelling salts. Worse. But that's what brought me back to life. Then I could see. His face faced mine. Too close. A hard face for a medical orderly. He said the bullet 'only' grazed me. But it delivered the blow of a bare-knuckle boxer. Bashed me numb. It ploughed a deeper furrow along the same scar I acquired at Le Cateau. Two injuries, only one scar to show for it. A thick wad and tight bandage stopped the blood flow. The headaches and dizziness lasted longer.

***

It seems the days of combat in the open, from field to wood, hill to vale, through village and town, are gone. Day after day we dig. We say we're more like moles than men. We even sing about it: *'Digging, digging, digging, always bloody digging.'* Trenches have become more intricate than a spider's web. Because chaps became lost, even in daylight, we named trenches with signboards to help find the way. Even this caused confusion at first because we came across several High Streets, Oxford Streets, Piccadilly Circuses and Hell Fire Corners.

Trenches are dug deeper too, saving many lives. I'm five feet ten inches. Men six feet or more have often been shot. Most trenches are now eight feet deep, some deeper. Unlike the start of this trench warfare, many of the firebays are now supplied with periscopes to keep an eye on Fritz. Too many men had died looking over the top of a trench. Many chaps made their own periscopes with two mirrors fitted to their rifles. But our No 9 periscopes, encased in a tall and darkened wooden case, provide a better view. For me, for all keen riflemen, we prefer to look through loopholes. Then, when we glimpse a Hun, we can shoot without delay. If a rifleman uses his own periscope, by the time he's withdrawn it, positioned the rifle and aimed, nine out of ten times the target's vanished. But our 'spotters' use periscopes and tell us if they see any movement.

In the early days of the war we didn't have trenches like today's. For one thing, there wasn't time to dig as we chased or faced the invading Hun. We hastily dug scrapes, but these small ruts and hollows hardly covered our backsides. And a lot of backsides got hit, which is excruciatingly painful and debilitating. A wound in the rump is as painful as anywhere else - not at all like 'six of the best' from the headmaster's cane, as some chumps joked. However, as the fighting balanced out, both sides dug in. We haven't stopped digging. And when we're not digging, we're repairing. In many locations near Ypres, in the low flatlands of Belgium, it is often impossible to dig a trench without it filling with water, even in summer. Our 'trenches' then were built-up barricades with sandbags, millions of them.

We only made trenches at first at the front to fire at the enemy, and to protect us from their fire. With artillery playing an ever-bigger part in the battles, men and supplies needed protection much further back from the front. Hence we started digging a second line trench, anything from five hundred to a thousand yards behind the fire line. We call these 'cover trenches' because we construct overhead shelter wherever possible. A trench 'roof' does little to protect us from a direct hit, but the more covered trenches we build the more lives are saved and injuries reduced from shrapnel.

Royal Engineers tell us this is only the start of the trenching system. Orders are coming through all the time for yet more complex trenches. These will have more firing bays, trench mortar positions, deeper dugouts for rest, dressing stations, kitchens, storage and latrines. Maps are made of the trench network numbering each new alley. Most trenches, apart from the communication trenches, are zigzagged at right angles which form separate bays. This design has saved many lives. For when a trench takes a shell directly, only men in that firebay are injured. Likewise, when Fritz sneaks up at night and places a machine gun at the end of a trench, the damage is mostly limited to the nine or so men in that bay. Had the trench being long and straight far more would have suffered.

To move to the front from the cover trenches, we've dug CTs, communication trenches. For speed and ease of movement these are not zigzagged, although overhead cover is provided in sections along them. Latrines are usually sited in bays and corridors off the CT. This additional trench network means we can move men and materials anytime rather than overland under the cover of darkness. Even movement at night was, and still is, hazardous. The slightest noise attracts an outburst of enemy fire. And when a 'star' shell lights the sky, anyone exposed, even in silhouette against the skyline, could expect a rake of bullets at his heels. More accidents happen at night too. Chaps often slip suffering cuts and bruises. Breaking bones falling into a trench or crater is also a regular occurrence.

Now trenches are a permanent feature, we've tried to make them more comfortable. When dry in summer, trenches become dustbowls; in winter, mud baths. To help prevent both conditions we line trenches with wooden duckboards. Bathmats, we call them. They reduce the quantity of mud under foot, but after a while they too become clogged-up. And after heavy rain, nothing keeps the ground dry. The slopes are also being shored up better than before with corrugated sheets, planks, chicken wire, or wattle woven between stakes driven into the ground. Construction depends on how firm the ground and available material. However they are made, trenches need constant maintenance and repair. Shells shake the ground and cause collapses, not to mention the wear and tear thousands of troops cause moving in and out of them.

The earth extracted from trench digs is used to raise the parapet, which is often firmed up with sandbags. To fire rifles through five-inch wide loopholes in the parapet we stand on a ledge, usually two feet high and eighteen inches wide. We hope our loopholes remain hidden from the enemy. The angle of the sun at certain times can however reveal their location. Gun barrels themselves can sometimes be spied. If loopholes become exposed, at night we go over the bags to hide them by remodelling the earth or replacing dislodged sandbags. Failure to disguise them would result in a Hun marksman placing his bullet through the gap. We can't complain, we do the same to them. There's no New Testament 'turn the other cheek' in war, it's Old Testament 'an eye for an eye'. Indeed, when shooting into loopholes, it is the eye that often takes the bullet. Men can survive if the bullet misses the brain, spine or windpipe. But jawbones often get shot away: a terrible injury, although not fatal.

Men routinely talk about good or lucky injuries, as well as bad and unlucky ones, as they discuss a good or bad death. When our number's up, everyone agrees that the best death is instant, unexpected, painless. Those who've witnessed the alternative know it's not pleasant. The word 'luck' has become almost meaningless to me. Nobody fighting in this conflict is lucky. Perhaps the only exception we make is reserved for the chaps given a ticket home: wounded seriously enough to end their fighting days, but their injury doesn't hurt too much or prevent them living a reasonable life. If anyone's lucky, they are, and many consider themselves to be fortunate. I've heard men say, 'I've *only* lost an arm' or 'I've *only* lost my foot'. One fellow in a bed near Bertie said he was pleased his leg had been chopped off below the knee. Sawbones say amputation below the knee makes life far easier than if taken off above it. I couldn't share the same fortitude as these fellows.

Although we once denied it, British troops have learnt from bitter experience the best German snipers are as good as ours. The Hun's main rifle, the .312 Mauser, is as accurate as our Short Magazine Lee-Enfield, perhaps more so at over fourteen hundred yards. We ranged captured Mausers and found them to be very good indeed. Their pointed *spitzer* bullets shoot more accurately than ours, delivering a more consistent closer grouping on the target. But the

Mauser, being nearly six inches longer, is more cumbersome, and I wouldn't swap one for my 'smelly'. Shorter chaps, especially those under the Regular Army minimum standard of five feet three inches in the new Bantam Regiments, would find the longer Mauser awkward to handle. Where the Germans found our left-behind Lee-Enfields and ammunition, they used them. We've occasionally found British rifles in the arms of dead Germans. But because of the different calibre size and cartridge shape, we can't use their ammunition in our rifles. Nor can the Germans use our ammunition in their Mausers. Our cartridge has a bottle-neck casing and the Mauser bullets have straight walled casings. For both sides, gun and bullet must work together

CHAPTER 18

TRENCH LIFE - RATS AND CHATS

Promoted last week to Captain, Simon Harcourt sat in the officers' bunker playing a record on his new gramophone. Many officers have purchased these contraptions. It's heartening to hear music, even when accompanied by an additional percussion section of bombs and bullets. When shells land too close the trembling ground jerks the needle from the record's groove. When the shelling becomes uncomfortably close, officers pack their precious box away. Cockney Private Earlsfield, a salesman at Gamage's in London before joining Kitchener's Army, said these Decca Dulcephones cost £8, £13 for a posh cowhide casing. Even on my sergeant's pay, I'd have to save for a very long time to afford one. And I certainly wouldn't risk it being damaged by a Boche bomb.

When men are at their wit's end, even an innocent gramophone causes conflict, or, rather, the music it plays. A cavalry captain visiting the trench yesterday took offense at Capt Harcourt playing German music. He didn't think it 'appropriate' that, as we are at war with Germany, we should 'provide succour' to the enemy by 'supporting' German composers.

'Good music is good music,' our Captain told him in no uncertain terms. 'Beethoven didn't start this damn war. And when he wrote this piece he hated Napoléon Bonaparte then for what the Kaiser is doing now - invading other people's countries and declaring himself "Emperor".'

'What the devil are you talking about, man?'

'It's Beethoven's *Eroica* symphony, which he'd planned to dedicate to Napoléon - until he declared himself a dictator in all but name.'

Embarrassed, although trying his best not to look so, the snooty captain mounted his horse in a huff and galloped off. We were proud of our officer for putting a flea in the cavalryman's ear. One up for the infantry!

War changes many things, most of all the men who fight in it. That thin, smooth-faced nervous boy, our platoon lieutenant of thirteen months ago, Simon Harcourt, has grown into a strapping man full of confidence and common sense. He now commands a full company of over two hundred men. I say men, but some of the new chaps seem mere boys to the few remaining regulars, here since this war started. From my original platoon of forty who landed in France, only a handful remain in frontline infantry positions. About half have perished, such as Thwaites, Meadows and Smith. About a quarter have been reassigned to other parts of the army such as communications, transport and supplies. Two corporals returned to England, promoted to sergeants, and now instruct new recruits. Several are missing, presumed dead, although we hope some taken prisoner. The remainder received injuries that rendered them incapable of active service again, such as Bertie Dale. He returned to England but not to Haworth or thereabouts. No-one in the village seems to know where he is, not even his family. I regret he has not written to me. Perhaps he still resents my rescue of him from Le Cateau. Perhaps he really did wish to die at the battlefront than live with one leg in Civvy Street. Wherever he is, I trust he's looking to the future and not dwelling on the past.

For those who eventually return home - in one piece, or injured in body or mind - I doubt men will want to talk much about life here in these terrible trenches. Silence heals quicker than speaking. Talking only serves to bring back painful memories. Why dig up bones from a grave? Personal pain shouldn't be shared. I can understand why Bertie has left his past behind. I see the sense in seeking fresh fields, new friends, people who know him only as he is now, not how he was. His future may well be better without a past.

Unless the enemy is very active, or we plan an enterprise against them, infantry usually serve a week in one go at the front. When it's bad, it's very bad. We live with neighbours who snipe and shell. There are periods when little happens. But there is the ever-present awareness that a bomb will fall out of the blue and your number's up. Worse, the Germans launch an attack across no-man's-land into our trenches. If they make it and jump down on us, then it's close-quarter fighting with guns and bayonets and daggers and clubs. If these tools are lost our bodies become weapons: legs kick, fists thump, teeth bite, fingers gouge, hands throttle. We do that to them, they to us. Both Tommy and Fritz fight to kill, not injure.

After about a week at the front we withdraw either to reserve trenches or, far better, to rest camps or billets in towns or villages. These are several miles back from the front and out of range of most German artillery. Even away from the front we can be ordered to 'stand to', usually in the middle of the night. Minutes later we find ourselves marching to help repel a heavy infantry attack or reinforce our counter-attack. The compulsory slow march to the front is daunting. Then, when stepping down onto the trench duckboards and the slopes enclose us, it's like entering a huge grave. For thousands, the trench has indeed become their tomb.

Once below ground level, if it's dry, walking is easy. But if there are no duckboards, or if it's wet, muddy or flooded, we slip and slide our way to the front. At worst, we can be up to our waists in mud-soup. Everyone's priority is to keep his rifle clean otherwise, before the next inspection, time will be spent cleaning 'smelly' with Russian petroleum and our oiled flannelette pull-through. From the support trenches, we move through the communication trenches to the fire line. Each step is a step closer to danger.

The more times you march to the front, the more you know your chances of return are reduced. If there's an action on, fear as heavy as lead grows in the stomach. Everyone's edgy. Tempers fray. Some go quiet. Others talk more, faster, louder. They're quickly told to pipe down. A few stroke their silver Fums-up or rub their Tommy Touchwud good-luck charms. Hands rummage through tunics seeking a crucifix to hold and kiss. Fear diminishes a little if there is no immediate threat, but apprehension remains. And the same questions travel to the trench with you. Will we be ordered over the bags and face a barrage of bullets? Or will our platoon be chosen to stay and offer covering fire? And always the question of questions: will I be killed or maimed?

Unless there is an enterprise into the trenches by either side, the enemy has become largely unseen. Occasionally, looking through a periscope, you might glimpse enemy movement in the distance - too fleeting to get a shot in. But Fritz has become almost invisible, as we have to them. They are there. We are here. It's a very peculiar situation. In trenches, often as close as fifty yards, there's chaps wanting to kill us. And, here, we're waiting to get them. It's a strange way to live. Shouldn't we be working on farms and in factories, shops and offices? But no, we're here to kill and be killed because the Kaiser - who is not here and never will be - has decided he wants to expand his empire. If ordinary folk were left to decided what to do, we'd probably agree a ceasefire right now. Let's all go home. We can sort this mess out over a cup of tea after we've had a wash and brush-up and good sleep.

We face a less dangerous yet more irritating enemy in the trenches: lice, which we call chats. These little biting bugs are everywhere on almost everyone, including officers. They however attempt to disguise their infestation. Senior officers particularly pretend they're adjusting their clothing, probably to 'maintain decorum' in front of the men and fellow officers. But we know they're scratching chats alongside the rest of us. We're constantly told scratching only leads to more irritation. It's best to ignore them, resist the temptation. Easier said than done, especially when settling down to sleep and these little yellow-brown buggers start biting. Their nip leaves a red pin-prick mark and, after a few bites, there's a slight sour smell. It's almost impossible to resist a good scratch, even when we know the pain later will be worse than the immediate pleasure!

Officers seem to take more baths than us, but the bugs are soon back. We ORs, other ranks, usually get one bath a month in our billets, so we stand no chance of ridding ourselves of these pests. In desperation, some chaps use a Trenchman's Belt. Worn around the stomach, these belts, which cost one shilling and sixpence, are supposed to keep lice away. They might for a few days. After that some users claim the belts just provide another hiding place for the biting blighters. I find a 9d tin of vermin powder (plus 3d postage) from Boots the Chemist to be effective, if you keep the talc-like power dry. But keeping things dry during winter in a trench is as hard as avoiding lice.

Some chaps hold chat hunts, or chatting parties. They light candles, remove items of clothing, and run seams over the flames quickly. Lice congregate in seams and folds and in the nooks and crannies of skin. If it's quiet enough we can hear the chats explode as they burn. For some reason, probably because we're surrounded by so much squalor and horror, we find this trivial act of popping chats very satisfying and amusing. Resembling children playing in the street, chaps count chat pops. It provides a little light relief, a moment of harmless silliness. All things considered, I don't believe we should be denied such small pleasures and sensible officers turn a blind eye to these activities. As a sergeant, I too have learnt there is a time for discipline, mainly to avoid danger, and a time for distraction, from the drudgery of daily life.

Another enemy is the rat. Black and brown and grey, large and small and vile. It would be no exaggeration to say that some chaps hate rats more than Germans. If rats were the real enemy, or fighting on Fritz's side, we would have lost the war already. We can't hold them back. We can't kill enough of them. No man can live in the trenches and avoid them. They are everywhere, day and night, summer and winter. Unlike hedgehogs, they don't hibernate to give us a break. Unlike swifts and swallows, they don't leave us for a few months. When you can't see rats, you hear them during lulls in the shelling. They share our space, as numerous as lice. Rat holes in most slopes. Always some scratching, digging, gnawing and fighting each other. Rarely can you walk more than a few paces before one or more dart across your path. Worse, every month or so, we get rat attacks. Hordes of the filthy flea-ridden blighters storm through trenches as if chased by ferrets. Hundreds scurry in a stampede, perhaps thousands in a mad frenzy. We trap 'em, drown 'em, bash 'em, stab 'em. They breed like, well, rats! Whatever we do, they just keep coming, an endless army of rat evil. At Stone Booth Farm Mr Booth reckoned a pair in a year, without vermin control, could produce approaching a thousand offspring. At least there we could shoot the buggers. Great sport around the farmyard and barns we had. The terriers and ratting cats helped us keep on top of them. Owls, hawks and foxes snatched a few too. But despite their enemies, like Huns, rats just keep appearing. We don't leave food around in the trenches, not even a crumb of biscuit. But rats rattle the empty cans thrown onto no-man's-land rummaging for the smallest morsel. Their noise at night is often mistaken for an enemy raid, causing alarm and an outburst of musketry.

One grim truth we've stopped talking about, because it's so nauseating, is that on no-man's-land rats feast on fallen flesh. They chew the corpses of comrades we've been unable to retrieve. Helpless, we watch the filthy rodents through loopholes and periscopes with disgust. Most can't watch for long, and eyes turn away. We throw stones and handfuls of soil over the trench to those bodies within range, but to no avail. The vermin return within moments undaunted by our missiles. If they can't find soft flesh of open wounds, rats tunnel into mouths, scratch and bite eyes, to start their rabid feasting. One chap, so distraught by the scene, ran out in a pointless bid to chase the rats off a friend's body: he died at his side seconds later, ripped by machine gun fire. More rat food.

So invasive have war rats become, when there are no corpses above ground, they tunnel into graves and gorge themselves on rancid remains. With such a surplus of food, it's not surprising there is a constant plague, and big rats at that, larger than any I'd seen back home. Knowing these rodents have been feasting on the dead, it is particularly revolting when they brush past our heads while sleeping. They are also becoming more daring. On the farm in Yorkshire they back away from people, as they once did here. But lately they've become as bold as brass. They don't think twice about snatching food off the table unless it's right under your nose.

Of all the never-ending horrors of this war, the most sickening sight I've seen are injured men, stranded on no-man's-land, fully awake and aware, attacked by rats. When unable to move through injury, they are defenceless when vermin approach. The rats move cautiously at first; a quick bite here, a nip there. Then, like the fox realising the crippled lamb is powerless, rats grow bolder and attack without fear. Injured men, some known to me, have neither the movement of limb nor strength to brush the rodents away. We watch, also powerless, pinned down in trenches or bomb pits, our anger and frustration unbearable.

There is one action we could take, but we're not allowed. Shooting rats, even on no-man's-land, is forbidden. It's pointless, for another rat instantly replaces a dead one. Unless it's nearing dusk, when there is a prospect of a rescue mission under darkness, our only option is to shoot the suffering soldier. It is an act of kindness, a soldier's responsibility to a fellow soldier. Soldiers want their suffering to end when there's no hope of survival. Not every man can bring himself to this gruesome task. These chaps can shoot a faceless enemy, but not a known ally. But if a soldier is prepared to kill a healthy enemy in battle, he can surely shoot a fatally wounded friend to end his agony. Instant death by a friend's bullet is far better than being eaten to death by rats. One is an honourable death, the other is just horrible.

***

Some say killing an unarmed man turns war into murder. When a man is pleading to be shot to end his misery, they say doing so is abetting suicide. God has 'spared' him from death during the battle for a reason, they argue. If so, the reason is unreasonable. Quakers here, working as ambulance and medical orderlies, stick to the Bible's commandment, 'Thou shalt not kill'. I respect it, although I disagree, because we have a higher duty. When a tyrant such as the Kaiser goes on the rampage someone must protect our children, women, infirm and older folk.

Murder and suicide are against the law of man. But politicians in parliament, wig-wearing judges at court, can't make laws for lawless wars. Rules made in peace at a safe distance will be broken in battle facing danger. Ideals are trodden in mud, smashed to pieces, drowned in blood. The man with the gun becomes the judge and jury. You must at times pass sentence in a split second. Later, when fear has faded and facts become clearer, you discover you were right, perhaps wrong. But the decision, right or wrong, has been enacted.

War Law here among most men means that, should we be severely injured and destined to die in pain, a fellow soldier's duty is to despatch you with a bullet to the brain. That law is unwritten, rarely mentioned, but generally understood. We end the suffering of horses on the battlefield, so why not our brothers-in-arms? It is an act of mercy: the duty of the living is to help the dying die painlessly.

CHAPTER 19

HULLUCH, NEAR LOOS

Our Company's four rifle platoons, each with about forty men, have for the past week been stationed near Hulluch, a village two miles north-east of Loos. The nine men in my squad, Red, have escaped serious injury, just a fractured wrist and cuts to three chaps when fixing entanglements over broken glass. Blue squad with ten men suffered two deaths and five injured, one serious. Orange, like mine, had no deaths but three injured, two severely after their legs took mortar shrapnel. Green drew the short straw. They lost eight, killed outright by machine gun and grenade on a night raid. Only the corporal escaped, although he too nearly fell victim. Crawling back to the home trench the sentry, a nervous lad new to the front, opened fire. He missed, as you'd expect firing into the dark.

The corporal called out the night's password, but obtained no acknowledgement - except a bullet whistling overhead. The nervy lad said he hadn't heard the corporal's call, although others nearby had. The excuse was deemed unsatisfactory by Company Sergeant Pratt. He gave the lad a right ol' rollicking and a week's extra duties on 'sanitary', the worst of the worst work details. Nobody likes carrying slop buckets, burying the contents and spreading chloride of lime disinfectant. It will be a lesson the lad will never forget.

Going over the bags at night on an enterprise is now routine. An exception was last Sunday, our first night back at the front. Light from a full moon on a cloudless night becomes a spotlight, almost as dangerous as going over the top in daylight. Hawk-like night-eyes of a sniper would easily pick out a man at up to four hundred yards. Cloud the following night however dimmed moonbeams and it was considered 'safe' to attack the enemy's trench. Without moonlight the Germans, like us, use star shells to throw light over us. These 'fireworks' or 'light balls' expose men out of the trenches for several seconds. Anyone lit directly or in silhouette can expect an immediate outburst of gunfire. Everyone drops or scurries for cover. But even the fastest find it hard to beat a bullet cutting the air at nearly one thousand yards a second.

Unless an enterprise is planned on an enemy position, most night work on no-man's-land includes reconnaissance, adding to or improving the position of our wire entanglements, and making good any damage to fortifications. Sometimes we come across casualties who played dead or kept low. And corpses. Always corpses. This night, one section from each of the four different Company platoons received special orders: a big push must be in the offing. My Red section had to approach German entanglements, three hundred yards over no-man's land, and cut the wires. These attack points would be approximately fifty yards apart along a two hundred-yard stretch. Nothing unusual in that. We had cut wire many times during assaults. But this time we had to 'repair' our damage with wire clips to make the enemy's entanglements appear intact. We also had to record the exact location of our work and, on this almost flat and featureless landscape in darkness, this proved a tough task. Come the moment of the big push it was vital we knew precisely the breakthrough point on the wire. We had good reason to know: the platoons who 'repaired' the wire would be leading the attack.

Cutting through barbed wire is a tough job at the best of times. But to cut and 'repair' them while disguising the feat is very difficult. Would the Germans notice our repairs? If so, we'd be walking into a trap of our own making. They would know precisely where to aim their machine guns, mortars and grenades for when our attack begins.

But such action is needed because artillery bombardment often fails to break entanglements. We certainly need to try other ways of breaching barbed wire. This trench stalemate must end, otherwise the war will go for ever. But both sides are digging more trenches, longer and deeper by the day, along the whole front from the English Channel to the French border with Switzerland. A good trenching party of, say, four hundred and fifty men can construct a trench eight feet deep, six feet wide, two hundred and fifty yards long, in little over six hours. Back-breaking blister-making work for everybody, even manual labourers, until blisters and backs harden to the task.

Pity poor chaps from soft indoor jobs who don't know one end of a shovel from the other.

Our task was, as Capt Harcourt described, a daunting and difficult undertaking. And damned dangerous, a thought I kept to myself. This would be the day my section copped a packet, including me. I continued to defy death, but Grim Reaper must be getting closer. If I remained alive, I would have to start believing in miracles. But death in the open, fighting, even this coming night, would be better than dying doing nothing in a dark rat-infested dug-out.

I reckoned this cut and repair task would take the best part of six hours, not counting the slow and stealthy stalk necessary to reach the wire. Most of the German entanglements stood five feet high and, in parts, as thick as fifty feet. That's a lot of wire to cut, repair, and cover up our trickery. My estimate also assumed we didn't bump into any Hun crawling their way to us. No-man's-land fighting at night is an ugly business, with death and injury to many on both sides. Looking at the sky, I also feared our cloud cover would break at times: we'd be lit by the full moon as bright as performers on a music hall stage.

Nightfall, dark enough to work under, arrived by 9 pm on September 18th. To match the night, we smeared our faces and hands with mud and ash and donned dark woollen caps or balaclavas rather than our usual caps. The ten of us from Red section crept forward. Six carried rifles with bayonets fixed and various tools. The rest of us lugged wire cutters, bags of repair clips and thick hedging gloves for protection from the barbs. Our plan was to have one team of five cutting and 'repairing' while the others stood sentry. We would change teams at each break-through point. Our two strongest men had arms as thick as thighs and I gave one to each team. At either side of the cutter, a man would hold the strands to prevent any noisy and dangerous recoil. If not restrained, barbed wire can whip back slashing arms and faces. And attract gunfire.

In case of a hand-to-hand, the chaps carried their favourite self-made unofficial weapons, mainly knobkerries. Most had been weighted with lead at the business end and spiked with nails. One chap fixed an old cog wheel to his cosh, ensuring a stunning blow to any Hun head. Many chaps carried claw hammers and most of us had a dagger just in case our rifle jammed or broke. In close-quarter fighting, especially at night in the confines of a trench, small hand-weapons often prove more practical than forty-four inch rifles - nearly five feet with the bayonet attached. We all carried two grenades, a new type called Mills bombs, or No 5s. They work a lot better than the grenades we made ourselves in jam-tin cans.

Night enterprises across no-man's-land had been practiced by new recruits on training grounds. But to complete the same tasks yards in front of a trench with *real* enemy is quite different. One slip, cough, sneeze, clink of metal, dropped tool, ping of wire, dislodged rock and *stielhandgranates* - stick grenades - will be lobbed in your midst. (Men with coughs and colds are excluded from raiding parties.) As they explode sending shrapnel in all directions, a wave of bullets will also cut through the smoke, dust and dirt. Repelling action usually lasts for several minutes. So far from your home trench, and so close to your enemy's, the chances of surviving are slim.

For those who escape death, we stay as still as the nearby corpses. I've played dead quite a few times on no-man's-land. One slight noise, from rats rummaging among old tin cans, or a groan from someone injured, will spook Fritz, and another shower of stick grenades will fall around us. If able to move, we must start back to our home trench before a hint of dawn light. The first time I 'returned to life' after being 'dead', strong wind and rain provided plenty of noise to mask my movement. Even with the help of the elements, I moved as slow as a slug, face down through cold mud – and cold corpses.

The night of another 'resurrection' was not so easy. Until recently barbed wire entanglements used wooden posts to support the wire. These were bashed into the ground with mallets. Even though we used rags to muffle the blows, sound and vibration attracted enemy fire. We now, thankfully, use metal looped rods, picquets, which screw silently into the earth. That night, last January, the snowstorm stopped suddenly. It left our platoon's entanglement party exposed in clear, still air. As the clouds took snow elsewhere, the moon's light shone on us. Fritz was ready. They'd heard our handiwork. Now they could see our outline. Two lieutenants, four sergeants and thirty-two men that night were caught red-handed erecting entanglements on the bald white surface of no-man's-land. Fritz, thirty yards away in a new trench unknown to us, let rip. Grenades fell about us like rocks in an avalanche. Bullets whizzed past our ears and many found a body to bed in. We all fell to the ground, shot or not. The onslaught continued for several minutes. Then silence. The grenadiers and gunners stopped. But they were still there, listening and watching like nighthawks for the slightest sound or smallest movement. And should a pin drop...

Most of the chaps had been killed. With experience, you can tell. You remember who was where when grenades went off. You see how heavy the fall, how peculiar a body's position. You sometimes see where bullets struck and know he's had it. If a chunk of head is missing, limbs gone, guts spilled, there is little hope of survival. From our party of thirty-eight, I reckoned a dozen or so of us remained alive, keeping our heads down. And some, if not all of us, were destined to die before the night was over. A few, like me, I think remained uninjured. But you can't risk moving to check. And in the heat of battle you often don't notice your injuries. Pain can hold off until you're home safe in your trench. I breathed heavily and slowly through my mouth; quieter than using the nose. But my breath created a vapour in the cold air for a sniper to see. How odd, I thought, that my breath could be the cause of my death. Slowly, very slowly, I turned my head into the ground to disguise the breath-cloud. And then I 'died'.

Those fallen nearby unable to move will hope they are picked up later. If time before dawn, a rescue party may be dispatched. But only new lads count on these. Old hands know such rescue missions are rarely worth the risk: double the number can end up dead, and many officers are loath to mount them. If the disabled are not rescued soon, their hope will turn to despair. Then, when a pack of rats encircles them, they will welcome death. If you can move an arm, you can drive them off. But if semi-conscious, paralysed, trapped in mud or under rubble, rats show no mercy. They will happily eat you alive. Some chaps have been roused from unconsciousness by biting rats. Last month, my section on reconnaissance in no-man's-land, stumbled across a young lieutenant presumed dead. It was his first, and last, enterprise from two nights earlier. He was propped against a broken tree stump with his entrails spilling out. Without the will or energy to stop them, he watched rats eating his own bowels. As I knew would happen, he died the moment we moved him. Many men, left injured in agony, have cried out in the hope of attracting death from a benevolent sniper or bombardier. It didn't matter whether their merciful executioner was Tommy or Fritz, they just wanted to be free from pain, free in death.

Towards the end of an escape from no-man's-land, there is one final danger to face: your own front line. Chaps have been shot by mistake as an aggressor. It had taken me about two hours to wriggle inch by inch like a legless lizard the mere hundred or so yards to our lines, a distance walked in less than a minute. Eventually I reached our entanglements, approximately twenty yards from the fire trench. I crawled into a crater to rest and gather my wits.

Then I remembered I'd forgotten that night's password. (You were not allowed to write it anywhere.) Without it I could be the enemy. It was one of Fritz's ruses to pretend he was one of us, as common as dressing in French or Belgium uniforms. As entanglements are opened, they attack the chaps opening the barrier and rush our trench. I tried whispering my name to alert our sentries. My voice croaked, frozen in the cold. I tried again, my call stronger. I hoped to be loud enough to gain the attention of our chaps, but soft enough not to cause Fritz to fire into my back. But no reply. I whispered again, louder. No reply. And a third time. Nothing. I searched for a stone with the idea of throwing it to raise attention. But my numb frozen fingers couldn't prise any stone from the earth's icy grip. Using my dagger, I chiselled out a fist-sized rock and threw it towards the trench. I heard movement, anxious movement. The rock gained attention, caused alarm. Several rifle bolts drew back ready to fire.

'It's me, Samuel Ogden,' I called using a loud whisper, if that's not a strange description.

After a pause, a reply, 'Password?'

I confessed I'd forgotten.

'Password?'

'Told you. I've forgotten the damn thing.'

'You can't come in without the password.'

'It's me 51890 Sergeant Samuel Ogden.'

Silence. Then, 'You still can't come in without the password.'

'Oh, come on. I'm 51890 Samuel Ogden of the Duke of Wellington's Regiment.'

'You could be a bastard German who tortured that information out of him.' I didn't recognise the voice. It added, 'Password?'

'Look, stop mucking about. I'm 51890 Sergeant Samuel Ogden, 2nd Battalion.'

'Password now or we'll send you a No. 5 for breakfast.'

In desperation, I cried, 'Go and get Sergeant Pratt or...or...even Captain Harcourt. They'll recognise my voice and...'

'You could have squeezed them names from Ogden.'

I tried a different tack. 'Get someone who speaks Tyke, Yorkshire lingo, an' knows "Ilkla Moor Bahr Tat". Thy knows Boche would never know that!'

Silence. I expected a grenade landing at my side.

'What's "yammer" mean in Tyke?'

'Talk. It means talk, chatter....'

The laughter started. I knew I was 'home'. Sergeant Pratt and others had fun at my expense. I haven't forgotten a password since.

Before dawn on September 19th, against the odds, all ten of my wire-cutting squad returned safely. None of us had to play dead. However, we only managed to cut and 'mend' two of the planned five attack routes through the enemy's entanglements. It took far longer to re-join the severed wire than we had calculated. One delay was caused by having to rub the sheen off the joining clips, which, after fixing, we noticed glistened as clear as shining stars. Each clip had to be weathered by quietly scraping it on the ground until it blended with the barbed wire. Even after our efforts, any close inspection would reveal our links. Come the big push I feared Germans would know exactly our points of attack.

I also sensed throughout that night the enemy knew of our presence on no-man's-land. Two of my squad, experienced chaps, thought likewise. Call it instinct as much as experience, but we could 'feel' Hun eyes watching, as an owl eyes a mouse before swooping to kill. All night I expected an attack. For some reason, best known

166

to them, they chose not to assail us. It was uncanny. After giving my report to our stick-thin new 2nd Lt Porter of the night's activities, he did not think it 'appropriate' to record my 'eerie feeling' in the log book. I wanted to tell him it could indicate the Germans planned a trap. Like many green officers, he'll learn to trust his hunches as much as the rule books. If he doesn't, he won't survive. I hope he does learn to listen to his feelings, he seems a pleasant chap underneath his stiffness.

At stand down we moved back to rest in a support trench. Before resting, men who wanted their rum ration joined the queue. Sgt Pratt, even as Company Sergeant, continued most days to administer our platoon's rum rations. He enjoyed the job. It was also a good way to check on the state of the men. The ceramic rum jars stood ready on the trestle table. Each was stamped S. R. D., standing for Supply Reserve Depot, and were filled at a dockyard in Deptford from rum warehouses alongside the Thames. Men made up hundreds of variations on these initials: Soon Runs Dry. Service Rum Dilute. Seldom Reaches Destination. Sergeants Rarely Drink. Silly Rum Do. Stomach Requires Double. Sailors' Rum Decent. Soldiers' Rum Deadly.

If a chap really wants to risk his full ration and test his sergeant's humour, he'll try, 'Sergeants Regularly Drunk.' It was also customary - unless it had been a terrible night when close chums had been killed - that chaps gave the dispensing sergeant a 'bit o' lip' when it came to their turn.

'Lord Kitchener told me I could have double rations.'

'As you're the best Sergeant in the Army, I'm sure you can see your way to an extra drop.'

'A big dose will help my sore throat, thank you, Sergeant.'

'I missed out yesterday, Sergeant, if you'd forgotten, so that's two tots today.'

'I killed three Huns in the night, Sergeant, surely that deserves three helpings.'

'Just in case of a mishap, can I please have tomorrow's ration today?'

Sgt Pratt had of course a spicy line to dash all their hopes of any more than their due ration. And the fresh-faced 2nd Lt Porter closely monitored proceedings with that youthful zeal experience will blunt. He reminded the men that rum rations could not be saved for later and must be drunk immediately. It was an unnecessary reminder.

CHAPTER 20

19th – 24th September 1915
BATTLE AT LOOS

It took a day to destroy the town of Loos. It took hours to flatten Hulluch village. Hardly a building remained untouched, most reduced to rubble. Town, village, history demolished. Its past only surviving in memories. Should they return, residents who fled the fighting would struggle to recognise their homes, churches, cafes and shops. It might be nigh impossible to find their bearings. Nothing was as it had been; nothing would be as it was.

Four days and nights of bombing from over five hundred guns had foretold 'the big push'. It would be the first large scale attack after months of stalemate. The British aimed to dislodge the Germans from two strongly fortified trenches. Their lines ran almost in parallel for over six miles in length north to south. We were flanked by the French Tenth Army for a coordinated assault eastward. Months of attack and counter-attack along this front had achieved nothing. No ground had been gained, none lost. It was clear the Germans had entrenched well. We had many new recruits. But even with one hundred and twenty thousand extra men in the zone, we were spread thinly. On Tuesday September 21st our artillery guns started. They didn't stop until the day we went over the top to rout Fritz from his trenches - four days later.

One hour of intense bombing from both sides is enough to unnerve new chaps. A few start to panic, the familiar signs showing. Private Samms, like many, must have lied about his age at the recruitment office, heeding Kitchener's *Your Country Needs You* poster. Recruiting officers increasingly turned a blind eye to these boys willing to join the colours and take the King's Shilling. If the lad was big enough, at least five feet three inches, and could puff his chest to thirty-four inches, with a nod and wink the boy was signed up. Samms insisted he was eighteen. He fooled nobody. Whatever his true age, I'll guess fifteen, he soiled his pants and cried, as embarrassed as he was frightened. To those of us who'd lived through artillery battles, we just carried on, only ducking when bombs became too close for comfort. I sent Samms to the latrines to clean up and ordered him to report back within thirty minutes. 'I'm all right now, Sergeant, sorry,' he said sheepishly on his return. His panic was over, for now at least. To others who looked worried I always advised breathe deeply, it's the best thing. Keep your head down. Don't be tempted to look over the top. You'll be all right. Some chaps don't need a word, just a smile - even from their sergeant! - and a pat on the back. Others require something to do as a distraction, and I get them cleaning, repairing a damaged slope, or making mugs of tea on our little stove. One lad, trembling and on the edge of tears, I sent along the trench to Sgt Pratt to ask him for the Army's secret glass hammer. He sent the lad back asking for the special bucket with holes in it. And don't dawdle! Confused at first, the lad eventually saw the funny side. He stopped shaking.

We are all on edge. Can't be helped when the bombing is unrelenting. Our artillery reported a shortage of guns and ammunition. That's hard to believe when they continued firing around two thousand six hundred shells every hour round-the-clock. The Germans replied, not tit for tat (or *quid pro quo*, as 2nd Lt Porter said), but enough. And it only takes one of our shells to fall short, or one enemy bomb to find our trench, and life or limb could be lost in an instant. The new chaps are scared, some terrified, but their nerve held, even the youngest. They are imagining going over the top, meeting the enemy, facing their death or injury, as we all do. It's best not to tell them the reality will be worse than they imagined.

The sky is not only busy with shells. Aeroplanes are increasingly employed. It seems the generals are relying heavily on them for reconnaissance. Cavalry troops and scouts have traditionally been our eyes and ears on enemy activity. Scouts, often working alone and behind lines, gather intelligence on the enemy: troop numbers, position, movement and weaponry. It takes a lot of courage and cunning. But aircraft cover far more ground than horses or vehicles and see much more from high in the sky, weather permitting. New and different types of machines appear almost daily, French, British and German. France, for example, has a new aircraft, the Nieuport 12. We're told it can reach the frightening speed of one hundred miles an hour. That's thirty miles an hour faster than our BE-2s. Aircraft are also being used for more than observation: they have started dropping bombs and firing machine guns. Another new weapon of war, another way to kill.

Two days before the bombing started on the 19th, we noticed chaps bringing crates marked 'accessories' to the front trenches. The men, neither talkative nor friendly, came from an army unit we had not seen before. They'd clearly been ordered to stay aloof. They removed from the crates what looked like small bombs. Those of us who had been at Ypres in April realised these 'bombs' were gas cylinders. As the news spread, the mood along the trenches grew uneasy. Faces reflected every emotion from horror to sadness. Now we understood why offices had recently stressed we received instruction how to don the new 'P' model gas helmet. It was *not* that we were expecting a big gas attack from Fritz, but rather we planned to attack with our own clouds of poison.

Each 'P' tube helmet came with a small sheet of directions. This was of no use to those who couldn't read, or read well. To make sure everyone knew how to don the helmets, each sergeant gave instruction to his men. We used a dummy helmet to practice. (Real masks couldn't be worn for drill because this would use up the chemicals neutralising the toxic gas.) Some naturally thought the tube valve was to be used for breathing in. But it was for breathing out, keeping the tube cooler and reducing condensation. Service caps had to be removed before pulling the helmet over the head aligning the goggles to the eyes. This is common sense. But we've seen a few dimwits attempting to don the tube helmets with their caps on. One chap tried with a cigarette burning! As Sgt Pratt says, common sense isn't that common. Once over the head, the helmet's skirt must be tucked in under one's collar and the coat buttoned up to the neck to form a seal. Frankly, however you wear tube helmets, they are uncomfortable and stifling.

Judging by the number in our Battalion's section alone, several thousand cylinders must have been positioned along the British front of over six miles. It had been hard work bringing the heavy cylinders forward through the narrow trenches, which had become busy and crowded in the build up to our attack. Our company's 'Green' platoon had been selected to man the 'accessory emplacements'. (Officers continued to avoid the 'gas' word.) The men received instructions on how to operate the 'accessories'. It wasn't a complex task: you turned the cock on each cylinder. 'But only when ordered to do so,' stated a pompous Gas Company sergeant, as if that wasn't obvious to even the dumbest new soldier.

A violent thunderstorm added to the noise on day three of the artillery attack, Thursday September 23rd. The artillery, dug in a mile behind our position, were delighted at the downpour, whereas we in the trenches clearly did not welcome rain. Heavy rain turns a trench into a sewer. And rising water can bring an invasion of rats. Artillery chaps prefer wet conditions because it helps them range their howitzers. When the land's dry, especially here in Artois where much of the topsoil is chalk, clouds of dust after a strike make it harder to see the exact point of impact, needed to gauge an accurate trajectory.

It seemed nature had become envious of man. Her forces of thunder, lightning and thrashing rain competed with man's bombardment. But nature knows when enough is enough. Her violence ends and returns peace to the land. Our bombing however continued around the clock into another day, and another. It affected us all: grumpiness, gloom. Surely no-one has ever undergone four days of continual bombardment on anything nearing this scale. Tension gripped as tight as I'd ever known. Sleep had become almost impossible. A few minutes snatched until a shell landed so close as to shake you awake was the best you could hope for. Surely the attack would be ordered soon. If not, we'd be too tired to fight, or fight well. Our barrage is supposed to be damaging the Germans in their trenches, and we hope it is, but it's harming us too. Eyes are sunken, faces pale and drawn.

Standing Order 28 states: *'All men must shave daily. Discipline as regards saluting, standing to attention, &c., will receive as much attention in the trenches as in billets.'*

But Capt Harcourt told our Company's junior officers and sergeants to cut the chaps some slack. 'Remember such orders only apply "as circumstances allow". It's safe to assume that four days of round-the-clock bombing provides sufficient "circumstances" to ease our usual protocols.'

And shells kept firing and falling, never-ending man-made thunder. How much longer? What are we waiting for? Everyone asks. Since this war betwixt trenches began, the greatest fear has been going over the top. With just cause. But after four days of body-shaking bombardment, most think let's get it over with, one way or another. Recently, when climbing the ladder to no-man's-land, I've found myself in a dreamy trance. I think myself into thinking that it's not me, but me watching myself. I concentrate hard on where I'm going, what's next. As sergeant, I direct the chaps about me, telling them to go here, or there, what to do. Worrying about them stops me worrying about myself.

When the chap on the ladder above you cops a packet and falls, dead or injured, you must elbow his body aside like a tumbling bale of hay and continue climbing the ladder. Climb the ladder, keep climbing the ladder. Don't think. Don't hesitate. Just go. You know the rifleman still aims at the same spot, waiting for you to fill his sights. We hope, often hopelessly, he's aiming elsewhere to claim another victim. Or he's reloading, gaining you three extra seconds to get off the ladder and forward. Or he misses. Even the best of us muff shots for any one of a dozen reasons: a distraction, nearby blast, jammed cartridge, a simple misjudgement.

None of the new drafts have experienced an all-out attack across no-man's-land, although each knows the danger they face. A few, foolish fellows, see going over the top as the time when they become a 'real' soldier: the boy becomes the man. Sadly, for many, no-man's-land is where the boy becomes dead: the boy dies a boy.

But, after four days and nights of shelling, the new chaps believe hell on no-man's-land cannot be worse than hell in the trench. They'll find it is. At least going up the ladder over the bags bring one thing to an end - the waiting. To 'do and die' is better than to do nothing and die.

CHAPTER 21

25th September 1915
FORWARD TRENCHES NEAR LOOS

At 4 am on Saturday September 25th the storm of shells became a blizzard. Fast fire became rapid fire; the canter a gallop. Surely the artillery guns would melt. At 5 am men assigned to release the gas received the 'stand by' order. This worried those of us who watched how gas clouds behaved at Ypres. There seemed little wind, not enough to glide the gas to the Germans. I said nothing. It wasn't my place to do so. I didn't want to worry my men. Capt Harcourt and the three other company commanders would know what to do. 2nd Lt Porter and our company's other three 2nd lieutenants had however yet to experience a major assault over no-man's-land. Our Company's four rifle Platoons, each with a full complement of forty men, received orders to prepare for an attack 'within the hour'. Now was the last opportunity for each man to visit the latrine, shave and wash if he wished, fill his water bottle, sort out his bits and pieces. Every man checked his rifle and ensured he had one hundred and twenty rounds of ammunition and two No. 5 grenades. Bayonets had been fixed throughout the night, complying with Trench Order 3(f). There was an exception, Trench Order 3(i): *'In very cold weather sentries will occasionally work the bolt of the rifle to prevent the striker becoming frozen. For the same reason, in cold weather men will sleep with their rifles close to the body.'*

Even at this dreadful time, perhaps because of it, many showed great spirit. 'Can't die unshaven, what would my wife say?' said Peters, smiling, 'I'd never hear the end of it.' Pte Skene provided more laughter. 'There's no point in going to the lav. I'll be pissing my pants anyway!' Pte Black added, 'Not sure we'll still have trousers at the end of this bleedin' caper - nor the dangling bits inside 'em!' During the banter, I enjoyed a breakfast of bread, cold soup and two hard-boiled eggs. Some couldn't face food, their stomachs too tight, although I encouraged lads to eat what they could. There was no hot food, the cookers had been withdrawn overnight to Divisional HQ.

Our four thousand-man infantry Brigade became positioned in trenches two miles north from the ruins of Loos and a mile west from the flattened village of Hulluch. Four Companies with a total of six hundred and forty men, including mine, had advanced through flooded trenches to our forward position, half a mile nearer Hulluch.

In these trenches our gas cylinders stood, their long rectangular nozzles poised to discharge the chlorine clear of the parapet. The venom was to be released in clusters at different times along the front line. At 5.30 am that moment arrived for us. The gas men donned their tube helmets. The rest of us were ordered not to wear ours unless needed, to preserve the neutralising chemicals, and the gas should blow away from us. With first light the wind picked up and my fears for the correct dispersal of gas abated, although the breeze wasn't a consistent flow eastwards. From our fire bay we couldn't see the cylinders unscrewed, but shortly a cloud of chlorine formed a rising blanket to around forty feet over no-man's-land.

We had sunk as low as the Germans in fighting dirty. For the greater good, and to stand any chance of victory, we had to match their ways of slaughter, however repugnant. Never again it seems will soldiers face each other across fields in a gentlemanly fashion, as men of honour fighting a duel. Never again will opposing lines of cavalry on fine mounts await the bugle to commence their charge at the agreed time. Never again will the cannons wait until the opposing side is equally ready, as a courtesy. War now knows no dignity, even if battles once did.

The chlorine cloud drifted forward slowly. Too slowly. The enemy had more than enough time to fall back or ready themselves for our attack. 2nd Division, a mile north towards La Bassée, launched their ground attack. All our Company had by now returned to the front in readiness for the attack. Sgt Pratt said one chap, and not a lad but someone in their thirties, had panicked coming through the communication trench and needed a slap across the face to bring him round. A handful had vomited or experienced collywobbles, but recovered and put their front foot forward. Chaps in my squad stood firm, everyone being brave for everyone else.

Capt Harcourt walked the line in and out of the bays. He had a quick word with each of his key lieutenants, including Porter, stood ten men to my right. The Captain asked if my lads were all right and ready for the attack.

'Yes, Sir, as ready as they can be,' I said. 'My chaps will give Fritz a good fight.'

'Good man, good man. How's that diary of yours? Has your French spelling improved?'

I was completely taken aback. He'd remembered about my diary! It had been thirteen months since we'd talked about it at Amiens railway station. I was even more shocked that he chose this moment to ask - minutes before our Battalion's biggest attack of the war.

'Now and then, Sir, when I get around to it,' I said. 'And, yes, my spelling's a bit better.'

'Good chap, good chap,' he said, alongside a short nod and tight smile. I took this as recognition of a special relationship: he and I, alongside Sgt Pratt, remained the only men in the Company from our original band of Dukes entering France from Dublin.

'Look after our Sergeant,' he told Pte Samms, standing next to me. The lad was equally taken by surprise that his Commanding Officer spoke to him at all, and so pleasantly.

'Oh, I shall, Sir, count on me, Sir,' he spluttered. The boy grew in stature and resolve. If he'd reached fifteen, he'd aged to twenty-one!

By 6.10 am the gas canisters had emptied and the smokescreen put down. The non-stop shelling of four days stopped. Oh, the peace! No more pounding! The order 'don gas masks' went along the line. We obeyed, some fumbling more than others in their nervousness. This was it, the big push. Ladders placed against the front slope allowed the first man, Cpl Treeman, to stand with one foot on the bottom rung. The rest of my section would follow. I would go last to ensure nobody was left behind. Duckboards slid over the trench to form a bridge for men from the back trenches to cross. These helped men get forward more quickly than would have been possible through boggy crowded trenches. In the distance, the first whistle blew. Then another. 2nd Lt Porter raised the Hudson's whistle to his lips and removed his revolver from its holster. After the whistle in the neighbouring fire bay, our lieutenant blew. I shouted go, go, go! 2nd Lt Porter removed his cap, donned his gas mask, climbed a ladder and went to war.

Cpl Treeman climbed swiftly without hesitation. Others followed. One chap slipped and injured his ankle, but insisted on climbing the ladder once he'd caught his breath. Pte Samms went and my Lance-corporal, then I stepped up. No-man's-land was suspiciously quiet. No firing directly at us, although fighting was going on in the distance on both sides. In this zone the chlorine and smokescreen had fulfilled their job at keeping the enemy down. The masks made it tough to see and we all stumbled about gasping for breath. Enclosed in the hood with such a limited view, I felt cut off from the surroundings, as if this vast war involving millions had become my small, private, intimate battle.

The tube mask become too confining for one fellow. He ripped it off in sheer panic screaming for air, regardless of its poison. I didn't recognise him, most likely a new draft who'd drifted from his platoon. He should have kept his nerve. He fell in a deep crater and I lost sight of him. I doubt he ever came out of that gas-filled sump. Just ahead of me Pte Skene stupidly took off his helmet believing the gas had dispersed. He immediately went blue in the face. I ordered him to put the mask back on. Too late. The gas had got him. He fell to the floor coughing violently and his eyes turned red and watery. I ordered him back to the trench dressing station. That was the last I saw of him.

The precious minutes of peace we enjoyed ended in one mighty burst of bombs and bullets. Shells cracked overhead scattering shrapnel over us. I honestly didn't know whether they were German or ours, probably from both sides. Machine gun and rifle fire whistled through the thinning smoke. Each one left a whirling trail of its trajectory through the cloud. Men fell in front of me. Men fell to the side of me. I didn't look behind. The smokescreen started to thin exposing hundreds of us. We moved forward, heads down, bodies bent, bayonets ready. I could just make out the enemy's entanglements about fifty yards ahead. Some had already reached the web of wire. They'd been told to look for the 'repairs' and break through at those points. But swirling smoke and the restricted view through the masks' goggles made them hard to find. Apart from one point, our earlier efforts had been a waste of time. Ladder parties and wire cutters worked in the usual way to break though the entanglements.

With Skene gassed, and three others of my section down, six of us remained approaching the enemy trench. I expected a volley of stick grenades, but not one was lobbed. The Germans had decided to stay dug in and wait for a hand-to-hand in the trench. Reaching the precipice, we could see their trenches dropped a good two feet deeper than ours, too deep to jump in safely. We retrieved a ladder left on the entanglements and descended the warren expecting a rush of Hun brandishing bayonets. But the trench remained eerily empty. At a dugout, the door was slightly ajar. I sensed a trap. I was momentarily distracted by what I saw: blinds, wooden venetian blinds in a bunker 'window'! And, inside, curtains. Curtains! Soft chairs! A table, set with fine-looking plates and cutlery. This hole in the earth had been turned into a dining room, almost as neat and tidy as any I'd seen above ground. Such luxury was about to be destroyed.

I pulled out the No 5's pin, released the lever and rolled it inside. We turned our backs and ducked in readiness for the blast within four seconds. It didn't fire. A dud. Young Samms quickly handed me one of his grenades. That worked. We rushed into the smoke with bayonets ready to finish off surviving Fritz. But the bunker was vacant. We continued moving along the trench in accordance with the latest orders on trench tactics. Two bayonet men went first, followed by two grenadiers with bombs ready. I went next, as the sergeant in charge, followed by anyone remaining. We had been ordered to clear five fire bays to our right. A grenade was supposed to be thrown around each corner before we rushed into the bay. But in the confusion caused in equal part by the smokescreen, restricted sight through gas masks and battle panic, I worried that many of our men had entered the trench at random points and we'd end up blasting our own. Indeed, in the very next fire bay, we met 2nd Lt Porter and lads from 'Blue' and 'Orange' squads. Had a grenade been thrown, they'd have copped it. I asked the whereabouts of 'Green', knowing them to be on the lieutenant's right as we advanced. He shook his head. Everyone? He nodded. 'Green' all gone - again. The men believe Green squad jinxed. 2nd Lt Porter confirmed all the bunkers empty. The trench had been abandoned.

Corps orders for the big push had been clear: keep going forward. Capt Harcourt put it simpler: advance. So up and on into the new no-man's-land we went, now without smokescreen cover. On leaving the German trench we faced grazing fire from a solid line of machine guns. Hundreds of us stumbled forward, unsure of our footing with these damn tube masks. Within seconds a quarter of us became riddled with lead. The ruins of a row of cottages provided shelter for what remained of our company. With our mask goggles obscured by condensation, it was hard to tell who had copped it. The strongly defended German second line looked about two hundred yards away. Even though most men had hit the ground, dead or catching their breath, Fritz did not cease firing.

As if the dead were not dead enough, they continued to fire, making mincemeat out of men.

Companies behind us started their advance. Most men fell within seconds of standing. To stand was to die. Many stood. More men came forward line following line. More fell. Unless our artillery could pinpoint the German second trench and blast it to kingdom come, we were going nowhere. But restarting our cannon fire would mean some shells falling short, slaughtering our own. It would be a risk worth taking. Anything was better than this carnage. Surely the order will be given to fall back, although a bullet in the back is no better than one in the front.

But no bugle sounded retreat. No order to withdraw was passed along the men pinned down in holes and hollows and behind ruins. Men kept advancing, falling after a few yards. A horizontal hail of bullets stopped them. Brave men? Stupid lads? Sane? Insane? If there was the slightest chance of overwhelming the German trench, the risk would be worth taken. But the odds stood overwhelmingly against them. Not one single man could advance. Could nobody stop this madness?

It was hard to recognise anyone, even my own lads, through these abominable steamed-up gas masks. Three for sure had copped it. Hopefully two fell with repairable injuries, but I knew for sure Pte

Saunders, a tall skinny chap from Huddersfield who joined us last week, was a goner. Bullets ripped out his heart and lungs and travelled through to down a chap behind: a two-for-one bargain bullet. Cpl Treeman and Pte Samms survived. 2nd Lt Porter, gripping his revolver, could be recognised. Treeman said something. His words muffled, he pointed to my leg. Unknown to me, a bullet had torn flesh from my right thigh, although it didn't hurt a bit. A standing - and unfair - joke was that there's never a medical orderly around when you need one. And there wasn't. Fortunately, I carried rolls of very good German *krepa binde* I'd taken from a dead Fritz orderly and kept for just such an occasion. (German bandages seemed more absorbent than ours.) I smothered Zam-Buk on the crepe bandage and slapped it on the wound. It stung then!

The German machine guns stopped. We knew what this signalled. Within seconds hundreds of Hun came at us. Their counter-attack began. We raised our rifles over the rubble and fired rounds as fast as we could. I missed as many as I hit because of the restricted view through the wretched goggles. Several chaps tore off their tubes in frustration. Damn the consequences. They could aim properly. They seemed unaffected. None of the Germans wore gas masks either, so I tore mine off and what a relief! I did not miss one of my next five shots. The Germans started throwing stick grenades which knocked down our lads at the front. We retaliated with No 5s, but our grenades didn't seem to have the same stopping power.

Too close now to use grenades, our forces came face-to-face. It was time to stand and fight, kill or be killed. Rifles and revolvers fired at point blank. Bayonets clashed, slashed, stabbed. Men grappled on the ground, in pairs, in groups. I was surrounded by a frenzy of fists and knives and clubs. You could smell gore and guts that gushed and spilled everywhere. Men shouted and screamed in fury and agony. My first bayonet kill went into the German's back. It saved the lad under him being clubbed to death. I pulled the boy up. He fell again, stabbed by a huge Fritz. Before this monster could retract his bayonet, I thrust mine into his eye. I'd aimed at his neck. But a Hun on my back caused the deflection. His forearm wrenched my head back and I could see the knife swinging to my throat.

A rifle stock came between the blade and my head to halt its thrust. It was young Samms. He'd saved my life. I twisted out of the arm-lock and grappled with the German. Samms gave Fritz a withering blow to the head with his rifle butt. Teeth flew from the German's mouth and his body went limp in my arms. To make sure he didn't get up again, Samms put a bullet into him. 'I owe thee a pint,' I said breathlessly, as another gang of Hun charged at us.

I retrieved my rifle in the nick of time to face the attack alongside Samms and others. The first Fritz was another giant of a man, too big to move nimbly and plenty of body to aim at, and he was easy to pierce. The next could not have been more different, a little terrier of a chap. He leapt around as if his feet touched hot coals. He jabbed one way and another, running all around me. His blade nicked my 'good' leg. Suddenly, with one skip too many, he slipped in a pool of blood-mud, and my bayonet was in his throat. With a gurgle and a spurt of bright red blood, he stared at me wide-eyed before falling face first to the ground. We got the better of this battle of the bayonets, although we lost chaps too. One was stabbed in the chest and coughing blood. Pte Black had taken several thrusts of blade to his guts and groin. Both realised their days were over.

The Germans retreated after about ten minutes. They'd decided to sit tight for now, which made sense. They had no reason to lose more men in open counter-attacks. And it was clear we could not penetrate the German's second trench, nor advance beyond it. Had we ten times the number of men, I doubt we could overcome them at this point outside Hulluch. They seemed indomitable, too well defended, with dozens of machine gun redoubts and their superior stick grenades. With every assault more of us got mown down. No one survived within twenty-five yards of the Hun's trench. Menacingly, we could see hundreds of German reserves amassing behind their lines. If they attack, we're done for. Six of my squad had gone already. Only Cpl Treeman, my life-saver Pte Samms, and Scotsman Pte Gavin Peters remained.

Sporadic fighting continued into the night. Several platoons, even foolhardy individuals who had been lying low in craters, continued to attack the enemy's second-line entrenchment. All failed, every man cut down. Each endeavour towards the enemy line seemed more pointless than the previous one. Pte Peters observed, in his dour Scots, that those attacking now might as well shoot themselves. I replied, lamely, orders had to be obeyed. But I started to doubt the wisdom of that. Sensibly, our CO decided not to advance from this hopeless position.

CHAPTER 22

Sunday 26ᵗʰ September 1915
LOOS

New orders arrived at dawn. They were needed. Confusion had set in. Behind the lines many men, alone and in clusters, looked bewildered, unsure about what to do. Each with his battalion broken, his body weary, his mind bewildered, firm direction was the required cure. Senior officers from Division assigned men to new units. Stories emerged how hundreds of our own had become casualties of our asphyxiating chlorine gas. One can't control the wind, an officer said offhandedly by way of an excuse. Scottish units had suffered exceptionally heavy losses.

An order from Brigade at 8.30 am instructed several companies, including ours, to 'drift north'. It was believed that at La Bassée, two miles away, we stood a better chance of breaking through the German defences. The Royal Flying Corps had dropped bombs on the railway supplying the enemy throughout the sector. We had already broken the German line to the south and entered Loos, whatever was left of it

We scrambled back to the trenches from where we started our attack twenty-six hours earlier. With no smokescreen cover nor gas drifting over the Germans, it was almost as dangerous going back as it had going forward. At least we could see better without the damnable tube helmets. As always crossing no-man's-land, we dashed between holes and hollows, pausing occasionally to catch breath or stay down if gunfire grew hot. Each rush invited bullets to your back. None of us liked sheltering behind a dead body, even a German one, but it couldn't be avoided. Several men however got picked off as we retreated.

2ⁿᵈ Lt Porter was one such victim. He took a shot two yards behind me. He yelled in agony and fell into a ditch, his face squelched into the dirt. I instantly rolled into the next crater. He spat out mud cursing his bad luck and writhing around; a good sign in my experience. Chaps who fall still and quiet are usually the more serious casualties, unless they've kept a cool head to play dead. He was holding his leg; another good sign. Limb injuries, unless an artery has been hit, are easier to survive, if you can avoid gangrene.

'How bad is it, Sir?'

'It's smashed my tib and fib, my bloody tib and fib,' he shouted. 'Damn it. Damn it. Damn it.'

Snipers continued working, their bullets striking the ground inches above us. But, while the machine-gunners took a break, I dashed towards the young lieutenant.

'Get back!'

'Too late, Sir.' I was in the hole with him.

'You need to get back,' he winced. 'Think you'll have to lead the platoon towards La Bassée. I believe I'm the last lieutenant standing in the platoon, if not the company. And now look at me. Damn it.'

'Let's get you back to our trench, Sir, you'll be safe there.'

'No, leave me.'

'Can't do that, Sir, you're too good an officer to lose.'

'That's an order, Ogden, get on man. I'll get picked up later.' He lied. He knew as well as I did that nobody would be searching this patch of no-man's-land for many-a-day, if ever. He'd be stranded and bleed to death or, as others have done, shoot himself. Either way, rats would enjoy a feast.

I gathered his arm around my shoulder and dragged him up. He hobbled along through his agony and we made it to the next hole, chased by a few bullets.

After several deep breaths, he said, 'Didn't you hear what I said, Sergeant? Leave me. I'll be fine.'

'Three things, Sir. One, after five days of shelling, I'm deaf. Two, you're not bleeding too badly and you can get that injury sorted. Three, I'm very experienced at rescuing chaps with leg injuries!'

'My tib and fib are shattered, Ogden.'

'Sir, I've seen chaps come back from worse. Surgeons are getting better at fixing things. Not surprising with all the practice they're having. And, look, we're only a few yards from our trench.'

'I'm a medical student, Ogden, or was, and I know...' Porter's speech slurred to a stop. He fainted as the pain got him.

I took my chance, abandoned my rifle, threw the lieutenant over my shoulder and bolted thirty yards to our trench. His skinny body seemed no heavier than sheep I'd rescued from moorland snow. German bullets whistled past us as I unceremoniously slid the lieutenant down the slope into our trench. I leapt in behind him as, I swear, a bullet skimmed my ear.

The trench was packed with men, as many injured as able. Everyone jostled past each other and over casualties. Any officers about? I asked. No. Captain Harcourt? No. Sergeants? No. But there were two medical orderlies and I persuaded one to help 2nd Lt Porter. 'He'll live,' the MO said after a quick inspection. 'When the stretcher bearers arrive, and God knows when that will be, we're evacuating the chaps with a chance of living to the field hospital at Vermelles.' I didn't need to ask about the fate of those without a chance.

Unexpectedly, with no officer in sight, I found myself in charge of nearly eighty men from several units. Some had become lost during the big push due to the confusing combination of tube helmets and smokescreens. The strays include four from the 2nd Oxford & Buckinghamshire Light Infantry, two from the 1st Queens, and one chap from the 6th London Regiment. Pte Tracy, from Lambeth, said he should be two miles away near Loos and didn't know how he'd ended up here. I walked down the line gathering everyone from our company. I explained we'd been ordered north towards Haisnes and La Bassée. Those not in our company should stay, hold ground and offer protection for the injured, although I didn't believe the Germans would attack. I told those remaining that I'm sure they'll be joined by chaps keeping low in no-man's-land.

'What shall we do with these two?' asked the Londoner. I had no clue what he was talking about - until Pte Tracy stood aside to reveal two Germans huddled together in a funk hole. (These are little shelters we carve out of trench slopes. Trench Order 8(a) stipulates *'the undercutting of trench sides to make shelters is forbidden'*. Thankfully some officers conveniently 'forget' this rule, knowing it's been written by a staff officer in a cosy office rather than someone who has lived in trenches under downpours.) 'An' there's a spare one of these, Sergeant, if you'd like it,' said Tracy, smiling. He held out a *pickelhaube*, a much-prized spiked German helmet. Most of the lads wanted one. Ignoring Tracy's nonsense, I asked if the prisoners had been searched. They hadn't. He said sorry. I reprimanded the Londoner for flouting Standing Orders: prisoners are to be searched immediately and, should any documents be found on them, these are to be forwarded to Brigade HQ without delay. Tracy's excuse, 'They're only privates, Sergeant, they won't be carrying top secret battle plans.' I made the point, in front of all the men, that one of the prisoners could have been a messenger. 'And never spoil an apology with an excuse,' I added. Tracy started searching immediately. In the skirt pockets of their tunics he found their identity papers. One, quite an elderly chap aged about forty, also carried an official-looking letter with the German eagle at the top. It had been neatly folded in four and tucked inside his identity papers. Tracy handed the documents to me. 'Anyone understand German?' I asked, not believing for a minute anyone would. (If a chap understood the language so well he wouldn't be a 'poor bloody infantryman' at the front.) As expected, everyone shook their head. 'Do...you...speak...Eng-lish?' Both prisoners guessed what I'd asked. They shook their heads too. 'Och, Sergeant, they would nae tell thee even if they spoke the King's English as good as myself,' Pte Peters said.

2nd Lt Porter had colour back in his cheeks when I went to wish him well and leave the prisoners' papers in his charge. 'Thanks, Sergeant, for disobeying my order out there,' he said. 'What order was that, Sir?' I replied. He smiled. I told him my plan was to follow Capt Harcourt's last instruction to 'drift north'. He confirmed it was the right thing to do. Now he'd recovered his senses, he would take charge of the chaps who remained until a senior officer turned up, or until the stretcher bearers came to cart him off. 'Good luck, Sergeant,' he said, and then held out his hand to shake. 'You'll be back out here as right as rain within a couple of months, Sir' I said, 'you'll see.' For once my reassurance to an injured man was truthful: young men's bones heal quickly and, if he avoids the gangrene, he'll be fine.

The forward trenches in this sector comprise of a string of separate diggings, not a single line. They had been quickly constructed in preparation for the big push, not well maintained, and used mainly as forward listening posts to see if we could learn what the Germans were up to. Following the thunderstorms each trench had become a trough of yellow muddy water, from knee to thigh high. We waded carefully through them to maintain our footing and avoid stirring up yet more mud. But inevitably in this sludge-soup most of us slipped at some stage and took a soaking. The priority was to keep our rifles above the waterline, including my replacement of the one abandoned to carry 2nd Lt Porter.

We stepped on all manner of objects in the mud, corpses being the worst. The bodies, some bloated, belonged to those who had copped it going over the top and fallen back into the watery grave. The best we could do was leave each body propped up across the slopes to help prevent the corpse sliding under the water again. It was an unpleasant and upsetting task, even for experienced chaps. To see corpse after corpse is the saddest of sights: the waste of war. Many of these chaps joined pals' battalions and stared into the faces of friends. Knowing the victim, the pain becomes personal. Part of you has died with them. Their memories of you, gone. No more shared smiles. They can no longer be part of your future. Nor you, theirs.

Heading north I assigned two chaps to keep an eye on no-man's-land with box periscopes. Look every minute, I ordered, we don't want to get surprised by Fritz. We came across a few able men holding positions in the forward trenches. But more laid seriously injured, including two lieutenants and a major from the 2nd Ox & Bucks. They were too ill to talk, or talk sense, and I doubted they would survive the day, if the hour. They desperately needed medical attention or a stretcher party. I ordered two of the able-bodied to make their way back to our lines and summon help. The rest should continue to defend the position and comfort the casualties until further orders.

The hazardous moment arrived when it was time to leave trenches and venture onto open ground. We soon found ourselves in a battle inside a complex of quarries. It was chaos, impossible to predict who was going where. Cannon and mortar shells from both sides fell haphazardly. The situation seemed senseless. Pockets of men, perhaps twenty or so, fought each other, battles within battles. We saw German medical orderlies giving first aid to our wounded. At first I assumed they had been captured. But no, behind them the Boche fired at us over the heads of their own first-aiders. It seemed the Germans helped our injured of their own free will. It was the only gesture of humanity that day. For the next two hours, the quarries became the scene of the worst man-to-man violence I'd witnessed since Ypres and Hill 60. I cannot say what I saw. I cannot say what I did. I cannot say what I felt, which, at the time, was nothing.

Contrary to what we'd been told, it was the Germans who exploited our undefended gap north of the quarries. Boche swarmed in. They started to get the better of the battle. Close-quarter gun fights merged into hand-to-hand combat with bayonets, daggers and knobkerries. The violence continued into the afternoon. It was clear we were done for. The Hun killed many of our chaps. They captured quite a few too, including a Brigadier-General from the 27th Brigade.

Alongside the 1st South Staffordshire my chaps halted the German advance by excellent musketry, good positioning and timely use of grenades. But it was only a question of time before the Germans would sneak around our flanks. We watched as they destroyed unit after unit getting ever closer. They killed or captured all in their path. My chaps stayed together well and, after the hand-to-hand, the fifty or so of us left clambered to the head of an escarpment. We picked off some advancing Germans. But we faced a major problem: each man had just a few rounds left for his rifle. And, between us, we possessed six precious grenades. I ordered to fire only when certain of a kill. Even so, for every Fritz we shot, others sprung up. They'd be on us in minutes.

It was midday, Sunday. Thoughts flashed to home in Haworth. Would I like roast beef, pork or lamb? Horseradish, apple or mint sauce? Yorkshire pudding, certainly, soaked in thick gravy. Alice. My sisters. Skylarks. Windswept moors. Woods. Streams. Rivers...

When things are bad, imagine good things.

But duty calls. Five bullets left. I can do something, something practical before I die: kill five Hun to save those after me killing them, kill before I'm killed. Forget home, Sunday roast, even Alice.

When stuck in shit, don't think of roses. Accept the mess you're in, otherwise you're dead. I fired the first of five rounds.

The situation looked hopeless when Blue platoon and others approached from behind, about sixty men. Capt Harcourt dropped down beside me and fired the rifle he took from the dead man next to him.

'I'm very pleased to see you, Sir!' I fired three more bullets leaving one left which, by tradition, I might keep for myself.

'Likewise, Sergeant. I thought all but Blue had been done in.' He pulled the trigger on an empty breach. 'Damn it.'

'We'll be done for soon too, Sir. I doubt we can hold here ten minutes longer, even with more ammo.'

'I agree,' Capt Harcourt said. 'What happened at Hulluch?' He reloaded his revolver in readiness for the face-to-face fight.

'We got pegged down at the crossroads when 2nd Lt Porter received the order to drift north. We started to withdraw when he got hit...'

'Is he a goner?'

'No, Sir. Took one in the calf. He'll live, I'm sure. Gave a good account of himself too.'

'That's good. Lieutenant Porter's tougher than he looks. Who's left?'

'What you see, Sir.' I scanned my chaps and fired my last bullet when an easy kill appeared: the Germans could pay for the bullet to finish me. 'Of the rest, I'd say half copped it. Some made it back, injured, and a few might be lying low until nightfall.'

'That bad, eh?'

'Worse. The fiercest fighting I've seen, Sir.'

'And you've seen more than most.' The Captain surveyed the quarry basin with his binoculars and watched the Germans advancing in strength. 'You're right, Sergeant, it's hopeless here. They'll be on us any minute. Oh shit!'

'What is it?'

'Christ! They're not taking prisoners. They're just killing chaps with their arms up!'

'Bastards!' It was the first time I'd blasphemed in front of an officer since joining the Army.

'If we stay we die. Do you want to die, Sergeant?'

I couldn't answer. Not immediately.

'Well, Ogden?'

'Not if I don't need to, Sir, if it doesn't serve any purpose.'

'I assure you, Sergeant, it won't. We've lost thousands already. Let's get out of this hell hole.'

CHAPTER 23

November 1915
LOOS – IN SEARCH OF BODIES

Back where we started five weeks ago, everyone except the new drafts appears despondent. September's big push pushed nowhere. Days of relentless artillery fire, using a quarter of a million shells, failed to dislodge the Germans. Our infantry advances likewise met stubborn resistance, and eventually repelled. We enjoyed early success at the southern end of our attack line, taking Loos and Hill 70. But the late arrival of reinforcements and lack of munitions helped Fritz retake the hill and most other positions. By September 28th all our gains had been abandoned.

We attacked again on October 13th. Within minutes, the 46th Division alone lost one hundred and eighty officers and over three and a half thousand men trying to take the Hohenzollern Redoubt, two miles north-west of Hulluch. This was a well-built complex of trenches, shelters and machine gun nests. Gas was again used to open our assault. And, as last time, the weather worked against us. The heavy fighting around Loos ended on November 4th. Since September's big push started, thirty thousand British men have suffered injury serious enough to keep them out of service. Around twenty thousand perished. Most of the dead remain where they fell, despite a few attempts at body retrieval.

Our chlorine gas caused as many British casualties as German, perhaps more. In several sectors the toxic cloud failed to blanket the enemy and, worse, drifted back over us. A change in wind direction took the blame. But many chaps ripped-off their steamed-up gas masks. A few died and over two and a half thousand rendered themselves useless by their folly.

Reluctantly, I must admit our new drafts, although keen and courageous, are not as good as regulars. With the training, expertise and discipline of our original force, we stood a chance of breaking the Boche at Hulluch. I don't blame the new men. Most had just arrived at the front. None had seen action. If they had experienced a few skirmishes, they would have been better prepared. It is easy at first to get confused in battle with the sheer level of noise, movement, destruction, death and injuries all around. Panic sets in. Fear takes over. What you thought would happen, doesn't. How you imagined you'd act turns out not to be the case. You discover your every weakness. You may also discover a hitherto unknown strength. Rarely do things go to plan. Fighting, like any skill, needs training, practice and, most important, experience. The new chaps had basic training in Britain and some had extra here. But none had experienced true battle. None had killed real men: targets don't cry, bleed, die. None had slain with or faced slaughter by the bomb, bullet, bayonet and club.

From our four infantry platoons at Loos, totalling one hundred and sixty men, only seventy-five remain fighting fit. We lost three 2nd lieutenants, four lieutenants and two experienced regular sergeants. Fifty-one men died, the rest injured. Some lads are missing, possibly captured. Many will remain unfound, their bodies blown to buggery, left to rot, or sunk in Flanders mud as sure as torpedoed ships at sea.

At nightfall September 27th, the day after our withdrawal from the quarries near Hulluch, Capt Harcourt asked - not ordered - if we should attempt to search for survivors. Haunting cries of help and groans of pain from casualties could be heard from no-man's-land. The Germans had returned to their deep trenches and it was thought unlikely they would mount any attacks. I gathered a working party of twenty, all new to the front from reserves. Not one had seen a scrap of fighting. Corporal Treeman, Pte Peters and young Pte Samms volunteered for the mission. I gratefully accepted Treeman and Peters' help, but Samms, despite his enthusiasm, needed rest.

Our priority was the living, I explained before we set out, we would collect corpses only after we'd retrieved the injured. And because it was the first time any of them had ventured onto no-man's-land, I stressed they had to keep sound and speech to a minimum. Preferably not even a whisper. If Fritz hears a murmur they'll fire at us with everything they've got. They might fire anyway, just for the hell of it. And if a star shell goes up, hit the ground and stay still. Don't go running around looking for a hole, their machine-gunners will have you before you find it.

By fifty yards into no-man's-land, the new chaps had learnt the main consequence of war: dead, disfigured, dismembered bodies. Then they discovered their first feelings towards it: horror, disgust, fear. (Hate, anger, regret, helplessness, guilt and emptiness would come later.) Two vomited. Others gagged and brought up bile. The sight and smell of bodies blasted, shot and slashed is sickening. Watching these fellows, I felt as sorry for them as the men whose bodies, dead or alive, they carried. Nobody told us it was as bad as this, they whispered, shaking heads. No, of course not, I thought. If Army recruiters or the politicians had told you the whole truth, you may not have volunteered. Sensible fellows would turn a blind eye to Lord Kitchener's recruitment posters.

One lad said he felt sick at the idea of touching a dead body. He asked to be excused from this task. 'You'll get used to it,' I said. 'Don't look at the face.' This was the best advice to get him and other squeamish chaps started. After carrying several corpses, his loathing would lessen, if not go away completely. However, I told the men to remember they were moving people, people who are dead. This is easy to forget when you're regularly carting corpses away. For some, bodies become like sandbags, another heavy weight to pick up, move, throw down. To see a corpse as anything but human is their way of coping. I give them some leeway, but ask them to be more respectful. It's how they try to forget their own mortality. But clearing corpses is not a funeral, nor a ceremony. It's a job. You do what you need to do as fast as possible. Get it over with. As one chap said, 'I suppose someone's got to do it, Sergeant, and it's better than carrying buckets of piss and shit on latrine duty!'

We carried the survivors who couldn't walk on stretchers to the first aid post, including seven Germans. We searched every Fritz and found nothing of significance, even on a junior officer, who seemed uninjured. He spoke a little English. 'Thank you, thank you,' he whispered, aware his own line would be listening, 'I be good prisoner. No trouble. Do not shoot me, please thank you.' He could easily have crawled back to his own line but, for reasons known only to him, he preferred to become a British prisoner of war than remain a German soldier at war.

Some 'corpses' come alive. Injured bodies, especially in the dark of night, can appear dead - until you move them. I had warned the chaps about this before we set out. But it always takes a man by surprise when someone you think dead speaks!

My squad cleared the corpses we could find from about twenty acres of shell-scarred land. Most of the Loos battleground was however never searched for bodies. We rescued twenty-eight casualties, perhaps half will recover with their limbs and organs intact. One lad didn't appear to have a scratch, but he had lost his senses. I'd seen this mind-loss a few times. There's nothing you can do to snap them out of it. You talk, they don't hear. Their eyes are open, but they don't see. They're threatened with death for cowardice, they don't care. They wouldn't know if you stood them in front of a firing squad. They would starve if not fed like babies. And, like infants, they soil themselves freely. They live inside their own skin.

On our final sweep of the area, we stumbled across a severely injured lieutenant, his face scorched by shrapnel. Blood and pus leaked from his raw head, neck and shoulders. The rest of his body had also absorbed sizzling shrapnel. I will never understand how he survived with such terrible injuries. I would have thought myself dead, used willpower to cease breathing. With his mouth torn and teeth smashed, he struggled to speak. He was fully aware talking would sap the last of his life, but he had survived to say something. His voice weak, I put my ear close to his disfigured lips. He asked me, speaking quite clearly, to tell his father and mother that he loved them. Between gasps for breath, he wanted me to thank his father for 'pulling strings' to get him in the Army and that he had 'no regrets'. The strain of speaking caused him to cough. His blood spattered my face. I thought this was his end. But no, he carried on, though his words became slurred as he slipped towards death. I asked his name and regiment. But it was impossible to detect what he said. I gave him a sip of water from my bottle hoping this would oil his words. He mumbled something like 'kipping' or 'kippers'. He became agitated, frustrated at his own inability to talk clearly. In desperation, he took one long intake of air and, on his dying breath, seemed to say, 'ruddy kippers'.

He was of course struggling to say something else, but what? Once we know his name perhaps all will become clear. But there was no metal or red fibre identity disc around his neck. I also inspected his wrists for a copper identity bracelet, which some officers had recently taken to wearing. The Army-issue fibre discs soon rotted with sweat and damp. (As a regular before the war my disc is stamped aluminium with my name, rank, serial number, regiment and religion.) In keeping with Standing Orders, the young officer carried no papers. In his blood-soaked tunic, however, he carried a photograph of an elderly couple, presumably his parents. They stood, quite distinguished-looking, in front of a stone-built house. The picture only showed the front entrance, but it was clearly a far grander house than our terraced cottage in Haworth. A heavy oak door filled the arched porch and above it, carved in the stone, the date 1634. I returned the photograph to the officer's top left pocket, their faces facing inwards. It's the place all the chaps choose to keep pictures of their nearest and dearest - the pocket closest to their heart.

The corpse of this unidentified officer was the last we stretchered away that night. Near where he fell I found a top-notch officer's cap by Burberrys of Haymarket, London. Its badge was the distinctive shamrock within an eight-point star of the Irish Guards. But it was one of many items that always litter no-man's-land and impossible to say with certainty the cap belonged to this officer. Unusually, it had no name inside, but I placed it on his chest. He deserved a cap, even if not his own. He will be a soldier unknown, one of many.

My party returned to Back Alley, the communication trench, exhausted. Six hours collecting casualties and corpses from no-man's-land is tiring work. Most of the lads did well and I praised their efforts. Two moaned under their breath about how hard it had been without a break. I didn't single out the grousers, but addressed the whole party, saying that we had been extremely fortunate on this occasion because Fritz left us alone. We had been within twenty-five yards of the Germans at one point and they had not fired at us or thrown grenades, nor sent out an attacking party armed with bayonets and coshes. I knew they knew we were there, but again they left us alone. I added for good measure it had also been a dry and mild night. If you think tonight was hard, try it in rain, a howling wind, ice or snow - and under fire. Under such conditions grousing might be in order. The complainants looked sheepish and buttoned their lips, certainly within my hearing. Their first night at the front had been an easy introduction to this war, as they will soon realise. The casualties we rescued were handed over to the orderlies of the medical corps. All manner of transport was used to get the injured to the nearest field hospital near Vermelles, three miles to our west, including several new motor ambulances.

Marching the lads to the kitchen for breakfast, the night's unwritten truce ended in a mad minute of small arms fire. These chaps, new to the front, got the wind up and ducked their heads. Some put their rifles to the ready. I reassured them that so far back from the front we should, hopefully, be out of harm's way. Some didn't look hopeful! I explained that it had become routine to experience a 'mad minute' of rifle and machine gun fire at dawn and dusk. It's called the morning or evening 'hate'. The 'minute' could, of course, last for several, and sometimes every minute of the whole day. These outbursts represented one side saying to the other, 'Hello, remember we're at war'.

Arriving at the kitchen after a hard night's work, it was disappointing to discover there was no bacon and bread. No hot food at all. Rations had not been brought up in the night. The kitchen fatigue had apparently other priorities. There was, as always, bully and a table full of tinned pork and beans. The tea was lukewarm and tasted particularly badly of petrol, the water having been carried in old petrol cans. I found myself reassuring new lads that today's breakfast wasn't too bad. You'll find when posted on the front line you might be having, if you're lucky, a duck's breakfast. For those of you who haven't heard, that's a face wash and a drink of water!

After rum, the men enjoyed a smoke before settling down to sleep wrapped in their groundsheets. Before I put my head down, I went to the dressing station to have my injured leg cleaned and re-bandaged. In the queue of walking wounded there was great excitement. The cause? Two lovely ladies, a chap cried excitedly, as if he'd just found a big blue diamond. Two nurses were indeed providing care. Like snow in August, it came as a great surprise to find women so close to the front. Chaps egged each other on like silly schoolboys. For the newly arrived to see a woman surely was not unusual, having left Blighty only a week or so earlier. But for men who hadn't enjoyed female company for some time, their presence provided a pleasant surprise. The nurses had one notable effect: the men stopped swearing within their hearing.

When my turn came, a Miss Chisholm cleaned and dressed my wound. She told me that alongside her colleague, Elsie Knocker, they normally worked in Pervyse, Belgium. They had been asked to come here temporarily knowing the big push would result in many casualties. With over two million men having enlisted - and many more would be needed, she added quickly - Miss Chisholm was proud that women were now working in factories, driving ambulances and wagons, even repairing them. Many girls have also started doing the jobs men used to do on the farms, including working the horses at plough.

'Women who wish should be allowed to fight too,' said Miss Chisholm, who told me her first name was Mairi. 'Russian women fight in a unit called the "Legion of Death" and can shoot just as straight as any man!'

Of that I have no doubt. Farmer Booth's wife could hit rooks and rats as good as anyone - and better than most - with shotgun or rifle. But most men believe women shouldn't be involved in fighting and killing. In a perfect world, war wouldn't happen at all. But the world is not perfect.

War provides clear proof of human imperfection. Some chaps are saying these two ladies - any lady - shouldn't be anywhere near the front. But if women are determined to be here, they are brave enough to serve alongside men. And unlike many of the new lads, I noticed neither Miss Chisholm or Miss Knocker flinched an inch when whizz-bangs or even Jack Johnson's crumped nearby. They carried on like old troopers, and treated many men very efficiently.

CHAPTER 24

February 1916
AMIENS

I've refused home leave since August 1914. A feeling nags me that, should I return to Blighty while the war rages, the spell of my good fortune would be broken. It's a stupid sentiment, nevertheless a feeling I can't dismiss. In letters my family ask when I'm coming home on leave. I say nothing, or explain things are presently too hot and I can't abandon colleagues. The warmth and safety of home would make the cold and danger here feel even worse upon return, the contrast too painful. Frozen hands need warming with cold water. After four years of Army service in Africa, my father understands this feeling. He doesn't press me to visit.

Until this Great War, as it is now being called, is over, I do not wish to experience peace. I want to get the fighting over and done with, win or lose. I want the certainty of life, or no life. After eighteen months of war and countless brushes with death, I've started doubting whether I'll die. This worries me. Any frontline soldier assuming he will survive, will almost guarantee he won't. Believing I will die here is reassuring, because this belief meets my expectation of no expectation. There is no ambition to fill, no dream to come true, no journey to complete. I can be content with what I have now, not worry about what I might want in future. If anything has kept me alive it is the awareness of my mortality. Death, being my constant companion, makes life more alive. Should I forget for a minute death can strike anytime, that will be the minute death strikes.

Forced to take a break, I stayed in France. 'Sergeant, you are on leave from this instant and that's an order,' the Commanding Officer said. 'If I see you back here before the week is out, I'll have you shot!' The CO did not smile, although I assumed he was being light-hearted. So, off I went by myself, which created a strange sensation after so much time with crowds of men. I found lodgings and kind French folk often refused to take payment for my room or food, even though they could ill-afford such generosity. I insisted that unless they took money I would not return, and they reluctantly accepted. The French wished to show their gratitude for the sacrifice British and Commonwealth soldiers make. But from what they reported, French troops suffered even greater losses than ours. I never strayed too far from the war, not wanting to think it was over. The boom of howitzers could often be heard, and sometimes the ground trembled. I stayed in a couple of lodgings where British troops came through, gathering battle news from the chaps returning from the front, and Blighty news from those going to the front.

A sergeant in the Royal Engineers recommended a place on the western side of the city of Amiens, the Hôtel de la Paix, near Breilly. Approaching the château it looked too grand and expensive for me. I almost turned away to find lodgings elsewhere, thinking I should stick to the small billets I was used to. It also crossed my mind that officers might choose this class of accommodation. They, and I, might feel uncomfortable that I was somehow trespassing in what they might consider the officers' mess. But the RE sergeant said its prices were very reasonable. And, if the hotel was good enough for a sapper sergeant, it was good enough for an infantry one. The elegant three-storey house, set back from the road, sported rounded turrets on each corner. Even in these damp dull days of February the garden, set in a good four acres with neatly trimmed box and yew hedges, looked in good order. A drift of snowdrops lightened the ground under bare-branched oaks, elms and limes which encircled the house at the back and sides. To the front, an expanse of lawn with rose beds greeted guests, who approached the heavy double-doors along a broad gravel path.

'We should, monsieur, have thirty-six rooms,' explained the manager in clear English while I registered. 'But a shell landed on the corner of the property and four rooms are awaiting repairs. And, as you can understand, finding men to undertake such reparation while this war is on is extremely difficult.'

I said I was sorry about the damage and that German bombs had caused a great deal of destruction. 'Oh non, non, monsieur,' he insisted. 'I am pleased to say the shell was French! And we are delighted it helped repel the Allemand from Amiens. It's a small price to pay.'

Some chaps on leave in France took to drinking or women, usually both. Maybe I'm old fashioned, but the idea of visiting brothels repulses me. Many have caught nasty diseases, not to mention how horrible it must be for the women. Some seem proud - certainly not ashamed - to have caught dreadnought and received their injections of 606, or salvarsan, although this venereal disease cure makes some feel very ill. They say the brothel business is booming, fuelled by the war, especially here in Amiens. Although the Germans captured the city for about a month at the outbreak of war, it was recaptured by the French late September 1914. Because of its large railway junction, Amiens has become a major centre for both French and British military operations. There are many men looking for female 'company'. The older chaps, who should know better, take pleasure in encouraging the younger lads to 'have a go'. The boys are told they can't die without having jig-a-jig. To stop embarrassing encounters, officers look for blue lamp establishments. ORs, other ranks, seek places with red lamps in the doorway or window, where 'services' are also offered much cheaper.

With time on my hands I discovered a new pleasure: reading. It was inspired by a wonderful gentleman I bumped into - I did in fact knock him over - in the hotel corridor. I had preferred learning by watching, listening and doing, rather than by reading. The lure of adventure outside always appealed more than the dull prospect of sitting inside with a book in hand, whatever the weather. Indeed, the worse the weather the greater my desire to be out in it, especially high winds and stormy nights. 'The wetter the better,' I used to say. After five years of Army life and over twelve months living in trenches like sewers, I no longer hold that view!

My introduction to 'literature' came courtesy of a soft-spoken Indian gentleman working for *The Times of India*. Mr Prem Unia had become a regular at the hotel. He was reporting on, as he put it, the fortunes and misfortunes of the many thousands of soldiers from India fighting on the Western Front. The British had fought alongside many Indian fellows, even from the early days of the war. The first winter for many of them was a terrible ordeal, many more of them suffering frostbite than our lads. These poor blighters continued wearing thin tropical cotton, not at all like our heavy serge. Out of pity we gave spare warm clothing to Indian Corps sepoys, the ordinary soldiers.

At first I thought it strange that I should be taught the true value of my own language by an Indian. But Mr Unia was far better educated. He had attended the University of Oxford. He knew many more English words than I did, and spoke them in the creamy cultured tones of the highest English upper crust. He knew about so many things, especially politics and history. He talked about socialism, communism, colonialism and economics, words and matters I'd never even heard of. I often felt embarrassed by my ignorance. But he was far from snobbish, always kind, patient, and gave freely of his time to explain things. 'We Hindus believe it is far better to give than to receive,' he said gravely, like a wise old man, although he was only several years older.

We first met in the main ground floor corridor of the hotel. Old portraits and countryside paintings, with hairline cracks running through them, hung on either side. I hovered outside a room wondering whether guests were allowed inside. The sign BIBLIOTHÈQUE was painted in gold on the door. In my ignorance, with the word near-enough to 'Bible', I thought it might be a prayer room. Not wishing to disturb anyone praying, I turned to walk away when I bumped into Mr Unia. I knocked him flying flat to the floor! He apologised immediately, although the collision was clearly my fault for stepping away quickly without looking.

'Did you not find anything of interest?' he asked while dusting himself down and readjusting his collar and tie.

'Sorry?' I must have looked completely stupid. Certainly felt it. I simply didn't know why he'd asked that question.

'In the library,' he said, smiling, gesturing towards the door. 'I could spend my whole life in there. But I would never complete a smidgeon of work.'

'Ah, it's a library, is it?' I believe my mouth remained open.

Mr Unia held out his hand, introduced himself, opened the door and invited me inside as if he owned the place. I later learnt Mr Unia spoke French fluently. But to save my embarrassment, and because he was a modest man, he rightly observed I had just discovered the French word for library. No translation from him was necessary. The château rooms had tall ceilings and on all four walls from top to bottom were books, books and more books, stacked in corners and on eight reading tables. Each wall had its own stepladder, built on a wooden frame with running wheels for ease of movement, to reach the uppermost shelves. I had never seen so many books, large and small, and in what looked like different languages. Like school on a wet Monday morning, the library held that heady tang of mustiness and beeswax polish. I started to whisper as in church, despite nobody else in the 'biblothèque'. But Mr Unia spoke with confident enthusiasm. He *was* 'at home'! He explained the 'volumes' to the left were in Greek, these Latin, here we have Persian and Arabic. The hotel's proprietor even has several fine quite ancient texts from India such as Sanskrit. Of course, most of the books are in French, Italian, Spanish, and, Mr Unia hesitated, German. 'I do hope we don't condemn the literary giants of Germany and Prussia for the Kaiser's recklessness,' he said, almost as if speaking to himself.

'And here,' Mr Unia said with a small bow and a flourish of his arm as if introducing a star act onto the stage, 'the English.'

A wall of books confronted me. How did anyone find the time to write all this? Who could possibly read all of them?

'Or rather, Sergeant Ogden,' he continued, 'to be more precise, these are books printed *in* English. Even the Americans and Australians write in English.' He smiled broadly. I didn't know why.

He paused and watched as I looked at the barrage of books, a wall of words, whether in complete awe or total dread, I wasn't sure myself.

'Everything is here from Chaucer to Marlowe, Shakespeare to Trollope. He's so amusing. Or perhaps you would prefer something more contemporary? I hear Thomas Hardy is now enjoyed outside his Wessex and, of course, the wonderful Rudyard Kipling. He was born in Bombay you know and...'

Mr Unia curbed his enthusiasm. He realised, of course, I knew little of these writers nor read any one of their 'volumes'. The gentleman that he was, he didn't wish to embarrass me.

'Oh, do forgive me, Sergeant Ogden,' he said kindly. 'I can be quite an ass at times. I should have realised you've enjoyed too little time to read anything since this abominable war started, apart from orders issued from on high.'

We both knew the truth. And that wasn't it. But his love of books was infectious and it inspired me to show interest.

'Please, Mr Unia, go on,' I said. 'I really would like to start reading some of these "volumes".'

'Before I say another word you must stop calling me Mister Unia. Prem would be far preferable.'

'And I'm Samuel, and on leave, so we can forget the "Sergeant" too - otherwise I'll be ordering you on a fatigue or, more likely, I'll end up calling you "Sir"!'

We laughed in friendship.

Prem advised that, as a newcomer to the novel, I should start with what he called a jolly good yarn. I said in Yorkshire we often use the word 'yarn' instead of 'story'. From my accent Prem had already accurately assessed my origins. And that, of course, is exactly why he used 'yarn'. When he asked where in the county I was from and I replied Haworth, he jumped as if a whizz-bang had exploded under him.

'The Brontë sisters, the marvellous Brontë sisters,' he cried. 'How wonderful you walk in their footsteps!'

Prem recommended that I did not however start my novel-reading 'adventure' with the sisters' novels. 'But when you do,' he said, 'start with Anne's *Agnes Grey* or *The Tenant of Wildfell Hall,* leave Emily's *Wuthering Heights...*'.

Like an over-excited child, I interrupted Prem, telling him I knew exactly where the *Heights* were!

'That's good. Yes, leave *Wuthering Heights* and Charlotte's *Jane Eyre* till last. You'll see why.'

Prem and I moved closer to the 'English' wall. I had heard of Charles Dickens, of course. (Even the daftest farm boy in Yorkshire would have *heard* of him.) But apart from extracts from *A Christmas Carol*, which we had to read at school, I'd never opened a Dickens' book. To my shame, I'd not read a storybook at all - apart from the Bible at Sunday school. Of the twenty-one volumes of Dickens in the hotel's collection, apparently filed in the order in which Dickens wrote them, I plucked the one in the very middle, *David Copperfield.* I read the opening: *'Whether I shall turn out to be the hero of my own life, or whether that station will be held by anybody else, these pages must show.'*

'Samuel, my good fellow, you could not have picked a better book with which to start,' Prem said. 'It is one of the greatest stories ever written, and Mr Dickens' personal favourite.'

Despite several words I didn't understand, over the next two days I stuck my head in the book and turned each page hungry for the yarn's every twist and turn. Frustratingly, the day came for me to return to duty having only reached the point where Jip, the old dog, dies. And, glancing at the next chapter, I saw Copperfield planned to return to Canterbury to see Mr Micawber. When I explained my dilemma to Prem over breakfast, he grinned broadly. He then reached towards a brown paper parcel tied with brown twine on the vacant chair between us. Still smiling, he placed it on the table and slid it towards me. I opened my present to find two books, *David Copperfield* and a new novel by a John Buchan, *The Thirty-Nine Steps.*

'Now, Samuel, you have no excuse not to complete one novel and continue reading with another.'

I had read all these wonderful words of Dickens over the last two days, but I couldn't find any to say at this moment. I simply shook Prem's hand as my 'Thank you'.

CHAPTER 25

February 1916
VERMELLES - NORTHERN FRANCE

Delays beset my return to duty. A train journey of fifty miles from Amiens north to Bethune, which usually takes one hour ten minutes, took five hours. Many complained. They worried, with reason as they'd cut it too fine, they would be punished for returning late. Overhearing them, a pompous young lieutenant told them in a voice shrill enough to fill the whole carriage, 'There is a war on, don't you know, one must expect this sort of thing'. The men, many of whom had experienced months in trenches and survived Loos, gave the prig dirty looks. He'll find out soon enough there's a war on, was doubtless the thought in everyone's mind. Hopefully the subaltern, obviously fresh from officer training, will quickly learn how to gain respect from ordinary soldiers. But I doubt he ever will.

The French guard elbowed his way through the crowded fug-filled carriages checking tickets with tedious regularity, even when the train had not stopped at a station. When asked the cause of the delay, he waved his arms around shrugging his shoulders shouting *'neige, neige'*. A dense wall of white engulfing the landscape provided the likely translation. Those returning to our rest camp at Vermelles did not welcome the prospect of a seven-mile trek from Bethune in this snow blizzard, although I looked forward to a bracing walk after my recent idleness. Eventually we arrived and when leaving the station, to the men's surprise and delight, a convoy of 'body snatchers' rolled up to meet us. The temptation to ride in one of the six canvas-covered wagons proved too much, and I joined the grateful pack of passengers. Our stretcher bearers, to address them properly, had earlier unloaded their 'cargo' at the nearby Casualty Clearing Station or, for those who died on the way, a burial site. It was also fortunate for us the bearers had just laid down fresh straw after hosing and brushing the wagons - to rid them of gore and bodily waste.

Two matters greeted me as I reported for duty, the first troubling, the second tragic. The disturbing piece was an order to report to Battalion Headquarters in three hours at 6 pm. The message had been delivered by yet another fresh-faced staff lieutenant I'd not seen before. When I asked the reason, he didn't say, and he probably didn't know. He just barked, 'Look as smart as you can, Sergeant, and that includes your dress cap.' (Did he genuinely think I wouldn't know which cap to wear?)

The terrible news I received in the sergeants' mess; the Allies had withdrawn completely from the Gallipoli peninsula. British and French, alongside commonwealth troops from Australia, New Zealand and India, had failed to capture Constantinople, the Ottoman Empire capital. We had already evacuated many troops in December, but hoped for a breakthrough later. It was not to be. It was hard to accept that Turks had beaten us. One bold chap asked the question the rest of us thought but were afraid to ask openly: if we can't beat the Turks, how can we beat the Germans?

The Allies had formed the Mediterranean Expeditionary Force to take Constantinople and defeat the Ottomans. British regulars had gathered from around the Empire, joining the 29th Division. But as we found on the Western Front, this industrial scale war was not the same as controlling small-scale rebellions and fighting skirmishes in troublesome parts of our Empire. A major part of the MEF was the French 1st Division of the Corps Expéditionnaire d'Orient. They had a full and experienced artillery battalion and were by all accounts excellent fighters. Unfortunately, most of the Australian and New Zealand chaps had virtually no experience as soldiers. They resembled many of Lord Kitchener's pals' regiments and new recruits joining us now. Although keen and eager, fit and strong, they lacked the discipline of regulars and experience of fighting together as well-practiced units. They too had not faced the force of big-gun warfare that we had suffered on the Western Front. Only chaps with the most vivid imaginations would come close to the horror of that reality. And then, come the day, it would be far worse: the killing greater, the injuries more horrendous, the noise louder, the smells more sickening, the depravity of man darker. On 25th April 1915, the day they landed at Gallipoli, they faced that truth. And after nine months without progress, we had pulled out of the Dardanelles Strait leaving behind goodness knows how many good men dead.

Battalion HQ was housed in a château similar to the hotel in Amiens, although smaller. It had been severely damaged by shelling - German, French and British - and a good third of the house lay in ruins. German officers had also commandeered the building during their advance in September 1914. As I waited on a bench outside the Commanding Officer's office, I worried about all the possible reasons for this reprimand. Whatever it was, it must be serious for the CO to be dealing with me. I couldn't think for the life in me what I'd done wrong. I hadn't turned a blind eye to any lazy or work-shy skrim-shankers. I did not know of any misconduct going on. Actually, I thought I'd done a pretty good job since becoming Sergeant. But my three stripes now looked in jeopardy.

Then a truly terrible thought struck me. It shook me harder than any shell had done. The CO had received news from home. Bad news, it must be. Someone in my family must have died. That's it. That's why I'm here. And they are going to order me home whether I like it or not. And I suppose, in those circumstances, I should return.

The CO's door opened. Three officers carrying thick brown files departed from the room talking so intensely they didn't notice me. I half-stood intending to salute, but they had passed by. Well, I'll soon know the worst, I thought. The staff lieutenant marched and stood me to attention in front of the CO's desk. But it wasn't the major I was expecting; it was the Battalion's Lieutenant-Colonel. 'Sir, Sergeant Ogden, Sir, The Duke of Wellington's Regiment, 2nd Battalion, Sir,' the Lieutenant barked. 'Thank you, Lieutenant, that will be all,' the Colonel said, and the subaltern marched himself smartly away.

To my surprise, Captain Harcourt sat to the side of the Colonel's large leather-top desk. And on a chair at the edge of the room I was delighted to see 2nd Lieutenant Porter, back from his calf injury, but with a walking stick and doubtless on light duties.

'At ease, Sergeant Ogden,' the Colonel said in a deep but friendly voice. The news must be bad. He looked at the Captain and the 2nd Lieutenant and told me they needed no introduction. 'I suppose you are wondering why you're here, Sergeant.'

'Yes, Sir.' I worried I'd spoken too loudly, or not loud enough.

'Two reasons, as a matter of fact. Can you guess?'

'No, Sir.'

'Have a go, Sergeant.' He was enjoying a game.

'Sir, I haven't the faintest idea.' I realised by the Colonel's tone that, to my relief, it couldn't possibly be bad news.

'Well, I'll ease your suspense. Both officers present here, and another officer, have officially cited you for exceptional bravery and dedication to duty above and beyond. Lieutenant Porter here also mentioned your rescue of him in September at Loos from no-man's-land under intense fire when you could have saved your own skin. As you know, for that alone you have already been Mentioned in Dispatches and named in the *London Gazette*. In addition, I have endorsed their recommendation and put your name forward for a further award. What that will be exactly shall be determined at Army HQ. But take it from me, Sergeant Ogden, a medal will be forthcoming. What do you say to that, eh?'

'Well, Sir, I...I don't know what to say, except that I'm honoured. But I've only done my duty like thousands of chaps, Sir.'

'Ah, you're modest too, Sergeant. But, frankly, all the medals the military can offer would not repay sufficiently the sacrifices you and many of the men have made at the front. Well done.'

To my surprise the Colonel walked around the desk and shook my hand. I'm sure this was against Standing Orders. But I suppose when you're a Battalion Lieutenant-Colonel in your own office you can more or less do what you damn-well like!

'Now, another matter, Sergeant,' he said returning to his seat. 'Captain Harcourt tells me of your progress throughout the duration of this war. I have also read the Captain's and Lieutenant Porter's reports of your leadership action at Loos. With not an officer present, or injured like the poor Lieutenant here, you effectively commanded what remained of the Company for two days in the face of the fiercest of fights.'

I remained silent. I had not been asked to comment. Regulars know that. New chaps don't. It was clear the Colonel understood and appreciated the 'old' discipline.

'Well, man, let's hear what you have to say to that?'

208

'Thank you, Sir. I'm flabbergasted, Sir, if that's the right word to use. And thank you all very much. But I did what I had to do, Sir.'

'Ah, you've done far more than that, my good man,' the Colonel said. 'Chaps like you with dozens of battlefront experiences are becoming extremely rare. And it's damn obvious why, sadly. That brings me to the second reason why we've called you here. Captain Harcourt, if you please.'

The Captain stood. 'Thank you, Colonel. Sergeant Ogden, I won't beat about the bush. Not only I but several officers have reported your skills as a soldier and, as the Colonel has already made clear, your courage is without question. It is also evident that all the men who have served alongside you recognise your leadership qualities...'

'If I may interrupt, Captain, and that includes Lieutenant-Colonel Arnold Allen. Do you remember him, Sergeant?' the Colonel asked.

'I recall a Captain Allen of the Royal Irish Rifles, Sir, on the retreat from Le Cateau.'

'The very same, don't you know,' the Colonel said with a broad grin. 'He dines out on the story how you shot a German sniper. A thousand yards away in a field, he says. And you sniped him with only half a second to aim and fire with a rifle you'd never used before. Best goddamn shot he's ever seen, he says. And it sounds like it to me. Without your shot, he says, that sniper would have pinned down most of those men until nightfall, by which time they'd have been captured, don't you know.' The Colonel slapped the palms of both hands down on the table to express his delight at the tale. 'Captain, my apologies, please continue...'

'Yes, Sir.' Capt Harcourt shared a quick smile with me at the Colonel's enthusiasm. 'So, Ogden, what do you say to that?'

'With all due respect to Captain Allen, well, Colonel now, I don't think the sniper was a thousand yards away, Sir.'

'Anyway, Ogden, we are going to make you an offer, a request actually. We can't order you to do this. But all three of us in this room would be bitterly disappointed if you refused. And you have no cause to decline our request because we are absolutely certain...

The Captain paused abruptly, deliberately.

'Because we know, Sergeant, you will make a damn fine officer.'

CHAPTER 26

March 1916
OFFICER CADET BATTALION

We served one Army. We shared the same enemy. We faced the same danger. But on arrival at the Officer Cadet Battalion's training school I found two camps. The gulf was, at first, discreet. To mention such matters would have been bad form, perhaps impolite, not done old boy. Even among 'them' divisions existed, although not with 'us'.

My Indian friend Mr Unia had talked about the *jati* class divisions in his native country, from high caste Brahmins to lowly Shudras, who mainly work the land. There are others considered so low they are outside any caste. Even the shadows of Untouchables are believed to be unclean and best avoided. And here, among the British officer class, struggling for survival against the Kaiser's Boche, we have division. They may not be as extreme or complex as those in India, but they are just as active. At one end, which they would consider the top end, we have chaps from 'good' public schools. Next we find those from 'minor' public schools. The likes of us couldn't tell one from another. The middle caste seemed full of former teachers, solicitors and the like, who had not attended any public school but served a profession. On the step below are the cadets who, although educated, had neither attended public school nor held a position considered professional. Many of these fellows are however very well off. Their fathers ran businesses such as shipbuilders, cotton mills and engine-makers. Many had made a fortune. Their fathers generally believed working in the family business provided a better education than any university. What's the use of Latin and Greek or poetry and plays when there are carpets to be woven, engines to build, coal to mine, fruit to import?

'Us' rankers, men like me promoted from the ranks to officership, represented outcastes. Not to all the others, but to many. We became officers 'for the duration of the war' and our papers clearly marked in bold red ink 'Temporary'. Our standing in society it seems would be as fleeting as that in the military, not only called Temporary Officers but also Temporary Gentlemen. This annoyed most rankers, who argued it was unfair. It was. And as junior officers, we were now more likely than senior officers or chaps in the ranks to die. Platoon commanders, lieutenants and captains, lead most enterprises and are usually first over the top and the first to attract bullets.

Mr Unia said socialism (or was it communism?) aimed to iron out such differences between people when property and businesses are state owned and wealth shared equally. I could not see that happening. People are different. Some are cleverer, work harder and therefore receive greater rewards. Others are just plain lazy or dim-witted. I can't see a day when the wealthy are going to share their wealth. Land-owners don't give land away. They had a revolution in France for liberty, equality and fraternity. But here the rich continue to live in mansions eating plenty while the poor live from hand-to-mouth in cottages little bigger than a sty. There are those who lead and those who follow, the strong and the weak. It is the order you see in nature, from birds to fish, dogs, cats, pigs, poultry - the pecking order. As with animals, so it is with officer cadets. Public school chaps mixed with rankers during formal activities. We all rubbed along well in training, especially during the practical activities where cooperation was vital. And we could hardly divide ourselves during the endless hours of drill. But off duty chaps of a similar background clubbed together, like birds roosting with their own kind. Rooks with rooks, starlings with starlings.

Among the four hundred new Officer Cadets, another gulf existed, regardless of wealth, education, background or breeding: those who had fought, those who had not. That difference also applied to the staff and instructing officers, including former soldiers brought out of retirement, dug outs, they are often called. Men who had not fought stuck rigidly to the instructions contained in the numerous manuals, Field Service Book and various Trench Orders. They knew no better. Those of us experienced in trench warfare realised some written theories fell apart once the bullets and bombs start flying. Regular soldiers, rare now, could be relied on to follow discipline. We had practiced numerous times together and everyone drilled in their role. Each knew his job.

Chaps in the pals' regiments rarely maintain discipline as full-time soldiers. And recent drafts have been hastily trained and there is more ill-discipline, certainly less willingness. A few chaps are positively surly. This could be because they are the first conscripts, men forced to join up since the Military Service Act came into force in January. Despite over two million volunteering since the outbreak of war, we need more men. I'm sure these conscripts, unmarried and aged between eighteen and forty-one, will serve their King, Country and Empire. But if they've been reluctant to fight so far, they won't be as keen for the fight as volunteers.

From now, most of the men joining the colours will have been compelled to do so. Many conscripts will take to Army life. Some will enjoy their time with us, especially if they are in roles not required at the front. But for those forced into the trenches, they will take no pleasure from living with the lice, rats, mud and foot rot - and the Boche constantly trying to kill you. And what will happen when all the male conscripts are used up? Will we, like the Russians, use women to fight? Some chaps say women don't have the will to kill. But I'm sure if home and family became threatened, they would fight as fiercely as any man. Game hunters say the tigress is more fearsome than the tiger, especially protective if her cubs are endangered. And women murder.

***

Having said farewell to some of the chaps, Capt Harcourt and Sgt Pratt, I cadged a lift to Brigade HQ on a mail wagon. It was a sad departure, having served together from the start, and it was unlikely I'd see either of them again. I had been told I would not be returning to my Regiment. The Army believes all newly commissioned officers from the ranks should return to different units. It helped 'maintain distance from the men', a phrase I came to hear frequently.

At Brigade HQ, awaiting transport to the officer training camp, I found myself amongst about fifteen chaps chatting away who, like me, had been selected for officership. Apart from one private and two corporals, the rest of us were sergeants. It was the private who stood out from the crowd, and not just because he was the only one without a stripe. He was extremely tall. He would have found living during the early days of shallow trenches tough indeed, deadly if he stood up. He was also as thin as a pin and spoke with the cut-glass accent of a lord. But he put on no airs or graces and got on well with one and all. Indeed, his confidence helped settle the room of anxious officers-to-be. He had seen action at Loos and could tell tales, sad and humorous, in an engaging manner. His father was a poet and encouraged story-telling out loud. Rumour at the far end of the room was that 'Private Toff', as the chaps from London had already dubbed him, had been posted to the ranks by mistake. I suspected that he wanted to serve in the ranks and had changed his mind. I had already come across a few upper-class men determined to serve as ordinary soldiers. For reasons I cannot fathom they rejected officership to which their status entitled them. They chose to follow rather than lead; to be told rather than tell; to be ordered onto no-man's-land and die than order others to the same fate.

Bitter easterlies in March delayed the onset of spring 1916. Drifts of snow remained tucked into nooks and crannies of buildings and hedgerows where the sun never touched. That freezing wind blew through the canvas flaps of our lorry all the way to our training camp near St Omer. Only twenty-five miles from the front line, but it seemed another world. It was, for me.

***

Officer training camp, our base for the next four months, enjoyed generous acreage of countryside. Most of the land was set to grass except for sixty or so acres of wood. A river ran across the southern boundary and, beyond that, farmland as far as the eye could see. In the centre on the highest ground stood a large house solidly built in a grey stone: Officer Cadet Battalion HQ. To the rear the stables looked as if they could comfortably house a hundred horses. Depending who you believed, the property had been a school for orphans, a home for lepers, a hospital for consumptives, an asylum. It appeared an austere building, so perhaps it had served as all these, the walls imprisoning its history. Upper floors accommodated senior officers and teaching staff. Ground level provided a chapel, main hall, several classrooms, kitchen and long serving hatch to the dining room. We later discovered a room designated Officers' Mess. Until now an officers' mess had been strictly out of bounds. For the first few times I entered, it felt like trespass on hallowed ground. Cadets were housed in huts, some of which were still under construction on land behind the stables. All the completed huts had been occupied by cadets arriving from Britain, none of whom had experienced frontline service. Most of we rankers, Temporary Gentlemen, found ourselves sleeping in tents. Several complained among themselves - never to anyone senior - that this was deliberate, the privileged getting the privileges. Sensing the disquiet, the major apologised and explained that sufficient accommodation huts would be completed within two weeks. Bad weather had delayed construction and, because of the war, there had been a delay in acquiring the boards. ('Whatever the problem, blame it on the war,' became a popular chorus.) But, for now, it would be tents, although a few chaps could be accommodated in the classrooms. Several chaps immediately requested these places indoors. I remained silent, and I noticed the pin-slim private didn't jump at the chance either. Frankly I didn't mind sleeping in a bivouac. Compared to most nights in the trenches, a bivouac was luxury. It provided privacy and peace, despite the howling gale and hail that blighted my first night as Officer Cadet Samuel Ogden.

Next morning, our first day, and every day in camp thereafter, everyone underwent marching drill. It was conducted mainly to knock those new to Army life into shape. Drill promotes discipline, brotherhood, unquestioning obedience, coordination, steadfastness. Fitness drill was also essential. Several cadets quickly proved weak, running out of breath after a few minutes, and not just the older men in their thirties. Two chaps in their early twenties were discharged as unfit to serve during the first week. They had no strength or stamina and couldn't run a few hundred yards, even without a backpack. These lads should not have passed the medical, the officers complained, and the doctors need to pull up their socks and be more vigilant. One fellow was so uncoordinated he appeared not to know left from right and got into an awful pickle. Clumsily, on parade, he bumped into others causing chaos. He once dropped a rifle, fortunately not loaded. He too had to go. Can you imagine him handling grenades? A few portly chaps, who found it tough at first, soon found themselves in shape with the daily fitness exercises, running and sport. For me however each hour of drill seemed a waste of time. But I bit my lip and carried on cheerily. 'Unless you can take orders, you can't give 'em,' was the drill-sergeant's creed, and I agreed.

I craved to be learning new skills, not boot-bashing the parade ground. Fortunately, and to save any embarrassment, it was reassuring that all we rankers performed well as officer cadets. No-one let 'our side' down. In some areas, especially handling small arms and battlefield tactics, we excelled because of our experience. Although we gained respect from most fellow pupils, whatever their background or schooling, there remained a small but stubborn group who resented our promotion. These snooty toffs considered being a 'gentleman' more important than any ability at soldiering. To them holding a knife and fork correctly, speaking eloquently, using short phrases in French or some other foreign language, appeared more crucial than defeating the Hun. We had no 'right' to be officers, one boomed after a drink too many in the mess. 'Working class soldiers will simply not respect working class officers,' he slurred before his more sensible chums steered him into a far corner. His friends thought, wrongly, that we rankers might set upon them. Had we done, it would have been an unfair fight. That small group of toffee-noses posed no match for hard-knuckled chaps who'd fought many-a-Fritz on no-man's-land and in trenches. It goes without saying that young loud-mouthed 'gentleman' had not yet been to the front line. When he does, he'll learn German bullets don't give a damn about his table manners nor which school he attended.

Our training progressed. It was fascinating. I enjoyed every moment, especially in the classroom. Over the weeks we were told of and taught about the deployment of new weaponry on land, sea and in the air. Rapid progress was being made on aircraft. Gone the days when aircraft were used only for reconnaissance, although that was still important. Cameras and their photographs had improved making it easier to spot enemy positions and activities. Significant developments came along almost every month. Larger aircraft, 'bombers,' were being built to carry heavier payloads. 'Fighters' now fire machine-guns at enemy aircraft and targets on the ground. 'Pusher' fighters, so called because the propeller is mounted at the rear to avoid the wooden blades being shot to pieces by the machine-gun, are being replaced. We first saw Vickers FB-5 'pushers' overhead last summer. But they flew slowly and became easy prey for German pilots.

A clever French pilot, Roland Garros, invented a mechanism last year which allowed machine gun bullets to pass freely through rotating propeller blades. Within two weeks he'd shot down five German aircraft with his ingenious device. An American newspaper called him an 'ace', a term now used to describe pilots who down several aeroplanes. Unfortunately, the Germans downed an aircraft with Garros's mechanism and copied the engineering. Aircraft manufacturers Fokker then improved the device. For a while our advantage had been lost. We've gained the upper hand again however with aircraft called biplanes, which have two wing layers and two machine-guns. Doubtless the Germans will copy this design too within a few weeks. We know for sure all aircraft – British, French and German – are going to fly further, faster, higher. Air power is going to play an increasing role in this war. And you don't need to be a General to realise that.

As an infantryman, I like my feet on firm ground. *Terra firma,* one of the friendly public-school chaps called it. In battle, I appreciate chaps at my side. Pilots in the sky have a special courage. To be flying mountain-high relying on an engine, and have guns on the ground taking pot shots, or an enemy aircraft sneaking up behind, is not my idea of fun. There's no hole to hide in, no wall to hide behind, no trench cover. It is going to get tougher for the pilots too; both sides are developing anti-aircraft guns.

The Senior Service doesn't appeal to me either. A sailor however stands a better chance of survival should his ship sink than a pilot whose aircraft is shot down. You can float in water, but not in air. As Army officers-to-be, very little time is spent teaching us about sea warfare. This war will be won or lost on land, not at sea. Britain rules the waves with twice as many ships as any other country. Soldiers on *terra firma* know nevertheless our water-borne Royal Navy comrades play a crucial part in the war. German U-boats are causing many problems. Hundreds of ships have been sunk, many of them innocent passenger liners, such as the *Lusitania*. Over three thousand passengers and crew died off the Irish coast when U-boat torpedoes struck on 7th May 1915. With one hundred and twenty-eight of their citizens on board, this appalling act angered the Americans. Until recently we seemed powerless to stop German U-boats sinking ships. Underwater steel mesh barrages between Dover and Ostend constructed last year have had some success. And our mines have become more effective. Although not given details, we cadets received assurance that measures were being taken to reduce the U-boat threat. It was crucial the British fleet kept the seas open for merchant ships bringing food and materials to Britain - and stop supplies reaching Germany.

Our Battalion officers became far more open than I had expected. We had to face facts, they said. We must admit when things go wrong or don't work properly. Otherwise we can't put things right. For example, we had been slow to deploy heavy artillery at the start of the war. We wrongly assumed our 5" 60-pound shells would serve us sufficiently. That was until we saw the damage at Liège caused by Germany's 16.5" 2,050-pound shells fired from their 'Big Bertha' howitzers: thirty-four times heavier than our 'heavy' shells. Our bombs are getting bigger and we'll be matching and hopefully exceeding the German shells pound for pound soon. Now both sides are entrenched, the use of our horse-drawn field guns has declined in favour of the big guns. When we push forward and are on the move again, perhaps field guns will come back into play.

The instructors also admitted German snipers had been better than ours, or rather their equipment superior. (Some of us had discovered this a long time ago.) But we were catching up. Our .303 bullets lacked the power needed to pierce German steel loopholes used by their snipers. We had not developed telescopic sights as good as the Hun's. An intelligence officer, Major Hesketh-Prichard, came and addressed us. He said, 'we needed elephant guns with calibres such as .450 to .600 that will pierce German plates like butter'. Snipers with these rifles, which produced an almighty crack, had started to arrive at the front last year. Some of us avoided been positioned near these snipers because they often attracted strong counter-fire! Major Hesketh-Prichard told us that in October last year he ran the first course for sniping officers. He was looking to establish a sniping school either here in France or at home, ideally both places. I looked forward to having a go with a large calibre elephant gun with telescopic sights, although I'm told they kick like a mule. Compared with machine guns and artillery bombing, snipers killed very few. But, as the old joke went, snipers kept everyone on their toes with their heads down. One battalion recently did however lose eighteen men in one day to Fritz sniping.

Germans also used superior mortars, an essential weapon for lobbing death and injury into enemy trenches. One lecturer was convinced the Germans, being so well prepared, had been planning this war for many years. We nor the French had any reliable mortars when the war began. We used 'toffee apples' but they were unreliable, cumbersome, and took too long to prime. But once again we have been given hope thanks to many clever scientists and engineers. We enjoyed a demonstration of a new mortar, designed by a chap called Wilfred Stokes. This was a wonderful contraption and caused great excitement. It was light to carry, quick to assemble, and took only two men to operate. It fired a three-inch grenade and, the best news of all, the Stokes Mortar was on its way to our front line.

New gases were being developed too, including one which caused sneezing. Amusing as that may seem, constant sneezing is very debilitating, even dangerous when stealth is required close to enemy positions. Other gases seemed more sinister. They burn skin, cause blindness, induce vomiting. If inhaled, the lungs flood. Victims drown in their own mucous. To counteract whatever the Germans planned, we had improved protective masks, including respirators for our horses. From now gas would not only be dispersed by canisters in or near our front line. Shells will be fired containing a liquid agent which evaporates on impact to form a killer cloud. Many British soldiers still harboured queasy feelings about using gas. But as we kill with little conscience or concern with bullets, bombs, bayonets and clubs, why should gas be considered a means of murder too foul? The result, death or injury, is the same. Everyone detests gas and prefer battle without it. But tell that to the Hun. It was Fritz who started using gas and, as they continue to do so, the Allies consider it right to do likewise. Think of the greater good, senior officers said.

If gas as a weapon caused anger, Hun's use of flame caused fury. Flamethrowers spit fire nearly thirty yards to scorch all in their path. Thousands of men have already been burnt alive or left scarred for life. Again, it was Fritz who deployed this evil weapon first. The French suffered an attack in October 1914, a month after the war began. Our chaps were first torched in a surprise attack at Hooge in Flanders in July last year. Over thirty officers and seven hundred and fifty other ranks died in two days of fighting where flamethrowers led the enemy charges. Intelligence officers say the Germans have had at least three specialist battalions dedicated to using *flammenwerfers* since 1911: another sign the Kaiser and his henchmen had planned this war well in advance. Flamethrowers, usually working in teams with six torches, often start an attack across no-man's-land. They spray our forward defenders with sticky burning oil. Men ignite, scream, sizzle and die. If their charred bodies are found after the battle, their identity has usually burnt too. Victims have no face. Black burnt bodies are as hard to identify as bags of bones.

To help maintain morale, officers had been asked not to mention the frequency of flamethrower attacks to the men. As if we didn't know! Since joining the Officer Cadet Battalion, it has surprised me how some senior officers believe they can keep such information from other ranks. It's as if they believe ordinary soldiers don't talk to one another. We gossip as good as fishwives. Like the silly ploy of calling gas cylinders 'accessories' and thinking nobody but an officer could figure out what they contained. I asked a training officer if we or the French planned to employ flamethrowers. Wait and see, he replied. I had the answer.

Although our trenches had improved, being deeper and more resilient, every experienced soldier realised this war could never be won from them. Methods were being devised and developed to break through trench defences. Large armoured machines which moved forward slowly were being constructed. Our officers believed such vehicles would 'break the deadlock'. Hopefully they'll work better than the armoured cars currently in use. Being heavy and underpowered, they are useless in mud or soft ground. They cannot tackle the shallowest rut or smallest mound and only drive on compacted roads. One enemy bullet or a shard of shrapnel in any of their pneumatic tyres and they shudder to a stop. German elephant calibre bullets easily penetrate the car's armour. They also break down regularly, whether they are made by Austin, Lanchester, Talbot, Wolseley or Rolls-Royce. Horses continue to provide the muscle-power for most of our transport, although motor vehicles are becoming more commonplace. Like our aircraft, motors are becoming bigger, better suited for the task, more reliable.

CHAPTER 27

May 1916
2ND LIEUTENANT OGDEN

Why would the Kaiser, with vast wealth and power, wage war? He could do whatever he wants, anytime he wants. He could sit in front of a roaring log fire enjoying the best beer reading a good book. He could shoot grouse or pheasant, hunt deer or boar, fish salmon or trout. He could travel the world in luxury, see its wonders. What more could he possibly want from life? But he's chosen war. Doubtless, at this very minute, he is still living comfortably. Yet the Kaiser's greed or fear or jealousy or rage has caused wholesale death and immeasurable suffering for millions. It's beyond reason, therefore beyond explanation. Many colleagues present all manner of complicated arguments explaining the Kaiser's behaviour. I just believe he's mad.

There also comes a time to stop asking unanswerable questions. Just get on. Beat him and his army. Do what needs to be done. War has turned the world upside down and inside out. It has changed me and my life, as it has that of many.

Besides military abilities, Officer Cadets raised from the ranks underwent 'gentlemanlification'. It's a word I'd never heard before, perhaps coined specially for this conversion from man to gentleman. Exceptions existed, such as the tall skinny fellow I'd met at Battalion HQ. That private, now Officer Cadet Robert Graves, clearly needed no tuition in being a gentleman. He was already from the top drawer. Those thought to need 'gentleman training' had been taken aside after several days in the Battalion. I, of course, was one of them. I remember clearly my first interview.

'Your problem, Ogden,' the Major told me sat behind his desk as I was kept at attention, 'is your bloody Yorkshire accent. You sound like a country bumpkin. My skivvies speak better English than you. I doubt if anyone outside the Ridings will understand a bally word you say.'

I didn't move an inch. My eyes focussed straight ahead. Anger churned my stomach.

'Your military record speaks for itself and, from what I've already seen, you are a jolly fine soldier. But, Ogden, you must realise the men need to understand what the hell you're saying, what? We can't have the ranks taking orders from someone who sounds like a bally stable lad, can we, what?'

'Yes, Sir, I...I...mean no, Sir' I whimpered. I wanted to say more. Much more. Tell him I'm not a country bumpkin. Tell him I've killed hundreds of Germans protecting him and his family and his bloody servants. Tell him he's not put his toe near the front line. Tell him that soldiering *is* more important than 'gentlemanlification'. Tell him everyone from everywhere in Britain understands what I say. But I chickened out. Lacked the confidence. What a coward! I could face a charge of Boche with clubs and bayonets, but I couldn't challenge a Major with his insults.

'To be good officer you have to be a good gentleman. Military techniques, strategy, tactics, knowledge of weaponry are one thing, Ogden. Being a gentleman, even a temporary one as you are, is quite another. What?'

I remained silent. Silence meant acceptance. Like conscientious objectors on the streets at home, I should have been handed a white feather for my lily-liver.

'So, Ogden,' he went on, 'work hard on your pronunciation. Just as you stand your body upright at attention, stand up each of your words when you speak. Got it my man?'

'Sir.'

'We've taken you out of the farmyard in Yorkshire, but I doubt we'll ever take the Yorkshire farmer out of you. Well, not all of it. But try, Ogden, have a damn good try, at least for the duration of the war.'

That interview was the saddest moment of my Army life. I'd been grazed by gunfire, slashed by shrapnel, ripped by barbed wire. I'd been frozen, soaked, hungry, filthy, gassed. School friends and battlefield brothers had been slaughtered at my side. I'd inhaled the sticky odour of sour flesh and choked on the fumes from burning bodies. Guilt weighs heavily in my stomach knowing my inept actions and orders have caused others to die and be injured. But the Major's words hurt more than anything this war had yet inflicted. At that moment, I hated him more than the Kaiser. I resented him more than any Fritz who'd killed or maimed my pals. And instead of counteracting his insults, I just stood there like a weakling in front of a bully and absorbed his kicks and punches.

Over the following weeks our 'gentlemanlification' continued. To my shame, I obeyed the Major's order and worked on my pronunciation. Reluctantly and grudgingly at first, then thinking perhaps there was nothing wrong with speaking proper - speaking properly! It was not easy, as if learning French or German: a new language. Many words I just couldn't pronounce like the upper-crusts, nor wished to. I spoke self-consciously. Real toffs recognised instantly this 'affectation', as one called it. Rankers knew we would never fool them into believing we had become real gentleman. Our improved pronunciation wasn't of course aimed at the higher classes. Our elocution lessons, as the Major called them, intended to give us greater authority when speaking to the ranks. We accented rankers did gradually adjust our speech. It became a joke amongst us at first, perhaps hiding our embarrassment, but we adapted, with varying degrees of success. For Northerners, our 'bath' and 'grass' retained the short 'a'. Anyway, as one chap from Manchester quipped, who wants to talk like a sheep saying 'baaath'? To pronounce either word like a Southerner would be a compromise too far. Even so, speaking as I've started to do, the leg-pulling from my former chums at Stone Booth Farm and friends in my Yorkshire village, should they hear me, would be relentless. I'd have to backslide and talk 'Tyke'.

Even the way we walked became the subject of instruction in 'gentlemanlification'. 'Head up, chin out,' the Major barked at the rankers. 'Stride forth as if the whole bally street belongs to you. The way you walk is the way you command.'

In preparation for the Battalion banquet, we received instruction on how to sit and eat at table. We can't have you dining in a slovenly fashion in front of the Brigadier-General. As if we had been pigs at the swill! Unlike men in the ranks, we couldn't simply ask for the salt or sugar without first adding a phrase such as 'Would you mind awfully if you could...' or 'May I trouble you to...'.

Without any choice in the matter, we had to drink wine, or at least appear to do so. Eventually, however, I came to enjoy gin with bitters before meals, and a whisky or brandy afterwards, alongside the almost-compulsory cigar. Slowly, as with my way of talking and walking, I changed. My self-consciousness gradually departed, resistance to change reduced. I grew into an officer and gentleman, even if only 'temporary for the duration of the war'. I confess I rather came to enjoy it.

The most distasteful part of officer training came when told to 'distance ourselves' from the men. A divide between officers and men was considered necessary 'to establish and maintain discipline'. Men had to know who was in charge. They must follow orders and instruction without question. Hence drills. The unthinking instant obedience was the aim. You must show absolutely no doubt in your own decision or when imparting orders from superior offices. The best units have the tightest discipline.

The lecture on the Ten Golden Rules of commanding a platoon, to gain and maintain respect of our NCOs and the men, went as follows:

1. Be, or try to be, the best man at arms in the platoon.

2. Be the first to take command issuing clear orders and ensuring they are carried out.

3. Be a good example by being well turned out, punctual, cheery, even - or especially - under adverse conditions.

4. Enforce strict discipline at all times. This must be a willing discipline, not a sulky one. Be just, but do not be soft. Men despise softness.

5. Recognise a good effort, even if only partially successful. A word of praise when deserved produces better results than incessant fault-finding.

6. Look after your men's comforts before your own and never sparing yourself.

7. Demand a high standard on all occasions. Never be content with what you take over, be it on the battlefield or in billets. Everything capable of improvement try to make it so, from the information on the battlefield to the cleanliness of latrines and washing places in the billets.

8.   Be bloodthirsty. Be ever thinking how to kill the enemy and help your men to do so.

9.   Be the proudest man in the Army. You are the Commander of the unit of attack. You are the only man who can know intimately the character and capabilities of each man under you.

10.   Build an *esprit de platoon.*

A big blow for me and many new officers, and not just to rankers, was the obligation to buy our own uniforms and kit. Although my sergeant's pay almost doubled as a 2nd Lieutenant to forty-nine shillings a week, the outlay came as a shock. Even a basic khaki shirt and collar from Debenham and Freebody in London's Wigmore Street cost twelve shillings and sixpence. A staff cap, three pounds, three shillings and thruppence; more than a week's pay. A warm coat, six guineas; over three weeks' pay. I removed the three stripes from my old greatcoat and gave it a good brush down. After a few minutes in the trenches it will be so splattered with mud few will know or care whether it's standard Army issue or the finest Tielocken Burberry. Some officers pay much more for their uniforms, having them made-to-measure at leading West End outfitters. Several stores in London offer to supply complete kits within a few days; faster if you order through Burberry's branch in Paris. The firm even has a fitting room in Flanders. Some of these new chaps clearly have no idea about real fireline life: dressed as a dandy, Fritz the sniper will have you first.

Most new officers looked to purchase all sorts of additional paraphernalia. Bullet-proof jackets made by The Wilkinson Sword Company are much talked about. If these chaps had spent time at the front, they would not rely on them for protection. Officers reported they were heavy and restricted movement. If so, they would be as much a hazard as a help. You need to be as nimble as a squirrel. Boxes from Harrods arrived with hipflasks, collapsible cups, penknives and service knives, forks and spoons. Wristwatches and military lamps delivered by Gamages in Holborn. Fortunate fellows, or those with wealthy parents, received hampers ordered from Fortnum & Mason's in Piccadilly. These arrived stuffed with pies and puddings and Nestlé's deliciously-sweet tinned milk for their tea. My family sent more modest but much appreciated provisions such as Bovril, Gong Soups, Oxo and Ovaltine milk tablets. And everyone appreciates Lea & Perrins Worcestershire sauce to spice bully. For me, the most important luxury from home is soap. A 4d tablet of Wright's Coal Tar lasts a month: a prized possession.

A week into my officer training I received a parcel, with no indication of the sender. I had not told my family that I was here, wanting to secure my officer position first. The parcel therefore could not have been despatched by them. I asked the post office sergeant if he knew the sender. 'No, Sir,' he replied. It was the first time as an officer I'd been called 'Sir', and it deflected my thoughts for a moment. I asked if he could find out who had sent it. 'No, Sir,' he said. 'It arrived with the rest of the parcels, Sir. Perhaps there's a delivery note inside.'

There wasn't. It did contain the highest quality leather single cross-strap Sam Browne belt complete with a four-inch barrel Webley Mark V service revolver and holster. The ammunition pouch contained seventy-two .38 bullets. I asked colleagues promoted from the ranks if they had received such a package. I wondered if the Army had generously issued these to rankers knowing most would struggle to pay for this kit, certainly before they had time to save the cash. None had. Perhaps mine has come through early, I suggested, you'll receive yours later. But none did. The sender remained unknown, a mysterious benefactor.

Throughout my four and a half months of officer training, we received reports about the biggest battle of the war so far. The Boche on February 21st this year, launched a massive attack on a fortified French city close to the German border. Verdun is vitally important. It is the gateway - hopefully barrier - to eastern France. If Verdun fell, the Major said, the Boche would set their noses on Paris like a pack of hounds on fox scent. We are told that up to a quarter of a million French have already perished. Attack follows counter-attack, day after day, a bloodbath on a scale history has never witnessed. No-man's-land is littered with not dozens, not hundreds, but thousands of rotting bodies. General Henri-Philippe Pétain, who took command of the French forces in Verdun in late February, has declared: 'They shall not pass.' Every man, woman and child in the civilised world will be hoping the General's wish is fulfilled.

At Officer Cadet Battalion we hear far more about what is happening than we could in the trenches. At the front our focus is facing Fritz. Here, away from the front and with senior officers constantly passing through, we gain a broader picture of the war. Since my arrival in February, I've learnt many things, and not just about military matters. I overheard some of the well-off chaps saying their families had been requested to give up their servants for the sake of the war effort. One complained his father had to dismiss two chauffeurs and close a heated greenhouse to conserve fuel for the war. Perhaps he thought growing oranges and lemons more important than stopping the Germans invading Britain.

March 9th saw Germany declare war on Portugal. The Germans have no troops there and we are told have no plans to invade, so their reason escapes me. The Kaiser must be crackers. And this madman is dangerous: Zeppelin bombing raids over London and elsewhere in England have killed innocent civilians. How evil are these people who kill old men, women and children who cannot fight back? This is not fighting fair. The Kaiser's U-boats continue to cause havoc to shipping in the Atlantic, North Sea, English Channel and the Mediterranean. America's President Wilson has threatened to break off diplomatic relations with Germany if it continues to sink ships in the Atlantic. There's growing talk - and great hope - that America will join the war and fight at our side. We need all the help we can get. A few officers however think France, Britain and our colonial allies can defeat the Boche, providing the Russians keep fighting on the Eastern Front. They may be right. But it stands to reason we would make a better fist of beating the Boche with additional troops from the United States of America.

As if the Germans weren't enough to tackle, some in Britain have been causing trouble. We could hardly believe the news that during March munitions workers on the Clyde went on strike. If not traitorous, certainly unpatriotic behaviour at a time when the nation itself is facing grave danger. Doubtless the three thousand strikers were whipped up by a handful of good-for-nothing extremists. If the rumours are right, German spies bribed the strike leaders to create disruption amongst these workers, who made much-needed heavy guns. The Boche are trying to beat us by the back door by creating unrest at home. The Clyde Workers' Committee claimed they wanted an end to the new law of conscription and wartime restrictions on pay and strikes. But anyone who goes on strike at home during this war are killing our men as sure as Fritz, or 'Jerry' as many chaps now call Germans. The strike ringleaders have been arrested. And everyone here said three cheers to that!

Reminding me of my father's experience during the eight-month siege that lasted to May 1900 at Mafeking, we heard that on 29th April, a siege, lasting one hundred and forty-three days, ended in our surrender to the Turks at Kut-al-Amara in Mesopotamia. It has cast dismay over our final days in the Battalion. Nine thousand Indian and British troops of the Indian Expeditionary Force surrendered. The Turks surrounded our chaps in Kut, a small town on the river Tigris, and starved them. Our Muslim and Hindu soldiers suffered even greater hardship: they starved rather than eat horsemeat, which is against their religion. Many died. All those who survived must have looked like walking skeletons. Royal Navy river steamers couldn't break the blockade. One boat, the *Junlar*, even fell to Turkish hands. British aeroplanes dropped packages of food, but these supplies proved insufficient.

An act of treason on our own soil took place where I know well, Dublin, Ireland. It was from where my Battalion of The Duke of Wellington's Regiment departed for France in August 1914. On Easter Monday, April 24th, rebels wanting an Irish Republic seized control of the post office in Sackville Street and several other buildings in the city centre. Like those causing strikes, these trouble-makers took advantage of the war raging elsewhere. Every Irish chap I've met in France has been bravely backing King and Country. They've fought well and many lost their lives. Now they've been betrayed by their own countrymen. Irish chaps in the Battalion have condemned these rebels, saying most Irish people don't want 'home rule'. Newspapers are putting the death and injury toll during the 'Easter Rising' at nearly eight hundred civilians, and over five hundred police and soldiers.

My intake of officer cadets received our commissions at the passing out parade on Friday 5th May 1916. I had rubbed along well with most of the chaps, even several upper-crusts. When starting as a pupil I had a quiet confidence in my own abilities at all the practical skills. They'd been tested often enough under fire since Mons. I was a decent shot. (I won second prize out of nearly four hundred men in the Battalion's rifle competition last week, missing first place by one quarter of an inch at three hundred yards!) As one of the few pre-war Regulars remaining, I could handle blindfolded all the small weapons. And with all my experience of real battle, field manoeuvres proved undemanding. During several exercises I was asked in front of other cadets my opinion on how best to tackle certain situations, but only by training officers who were not too pompous or self-important. I also followed some poor instruction without protest. I should have spoken out, suggested alternative action. I should have said to the officer that what he was instructing wouldn't work in real battle conditions. But I remained silent. I didn't want to upset the applecart, although what I would have suggested might have saved lives. But, like a raw recruit, my first sergeant's words still rang loud and clear in my head: 'Don't speak until you're spoken to, lad.'

Having survived so far, I know that when your neighbour's blood sprays your face, sizzling shrapnel shoots everywhere, hundreds of bayonet-brandishing Boche are charging your way, 'book-theory' falls apart. Only the most highly trained and experienced soldiers will behave as the book dictates under heavy fire. Most of these new chaps are brave, I'll say that for them, but their discipline breaks down. If new recruits had been at Mons, Le Cateau, Néry or Marne in the early days of the war, the Germans would have overwhelmed us much faster. It was our training, discipline, experience and fast-fire musketry which kept Fritz at bay against the German's vastly superior numbers. Those skills saved many lives and prevented thousands being taken prisoner.

If confident about my practical skills in the field at the start of officer training, the opposite was true facing written work in the classroom. Anything to do with arithmetic would be my downfall. I thought my failure would return me to the ranks quick-time. Fortunately, as most calculations were based on practical applications, such as the trajectory of missiles, map bearings or supplies, I struggled through.

229

During my time as a pupil officer, I enjoyed a sense of achievement, a feeling I'd never experienced before. This tragic war has thrust me from Private to 2nd Lieutenant in twenty months, which would not have happened in peacetime. Despite knowing millions of men, women and children have suffered death, injury and disease, the war has been good for me, an adventure, and it still is. But I also feel shame that I have only become an officer by filling the boots of a dead man: many dead men. Certain chaps, when drink gets the better of their tongue, admit they 'like' the war, 'enjoy' fighting, 'relish' the camaraderie, even those who have experienced war's horror and tragedy.

As our final day in the Cadet Battalion approached, speculation grew to fever pitch about where we would be assigned after passing out. I assumed most of us would be going to the Western Front, particularly as the battle at Verdun continued to rage occupying a huge number of French forces. And we had been told to expect another big push. But with British involvement in Salonika, Mesopotamia, Italy, Egypt and Palestine, we could end up there, or at a new operation. One chap said he had heard on the grapevine that I would be retained here as a training officer, or sent back to Blighty to instruct officers moving to combat roles, and raw conscripts. Some hoped for a staff officer post at General Headquarters, in a small chateau at Montreuil. This was apparently considered the 'pukka' job. Any young officer there would be at the heart of the British Expeditionary Force's operations and 'in the eye' of the generals. Second best, but still considered highly desirable, would be a similar position at Army, Corps or even Division HQ. For me and fellow rankers such cushy numbers were, as one put it, 'not appropriate'.

At the passing out parade we received our commissions from the Brigadier-General. I was now 2nd Lieutenant Samuel Ogden. Of the three hundred and ninety-eight cadets who started, three hundred and eighty-one completed. Of the seventeen who did not gain officership, five suffered injuries so severe during exercises they had to be set back. One died falling from a rope bridge. Seven were quickly revealed as unfit for service on medical grounds. Senior officers expressed their annoyance they had been passed A1 before entering the Battalion.

Four cadets mysteriously became 'unsuitable', the only word from our officers on the matter. Even Battalion staff, who usually enjoyed gossiping, sealed their lips. All they said was that the four had been removed quietly during the night. Somehow, although I don't know how, as nothing was said, it was made crystal clear that we should not talk about these chaps. We did, of course, in whispered tones among trusted friends. Speculation ranged from them being too reliant on drink, to being decommissioned by influential relatives to avoid the trenches. One gossip-monger whispered the four had indulged in 'unnatural acts'. This, he added with wide-eyed enthusiasm, explained the strict silence, the cloud of embarrassment, their sudden departure in darkness.

One fact I'm far from embarrassed to mention is that all the rankers passed out with flying colours. No serious injuries. No health problems. No unsuitability. And none of us had influential relatives to save us from the front! Most of our senior officers also seemed genuinely pleased. A few old-school types remained disgruntled, however. It appeared they disapproved of rankers becoming officers, even temporarily. They probably hoped rankers would fail in training to justify their low opinion of us. This went some way to explain why several rankers appeared to be put through particularly gruelling exercises and examinations.

On the parade ground podium the Brigadier-General, after a salute, shook every new officer's hand while presenting our commissions. He uttered a few words of encouragement to us all, usually, 'Well done. Keep up the good work'. Next to him, the Battalion's Commanding Officer, added a word of praise and wished everyone good luck. The next officer along handed each of us a sealed envelope. The letter inside would reveal our new posting. Where will we be? What will we be doing? Far afield? Back to Blighty? A safe desk job? Or, for most, a posting on the Western Front in preparation for the next much-discussed big push? If so, by this time tomorrow, many of us could be in the firing line.

We had been ordered not to open our envelopes until the parade ended and everyone had received theirs. Waiting wasn't too frustrating for Wade, Yellowlees and Zeppenfield, called towards the end of the ceremony. But it was extremely maddening for Atkinson,

231

Brown and Coulson: Ogden didn't have too long to wait. When the moment finally arrived, some opened envelopes nervously. Others delayed, savouring the expectation, like those who leave the tastiest morsel on their plate for the last mouthful. Most ripped open their letter tense with excitement. Faces smiled. Faces frowned. Genuine delight. Feigned pleasure. Honest fear. Chaps grouped together sharing their news with handshakes, back-slapping and laughter. Most seemed delighted with their placements. Time to face the Boche at last, some welcomed in their ignorance or bravado. A few walked back to their billets in silence, perhaps contemplating the future, one with his head down.

I was neither agitated nor excited about my post. What would be, would be. I had no yearning for one place more than any other, no expectation of what some considered a good or a bad role. Perhaps I should have ambition, a desire to be in a special position. I didn't, I don't, and that's it. Faithful to my oath when I joined the colours and swore allegiance to King and Country, I would follow the route mapped by the Army.

The Army is now my family. I am its child. The Army is my life. It will probably deliver my death. This Great War my job, my duty, my all. Like a blank page, I waited for the Army to write my future: it wrote I was returning to the Western Front.

CHAPTER 28

June 1916
RIVER SOMME

Although thoroughly baked in my battered mess tin, smeared with Picardy butter and sprinkled with fresh rosemary, I hesitated about eating her. She was too hot, I told McGavan, needed time to cool. I blew across the pale meat to back my story. This Lady of the Stream had devoured flesh from the fallen. At seventeen inches weighing nearly 2lb the silver grayling, with its large sail-like dorsal fin, had lived in the River Somme for several years.

Rivers run through land as blood in bodies. Here, near Amiens, its water washed away hundreds of dead during the German advance in August 1914. More lives were lost when the Hun retreated later that year as we and the French repelled them. Old folk, women and children, innocent civilians fleeing for their lives, also fell victim to the river or died in the surrounding marshland.

Fishing provides tranquillity to a troubled mind. Whether wading in the river or stalking from the bank, casting a fly and watching it float in the flow banishes despondency. The hopeful anticipation of a catch couldn't be further from the hopeless despair of war. Even after a thousand bite-less casts, the belief the very next one will hook a fine specimen keeps the angler going. Optimism is the fisherman's faithful friend. Fish for the fishing, not the fish.

However hard I tried to cast it out, the thought remained that in this fish flesh lived human flesh. As the Somme weaved its way from north of St Quentin to here outside Amiens, the river, its tributaries, marshes and swamps snared and consumed the bodies of many murdered by the advancing German First Army. The Somme became a sewer, a channel of human and animal sewage. This very fish must have swallowed human blood, bitten human flesh, swam with the dead. And on my spoon sat a morsel of meat that must contain a morsel of man.

McGavan poked our small campfire encouraging flames from the embers to hasten the cooking of his catch on a greenstick spit.

Despite my worries of cannibalism, I ate the fish, no longer pretending it was too hot. I kept quiet about my concerns, not wishing to spoil my companion's meal. Whatever else the grayling devoured, it gave off a slight smell of cucumber and tasted a little of thyme. McGavan, being well educated, said this was to be expected, the Latin name for grayling being *Thymallus thymallus*. Regardless of my misgivings, the grayling tasted good: there is no better meal than a fish fresh from water, baked, fried or spit-roasted.

River Somme has a gentle flow. My friend Mr Unia said 'somme' means 'tranquil' in Gallic. The fishing was as slow as the flow, our two grayling the only catches of the day. We returned for our last night of leave to the Hôtel de la Paix near Breilly, west of Amiens. Tomorrow McGavan, a fellow newly-commissioned 2nd Lieutenant, and I would be returning to the front. I assume I shall be commanding around forty-five men. Most of them will be conscripts, called up under the tougher laws introduced last month. All single men between the ages of eighteen and forty-one have become subject to conscription. And if these measures fail to attract fifty-thousand recruits a month, Prime Minister Asquith declared married men would also become subject to compulsory recruitment. The authorities are even re-examining men previously deemed unfit for active military service. Unfortunately, this means some of the chaps in my platoon may be reluctant to fight, unfit to fight, or both.

Almost everyone and everything is affected by the war. One change however came as a complete surprise: time. Apparently, by putting clocks and watches forward an hour for summer, the government believes it will save hundreds of thousands of tons of coal because of 'daylight saving time'. Frankly, I can't see it makes any difference. Surely folk can do what they need to do when they need to do it, regardless of the hour hand on the clock. It seems strange to put clocks forward an hour in spring only to be put back likewise in autumn.

Relatives and friends writing from home rarely mention their own hardship. They choose not to bother us with their worries. They struggle in silence knowing conditions here are worse, certainly more dangerous. We hear some at home go hungry, although not starving. The Germans continue to attack ships bringing in food and other supplies. Shortages are beginning to bite, although most families forfeit their own cravings to continue sending food to us. Some new chaps admit they are better fed by the Army than at home.

Giving one's life for one's country is a great sacrifice. For every man lost, a family endures grief. Mothers, fathers and wives with their son or husband away fighting must dread the knock on the door delivering news of death. The Long family, from Barking Town in London, has eight sons serving in the Army. The ninth is expected to go shortly. Their father appealed wishing to keep his tenth son for a while to assist at home. The tribunal granted the tenth son exemption from service - but only for three months and on condition he obtained work of national importance. If families are told their dear one is missing, they may at least have hope he is captured, however remote the chance. One day, perhaps, Tommy will return. The number of deaths has already reached such a level almost everybody knows somebody who has lost someone. Many parents have lost a son, sometimes more than one. Many women have become widows. Children, fatherless.

The most tragic news of late was shared by all: the death of Lord Kitchener, Secretary for War. Every true Briton grieved his loss. On 5th June, this great soldier set sail to Russia to discuss plans with our allies. His cruiser, *HMS Hampshire*, struck a mine off the Orkney Islands. A few survived, some bodies came ashore, but Lord Kitchener was not among them. Soldiers, especially regulars, adored him. We knew he was one of the few voices telling the truth at the start of this ghastly conflict. He told us straight the fighting would not be over by Christmas, or for a Christmas or two after that. For those of us who witnessed the Hun's rapid advance in August 1914, we knew assurances the war would be over within months amounted to self-deception at best, public lies at worst. The Germans had a huge army, one million seven hundred thousand; perhaps over two million with reservists. They had prepared for war for years. We had a small army, one hundred and ten thousand; of those, only seventy thousand were combat troops. We had not prepared for war, certainly not on this scale. Lord Kitchener could see it would take far longer than a few months to acquire forces large enough simply to hold the Germans at bay.

On the Eastern Front, where Russia faces the Austro-Hungarians and Germans, they have been pushed back through Poland into somewhere called Belarus. They have however enjoyed recent success against the Austrians in Galicia, north of the Carpathian Mountains. Russians are hardy and resilient people, we're told, if somewhat disorganised. Cavalry officers say the Cossacks are the world's finest fighters on horseback. They ride as if horse and rider are one. It's said Cossack children ride before they walk! Russia is a vast country, at least seventy times larger than Britain, a former teacher claimed. If so, it's hard to imagine how Germany could conquer or control the country. Thanks to the Russians, however, the Germans have two fronts to fight in Europe. Just a few days ago, more than a hundred trains packed with German troops left our front to counter Russian attacks. Reduced German numbers here must help our next big push. If Fritz had been fighting just one front, I fear we would have already lost in France. Britain's shores would have faced invasion.

Good news reached us about the Red Sea port of Jeddah. It has been captured by Arab forces from the Turks. Its seizure means our ships with food and other goods can now pass without facing bombardment from Turkish cannon. Our Arab friends have also captured Mecca which, we're told, means a great deal to the Muhammadan. A British Captain, T E Lawrence, who can apparently speak the local languages fluently and understands Arab ways, has been fighting alongside the Grand Sherif of Mecca and other leaders to secure their victories. Open warfare in the hot dry dusty deserts of Egypt and Palestine must be a far cry from the fighting from entrenchments in France.

***

Should they wish, the privileged may enjoy endless days of idleness without suffering the consequences. But most of us must work to make a few shillings for food and keep a roof over our head. Our leisure must give way to work, pleasure to duty, and, in my case, today's peace will become tomorrow's war. My week's leave with McGavan ended having fished the River Somme or one of its smaller tributaries flowing through thick woodland into the main watercourse. Several small lakes nearby provided sport too with good-sized perch, pike and carp. No fish we caught in France however could match the taste of a wild brown trout caught and cooked at the side of an English river. McGavan, as you'd expect, claimed Scottish rivers produced the tastiest trout. He was probably right, although it can't be admitted.

Hôtel de la Paix had become my favourite billet on furlough, a second home. Mr Prem Unia of *The Times of India* was still in residence and it was always a pleasure to meet him. As usual we discussed many matters. He would enquire about the books I had read and my views on them. He would suggest new authors or titles to try. My excuse for not reading quite so much fiction recently was because of all the manuals to read and studies to digest as an Officer Cadet. He was delighted at my 'much-deserved' promotion. Leadership should be earned on merit, not assumed by a privileged birth, he said. More generals need to get mud on their boots, he added, and more chaps with muddy boots should place them under the top table. Such an exchange of experience would have saved countless lives, and still could.

As a correspondent Mr Unia possessed a much wider view of the war than any one soldier at the front could possibly have. Although always polite in his presence, McGavan wasn't impressed by Mr Unia. He believed Prem to be 'a wee subversive', despite my insistence that he very much supported the British against the Germans. But Prem at dinner one evening said that India was Indian, not British. Although the British Raj had brought some good things to the country - a national political system, a unified legal regime and railways network, to name three - it was time, Prem said, for Indians to take responsibility for running their own affairs in their own land.

'After all,' he added, as always speaking calmly and politely, 'you gentlemen are here in France risking life and limb to keep France for the French. You wish to return Belgium to the Belgians. And you clearly don't want Germany to become the ruler of Great Britain.' This, as they say, put the cat among the pigeons. A couple of chaps coughed uncomfortably and quickly changed the conversation.

Later that evening a captain in the 2nd Essex Regiment, also on leave at the hotel, advised me not to 'associate oneself with that Indian chappie'. I thanked the officer for his advice, and ignored it. For reasons unknown to me he seemed not to like Indians or, as he put it, any 'Johnny Foreigner'. When thousands of men from Australia, Canada, India, China, New Zealand and the West Indies are fighting and dying for Britain in this war, I found his view unreasonable. Perhaps I should have challenged the captain's opinion, although he is entitled to his views.

***

In readiness for the big push, hundreds of thousands of men are arriving in France from around the world. Only yesterday I watched over a thousand men belonging to the British West Indies Regiment march through Amiens. Dozens of ships, hundreds of trains and thousands of wagons, vans, motor lorries and horses had brought men from Land's End to John O'Groats, from Canada to New Zealand. Millions of shells and bullets for every calibre of gun, large and small, were brought forward. As guns need feeding, so do men. Tons of food in bags, sacks, cases and boxes arrived on extended trains and wagon convoys day and night, all packed as tight as tinned bully. Alongside the food came non-edible supplies necessary to maintain an army at war. Roads and railways from the channel ports had been improved to handle all the men, horses, vehicles and materials. Engineers near the front even laid small-gauge railway tracks to convey men and materials closer to the impending fight. We appeared to be building a new city and supplying its residents with all their needs: a city of trenches and tunnels where every citizen was dressed in khaki with a duty to kill.

It was hard work trying to conceal all this activity from the Germans. They'll know about our build-up of men and machines from the many spies behind our lines, some of whom will have been in place before the war began.

One Fritz spy, dressed in British khaki, was captured by our chaps recently in a forward listening post. The German was returning to his own lines when he accidentally fell into our sap. Earlier that night the cheeky German had mingled as large as life with us in a trench working party and sneaked away before dawn. He could speak good English and had been ear-wigging amongst us picking up information. He would also have noted our machine gun and mortar placements, the line our trenches took, perhaps names of officers, and the state of our men. The spy had pretended to be shell-deaf and lost from his platoon, which was not uncommon. The men thought the chap was a simpleton and left him alone. Despite his offer to work for us as a spy, a firing squad dispatched him the following day.

CHAPTER 29

June 1916
ALBERT

The Virgin Mary, clutching her infant son, slumped to one side. Since the German shell struck the golden statue on the Basilica of Nôtre-Dame de Brébières, on 15th January 1915, people passing through the Picardy town of Albert predicted the next gale would bring Mary and Jesus tumbling down. But she held on. French fighters, as stubborn as the statue, successfully defended Albert in late September 1914, despite the Germans surrounding the town. Much of Albert, including its railway head, had been reduced to rubble. The Basilica, although battered, stood defiant amongst the ruins. A Jack Johnson had created a large hole outside the west door and its stonework had suffered shrapnel damage. The Madonna may be prostrate, facing earth rather than heaven, but she still clung to the church tower with Jesus safely in her arms. Locals who believe in omens say that whichever side causes the statue to fall will lose the war. Fritz probably thinks the opposite.

After leaving the Officer Cadet Battalion on 6th May, I billeted in Albert. Apart from my week's fishing furlough, I worked eighteen-hour days and grabbed sleep when I could. I was attached to the IV Army, commanded by General Sir Henry Rawlinson, in charge of the impending Somme Offensive, the next big push. The main British attack was planned along a fourteen-mile front from Maricourt to Serre. I was disappointed not to be placed in command of a platoon, the usual assignment for most new 2nd lieutenants. I thought someone, perhaps an officer who resented rankers, had put a bad word in about me. Perhaps because of my 'provincial accent'. Or that I had a basic education. Or had worked as, in the words of an old dug-out officer, 'a mere farm hand'. But the opposite was the case: I had been selected for special duties because of my frontline experience. The captain at IV Army HQ declined to say by whom. I suspect, as usual, he didn't know, but couldn't bring himself to admit it. This appointment was yet another strange occurrence that seemed to make no sense. I'd been chosen to become an officer. I'd received the gift of a revolver and the finest Sam Brown belt from some mysterious benefactor. Then, a week later, a pair of boots arrived: the correct size. It was as if someone was watching over me, controlling my progress in the Army. A guardian angel, Mother would say.

My first assignment as 2nd Lt Ogden was to survey an area of the impending offensive. I studied maps published before the war and, using a magnifying glass, I carefully viewed photographs taken by our aircraft. I spent many hours looking long and hard through field glasses and making sketches and notes. For the two-mile front allocated to me, I grew to know every trench and tree, farm building and field, rise and fall of the land. Our brave scouts also provided valuable information about German activity and the shape and features of the land behind their trenches. The smallest feature - a hill, ditch, wall, hedge, copse - can make a big difference to your fortunes in battle.

Having studied my attack zone, I was required to look at the surveys of others and offer an opinion. I was instructed to advise company commanders, especially those new to the front, where best to place machine guns, bombers, riflemen and rifle bombers at the launch of our attack. I aimed to seek sites offering maximum concealment before the fighting began and maximum killing fire advancing. I was left in no doubt by senior officers that I was not to even contemplate defensive positions or fall-back procedures. Forward was to be the only direction. I was also required to discuss the differences between trench-to-trench attacks and open warfare, which we would face if our major attack is successful. 'If' was not of course the word I used in these briefings, but 'when'.

My sector was south of a village called La Boisselle. I had been provided with a fine mare to get about on. She was certainly a smoother if livelier ride than any of the ponies at Stone Booth Farm; pot-bellied Dales, which we rode bareback. But I found it easier to walk or find alternative transport. Vehicles of all kinds constantly criss-crossed behind the lines and it was easy to hitch a lift, especially as an officer from Division HQ, even a lowly 2nd lieutenant. Although a new subaltern, my attachment at this level 'amongst the generals' commanded respect. An advantage of being on foot, or sharing transport with others, was that I heard things you can't hear from horseback, simple but significant nuggets of information. For example, a certain battalion commander - a lieutenant-colonel who should know better - reported that all his forward firing and communication trenches had been dug and fortified. Sharing a wagon with a working party, I discovered this was far from the truth. I suggested to my seniors that a random inspection of some of the trenches may be helpful. This revealed the true state of the lines. Come the assault, hundreds of casualties could have resulted from this 'oversight' and 'misunderstanding', as the colonel blustered later.

I had another reason for preferring Shanks's Pony and scrounging lifts: I didn't wish to build a bond with the mare. Although I've come to accept the loss of men, the pain of a horse's inevitable death would be too much. Having lost all but one of my childhood pals in the Dukes, I have been reluctant to become friends with any fellow soldier. I am friendly, but not a friend. The more you like someone, the more you miss them when they're gone. And here they will be lost. To avoid that heartache, it's best to avoid that friendship. Hundreds of men I've met in this damnable war have come and gone: killed, injured, captured, missing, transferred. Here today, gone tomorrow. Alfred, Lord Tennyson wrote: ''Tis better to have loved and lost than never to have loved at all.' Perhaps in peacetime the gain from love is worth the pain of loss, as I found with Alice. But in war, where loss is commonplace, it's better to live without love.

My role appeared to be appreciated by officers and men alike, especially by those who had never seen action. I was always tactful when talking to superior officers. I tried to be reasonable, weighing up the advantages and disadvantages of any course of action. Offering examples of what happened in this or that situation was considered helpful. I always stressed one battle was rarely the same as another. The men, their numbers, experience and condition, weapons, shape and state of the land, weather and so on all made a difference. And whatever *we* planned there was always an unknown factor: the *enemy*. How would they respond? What resources did they have? It was important to remain discreet. I never advised an officer if superiors or juniors were present. And I only offered opinions when asked for them. It was essential to preserve every officer's respect and self-esteem.

A surprise came three weeks into my posting when summoned to see a brigadier-general. I was told there was nothing to worry about, so I worried! A 2nd lieutenant called to an audience with a senior general was unheard of. I thought someone was pulling my leg, until the major delivering the order pointed to the waiting car. After the brigadier-general dismissed his staff and we were alone together, my heart raced at this unusual situation. What on earth could this be about? He invited me to be seated. He said this was to be an 'informal chat' and, observing my apprehension, invited me to be at ease. He started asking a string of detailed questions about life at the front. He was particularly interested in hand-to-hand combat. What happens? What *really* happens? What do the men truly feel? What could be done to stop chaps 'accidentally on purpose' shooting themselves to get Blighty wounds? How had I avoided this condition now called shell shock, which many frontline infantrymen suffered? How could trench warfare be improved? After an hour of questioning the general stood, making it clear the meeting was over. He thanked me, politely, and said our little chat had been very helpful. Then, in a serious if not stern tone, he added: 'Of course, Ogden, you understand the contents of our dialogue, and the very fact we have had this discussion, are to remain strictly confidential. Should anyone of whatever rank ask, as rumours spread like wildfire around HQ, simply say I wanted a detailed briefing about the condition of our trenches. Which, of course, is exactly what we have discussed. Not a word more. Understood?'

Criticism of armchair generals increased as more conscripts arrived and the war dragged on, much of it unfair. Some chaps seemed too ready to criticize our leadership. Critics however were unwilling to admit that Germans are formidable fighters. The enemy had good, often superior, weapons. Early in the war, probably before it began, Germans realised the importance of large howitzers, mortars and machine guns. We stuck to the rifle rather than the machine gun, and relied too much on cavalry instead of artillery. The Germans are excellent engineers, well organised, and their troops disciplined. They had prepared for war. We hadn't. Never underestimate the enemy, was often said, but some had done exactly that.

As if playing on familiar ground, it seemed the Germans also felt at home in France, even in trenches. It was as if we, the British and our Empire comrades, became the invaders, the visiting team. Germans lived on the mainland of Europe. They considered it their soil, whereas we had crossed seas and oceans to wage war on foreign land. I wondered if this made Germans feel more tolerant than us of the war's stalemate. The Hun appeared content to sit it out, make deep permanent trenches with many home comforts. (The general called my view 'a fascinating theory'.) Perhaps the Kaiser believed the day would arrive when the British and her colonial friends would tire of the war, pack up, go home. The Kaiser could play a waiting game. In his mind, he was home already, or at least in his back garden.

Mr Unia told me that countries had come and gone across Europe throughout history. Borders moved back and forth like tides on the shore. The Spanish once controlled part of the Netherlands. The Romans, Saxons and others had invaded England. Sweden possessed an empire in northern Europe, including much of Germany today. Most Finns resent their country being a grand duchy of Russia and want an independent Finland. Centuries ago, under the Plantagenet, the English ruled much of France. Germany, as it is now, didn't exist as one nation until 1871 when King Wilhelm I of Prussia accepted the crown of a new German Empire and became *Kaiser* Wilhelm I. Before then there had been duchies, states, small kingdoms, bishoprics, imperial free cities and a Holy Roman Empire.

'Remember, gentlemen,' Mr Unia said at dinner that last evening in Amiens, to the obvious annoyance of the captain who had taken against him, 'the French under Napoléon Bonaparte invaded much of Austria and German territory as it stands today.

'In 1806 he occupied Berlin. And if it hadn't been for the harsh winter of 1812, which entrapped his troops in freezing blizzards, he'd have succeeded taking Moscow. The weather, my friends, has determined borders as much as seas, rivers and mountains, besides the outcomes of war.'

244

Mr Unia revealed to me afterwards in the *bibliothèque* that the English had once fought alongside Germans! Their combined troops, led by the Duke of Cumberland, routed the catholic Jacobite forces at the Battle of Culloden in Scotland during 1746.

'Friends can become foes, and foes friends,' he said. 'History is a great teacher, we often hear. Unfortunately, Samuel, every new generation ignores those lessons and believes it knows best. "It's different this time," they say. Some things are, some things aren't. One fact is clear, those of us living now can't change history - we make it.'

***

Zeppelins. Howitzers. Toxic gas. Flame throwers. The Hun used them first. It was during December 1914 when we first learnt of another ghastly Boche weapon: mines. Around ten miles south of the French border with Belgium, near Festubert, underground explosions killed and maimed many Indian troops. Those who survived were too shaken to fight. Some remain gibbering wrecks, such is the effect of a blast under your feet. On 17th April 1915 under Hill 60 near St Eloi, Ypres, we too deployed underground mines. My memories of Hill 60 have never faded.

Tunnelling under enemy trenches to detonate large caches of high explosives is now routine on both sides. For this next major push, many tunnels are being dug along the front from Maricourt to Serre. Following my survey of the territory south of La Boisselle village, I was ordered to liaise with a mining officer, Captain James Young of the 179th Tunnelling Company, Royal Engineers. These specialist companies had developed since 1915. Captain Young wanted to know all I had discovered about the enemy's positions and how they constructed their trenches. We discussed the best possible spot for several underground blasts. Each explosion aimed to inflict the greatest damage on the enemy line and provide the maximum advantage for our advancing troops. One spot, half a mile south east of La Boisselle, was to be at the centre of a string of eighteen explosions. I blinked in disbelief when he told me it would be the biggest blast of the war, in any war in history. Two charges, one using over sixteen tons of high-explosive ammonal and another with over ten tons, would be detonated simultaneously under a strong German position called the Schwaben Redoubt. This spot would be the focus of our pincer attack. I asked how big the explosion would be. 'Think of the biggest howitzer shell you've seen explode,' the Captain replied, 'quadruple the size of the blast in your head, then double it again. And it might be bigger than that.' I didn't struggle with my poor arithmetic, I simply changed the word in my head, from big to massive.

Most of the tunnellers had come from our coal fields in Scotland, Durham, Yorkshire, Wales and Kent. Miners and specialist engineers had also joined the war from South Africa, Canada, Australia and New Zealand. Tunnelling, unlike basic trench work, needs knowledge and experience of driving shafts deep underground and securing the roof and walls from collapse. The conditions are, to say the least, arduous. It takes a special kind of man with extraordinary courage to labour underground. No natural light, air stale, space confined, ever-present danger, hazards all around. Until the pumps get going men will often work to their waists in water. Cold water, icy water. There could be poisonous gas, either from the earth itself or that released by the enemy. As in their coal mines at home, some miners carried canaries in cages down the shafts to alert them to toxic fumes. Also, as the Germans were almost certainly digging tunnels towards us, there was the ever-present danger of counter-charges, which the engineers call 'camouflets'. This would result in our chaps being buried in their own tunnel. Few escaped.

Miners tend to be short, stocky and strong, some skinny and sinewy. Hands that grip like a vice. Skin as tough as hide. Sunken eyes. Human moles. I admired them greatly. These tough little fellows - tall men, they say, soon start to suffer back ache - could dig at a rate which took my breath away. One of these chaps, alone with nothing but a spade, could construct a trench twenty-four feet long, three feet wide and eight feet deep in half a day. It didn't seem to matter whether they worked wet heavy clay or rock-hard soil! Their slopes would be neat and perfectly straight, their parapets perfectly angled and rounded. It would take a very fit infantryman at least two whole days to complete the same feat. And the results would not be as good. I often praised the miners' work and asked how they managed to achieve such perfection. We have the knack, they say proudly, with a knowing smile, a wink, and a tap of the nose.

Captain Young later asked if I'd like to visit the main mine south of La Boissell to see the progress they'd made. Most of the sappers belonged to the 51st Highland Division and had named their home trench 'Lochnagar', after somewhere in the Grampians. Despite attempts to disguise the diggings, it was clear the Germans knew from their observation aircraft the location of the shaft heads. Their bombs regularly targeted the entrance and occasionally struck home, creating much hasty repair work. Thankfully, on the night of my visit, the German artillery decided to shell the south towards the French across the Somme river.

After a few yards walking the gentle slope into the mine, I found myself looking down a deep vertical shaft. 'It's ninety feet, Sir,' said the corporal escorting me, answering before I'd asked. Stepping closer to the edge, cautiously, I saw a dim lone light at the bottom. 'Are you sure it's not ninety yards?' I asked trying to hide my trepidation. 'Feet, Sir, definitely feet.' He smiled. The rope ladder dangled into the shaft and the corporal pulled it towards me with an invitation to step onto it. At that moment, I regretted accepting the Captain's invitation: I didn't really need to see a tunnel, did I? But it was too late to turn back. And even in the low light, the corporal could read the expression on my face as clear as a bill poster on a sunny day. 'You can count as you go down, Sir,' the corporal said. 'Each rung is exactly one foot apart.' I half-hoped a German shell would land nearby offering a reason to delay my descent. But the Germans failed to provide my excuse and the French lines continued receiving the night's pounding.

I felt more afraid climbing down this shaft than going over the top onto no-man's-land. Why? The mind is a mystery. I'd used rope ladders on occasions in the open without undue concern. But this one, dropping deep into the bowels of the earth, was frightening. My admiration for the miners, and my pity for the tunnel working parties who are not miners, doubled. As on the battlefield, perhaps as in life, if you can't go back, and you can't stay where you are, it's best to go forward with hope and enthusiasm. So, without hesitation, if not with hope or enthusiasm, I stepped onto the ladder and it swung like a church bell until settling to my weight. The first few steps I gripped too tightly until I found the measure between each rung. Feeling more secure, I quite enjoyed the experience. And I remembered that, for my return, ascending a rope ladder is easier and less hazardous than climbing down.

It was nevertheless a relief when my feet touched the ground. A sergeant greeted me with a finger across his lips, reminding me to stay quiet. No talking. Whisper only if absolutely necessary. Swallow any cough. Suppress any sneeze. Walk slowly. Tread carefully. I hadn't realised sound travelled so easily underground until the sergeant presented me with the earpiece of a listening device. I could hear digging and scraping: he mouthed 'Germans'. Hun miners, thought to be just twenty-five yards away. It was eerie. Here we are digging a tunnel towards the Germans, and they're doing the same towards us. More unnerving was realising that, at any moment, the enemy could detonate explosives. It happened with frightening regularity. If the explosion didn't do for us immediately, we would drown in soil. Worse, I could be trapped in some underground cavern, a cavity which would become my coffin after I had died of thirst or hunger. Close to the big push, I doubt men would be diverted to dig for survivors, unless they could be heard or their precise position known. I lived with this frightening thought for the long, very long hour I spent underground.

These poor chaps work the mines not just hour after hour, but week after week. Not surprisingly, free men living like ferrets trapped in a drainpipe, a few go raving mad. They dash for light and air and open space. I too would go crazy confined below ground - it must be like working inside your own coffin.

Miners may not come face-to-face with Germans as often as infantrymen above ground, but they face an equally formidable enemy: sheer walls of rock and earth which they must hack and hew, scrape and clear. And often quietly, slowly, inch by inch. Their weapons are not rifles and bayonets, but picks and shovels. They may not scurry across no-man's-land on night forays to capture trenches, but build tunnels under the enemy that will blow the blighters to bits.

248

CHAPTER 30

July & August 1916
SOMME OFFENSIVE

Earth exploded. The debris fountain reached four thousand feet sky-high. Higher than the highest mountain in England. The blast could be heard in Britain. Our nearest shoreline one hundred and twenty miles away. Hundreds died instantly. Maybe thousands. Nobody knows the exact number, nobody ever will. We don't stop to count the dead in the middle of battle. If alive you fight to survive. And the nearly-dead can't count. Never in history has man killed so many men so quickly with one blow. The mine at La Boisselle exploded at precisely 7.28 am. The Somme Offensive began. Captain James Young detonated the charge, his mine-laying duties at an end - for now.

In front of my eyes the world changed. The landscape torn as a painting ripped from its frame. The horizon obliterated by a curtain of dirt and dust and bloody debris. As the bomb-cloud settled, the scale of devastation unravelled. A gigantic crater, with a perfect circular ridge, had been created. A new man-made power challenged the old forces of nature.

I feared that one day, when dust is all that remains of me, man will make ever-bigger bombs. If the destruction in Flanders and Picardy demonstrates what men at war can achieve, bombs will grow so large they will destroy whole countries. Craters could be created the size of England, Germany, France, even Russia. If God can take back what He has given, if Nature can reclaim what She has formed, Man can destroy what He has built. They said the *SS Titanic* was unsinkable - until the unthinkable happened when a lump of ice slashed its hull, as easily as a sharp blade across a soft throat.

Captain Young's bomb signalled the start of the big push. Months of planning had gone into this moment. Line after line of men emerged from the trenches. Determined, head tucked in shoulders, tight jawed, rifle ready, bayonet fixed, waves of men moved into no-man's-land. Our artillery bombardment started on 24th June, the infantry attack planned for the 29th. For reasons not explained to such lowly lieutenants as me, this was delayed until 1st July. Rumour had it that the French, positioned for attack south of the River Somme, had requested the postponement. This two-day delay cost us dearly. The men, cooped up in the trenches this extra time, had to suffer not only the racket of our own artillery but also German retaliatory fire. Then, worse than the shelling, a natural enemy of the trenches struck; rain, torrential rain. Many of the trenches flooded. The rats ran riot. Skin sores worsened. Leather boots tightened. Heavy kit became heavier with water. Guns and gear needed more protection, cleaning, oiling. Every man realised the climb out of the trenches would become a slippery scramble. The mud turned into a sticky cemetery for those who became stranded and shot.

No-man's-land became dead-man's-land.

Despite a week of shelling the German positions remained largely intact. Most of their barbed wire entanglements hadn't been broken. Captain Young's mine at La Boisselle and sixteen others exploded along the fourteen-mile front. One thousand five hundred and thirty-seven artillery guns - one gun to every twenty yards of front - had failed to break the Boche. Where mines exploded, the Hun's guns were stunned, but not silenced. Machine-gunners emerged from deep underground bunkers and massacred our men with enfilading fire. Row after row, man after man, cut down. Platoons, companies, battalions destroyed or severely depleted. Men in their dozens, hundreds, thousands killed. Machine gun tack-tack-tack-tack was the ever-present sound of the day between the bombs. What remained of Kitchener's Army, brave volunteers full of verve and bravado, shot to shreds.

Throughout the offensive most of our men had to move uphill, a great disadvantage, especially when carrying seventy pounds of kit. In addition to their rifle and bayonet, most men carried an entrenching tool, some also carried spades, wire cutters, gas helmet, over two hundred bullets, Mills bombs, groundsheet, water bottle, haversack and field dressings. And after the rain and floods, nature dealt another cruel blow on the day of our attack - hot sun and sweltering humidity. Mud under foot with your back laden, your head baking under a steel helmet, are not ideal conditions for fighting. The enemy had many look-out posts and machine-gun positions. We became easy prey, lame ducks in neat rows. The order remained the same, whatever words used: advance, move ahead, proceed, press forward, keep going, and always 'at a steady pace'. Shell pits, gullies, debris and bodies provided temporary shelter to catch breath. But orders to advance never ceased. Company captains and platoon lieutenants, following orders to the letter, steered each successive wave. Many officers fell first. Despite our best efforts at concealment over the preceding months, it was clear the enemy knew of our build-up of forces. Our attack came as no surprise. The Boche stood ready to receive us, not with the open arms of a loved one, but with loaded weapons full of malice.

Men stood not to fight, but to die.

Our week of shelling served as a signal to the Germans that an offensive was at hand. It had become standard practice, our *modus operandi*, the educated officers said. When shelling stopped, the enemy knew our infantry attack would begin. Every Fritz tensed like a spider on the edge of his web waiting for a fly. I thought we should break this habit, change the game, attack without any preliminary bombardment, at least on some occasions. But the lone voice of a junior lieutenant in this war is heard no louder than a raindrop in a storm.

For the offensive, I had been allocated to Brigade as an observer in the La Boisselle sector, half a mile north-west of where Captain Young's earth-shattering detonation reshaped the landscape. We called it Sausage Valley. My orders were 'to report and record the progress of our advance and the enemy's response'. After the mine explosion, I watched infantrymen of the 34th Division emerge from their trenches. Behind them around four thousand men came up from reserve trenches in battalions of the Tyneside Irish Brigade. At first the Tynesiders had the slight advantage of walking downhill, but it did them no good. Within minutes German machine gunners had cut them down. It was glaringly obvious our week-long artillery bombardment had not paralysed the Germans, nor rid no-man's-land of their entanglements, nor bludgeoned them to submission, nor collapsed their trenches. A few uninjured men of the 34th sought sanctuary in Captain Young's crater. As this stifling summer's day came to an end, they joined what was left of the 21st and 22nd Northumberland Fusiliers, holding a position between La Boisselle and the mine crater.

To my right platoons of the 11th Suffolks and 10th Lincolns advanced nearly half a mile beyond German lines to a place we named Wood Alley. They were joined by the 15th and 16th Royal Scots with the intention of guarding the left flank of the 21st Division's advance, expected within the hour. Reports came from evacuated casualties that men of the Tyneside Irish Brigade had even penetrated beyond the wood to the village of Contalmaison, a little over a mile east of La Boisselle. But they were forced back by the German counter-attack. The handful of battered survivors said the Germans killed every man from the Tyneside Irish. No mercy. No prisoners.

Towards the end of the Somme Offensive's first day, I was required by Brigade HQ to submit my assessment of the battle so far in the sector. One task was to estimate the number of casualties and remaining fighting strength on both sides. It's an almost impossible undertaking. Telephone lines are frequently cut by falling ordnance. Messengers are killed, injured or waylaid. Commanders are incapable of reporting because they themselves are injured, severely or fatally. Many platoon lieutenants and company captains had perished, often alongside their second in command. Roll calls obviously can't be conducted in the middle of battle. And no one pair of eyes can see all that's happening. Stretcher bearers count their collections, and casualty clearing stations keep accurate figures. But many men are left on the battlefield, unfound, hiding, buried, or in bits. Some survivors may be able to fight later, but are lying low for now, and others will have strayed into other sectors.

Casualty summaries are listed: Date, Time, Sector, Officers - Killed, Wounded, Missing. Other Ranks - K, W or M. I added together the numbers I'd noted over the past seventeen hours during each attack around La Boisselle. The totals didn't make sense. Again I believed poor arithmetic had let me down. Calculations must be wrong. Surely these numbers couldn't be correct? Even before eight o'clock in the bright morning sun, within thirty-two minutes of Captain Young's bomb, I had recorded nine platoons all but wiped out. Killed in Action, abbreviated to KIA, I had noted '360 approx'. On the following pages I found KIA 290 approx, KIA 450 approx, KIA 120 approx. Page followed page of unbelievable numbers. After checking my addition three times, the total reached KIA 6,380. I wrote 'approximately' in full, it seemed more respectful.

Estimating enemy casualties was clearly harder. Calculating the distance across the mine crater at around one hundred and fifty yards, and the number of men possibly in the tunnels and trenches affected, I entered 800 to 1,200 casualties. The majority near this huge explosion would be dead or incapacitated. Gigantic though the explosion under the Schwaben Redoubt was, its impact was surprisingly localised. The Hun's riflemen, machine gunners and infantry to the sides and behind the crater remained ready for the fight, even before the debris crashed back down to earth. For the rest of the day I reported 'only pockets' of the enemy killed or maimed, '300 at most'. The telephone wires cut again, I sent a messenger with my report. Two or three Brigade HQ officers would be disappointed in the difference between our high casualty figure compared with the enemy's. But I saw what I saw, and said what I saw.

A few officers occasionally reported what they believed their seniors wanted to hear, rather than report the facts. Or they would delay presenting bad news in the hope that good news would follow, as if the good would banish the blow of the bad. I recall overhearing a major give a totally false account to a colonel of a skirmish. He grossly exaggerated the German losses we had inflicted and falsified the time of our 'orderly withdrawal' by two hours. It was a bare-faced lie, for no other reason than to make himself look good in the colonel's eyes, and doubtless in the subsequent report to Brigade. It did not improve his already poor reputation among the men. I was then a corporal and standing to the side with my squad. It was not my place to speak. And, on principle, the word of an officer and gentleman would always be believed before that of one of the men. Even now as a 2nd Lieutenant it would be awkward to contradict a senior officer, even with the truth - especially the truth.

A handful of senior officers appear to deny bad news, pretending situations aren't as bad as they are. Junior officers too might play the game and report only what is wanted to be heard. But, like tumbling dominoes, one falsehood falls into the next. Pigeons come home to roost. I remember a platoon commander being briefed by the departing battalion's officer that a farm house and its outbuildings had been cleared of Germans. It hadn't. Six men died and fourteen suffered injuries in an outburst of bullets and grenades as the platoon approached. Had the truth been told, a cautious advance would have prevented most if not all those casualties.

The words we'd come to use for 'death' since this deadly war began has widened. Some avoid the word altogether, as if 'death' was dirty, dirtier than being dead. Regiments adopted their own favourites. 'Copped it' and 'done for' we Dukes used mostly. Some chaps describe the dead as 'daisy pushers' or 'land owners'. London lads often said a dead man was 'a loaf of bread'. They liked rhyming slang! Others used 'outed', a boxing expression, from knocked out I suppose. We all used 'gone west': it's in the west where the sun sets and the day ends in darkness. The word 'napoo' has become popular. With the help of a French speaker, I learnt it was an adaption of *il n'y en a plus* - there isn't any more. Killed in Action, even if the victim copped it sleeping, is a kinder phrase than the heartless if accurate word 'dead'. The Army believes 'Killed in Action' make bereavement easier to bear for relatives.

I regret to inform you that your son, Samuel Ogden, 2nd Lieutenant, originally of The Duke of Wellington's Regiment, was killed in action on.... will be easier on Mother and Father than the cold word 'dead'.

'Killed in Action' aims to give death glory, justify the loss, reduce the pain. But it fails to fill the void in the bereaving heart.

The French Sixth Army, to the south of the River Somme, enjoyed more success than us that first day. They pushed the Germans back through several villages before taking Herbéncourt and Asservillers by nightfall, despite ferocious counter-attacks. The French, more experienced than our Kitchener Army of volunteers or new conscripts, proved again that no amount of battle training amounts to real battle experience. Experience always beats inexperience, even if bolstered with enthusiasm. Besides having skilled troops, the French used a higher proportion of heavy artillery than us, and with more reliable gas and high explosive shells.

Perhaps the main factor in their greater success was their focus on a narrower front. This knocked the Germans senseless during the first phase of the attack. The French also delayed their infantry attack until ours got under way two hours earlier. This resulted in the Germans becoming distracted by our attack to the north and lulled them into believing the French would hold their line for some time.

***

The slaughter on the Somme continued, although no day's death toll was as terrible as 1st July. In around fifty separate incursions over the following weeks, almost all in vain, we suffered thousands of casualties. I completed reports on the action and outcome. Our aim had been to manoeuvre into position for the next phase of the big push: an all-out attack on the German's second line on the Bazentin Ridge. But many of our ventures became uncoordinated. Divisional commanders, even company commanders with a few hundred men, again took it upon themselves to launch attacks. There were times when I wanted to shout 'No! Idiots! What the hell are you doing? Stop!'

But one man's call in war, one voice in a chorus of chaos, would not be heard nor heeded. It seemed that certain commanders had a compulsion to do something rather than do nothing, even though each attack resulted in a loss of life for little or no gain. Nothing would have been better than something.

Eventually, on 13th July, on a two-mile east-west line between Delville Wood and Bazentin-le-Petit Wood, Fritz's second line was taken. Our victory came with the help of a simple yet ingenious device: white tape. Many attacks failed not only because of their piecemeal nature but because troops in battle become disoriented. Even in daylight, especially when wearing gasmasks, it was easy to lose your sense of direction. The tape, strung out under darkness, guided chaps along the final approach of one thousand yards. It was also stretched across at right angles to mark where the men should gather. These measures enabled men to start attacking at the same time and distance parallel to the German line of defence. Fritz then faced a tidal wave of XIII Corps troops, not a piecemeal platoon here and a company there.

From midnight the men, in long single files, moved forward following the tape. Our attack began in the deepest darkness before dawn, at 3.20 am. One thousand artillery guns, nearly one third of them heavy, started pounding the German trenches with concentrated rapid fire over a three-mile frontage. They would have expected the barrage to last hours, if not days, as usual. But this artillery onslaught lasted just five minutes. Within seconds of the cessation of the bombardment, our whole line moved in and overwhelmed the enemy. It was wonderful to witness. I felt very proud of the officers and men who executed this action. But it wasn't all easy sailing. The fighting was fierce through the villages of Bazentin-le-Grand and Bazentin-le-Petit, and especially tough through Longueval and behind it to the edge of Delville Wood. Over the following days, in close combat fighting as intense as any in the war, many South African colleagues in 9th Division died deep in Delville Wood.

Fighting in the Somme region raged on. But every success met a setback. On 23rd July the Anzac Corps - Australians and New Zealanders who had served in Gallipoli - together with our III Corps of the Fourth Army, launched an attack to take Pozières Ridge. Many Canadian troops joined the offensive and fought fearlessly. The fighting lasted two months and failed, unless you value a slither of land for the price of twenty-three thousand lives. More territory was however gained six miles to the east of Pozières. Two months of fighting acquired the village of Guillemont on 3rd September and, the following week, we secured a village a mile north, Ginchy. Secured is probably the wrong word, for all along the line bitter battles continued with ground being gained and lost daily. Guillemont and Ginchy lay in ruins beyond recognition. Not one building remained habitable. Should the locals ever return to this rubble, will they want to rebuild with blood-stained stones on blood-soaked soil? Captured Germans revealed the head of their First Army, General Fritz von Below, issued an order threatening all officers with a court martial if they conceded territory or failed to retake lost territory, which explained the constant counter-attacks.

256

We hear of deaths and injuries in numbers that strain the imagination. Bad as they are, the true figures are rumoured to be worse. But our political and military overlords have determined they must not be publicly reported. They say censorship helps maintain morale of fighting men abroad, and civilians at home. Whatever the true toll, if anyone had predicted this level of casualties at the outbreak of the war, they would have been shouted down, ignored as scaremongers, considered insane.

After this Somme slaughter, I feel vindicated in maintaining that personal no-man's-land between me and those I meet. Friends are lost as easily as farthings. War means loss. Much has gone. More will go. It's better to keep a distance. Enjoy perhaps the passing acquaintance or companion, but make no friend. Spare them the pain of your loss, and your own pain of theirs. The intensity of war can bind people together quickly, intimately, urgently. Too quick, intimate, urgent. Colours are brighter, emotions extravagant, passions aroused, music louder, time condensed. We strive to live a lifetime in the days and hours we might have remaining - as if we only have minutes and seconds. We accept that death, injury, disease and separation are waiting for us, because we witness what is happening all around. The men who think they are immortal are usually the first to prove they are not.

Guilt nor self-reproach serve any purpose on the field of battle. Neither helps survival, nor the mission. Sentiment and squeamishness are dangerous. Chaps die because they dither, wondering whether to kill or not. A split-second delay on squeezing the trigger may be the last second of your life. They saw the face of their victim, a person, rather than that of a soldier, an enemy. And the enemy did for them in that moment of hesitation. If you're about to kill, delay, and you're dead. Afterwards, conscience can play no part. Dwelling on the men you've killed only puts you in greater danger. And, later, disturbs your sleep.

As the weeks went by on the Somme, I became increasingly frustrated at not being in the thick of it. Being a Brigade Observer still had its dangers, many bullets and shells landed nearby. But I could keep my head down until the worst was over. I didn't have to 'advance, advance, advance' into shell hell. With few exceptions, the company and platoon commanders I saw demonstrated incredible bravery and skill. Some made terrible basic blunders resulting in more casualties than there needed to have been. A few commanders delayed a few seconds too long before advancing after an artillery barrage, or charged too early, or went forward in poor formation. Others instructed their men to follow a bad route, exposing them to greater machine gun fire and mortars. Many platoons just went over the top and walked forward into gunfire and shell bursts. If by some chance they reached within throwing distance of a German redoubt or trench, they were finished off by grenades. Platoon followed platoon in this senseless way, and their only achievement was to end their day dead.

Seven out of ten lieutenants had already become casualties on the Somme. My request therefore to take command of a platoon and return to frontline fighting surprised senior officers and colleagues.

Fellow fisherman 2nd Lieutenant McGavan, also serving at Brigade HQ, declared: 'You must be as mad as a mayfly landing on a trout pool! Why, why place yourself in so much danger?'

There are times when questions say more than answers.

CHAPTER 31

September 1916
MY PLATOON

Forty of the forty-eight men in my new platoon had not faced frontline action. Until now these men had served in the Reserve Army, commanded by General Sir Hubert Gough. My chaps were afraid. They should be. Fear helps keep a soldier alive. I was afraid too, and told them. A captain later reprimanded me for sharing my fear with the men. It was 'bad form', he said. To admit my fear would 'diminish the men's confidence' in me.

The captain did not understand how a man's mind works in war. Everyone in the company could see the fear written across his face. They could tell when his speech became fast, his voice thin, his mouth dry. They watched the captain wipe the sweat from under his helmet when danger approached. It's the *denial* of fear that diminishes a man's respect for his senior officer. Any man here who claims to have no apprehension is mad, stupid or a liar. And who wants to be taken into battle by an officer displaying any one of those attributes? Denying your demons doesn't rid you of them. True courage is carrying on despite your terror: walking into darkness with a fear of the dark, standing at the cliff edge fearing heights. Officers who share their own unease with the men find his troops give of their best. I have also found that when I admit I'm fearful, the admission itself provides some comfort. Mysteriously, saying one is scared helps one to be brave - or at least slightly less terrified.

It was this very captain who, a few days after his reprimand, I found wailing uncontrollably in a captured trench. I slapped his face and shook him in the hope of bringing him round: the treatment sometimes worked. But he simply sat on his heels and stared rocking forwards and backwards, his nerves shattered. Doctors now call this condition 'shell shock'. But, in this instance, it wasn't the shelling itself as much as the aftermath. It was the first time the captain had seen smashed corpses, tasted the stink of burning flesh, blood and guts at close quarters. It affects some people this way. He couldn't go

259

on. His mind rendered his body useless. Perhaps if he had not denied his dread, accepted his distress…

Breakfast arrived at night in the assembly trenches on 15th September. Meat rations, vegetables and plenty of hot tea cheered us all. While still dark my platoon, alongside the whole battalion of over a thousand men, edged forward in readiness for the main assault, set for 6.20 am. Our advance did not go unchallenged. At times, with explosives and star shells bursting overhead, the night became as bright as day. German machine guns got busy and peppered us. A handful of my platoon fell before they could find cover. Only one victim was an outright kill. A young lad, seventeen at most. A bullet found his heart. I was upset at his death, the first of my platoon command. But I was doubly dismayed at this lad's end - because I didn't know his name. I strived to learn the name of everyone in my platoon. Foolishly, for I was still in the line of fire, I removed the young man's Army Book 64 from his right breast pocket before moving on.

Later, during a short respite from the battle, I opened his AB64 to find his details: name, skill at arms, discipline record, sick record, next of kin and so on. From page thirteen onwards of every Soldier's Pay Book, blank pages were allocated for his Will. Every man was encouraged to complete this to bequeath any possessions and, should he wish, say a few final words.

John Smith, the lad with the simplest of names, had written: *'I have nothing to leave except all my love to Mother. I don't know who Father was. You never said, or you could not say. But he should not have abandoned you carrying me. Perhaps he was married. Perhaps you never told him of your condition. Perhaps you didn't know his whereabouts. But I am proud of you, dearest Mother, for it must have been a struggle surviving with me in tow. You said you had been foolish, didn't know what men could get up to, felt ashamed, and asked for my forgiveness. But you should feel no blame or shame, and there is nothing to forgive. Your loving son, John.'*

Bullets raking the ground inches from my feet brought me back to my senses and I bolted into the nearest hole. A German machine-gunner, perhaps thinking John Smith may still be alive, made sure he was dead - by riddling his body with bullets.

Back in the frontline, the first time since February, I was where I should be: with the men. But things had changed. I was platoon commander and should know the names of my men. My excuse was that, having been with this platoon for just a few days, it was impossible to have learnt all their names. I knew my sergeant's, the corporals' names and, now, John Smith. A few privates' faces I could put names to; the stand-out characters, the surly, the comedians, and the one paunchy chap, Pte Clegg, whose knees knocked together when he ran.

After advancing just one hundred yards, my platoon was already ten men down. Our company's captain remained a jabbering wreck. Two 2nd lieutenants scurried into the shallow trench alongside me. A volley of bullets followed them and we cowered holding our helmets tight to our heads. They had come for orders from the captain and report that 2nd Lt Nixon, the fourth platoon commander in our company, had been badly injured. The second officer started to speak, but stopped suddenly. Well? Spit it out, I urged. All his manhood has been blown away, he reported. It happens, was all I could say. It was then both lieutenants noticed the captain gabbling to himself, they turned to me and asked what to do. Our orders haven't changed, I said, we must advance. But go with caution. Move in darkness as soon as the Very lights or star shells burn out. Keep low. Use every nook and cranny. It's better to progress slowly and get there than rush and get shot. We need to be further up by dawn for when the main attack begins. One of the lieutenants asked, 'What about him?' The captain had curled himself into a tight ball oblivious to all that was going on. 'He's had it,' I said. 'We can't do anything. If he's lucky a body-snatcher - sorry, that's what the men call a stretcher bearer - will pick him up later.'

A morning mist lingered on the southern edge of High Wood filtering the morning sun, typical of mid-September. Autumn had arrived on time. Our Company, part of XV Corps, waited for the order to attack. We planned to advance clearing the wood of Germans and on towards the village of Flers. To our left III Corps was also ready to advance north to the village of Courcelette, four miles west of Flers. To our right stood XIV Corps. In its sights were the villages of Lesbœufs and Morval. This offensive, along a front of over seven miles involving around two hundred thousand men, hoped to push home all our hard work on the Somme since the beginning of the year. One key objective was to reach the high ground from Courcelette to Flers. This ridge would provide several excellent observation posts, an advantage the Germans had enjoyed for too long. Another aim was to push back the Boche a few miles north and east: anything to break the stagnant stalemate of the trenches. There was even talk that, if this big push got the Hun on the run, it might bring the Kaiser and his generals to the peace table.

At 6.20 am whistles blew along the lines. Men arose from their holding positions gained overnight and moved forward. We started to use the 'creeping barrage' method of advancement, hotly discussed during my officer training. Until recently artillery had largely been used to shell enemy trenches and positions. This had limited success. Trenches, especially the deep and well-built German ones, proved resilient to such attacks. We still shell trenches routinely. But when a ground attack now takes place, our artillery aim to drop their cargo on no-man's-land ahead of us. As infantry press on, artillery guns are gradually angled slightly higher enabling shells to land further forward. When it works, it works well. The barrage gives infantrymen more confidence advancing. It disrupts the enemy's machine guns, mortars and rifles because their line of sight is constantly interrupted by explosions and debris. Fritz continues firing, of course, but with reduced accuracy. When the creeping barrage doesn't work, it has one disastrous consequence: shells falling short land on us! We find ourselves diving for cover from our own barrage that hasn't 'crept' far enough ahead. The air turns blue when the PBIs, the 'poor bloody infantry', curse the RAs, the 'right arseholes' of the Royal Artillery.

As we commenced our attack the most amazing - perhaps historic - event unfolded. We heard their roaring power before we saw them. Out of the mist behind us emerged three enormous vehicles. The land battleships crept forward slower than walking pace. But forward they came, one hundred yards apart. Officers had been given orders to advance alongside 'tanks'. Most of the men had not seen these giant machines before, although gossip about this new weapon had increased in recent days. Some chaps couldn't believe their eyes, nor could have imagined these contraptions. Thirty-two and a half feet long, almost fourteen feet wide, 8 feet tall, these iron boxes on caterpillar tracks trundled towards the Germans. If these twenty-eight ton tanks inspired awe in us, what will the Germans feel when they see them? Outright fear, I would think! Our confidence was boosted. Chaps cheered and shouted these land battleships will have Jerry running back to Berlin!

Our joy was short-lived. One of the three tanks coughed and spluttered to a stop. Two of the eight-man crew from the Heavy Machine Gun Corps alighted to see if they could find the source of the breakdown. They could not. We advanced leaving the tank behind us. The mist started clearing and we came under intense small arms fire. The German artillery guns remained, however, strangely quiet. Partly thanks to our two remaining tanks, especially the way they crushed the German's wire entanglements, we made good progress. Our metal monsters sent many Germans into a blind panic. At each Hun trench the tanks fired large calibre Hotchkiss machine guns and two six-pounder naval guns along the Hun's line. They caused devastation. Where pockets of Germans survived, we lobbed in grenades. The German trenches here were not as deep or constructed with concrete as those we encountered on 1st July. Nor were they in orderly lines. This random nature of their defences made predicting where the machine gunners lay in wait harder. Their MGs accounted for many of our chaps, including a whole squad of six from my platoon. It was a cruel blow, because the chaps thought the hard work of fighting to Flers was over. They were hoping for a breather, even time for a quick brew, while those to our flanks caught up. But a crew of three enemy machine gunners emerged from a hole the squad had passed and cut them as a scythe slices straw.

Regulars and experienced men knew to clear every trench and hole before walking by to make sure no enemy remained hidden. The six dead simply forgot their basic training and reminders from me and their sergeant. A high price to pay for one act of forgetfulness, nevertheless. Some Germans would play dead and 'come back to life' to shoot chaps in the back, as these three had done. When in doubt put a bullet in the head to make sure they're dead, is a key rule of battlefield survival. I had stressed this essential task over the previous days to the whole platoon. But in their tiredness, following five hours of continuous fighting with bombs and bullets everywhere, and the prospect of a short rest, the six let their guard down. After their deadly deed, knowing they were surrounded, the three Germans immediately stood and threw their arms in the air to surrender. But their conniving murderous act was beyond mercy. I threw a grenade in their pit.

Hopes our mechanical monsters would roll on to Berlin were dashed later in the day. Shortly after the first tank broke down, the second became stranded crossing a shell pit. It rocked forwards and backwards in a desperate bid to release itself from the crater's jaws. The more it tried, spewing smoke and churning soil, the deeper it sank. The lame tank became easy prey for the enemy who quickly sought their revenge. Despite our heavy gun fire in its defence, a troupe of Germans crept towards the tank and threw a handful of grenades towards its undercarriage. If the crew of eight were not killed, they would certainly have been knocked senseless by the sequence of blasts. The frightening spell of the seemingly invincible land battleships had been broken, their awe diminished, the monsters belittled. Germans ran for their lives when they first viewed the tanks rolling towards them. Such was the dread these massive machines caused. Their half-inch armour plating provided protection against most shrapnel and standard rifle bullets. But the enemy soon discovered a well-placed high calibre bullet could penetrate the half-inch armour plating.

Tank crews reported wretched conditions inside their metal carcass: hot, airless, noisy, juddering, packed as tight as sardines in a tin. But it was the petrol fumes that caused most crews to be as sick as dogs. Four men manoeuvred the vehicle: the commander, two 'gearsmen', and one steering. Vision was restricted to a few peepholes. Not surprising then that a report came from up the line of one tank accidentally turning tail and opening fire on our own men.

Forty-nine tanks had been scheduled to fight along the front in detachments of two or three. But only between thirty-two and thirty-six tanks even reached their starting positions. Of those, many broke down or became stuck, as our company had experienced. Only one of our three tanks made it to Flers. The tank then 'posed' for pictures in the village ruins for gentlemen of the press for three days. I was delighted if not surprised to see Mr Prem Unia amongst them. Apart from a quick 'Hello', a handshake and a few words, the officers in charge of the journalists kept them away from junior officers and other ranks.

I was later asked, by a captain accompanying the journalists, if I knew 'the little brown fellow' from *The Times of India*. You seemed 'frightfully familiar' with him, he said, sounding mistrustful. After I confirmed my knowledge of Mr Unia, how we'd met in Amiens, the captain seemed anxious to find out what I'd told him. Had I disclosed any information, especially about the performance of the tanks? I assured him the war was not even mentioned and the word tank never crossed my lips, nor Mr Unia's. We simply and quickly discussed when I might return to Amiens and fly-fish on the Somme. I added, too grimly for the humourless captain it turned out, the odds stood in favour of the fish catching me in the Somme rather than me hooking one of them! 'By Jove, that's not the sort of thing a gentleman says, don't you know,' he said, before turning to leave.

My platoon was down seventeen to thirty-one. Nine wounded, some badly, eight dead. In addition to the six lads who died at the hands of the machine gun bandits, a John Glover joined John Smith listed as Killed in Action. Pte Glover's AB64 Pay Book recorded - wrongly - that he was born in 1898. But he wasn't eighteen. He'd lied. A lie the Army was happy to accept as truth. Looking at his scrawny body and pale skin, as smooth as a baby's bottom, my sergeant and I doubted the lad had reached sixteen when he voluntarily enlisted for service in June. Glover had scrawled one word in child-like writing on his Will page, 'Nowt', the Yorkshire word for 'nothing'. What killed Glover remained a mystery. We could not find a bullet hole or shrapnel wound. He had no bruising about his head. His section corporal reported Glover simply dropped his rifle and fell while running for cover coming into Flers. There was no gunfire nearby at the time. The stretcher bearer said this was happening more often, especially with the conscripts. 'It's as if their heart just packs up, Sir,' he said. 'Although it's usually the older blokes it 'appens to, especially if they've got a belly on 'em.'

Over the next ten days we consolidated our position along the new front. It ran east to west on the ridge from Courcelette to Flers, before our line curved three miles south through Leuze Wood, one mile west of Combles. Somewhere in this wood Major Cedric 'Ceddy' Dickens, the grandson of the great author Charles Dickens, fell to a machine gun on 9th September. Our Battalion commander also announced that a brilliant composer, well-known in music circles, had been sniped. Lt George Butterworth, 13th Durham Light Infantry, took a bullet to his head 5th August, somewhere near Pozières. His platoon, many of them Durham miners, admired the man and his bravery so much they named an assault trench Butterworth Alley. You must be very special to impress a Durham miner.

***

Since 1st July our advance in this Somme Offensive, albeit at a high cost in casualties, was thanks more to the aircraft of the Royal Flying Corps than the tanks of the Heavy Machine Gun Corps. Certain senior officers, sticklers for traditional ways, dislike the modern chaps in their flying machines. They believe airmen to be a law unto themselves: most without military training or parade ground drill and discipline. Experienced artillery officers especially seem to resent being told where to aim their guns from 'cavorting whippersnappers', as one complained. Like it or not, the RFC's reconnaissance flights and their photographic montages have made all the difference to our assaults. One aircraft can recce territory in a few minutes that traditionally a cavalry squadron would take a day to explore. Our spies in the sky have taken thousands of pictures. And when put together like a jigsaw, in what they call mosaic maps, they have revealed machine gun positions, dugouts, gun batteries and even command posts accurately. Aerial reconnaissance has changed the way both sides operate. We know for instance that we can't move large numbers of men or machinery within a few miles of the front without being discovered from the air. This means we must move forward faster from further back to wrong-foot the enemy.

Fuddy-duddy Army officers argue the RFC is half-civilian, not fully military. Some narrow-minded types still think aeroplanes are a flash in the pan. When in 1911 the Italians used aeroplanes against the Turks in Tripoli, our top brass concluded these machines had no place in our military. How wrong they were. Fighting in and from the air is here to stay, the sky a new space for combat. Dropping bombs from aeroplanes has never been done before. Nor being shot at from the sky. Nor sky fighting with one aircraft machine-gunning another. Airmen are not soldiers nor sailors. They don't have hundreds of years of Army or Navy tradition. They don't have shelves full of manuals and standing orders on how to fight. This air force must find its own way of warfare.

At the start of the war we rarely saw aircraft. Only sixty or so machines came to France at the outset. In recent months, unless the weather is particularly harsh, aeroplanes pass overhead many times a day, most of them on photographic reconnaissance missions. We are using around one hundred and eighty-five airborne vehicles of various types in this Somme Offensive. Our light bomber, the BE-2, which can fly up to ten thousand feet, seems to be the main type, although the engineers are constantly adapting them. They change so often it's sometimes hard to tell what's flying above.

Anti-aircraft guns, as all our weapons, are fast improving. Back in 1914 we simply aimed our rifles at enemy aircraft, usually without success. Many gunners in the early days also forgot the old game shooting saying: if you aim *at* the bird you'll miss *behind* it! You must move to hit a moving target. Birds don't wait for bullets. Nor do aeroplanes. Like birds, an aircraft will have moved since you pulled the trigger. Yet again gamekeepers and country chaps made the best anti-aircraft gunners. After all, if you can shoot a fast-flying grouse with wind up its tail, or a pigeon ducking and diving, a large aeroplane should prove an easy target. They're not, of course, and most aeroplanes are shot down by enemy aircraft. We are finding the main advantage of an anti-aircraft gun is that it reduces aeroplane attacks on us on the ground.

During this Somme Offensive, RFC pilots are increasingly dominating the skies. They've developed 'dogfighting' and use loops and side turns and rolls in their airborne struggles. Pilots have also discovered that aeroplanes working together in certain formations outsmart even faster and more manoeuvrable enemy craft. This combination of new skills, improved aircraft and on-board guns, started to outwit the Germans, especially their Fokker E III monoplanes. This damn aircraft over the last few months has shot down hundreds of ours, especially the Vickers FB-5. We called this the Fokker Scourge, usually in its rude variation. Despite the criticism from old school colonels and artillery, the RFC have done a fine job. The pilots improved our 'killing efficiency', words senior officers now often use, as if they are factory bosses.

How many yards of carpet woven today? How many soap bars produced?

Gruesome as it sounds, they are right. We are in business, the production of war: Killing Company Limited. Military forces are manufacturing death, injury and destruction as sure as Crossley's in Halifax make carpets, Cadbury's produce chocolate and Port Sunlight churns out soap. All sides are in competition to make as many dead as quickly and cheaply as possible. Our profit will be peace, not cash, but with debts of death and despondency.

***

My platoon, replenished with new conscripts, helped keep the enemy's regular attacks at bay north of Flers. We continued to suffer fatalities and injuries, but defending is less hazardous than attacking, unless striking with overwhelming force.

We thought all the villagers of Flers had fled. Yet somehow a few survived the occupation and the bombs and bullets from both sides. Even when fighting raged on the edge of their village, inhabitants returned. Like field mushrooms they appeared overnight in small clusters. Slowly, steadily, stone by stone, reclaiming fallen beams and broken doors, villagers started rebuilding their homes from the rubble. They seemed undaunted using blood-splattered stone on foundations of blood-soaked soil. Weather will wash away those stains over time, but not the pain in their souls. The villagers, mainly women, children and old folks, found battered pots and cooked watery soup and scraps of food. Squatting in front of a small fire of twigs and splinters, an elderly woman, her apron pocket full of flour, made flat bread from dough balls for her family and neighbours. Even though our food stocks fell short, especially when supplies had been delayed, my men shared their rations with locals. It was heart-warming to see their generosity. A small skinny girl approached me, the old lady's granddaughter I reckoned, and asked for *sel*. It was one of the first French words I learnt, and I persuaded Battalion cook to spare a ladle of salt. She returned later with a smile, a thank you in English, and a round of flatbread: the smile was appreciated most. I'll always remember her as Havercake Girl.

The French villagers' belief in a future gave me, and I suspect others, hope. Perhaps life can be rebuilt from the ruins of war. Normality can follow abnormality, sanity after madness. The citizens' presence provided a much-needed reminder of why this whole bloody war was necessary: old folk, women and children needed our protection from Hun hordes. We fight for people who cannot fight for themselves. In our daily quest for territory - a hill, wood, field, farm, river, village, town - I had forgotten it was not for the land itself we are fighting, but for the people who occupy it. The French, like the British and most people everywhere, just want to live normal lives. I bet that includes most Germans too. Everyday people wish to live everyday lives: work, rest, play, spend time with family and friends, marry, raise children, eat, drink and enjoy hobbies.

Alas, normal life can't be lived in war. Peace is ousted by violence; life with death; health with injury; hope with despair.

***

Autumn rains changed the landscape. Firm soil turned soft. Trenches flooded. Mud everywhere in everything. Somme mud became the bane of our lives. It dictated much of what we could do. The landscape, in and out of trenches, turned into a quagmire. Mud wasn't simply a nuisance, an inconvenience, it blighted our whole lives. Our world became a bog in which we fought, slept and ate. Pumps helped reduce water levels in some trenches. Duckboards, 'bathmats', helped movement but had to be scraped and brushed regularly. Almost every man, machine, horse, pony and wagon at some point became stuck. You could walk a few yards with mud at your ankles then suddenly sink in a soft spot to your thighs, sometimes deeper. Motor vehicles could only run on compacted roads and tracks soon churned to resemble deep plough furrows. Owing to the slippery surface and danger of sink holes, walking resembled wading. Progress was slow. The artillery found moving field and heavy guns especially difficult. And dangerous. Many chaps got injured, some crushed to death. Our only consolation, although a minor one, was that the Germans faced the same slimy sticky enemy.

With winter approaching and movement increasingly difficult, General Sir Douglas Haig decided that our final action of 1916 on the Somme would take place between the 13th and 18th November. The assault was planned on a two mile north-south line between the villages of Serre and Beaucourt. We also wanted to oust an irritating brigade of Germans occupying a nearby section of the River Ancre's south bank. In the weeks before the attack a team of miners dug deep tunnels under enemy positions. The mines did the deed. They blasted the Germans away allowing our chaps to advance. The offensive was however only two-thirds successful. Largely thanks to the mines, the 51st Division captured Beaumont Hamel and Beaucourt. But our third target, Serre, remained in German hands.

Several experienced officers and men regretted these gains. They argued that, having captured much high ground in September, we should have overwintered on it. We pushed further forward, but down into the lowlands and valleys. It was a reasonable argument, and I could see both sides. Our winter frontline would not have advanced as far. But it would have been on higher dryer ground. The Germans would then have enjoyed the pleasure of wallowing in winter mud and flooded trenches below. Being on higher ground would also have helped us keep a closer eye on what they were up to. But what's done is done. Forward was the only direction, territory gained the only way to measure success. Our senior generals, especially Sir Douglas Haig, believed we had the Hun on the run. Since 1st July we had broken most of their fortified trenches in the

Somme region. But in the coming months the only victor would be the weather.

***

We survived as slugs under stones during the winter of 1916-17 on the Somme. We lived as no human should live. Nature became our enemy as much as Fritz. On mild days we fought mud. Mud won. On cold days, when biting north-easterlies froze the pot-holed land solid, it proved an equally formidable enemy. We stumbled over surfaces of spikes and ankle-twisting gullies. We endured being constantly frozen, soaked, or both. Every day seemed endless. Every night longer, darker, colder than the previous one. Bitter winds cut so deep they froze our souls, numbed our minds. Even the happiest of chaps became drained of humour. It hurts to smile with skin frozen stiff to the skull. Snot icicles dangled from noses. Lips, raw and sore, cracked, despite a layer of Vaseline or Zam-Buk. Steam rose from every man's piss, expelled on every breath. Coats froze as stiff as straight-jackets.

Morale sank to the lowest I'd seen. But most of us kept going. What's the alternative? Two chaps in the battalion of over a thousand shot out their brains. Only two. A handful were suspected of causing cushy wounds to get out: to get out was to get warm. Owing to the conditions it was often difficult to distinguish genuine accidents from deliberate. Artic winds made bones feel as brittle as dry twigs, joints as arthritic as broken hinges. Frozen fingers fumbled to complete the simplest task. And when warmed by candle or lamp, better still stove or brazier, excruciating pain shot through limbs as frozen flesh regained its feeling. Slipping and sliding on sludge, ice-bound battlefields, snow swirling along our trenches driven by bitter winds, will provide everlasting images of this winter. Yet more memories I'd prefer to forget.

One event caused our faces to crack in painful laughter. The Padre, about to take Sunday morning prayers, found his false teeth frozen in a solid block of ice in his tumbler. He'd slept in a small hut with a stove going all night, but it hadn't prevented a penetrating draught. The service had to be delayed until Padre's teeth thawed out. To the delight of the men, he started prayers by referring to the Gospel of St Matthew, chapter 8, verse 12: 'Earlier this morning, men, I must tell you that there was indeed a "weeping and gnashing of teeth".'

The industrial-scale warfare of the Somme Offensive subsided during the winter as both sides dug-in against the weather. Fighting didn't stop, however, simply the 'production' of death, injury and destruction was scaled back for the season. Artillery shells still fired. Snipers still sniped. The rattling tack-tack-tack of machine guns was ever-present. Men still died from bomb and bullet, mercifully in far smaller numbers. As a frontline infantryman, because we suffer the most, it is easy to forget that most soldiers survive, despite the huge number of deaths and injuries. More live than die. So far.

We carried out several raids during winter when, we hoped, the Germans would be caught cold off guard. And they attacked us, doubtless thinking the same. Both sides however remained wary and vigilant. Over the winter a little ground was gained by us and no ground was lost. We straightened the lines in a few places along the battlefront. Even in the filthy muddled mess of war - perhaps because of it - military discipline demands order. Men, guns, kit, horses, huts, beds and bivouacs all in a nice neat row, please, gentlemen. Even our frontline it seems should be well-groomed, clean cut like the edges of a major's moustache! As if our straight lines and regular columns will provide an orderly war, a clean injury, a tidy death. Yes, corpses too end up in neat lines in their graves.

***

Germany's peace offer of 12th December was rightly rejected. Their terms, believing there would be no reparation for Belgium and France, were totally unacceptable. Most on our side believed the offer was nothing more than a trick. The Germans would use the lull to rearm and close the fighting on the Eastern Front. They would then reinforce their Western Front before resuming their invasion.

No football was played on Christmas Day 1916, not even amongst ourselves, so certainly not with Germans. Not near Flers, anyway. No carols sang out across no-man's-land, in English,

German or French. The mood along the five hundred-mile Western Front, from the Channel coast to the Swiss border, was not one for games or song. Not this year, nor last. 1914 was different. The war was new, almost an adventure with well-trained regular soldiers. The goodwill of Christmas 1914 never returned, the ill will of war entrenched. Christmas Day 1916 became just another fighting day.

If figures are to be believed, and at best they can only be estimates for now, British casualties during the Somme Offensive came to nearly four hundred and twenty thousand. Of these around one hundred and thirty-one thousand died. The French, especially at Verdun, are thought to have lost over three hundred and sixty-four thousand. German casualties are, for obvious reasons, harder to calculate. After the first weeks of July, when we lost far more than them, the tables turned. As we gradually uprooted Germans from their deep trenches, we calculated their casualties amounted to between five and six hundred thousand. We and the French took in several thousand prisoners, and many Germans died deep in our mine craters. Half a million is a lot of men to lose: dead, injured, missing, or prisoner of war.

At this rate of carnage, I wondered if my dream in Loos, where only two men remained alive on earth, would become reality. How long before we reach the last man standing? Where will all the men come from to fight? Will we raise a Boys' Army? At what age will they be considered too young to enlist? Twelve? Ten? Eight? Like the Russians, will we raise a Women's Army? Our women at home are already working in the fields and factories producing food and firearms. Tough jobs. Skilled work. And when they're done in, shall we raise a Girls' Army? This is all nonsense, of course, silly speculation, idle gossip. But every day you hear the question: when will this war end? Workers, men and women, are increasingly going on strike in Britain. If workers can down tools, what's to stop soldiers downing weapons? Doubtless Germans are also asking these questions. How many deaths will be enough deaths to stop the war? What level of carnage will the Kaiser and our new Prime Minister, Lloyd George, accept?

How many deaths can there be? The German Empire population at the outbreak of war was said to be between sixty-five and sixty-nine million. And for how long can this war go on? German Catholics and Protestants fought the Thirty Years War, although nothing on the scale of this one. Britain has a much smaller population than Germany, around forty-six million. Britain against German, man for man, death for death, we would run out of people first. Fortunately, we have the Empire to call on, with a population of around three hundred and fifty million. We also stand alongside the French, with around forty million citizens.

There's increasing talk of the United States of America joining the fray. Our Commanding Officer says their entry into the war would bring three Ms to the show: men, machines, money. Surely the Germans couldn't withstand the combined might of the British Empire, France, Russia *and* the United States of America.

If America declared war on Germany, some believe the Kaiser would accept he was finished. Perhaps President Woodrow Wilson will end the war with words, America's declaration of intent: a winning blow without a bomb or bullet.

CHAPTER 32

April 1917
ARRAS – ACTION AT FAMPOUX

They gassed the horses. At first I believed it to be an accident from misplaced shells. I was wrong. Horses, ponies and mules the target. Despite canvas respirators resembling nosebags of hay, hundreds perished. Many went berserk as the chemicals burnt their eyes, too wild for their handlers to control. The animals tried desperately to scrape the pain away by rubbing and banging their heads on walls, posts, vehicles, tree stumps. Gouged eyes and cut heads resulted, before they slumped to the ground, rolled, kicked, juddered, died. Their death helped our fight. Without these animals to bring forward heavy weapons and ammunition, the Germans became severely incapacitated.

No true Briton, certainly a farmer or countryman, likes to see an animal suffer. Not a rat. Even a louse! A quick death is acceptable and, if to be eaten, desirable. Slow death makes bad meat. Pain should not be part of dying, certainly not for animals. They can feel but can't understand agony. Animals know of danger, of fear. But they don't know of dying because they don't know of death. It was the horses' suffering which upset many of our chaps. This new gas used by our artillery did not deliver instant death to man nor beast, merely a slow and distressing one.

Horses, ponies and mules become animals of war when we are at war. They labour for us in peace. They suffer alongside us in conflict. They pull ploughs and haul guns with equal effort. Animals can be heroic, like Heracles, the goat who saved Bertie's life. Cattle, sheep, pigs and poultry have been victims too, killed in crossfire, or slaughtered to provide food for hungry troops. Carrier pigeons conveying messages are used in their thousands with lofts built into wagons. The French last year awarded a gallantry medal to a pigeon for flying a message vital to the defence of Verdun. We thought it was a tall tale. It wasn't.

I stopped counting how many men I'd shot a long time ago. Survival depends on concentrating on the next kill, not the last one. I also ceased thinking of how many died in bunkers after lobbing grenades. If I saw a victim's face, I tried to forget it. Yet I vividly recall every detail of the two dogs I shot. The first, crazy with rabies and riddled with mange, attacked a fellow soldier on the outskirts of a village. A bullet was the only way to release the punctured arm from its jaws, and the dog from its madness. The second was a large German messenger dog. She was leaping over a trench about fifty yards ahead when I fired. To my shame, it wasn't a clean kill. I'd shot her hips away and she rolled out of sight into a shell hole. I felt terrible knowing she would die a painful death. At thirty yards, forty at a push, I could have thrown a grenade to finish her. But the hole was too far, even for our best grenadiers to reach. There was nothing I could do to ease her pain. A minute or so later the dog's head appeared. Despite her disability and agony, she had crawled to the crater rim. She was determined to fulfil her duty and deliver the message in the canister on her collar. What courage and grit! I was grateful for a second shot. This time I found the centre of her head to relieve the animal's misery - and mine.

My wretched winter in the trenches came to an end early March 1917 with wonderful news. I received orders returning me home - to The Duke of Wellington's Regiment, 2nd Battalion. They too had recently emerged from the trenches and given a much-deserved month of rest. I joined them in billets in the small town of Corbie, nine miles east of Amiens, where the River Ancre flows into the much larger River Somme. Until recently the town had been the centre of two Casualty Clearing Stations which had treated thousands last year during the Somme Offensive.

Some officers maintained that rankers should never return to their former Regiment as an officer. They claimed chaps from the ranks could not command respect if he was remembered as one of the men. But someone at Brigade level clearly ignored that unwritten rule and reunited me with my Dukes. I had that strange feeling again that this was more than coincidence, but absolutely no evidence of deliberate interference. I made enquiries and was told my posting had been routinely signed off at HQ. Any concerns fuddy-duddy officers may have harboured about my conversion to officer status need not have worried. In the year since leaving the Dukes to join the Officer Cadet Battalion, only a handful of men remembered 'Sergeant' Ogden. And most of the officers in my Battalion were new to the Dukes, such was the rate of casualties. The men from the old days were excellent chaps and pleased at my promotion. Because they knew I was once one of them and served in the ranks, I was treated with greater respect. Only one man, Sgt Harry Pratt, would remember me as Private Ogden. He was the first to approach me with a full formal salute, a beaming smile, and a handshake that crushed finger-bones. 'Welcome back, Lieutenant Ogden, I'm very pleased to see you and I'm proud to call you Sir, Sir.' (He looked ten years older since we last met, and I suspect he thought the same of me.)

The Army's Commander in Chief, General Sir Douglas Haig, who replaced Sir John French during December 1915, designated March 1917 as a month of intense training on 'How to Kill Germans'. In 'rest camp' several miles from the front, every spare hour of the day was to be devoted to training. I was part of the instruction team in infantry battle tactics. My life became dedicated to drilling men on how to kill other men. Over the next four weeks our regiment gradually moved northwards into new billets and camps slightly closer to the front. It was as clear as a clean window that another big push was on the cards. We didn't have long to wait.

The Battle of Arras launched in earnest on Easter Monday 9th April along a ten-mile front. The Third Army, under General Sir Edmund Allenby, took the fight to the Germans. My Company remained holding a line in an area I knew like the back of my hand, Flers, fifteen miles south, close enough to hear the first major barrage of the year which commenced on 4th April. The ground shook when at least two mines opened the battle and obliterated any Germans above. Two thousand eight hundred and seventeen guns then commenced blasting the German's Hindenburg Line of trenches, redoubts and pillboxes. To the north of Allenby's Third was General Sir Henry Horne's First Army, ready to attack simultaneously forming a defensive flank. Most northerly of the attacking force came the Canadian Corps of the First Army under General Sir Julian Byng. Their four divisions planned an assault

277

alongside the British on the two-mile length of Vimy Ridge, important high ground six miles north of Arras.

Between our artillery's opening salvo and the infantry's advance at Arras, we received the best news since the war began. On 6th April the United States of America entered the war on our side. Many cheered when we heard President Wilson had declared: 'The world must be made safe for democracy.' Officers and men on hearing the tidings spontaneously shook hands and broadened their smiles. Heads were held higher, chests pushed out, confidence doubled and optimism filled the air. After the sinking of the *Lusitania* last May - and dozens of their innocent cargo ships - Americans decided it was in their best interests to help bring peace to Europe. Many Americans of German extraction and Irish-Americans had opposed the motion. So-called peace-loving socialists also opposed the declaration, as if those of us losing life and limb here were war-loving!

No-one wants peace more than those fighting at the front.

And with the revolution in Russia following Csar Nicholas II's abdication in March, the Americans needed to help stabilise events in the world. If Russia and Germany sign a peace agreement, all the German troops on the Eastern Front will turn their attention to us: the consequences could be calamitous.

Why is good news often soon followed by bad news? Our spirits lifted, then dashed. America joined the war. Hooray! But. And this bad news was a real surprise. Considering the size of the country, America retains a tiny army of just one hundred and thirty-one thousand officers and men. Then, given the effectiveness of German U-boats, it could be many weeks if not months before the first fighting Yank sets foot in France or Flanders. Let's hope we can hold out until their men and weaponry arrive, in whatever numbers.

On hearing the news of America's declaration, after their initial jubilation, some lads turned their attention to less important matters. They hoped the Yanks would bring fresh supplies of a gooey material called chewing gum. This strange substance went on sale here last summer. Some seem addicted to this novelty and at times it was hard to find supplies, even in Paris. Many officers look down upon its use as a common habit and order men to remove it. One captain went so far as to inspect the mouths of men suspected of concealing gum. Another declared it would 'engender poor discipline' in the front line 'and, come the fight, could cause men to choke'. Come the fight, I wanted to tell the inexperienced young officer concerned, there would be far more hazards than chewing gum. I can't see what the fuss is about. The gum loses all its taste after a minute and is a waste of money. Worse, it dries your mouth. Much better to suck a small pebble, especially if you're running low on water.

At 5.30 am on April 9th, five days after the general barrage, the creeping barrage began at Arras immediately ahead of our infantry advance. Our artillery attack, again thanks to excellent aerial photographic reconnaissance, was pinpoint accurate. Gaining that information had not been easy. Many pilots paid the price with their lives when their aeroplanes suffered airborne and ground attack. A dangerous German pilot we'd heard about, Manfred von Richthofen, had apparently flown above our heads for weeks leading many raids. His nickname, Red Baron, is because he's a Baron from Prussia who, we're told, often flies red aircraft. Our RFC chaps described Richthofen as an 'ace', having shot down at least ten enemy aircraft. He was respected and feared in equal measure.

On ground as well as in air, however, we appeared to have gained the upper hand. The new highly sensitive 106 shell fuse ensured bombs burst instantaneously on the slightest contact. This meant that, instead of a shell having to hit hard ground before exploding, it would burst as it touched entanglements to cut a swath through the wire. A gap in barbed wire is a sight welcomed by every infantryman. Eyes light up like a child offered a chocolate - even a whole bar of Cadbury's Dairy Milk! Our strides become longer, bolder, racing towards the barbed-wire breach. Open ground ahead makes the difference between success and failure, life and death. Thousands have died struggling through entanglements, snared on spikes like worms on hooks. Improved smoke shells, screening our advances with dense cloud, also proved effective at stopping German artillery and machine gunners firing accurately. We also deployed for the first time another clever device, the Livens Projector. This contraption throws barrels of gas over one thousand yards. The noxious fumes cover the enemy without any immediate danger of it blowing back on us. The gas virtually paralysed the German artillery. It certainly hampered their retaliation by forcing gun crews to work in their masks. But our gas killed their horses.

At Vimy Ridge the Canadians and, to their right, our chaps, started their advance. Twenty-four thousand men emerged from underground hiding places to surprise the Germans. And surprised they were: some caught in pyjamas! Within hours we had succeeded in taking most of the ridge. Eight miles south-west, the Third Army had advanced over three miles along Scarpe Valley to hills near Monchy-le-Preux, a village six miles east of Arras. Our advance was thanks largely to the Flying Corps. Aircrews continually directed artillery by signalling to the ground where to aim their shells using 'zone calling'. Within minutes of receiving a message artillery guns established their target and, with concentrated accurate shelling, any troublesome German position was knocked out. But success came almost too quickly. Artillery can't advance as fast as infantry. Big guns weighing tons are not as nimble as infantry boots and a rifle. Because the artillery barrage could not keep up, our infantry advance halted. A cavalry attack was quickly arranged to help our push. We gave the Germans a good bruising, but we hadn't broken their backs. Several company commanders argued that if our sixty tanks had operated closer together, a breakthrough could have been achieved. But the tanks had been deployed evenly across the whole front tempering their effectiveness. Had they formed an arrowhead the German line would have been pierced.

A few days after the general bombardment began on 4th April, four tanks rolled up at Monchey-le-Preux to help a battalion of 37th Division break into the village. And as tanks eventually moved into Flers, my Company received orders to move out. We were to join the main Duke of Wellington's Regiment to the east of Arras betwixt two villages, one large, Fampoux, and one small, Roeux. The Scarpe River flowed through both. The Dukes now formed part of 4th Division within Third Army's XVII Corps. The Regiment had experienced a tough time since the start of the Arras offensive. It was to get tougher. Another enemy unexpectedly joined the fight and favoured the Germans: snow.

Neige fell like blazes. In April! In France! We marched seventeen miles through snowstorms north towards our Regiment's main contingent. When spring should deliver warmer weather, winter returned to frustrate our movement. Springtime snow on the Pennine Hills of Yorkshire would not be a surprise. But to fall in France now, when Paris is said to be full of blossom, came as a blow. Locals along the road said it was the first snow in April for years. New drafts in the regiment moaned, some whispering it was a bad omen. I was sorely tempted to tell them this snowfall was nothing to what some of us had endured over the past three years and eight months. But I held my tongue. They'll find out come winter how wet and cold it gets in the lowlands of France and Flanders.

Bad weather impedes attackers on the move more than stationary defenders in their lairs, and the quick-thinking Germans took immediate advantage. They moved most of their big guns back and retrenched out of our range. They could pick us off as we advanced, but we could no longer get to them as easily, like a short-armed boxer struggling to land a punch against a long-armed one.

The Dukes, under the command of Lt-Colonel Alfred Garnett Horsfall, had been ordered to take Fampoux and dig in three hundred yards beyond the village. At 5.15 am on April 9th, during a heavy snowstorm, we marched to the assembly area. After enjoying a hot breakfast and rum ration we set out ready for the attack. A mile south of the Fampoux we suffered heavy fire from Hun howitzers. Most of us were unscathed, except for one private who died from a stray bullet. The Colonel said later: 'Lord knows where it came from.' But ahead of us the 1st King's Own Royal Lancaster Regiment suffered tremendous losses. More than half became casualties and many taken prisoner.

German machine guns restrained our approach to Fampoux until our artillery pasted them. A few Boche riflemen also got their guns on us. Just a few yards ahead of me young lieutenant Albert Taylor copped it and several men took hits in quick succession, none fatally. We took cover for a minute or so before the Colonel issued the order to rush the village. We took our chances and ran to the first line of buildings in Fampoux. I ordered my platoon not to stop or fire along the way. Just keep moving! The village was somewhat larger than we thought, although the Germans seemed in a hurry to leave. It would have been a tough job routing them house by house, building by building. We met no resistance until we approached the last street running through the village. A few Fritz decided to make a fight of it. We bombed them out of three or four houses and several weary fellows emerged into the street with their hands up. One pitiful prisoner could only raise one arm: the other had just been blown clean away. Blood poured down his left side like a red river before collapsing. Despite our medical orderly's best efforts, the fellow died within minutes.

The Boche did however make a stand with machine guns on the outskirts of the village. They held a railway embankment to our right, several trenches, and a line of cottages. The order to advance was still in place and the chaps, mostly first-time fighters, showed great courage as they moved forward. Around eighty men and six officers were lost within two minutes. The rest of us had to lie flat or find the smallest nook or cranny to survive the onslaught. Any man showing the slightest movement or an inch of body was shot to pieces.

Lieutenant-Colonel Horsfall, wisely in my view, halted the advance until artillery support could knock out the enemy's machine guns. But the game looked desperate. To the south a heavy Boche counter-attack had curved behind us. They could not have been a mile away. And to our left, where we had been warned an attack was expected, the rest of the Brigade had not come up the line. The game no longer looked desperate. It looked over. Death or capture seemed inevitable. We were struggling to hold the forward end of the village, and both our flanks had become wide open for the Boche to fill.

Somehow, by charm or cajoling, the Colonel managed to find and persuade a company of Lancashire Fusiliers to join up on our left. They provided the extra weight to keep the Germans at bay, on that flank at least. As if rivalry between English counties still mattered in this Great War, the inevitable light-hearted comment was made that Lancastrians had come to rescue Yorkshiremen! Darkness fell and we expected to be crept up on and attacked with bayonets, knives and clubs. Rope and wire may also be employed at first to strangle victims as quietly as possible until an alarm was raised. But the enemy stayed put overnight. I suspect they believed we would do the same. Few of us found sleep, although sleep found some of the exhausted. If not on sentry duty, I encouraged my men to catch as many winks as they could. Men differ. Some clearly run faster than others. Some stronger. A few chaps have an aptitude or special skill that others don't possess. It's the same with sleep, some chaps need more than others. I advised stiff-minded young officers to allow some leeway with their subordinates: let your men sleep if not on duty. Not all of them took heed and it was noticeable they or their men performed less well. Even after all this time at the front, I could rarely sleep when action was at hand. Nevertheless, I find it astonishing how refreshed I feel after just fifteen minutes of closed-eye stillness.

Dawn arrived and so too the rest of Brigade came into the line. Just in the nick of time. The King's Own Royal Lancaster Regiment, reinforced from reserves after their heavy losses the day before, came in support and held a bridge over the Scarpe River behind us. Over the next two days no territory was gained or lost. The Boche pounded all around and, for the most part, we kept our heads down. Occasionally a platoon made a foolhardy dash to do something rather than nothing. Being able to wait and watch in battle is crucial for survival - and to win the war. In such situations doing nothing is the better than doing something. Some officers, at all levels, don't seem to realise this. And, sure enough, Hun machine guns cut chaps down within seconds of breaking cover. Bravery and stupidity is a lethal combination.

We had been promised additional artillery support, but the guns had been directed elsewhere. We also received an assurance the cavalry would charge the German trenches for us to immediately follow behind. But, as the Colonel said, 'they've jibbed and nothing's going to happen'. We thus spent another day and night in the line lying low. General supplies hadn't turned up either. We only had basic rations to eat, and they were getting low, although water was in good supply. Men apparently couldn't be spared to bring up extra supplies. Some young chaps, as they do, failing to heed sound advice from more experienced heads, had already eaten all their rations and found themselves hungry, or 'clemmed' as the Yorkshire lads said. 'Serves 'em right,' one officer scorned.

With permission from Battalion, under cover of darkness, I led a squad of eight volunteers to return to our assembly area with the objective of replenishing our rations. For the first six hundred yards we moved carefully, crawled, or kept low in the shadows. Snow remained on much of the ground and, with almost full moonlight, snipers and even machine gunners would easily detect movement. Once away from the front zone we made good progress over the remaining four miles of road and track, although I instructed my lads to stay wary. Boche scouts or snipers could have sneaked around our front line and we, walking in the open, provide easy prey, as exposed as rabbits mid-field to a hawk after harvest.

Arriving at the assembly point the reward for me and my volunteers was a hot meal of generous portions. And pints of hot tea! We returned to the front with our haversacks full to the brim and, besides food, we packed in extra Gold Flake and Wild Woodbines. Given the choice, chaps often opted for cigarettes over food. When allowed, some men smoked almost one fag after another. It gave them something to do. I've resisted the temptation to start, but I've often welcomed the whiff of tobacco smoke: it masks the stench of rotting corpses and other terrible smells! Cigs have other uses too: keeping biting insects away. Captain W G Officer (his real name) joined us in February from the Regiment's 1st Battalion in India. He said cigarettes helped avoid malaria. Captain Officer explained he had met Dr Ronald Ross of the Indian Medical Service, who, in 1897, discovered mosquitoes spread the disease. The doctor stressed however that nothing prevented the disease better than sleeping inside a muslin net.

Before returning to the front with our provisions, I asked for my Company's mail and was handed a bundle. The top letter was addressed in a neat hand: '2nd Lieut. Albert Edward Taylor, 2nd Battn Duke of Wellington's Regiment ... '. As he died just in front of me, if the commanding officer would allow, I wished to write personally to his next of kin. I'll tell them how bravely Albert died leading his men proudly into combat.

Before we left with our supplies, I sweet-talked the quarter-master to allow me a jar of rum. We'd known each other since before the war and he a long-serving regular. 'As you well know, Sir, as you are now a "Sir", it's against Standing Orders,' he said with faked severity. 'You'll get me shot if I were to slip this 'ere jar into this spare sack of yours down 'ere.'

I told him not to worry, I never miss at close range!

After the night's foray, I did eventually succumb to sleep. The ten-mile trip, a good hot meal, plenty of tea and, for me, a rare tot of rum, helped my eyelids fall. On waking I felt greatly refreshed, even after three hours curled on a stone floor in the corner of a roofless cottage. Overnight we heard that at first light, with or without artillery or cavalry, we would make a move. However, instead of going head-to-head with the Hun, who will have strengthened their positions, we planned to drift right. This would take us to a railway embankment, the station, and houses at a crossroads north of the small village of Roeux. The ground immediately outside the village was swamp and deep mud, making this route almost impassable. The Colonel had managed to get artillery to offer a barrage, but it was too thin and fast. We couldn't keep up, although we captured a German trench held by Prussians. What remained of our company, about eighty able-bodied, climbed the embankment, which proved far steeper than it had looked from a distance. Only fifty-four of us made it across. We came under such heavy fire we could only lie in a low bank all day, or die. The Boche, unknown to us for they hadn't shown their hand, were strongly fortified beyond this point. Another Brigade was to have been on our left offering support. Days later I learnt an officer, quite a senior one, had 'misread' the order and gone elsewhere. Consequently, many Boche trenches, and all the buildings between the railway and the Athies-Plouvain Road, never came under attack, and all stiff with machine guns. Colonel Horsfall came to view the cause of the hold-up and noticed our predicament. We could see that he ordered movement along the river to support us and continue the attack. But the swamps were too deep and there was no cover. Adding to our woes, the snow started to again fall thick and fast. Each flake held a unique pattern, a soft white diamond of nature, too beautiful to be falling on fields of ugly fighting.

The men became exhausted, understandably so. For four days and nights we had secured little rest. And last night, experiencing two Boche counter-attacks, was the worst. Even the heaviest sleepers could not have snatched more than two hours in total. Over these days we had also launched two major attacks ourselves, each followed by digging in, all the while being heavily shelled and sprayed by machine guns. Marvellously, the chaps somehow found the reserves deep inside their bodies and souls and rallied to maintain the fight. Even though this war had become dull for me, I found myself in admiration of Tommy Atkins, every one of them. Relief finally came during late night on April 13th following over five days of frantic fighting with little respite. A fresh Brigade came up behind us and took on the task of attacking the buildings north of the railway. I was pleased to report that not one of my fifty-four men isolated on the embankment was injured in our time there, nor during our cold and wet withdrawal in darkness through the bog.

***

My Battalion of the Duke of Wellington's Regiment went into reserve and we marched about twenty miles to billets west of Arras. Considering the attacks we made and received, our casualties were light. Of approximately one thousand men in our Battalion only one officer - the young 2nd Lt Taylor - was killed. (I wrote to his family in Yorkshire providing the details of his death. A letter by return from his father expressed the family's gratitude for the time and trouble I had taken to write.) Ten officers suffered wounds, half of whom would eventually be capable of resuming battle duties. One hundred and eighty-five other ranks suffered death or serious injury.

Our 'rest' consisted of marching and counter-marching. We halted for four days in one village during which we received the next draft of replacements. I was again the designated training officer and assigned my best men to instruct new Lewis-gun teams, bombers and grenadiers. Watching and supervising their work, I was impressed by the general standard. We didn't always receive top-hole drafts. But this batch seemed all right. I spoke to the new chaps about what to do and not to do in battle. They had, of course, undergone basic training before crossing the English Channel. Most had undergone General Sir Douglas Haig's special 'How to Kill Germans' training too. But now, near the front, reality closer than theory, it was noticeable how they paid more attention to what was said. New drafts also looked closely at men returning from the forward lines fresh with flesh wounds - and old scars. Some talked of their battle experiences. Others didn't. New chaps listened to the men who talked while watching the ones who remained silent.

One new chap, through his platoon sergeant, asked to see me with a special request. Since becoming an officer I've found most of these appeals fall into one of three kinds. The first and reasonable plea is for compassionate leave. Mother, father or a sibling had died at home. The second, and usually ridiculous request, is to be excused from certain fatigues for one reason or another. One chap had the cheek to say digging gave him back ache! I told him that *everyone* got back ache digging trenches, including former miners. I recommended he carried out *additional* trenching - to build up his back muscles! (Nobody else in the Company then makes that request for quite some time.) The third reason for a meeting with their platoon or company officer comes in the form of a confession: the chap's done something wrong and, because he's voluntarily admitted the offence, hopes to receive a lighter punishment.

I waited to see what the new chap wanted. Sergeant Foster quick-marched him to the front of my 'desk' - a broken door resting on empty boxes - and stood him at attention. I doubted the boy was yet fifteen. Had someone said he was twelve, I would believe them. The scraggy lad was trembling from his lips to his knees and I thought he was going to burst into tears. '24436 Private Crossland, Sir,' he said. His voice hadn't broken and was as light as a little girl's. For the first time in my life I called someone 'son' when I told him to stand easy and explain why he'd asked to see me. Perhaps I was becoming long in the tooth - at the grand age of two and twenty - or because he looked so young. He glanced at the sergeant, standing to one side, but it would have been inappropriate for me to ask the NCO to leave, and undermine his authority.

'You can say whatever is on your mind, Private, nothing surprises Sergeant Foster these days,' I said, determined never to say 'son' again.

He remained silent. I looked at Foster.

'Come on now lad, spit it out,' the Sergeant said. 'The officer hasn't got all day.'

After a pause, he did, blurting his words loudly and all together like a burst of bullets from a machine gun. 'Can I please Sir make a special request to be allowed to become a sniper because that's what my brothers was and they're both dead now Sir but I think I will be third time lucky as they say Sir and that's what I wanted to say Sir thank you.'

Foster and I looked at each other bemused, not at the sad content in his request, but by the rapid-fire delivery.

'Tell me about your brothers,' I asked. He explained, in a slightly calmer voice, both had died within a few weeks of each other during 1915, one at Aisne and the other at La Bassée. I remembered both, but I didn't reveal my knowledge of them.

'How good a shot are you?' It was the obvious question.

The lad turned to the sergeant who reported that he was, indeed, an excellent rifleman. 'Despite his youth and inexperience,' Foster added.

'You do know, Crossland, that sniping entails far more than just being able to hit targets?'

'Yes, Sir,' he said. 'Me brothers told us how they had t' creep int' positions and stay still for 'ours, days on end even, sometime well away from rest of t' men. Tommy told us 'e spent loads o' time in a false tree. Didn't believe him at first till 'e told us engineers made models of 'em t' fool Germans.'

In memory of the Crossland brothers I felt obliged to help the lad fulfil his wish, despite his youth. And I admired his pluck. It took guts to go above the head of your sergeant to see an officer. I would never have dared.

'I'll promise you this, Private,' I said. 'Let's see how you manage for a month. You should be able to get some shots off at least, even if we don't go over the top, or the enemy doesn't rush us. And, if

Sergeant Foster thinks you're up to it after some action, we'll get you trained.'

'Thank you, Sir, thank you.' The lad smiled from ear-to-ear.

'But don't go shooting out of turn. Do so only when ordered unless a fight is on, otherwise you could cause an unnecessary bout of "hate" that we don't want or need.'

'No, Sir. I mean yes, Sir,' he spluttered, confusing all of us.

'Remember the secret of good sniping is to shoot and not be seen. The bullet should strike as a complete surprise. Your target should not know he's dead - if you see what I mean.'

'Yes, Sir. Thank you, Sir.'

'Meanwhile, do the best you can at whatever you're asked. Watch and learn from the good chaps and I'm sure you'll do your brothers proud.'

He cried, the mention of his brothers causing the tears.

'Now, now, lad, we'll have none of that,' Foster said.

The boy quickly pulled himself together with a snuffle and muffled apology. He wiped his wet face with the arm of his over-sized uniform. I couldn't help but notice his thin forearm.

'That's all, Crossland,' I said, and the Sergeant marched him out at the double.

His brothers had been excellent 'butt-notchers', so called because most snipers carved a scratch in the butt of their rifles with their clasp knife to keep a tally of their kills. When Sgt Foster returned it was obvious he wished to say something: the tell-tale sign was to clear his throat while lingering at his desk before sitting. 'Come on Sergeant, spit it out,' I said.

'Well, Sir, if you don't mind my saying, I can't see the lad becoming a sniper for a year or two, even if he makes it through. He's just not strong enough.'

'Nor can I, Sergeant,' I replied. 'You're right, he's as scrawny as a tight-fisted farmer's scarecrow. But after losing two brothers he deserves to live with hope in his heart. He needs to believe he'll be "third time lucky". Goodness knows the sacrifice his family has made and the sadness they've endured. Let's give the lad a chance. If he's only half as good as either of his brothers, he'll do well enough.'

289

'I see, Sir. Fair enough,' he said. Sgt Foster removed his cap and sat at his 'desk', constructed with four planks across the back of two burnt settees. 'You knew 'em then?' he asked.

'Yes, both brothers. Hard workers. Great shots. Tommy was in our team when we won the Regimental range trophy in '13, and Ernie in '14.'

The Sergeant paid attention to his paperwork. After a minute or so he said, 'I'll build him up a bit, Sir. The lad, I mean. I'll make sure he gets his full entitlement, eats it all up, doesn't swap grub for cigs and the like.'

'That's good, Sergeant, very good,' I said. 'Over and above. Thank you.'

***

By 14th April 1917 it was clear the first phase of our offensive east of Arras had failed to live up to expectations. The Allies had however advanced to better positions. In so doing we seized over two hundred artillery guns. Some will provide additional weaponry if shells were also captured. Those guns not usable will be melted to make more of our own. It seems the only thing in war going to waste is human life: life can't be returned, repaired or reused. At least horse meat can be eaten and their bones rendered for glue.

We also captured around thirteen thousand prisoners in the Arras action. Attitudes to them varied widely. A few chaps wanted *every* German dead out of hate and revenge, even fear. Hun prisoners, others groused, eat our food and use up supplies. Prisoners need men to guard them, depriving the front of fighters. But thirteen thousand unarmed captives can't be slaughtered in cold blood like turkeys for Christmas. Savagery must stop somewhere. Treating prisoners reasonably well is a good place to start, however much it sticks in the craw. Free soldiers with guns should respect captured unarmed soldiers.

But in the white heat and immediate aftermath of battle, when friends and comrades have suffered death and injury, restraining rage takes tremendous willpower. Some see nothing but red, especially first-time fighters. They're horrified, terrified, shaking uncontrollably, heart pounding. Panting. Sweating. Cold shivers. Some will have soiled their pants and seen sickening scenes that will stick with them to their dying day. Everyone will feel relief being alive, having been so close to death. It's understandable, if not always acceptable, to blow a brass fuse. Most of us have taken revenge on the nearest German at one time or another: sometimes a blind eye needs to be turned.

The Army teaches men to kill. It orders them to fight. You can't then expect soldiers to stop suddenly to become gentle saints, no more than a ship in the sea can stop dead or turn on a sixpence. It takes time for the fiery impulse of killing to cool, the icy fear of battle to thaw. Aggression and fear can't be doused as a candle flame. It takes more than a moment to calm down and see the world in normal colours.

Two days later, April 16th, we learnt our British and Canadian offensive around Arras was partly a diversionary action. The French, under General Robert Nivelle, launched a far larger offensive in the Champagne region across a twenty-mile ridge between the rivers Ainse and Ailette. When I heard where their attack took place, I shuddered: *Chemin des Dames*. It was near the Ladies Path in September 1914, several lifetimes ago, where the Expeditionary Force dug our very first trench in this war. We thought then the trench was merely a quick tactical defensive measure. Little did we know our simple shallow scrapes would develop into a complex underground fighting method: trench warfare.

April's unseasonal cold weather curtailed the French attack too. The Germans stubbornly remained entrenched at *Chemin des Dames*. We heard the French had suffered tremendous losses, around one hundred and eighty-seven thousand killed, injured or missing. Whatever we believed about the French at the beginning of this war, if actions speak louder than words, they have proved beyond doubt to be clever, cunning, brave and extremely resilient. Rumours circulate that the top French generals routinely disagree with ours. 'Stubborn' and 'obstinate' apparently often used to describe them. Perhaps it is exactly those qualities that have saved their country from being overrun by the Hun. Politicians and military chiefs will have their arguments, although almost every French person I've met has been kind and helpful. Some French women may have been *too* friendly to our troops, especially in the cities and large towns.

Venereal disease, a dose of dreadnought, remains a problem despite 606 injections and more 'short arm' inspections of men. And not just here. VD has become more prevalent in Blighty. A Royal Commission was established last autumn to investigate the problem. Doctors and politicians blame prostitutes for the spread of the disease. These women 'haunt the camps of men in training and beset their arrival at stations when they return from leave'. A Dr Mary Scharlieb in London told the newspapers these strong young men 'overflowing with animal strength and spirits' became 'easy prey for the prostitutes'. I'm not as clever as a doctor, but you can't blame the women alone for tempting the men: chaps can say 'No' and keep their trousers buttoned up.

The following weeks we waited, waited more, went nowhere. Inaction breeds boredom, so we kept the men busy. Besides routine repairs and improvements, we ran regular battle and fitness exercises. The Regiment returned to our routine of six days in the forward line, six in Brigade reserve and rest periods of a few days. On patches of less muddy land games of football and rugby were enjoyed. This quiet period was not however without danger. Artillery shells continued to fall, and not only at the front. Several landed as far back as the rest camps, thankfully without injury or significant damage.

My platoon carried out one successful reconnaissance mission during this period. We discovered an underground store of German gas cylinders. Being able to provide its location accurately, three RFC aircraft dropped several bombs on the exact spot and destroyed their deadly supplies. Intelligence officers believed Fritz was waiting for the wind to change direction and then we would have suffered a gas attack. It was a good feeling knowing we'd turned the tables on the Hun and prevented casualties.

The only sadness that night was losing one young lad. We believe he lost his way in the dark, perhaps falling into a shell hole breaking his neck or knocking himself out. It was easily done. We don't know if the lad died or was captured, the former more likely. The thought of writing to the Crossland family informing them that a *third* son was 'missing, presumed dead' filled me with dread. Pte Walker Crossland yearned to become a sniper like his two brothers before him. He hoped to be 'third time lucky', he told me and Sgt Foster. He wasn't. There is a fourth brother, Harry. He is or soon will be old enough - or look old enough to get through the deliberately short-sighted recruitment staff - to join up. I hope Harry doesn't fool the recruiters. I hope the Army tell him to stay at home, where one living son might bring a little comfort to his kin. Three sons are more than sufficient price for parents to pay in any war. My hope will prove futile. Harry Crossland will believe he can defy the odds. He'll be obsessed, like men who lose their shirt playing cards and believe the next hand will deliver four aces. He'll ignore pleas from his parents. He'll be driven to follow his brothers because he shares the same blood and be willing to spill it. War twists minds: Harry might feel a failure if he survives.

Snipers and machine gunners continued to keep our heads down in the fire line. But there's always one Mr Smart Alec who thinks he's invincible - until a bullet blows his brain away. There's always a chap who looks over the parapet 'just for a second' - and one second later his number's up. There's also always one unfortunate chap who's a bit dim-witted. He forgets to keep low in a shallow trench and gets sniped. When one of these simpletons is in my platoon, I ask his corporal to keep an extra eye on him.

***

A shared enemy as mighty as the German Army doesn't guarantee harmony and friendship among Allies. Our politicians and generals argue about what actions to take, priorities and policies. Jealousy, rivalry and disagreement continue as in peacetime. Men at the front too, even with Fritz lurking a grenade-throw away, have their squabbles, petty and serious.

Lieutenants Digwood and Michael could not get on. None of us understood the root of their constant bickering. Both are gone now. Their quarrels irrelevant, their disagreements as dead as them. Many in the junior officers' mess that night recalled the bitterness the first of many rows caused. Following arguments people often remember the resentment yet forget what the squabble was about: the feelings stay, the thoughts go. Hostility between the two lingered for the remaining month of their lives. Although divided in life they were united in death, killed by the same bomb.

One disagreement blew up when Lt George Digwood, 22nd Manchester Regiment, objected to Lt Michael's pair of shotguns. The twelve-gauge guns, both with twenty-nine inch barrels, had been made by the London gun-maker Watson Bros. They were as fine as any I had seen bagging grouse on the Yorkshire moors. Their matching stocks shaped from the finest walnut. Deep acanthus engravings adorned the metal sideplates. We local lads and farmers used basic guns, scratched and bashed, and usually thrown into the back of a hay wagon after shooting a few rook or pigeon. It was the toffs from London who wielded these wonderful weapons when I was beating for local gamekeepers. Servants cleaned their masters' valuable guns spotless before carefully packing them away. Even now, as a 2nd Lieutenant, such hand-crafted guns are beyond the depths of my pocket.

Lt Luke Michael brought his shotguns to the front, as many officers do. They may come in handy against the Hun, they all said. In fact, they hoped for a spot of shooting when off duty. French partridges were much talked about, although no bird in northern France could offer the challenging sport presented by grouse on a windswept Yorkshire moor. When Lt Michael opened the guns' oak calf-lined case, Digwood noticed the gun-maker's label on the lid. Printed on it were pictures of flags and medals and, in bold, an endorsement which read: BY APPOINTMENT TO H.I.M. THE SULTAN OF TURKEY THE SHAH OF PERSIA.

'How can you possibly use these?' Digwood snapped, his puffy face rage-red. He stood pointing at the label inviting all those around to view the offence and endorse the accusation.

'What?' Michael quizzed, taken aback.

'Using these guns is nothing short of traitorous.'

'Sorry, Digwood, old boy, as usual I haven't the foggiest idea what on earth you are talking about.'

'Turkey is our enemy, you damn fool,' Digwood stormed. 'They're in league with the Germans. Those bastards starved our chaps to skin and bone in Kut. Massacred twenty-five thousand of ours at Gallipoli. God knows what torture they're inflicting on those they captured. And you're using their guns!'

Michael laughed. Enough was enough. Digwood lunged at him. They fell to the floor fighting. Rolling one way, then another, arms flailing, legs kicking. I and others rushed to stop the scrap. After a struggle, with one innocent helper taking an accidental blow in the eye, we prised them apart.

'You're the damn fool,' Michael shouted, shaking and breathless after Digwood's assault. 'The guns aren't made in Turkey, you ignoramus. They're made in London. Only the walnut comes from Turkey. And that came over twenty years ago when my father commissioned the guns to be made.'

As if he hadn't heard Michael's explanation, Digwood struggled for his release to continue the fight. 'Even so,' Digwood yelled, 'you shouldn't....'

'What the hell is going on?' roared a senior officer, bursting into the mess on hearing the altercation. 'Well?'

After an embarrassing silence, Michael, still catching his breath, answered, 'A silly misunderstanding, Sir. That's all.' A trickle of blood escaped Michael's nose and gathered in his moustache, like paint on a brush.

'That's all? What do you take me for? It looks somewhat more than that.' The Major, from the Royal Horse Artillery, stood bolt upright, legs apart, thumbs tucked inside his tunic belt and fingers tapping, still clearly waiting for the details.

After a few seconds, Digwood confessed. 'Entirely my fault, Sir,' he said, shrugging off those still restraining him. 'I got the wrong end of the stick, Sir. I apologise. Unreservedly.'

'It's clearly not to me you should be apologising,' the Major barked, glancing towards Michael.

Resembling a resentful four-year-old, Digwood muttered, 'And to you, Michael, apologies.'

Digwood offered his hand to shake, and it was taken. All those watching suspected this was a well-acted gesture without sincerity to appease the senior officer.

'By Jove,' the Major said, 'haven't we got enough Hun to fight without these schoolboy tantrums? Thank heavens there are no men around. If they'd witnessed officers fighting each other like common urchins, we'd be having riots in the trenches, don't you know.'

'Yes, Sir,' Digwood and Michaels said simultaneously.

'Remember, you are supposed to be officers *and* gentlemen, not officers and ragamuffins!'

The officer's anger vanished as quickly as it had arrived. When he turned to leave, he noticed the shotguns and pointed to the Watson Bros label and the Sultan's endorsement. 'Do I take it this was the subject of the altercation?'

'Yes, Sir,' Digwood said.

'Ah, don't tell me, you mistakenly believed these guns to be Turkish.'

'Yes, Sir. I just didn't realise...'

'And these fine shotguns are yours?' the major addressed Michael without waiting for Digwood's excuse.

'Yes, Sir,' Michael answered. 'Well, my father's actually, Sir. He was rather hoping I'd blast a few Boche away with them.'

'However worthy your father's desire, I'm afraid it's going to take far bigger guns than these to shift the Hun out of their holes.'

'Yes, Sir, of course.'

'May I?'

'Be my guest, Sir.' The officer carefully lifted one of the shotguns from its case.

'Wonderful,' he said, admiring the weapon. 'Beautifully weighted,' he added, pointing the gun skywards to some imaginary bird. 'Such marvellous workmanship.'

The Major announced that he would take no action against Digwood on this occasion. Because of another big push days away, he didn't wish to be wasting senior officers' time dealing with 'this nonsense'.

***

As the war dragged on with no end in sight frustration festered, anger flared, squabbles erupted. More than a fist was thrown at times.

Under darkness, in the mayhem of battle, it was easy to 'accidentally' shoot your own enemy: a reviled sergeant, an officer who had deprived a man of leave or rum ration, a fellow soldier who had cheated at cards. In battle, what's one more death? At night in thick cloud - natural or man-made poisonous gas - with bangs, flashes, fire and gun-smoke, encased in gas masks, who would know it was your rifle that felled the fellow in front of you?

One of many rumours told of a chap shooting a colleague from his Pals' Battalion because he planned to marry the victim's wife. This extraordinary war creates extraordinary stories. Many false. Some unbelievable. Most true.

Chaps are driven to do unusual things unexpectedly in extreme conditions. I've found that not all good people always do good deeds. Facing danger, they can let you down. On the other hand, not all hitherto bad people are always bad. Under duress they can surprise you with their kindness and selfless bravery.

This war has also taught me that most people are at their best when the situation is at its worst.

CHAPTER 33

Summer 1917
TOWARDS YPRES

Dark clouds rolled over Belgium and northern France on the first day of the new offensive, the last day of July. They unleashed their weapon, rain. Yet again the weather played a major part in this war. Had the rain stopped, like summer showers should, success would have been ours. Except for three days of respite, it rained throughout August 1917. Some days it poured, other days, drizzle. Occasionally a fine mist descended penetrating every pore of your body, every fibre of your clothes. It gently moistened faces with droplets, as spray downwind of a distant waterfall. Like the unexpected snowstorms in April at Arras, locals claimed so much rain in August 'unusual'. An elderly Frenchman, skin as wrinkled as old boots, blamed the strange weather on the war. Shells disturbed the clouds, he said, explosions had interfered with nature.

A tall broad-shouldered Punjabi company sergeant-major from the Indian 4th Cavalry, sporting a fine moustache and beard, put it, 'Sir, it pelt down dog and cat every day'. I did think to tell him we usually say cats and dogs. However, at the time, surrounded by rotting human and animal flesh, such a point of order didn't seem important. Anyway, I thought, what's wrong with saying raining dog and cat? It's as sensible as raining cats and dogs, nonsense based on a legend that cats cause rain and dogs' howls whip up wind.

'Déjà vu,' the colonel said at Brigade HQ briefing, 'it's a feeling we've experienced before at Ypres.' I wanted to correct the colonel more than the Cavalry CSM: it was not a feeling, but a real experience. I was there the first time in Ypres, and I'm here now. Conditions are not the same as at the end of 1914. They are worse, far worse. And once again we began to exist in a mud-soaked world.

Most officers and men remained remarkably cheery. My platoon chaps especially were magnificent. Naturally they groused now and then, and rightly so. Complaining makes a person human, shows you want things better. Having a good moan provides an outlet for anger,

298

although it can worsen situations too. But my men gritted their teeth, got on with what needed to be done. As one of my four corporals declared in front of his squad: 'Sir, we lads have a choice through all this. We can frown or we can smile. We've chosen to smile.' And they all did!

It was acknowledged at Division HQ, perhaps at Corps HQ, that our Battalion's sector on the Passchendaele salient was the wettest of the wet in Flanders. Our trenches were hardly above the land's natural water table. In many places water seeped in the trench as soon as dug. We built sandbag breastworks to raise our defences. But even when it was not raining we still endured endless yards of trenches knee-deep in a thick brown soup of slime and slush. Nowhere lower for the water to flow existed. Trenches became permanent channels of water and, worse, human and animal waste. The stench as bad as the wet. As many men succumbed to sickness as the enemy's weaponry. All of us at some time suffered a bout of sickness and diarrhoea, compounding the problem. In our sector alone hundreds of yards of trenches became streams of sludge, most overflowing their banks. Trench walls caved in. Sandbag fortifications sank as easily as sandcastles on incoming tides. Dugouts and shelters suddenly flooded, often causing casualties and emergency rescue. To our disgust, we discovered the Germans deliberately dug ditches from their trenches towards us - sending their sewage streaming into ours.

Disease-ridden water with urine and excrement, another weapon of war.

In heavy rain men became marooned as trenches around them flooded. But they risked being gunned if they left the trench in daylight. Most lingered for hours until nightfall to make good their escape, often waiting up to their necks in cold stinking bilge. Men died in flooded trenches unable to escape the deluge, sucked under and drowned like unwanted pups in a brick-weighted sack in the canal. Brave chaps, usually under fire from machine gunners and snipers, tried desperately to rescue trapped colleagues as the swill rose threatening to drown them. But once a man had sunk to his waist, unless a rope, ladder, plank or suchlike could be quickly found, the chances of his rescue were slim. The deep mud of

Flanders grabs, grips and squeezes as if a hungry ground needs to eat your body. Men considered themselves lucky if, after slipping off the track or duckboards, they only lost their boots going to or from the trenches. They completed their journey in socks and hoped to find spare boots. An injured or dead man's boots would suffice. If boots were no longer needed, they would be left at the front for others. The fitting might be too tight or too loose, but any pair of boots is better than none. One boot is better than none, too.

Trench foot again became a major problem. It was to be expected, trying to survive in swamps like frogs. Nearly one in three men suffered to some degree in my battalion of four hundred and eighty officers and men. Feet first turn pale and the skin wrinkles. Catch it at this stage and recovery is good. If not, feet then become red, swollen and very painful. Legs are weakened and ulcers often form, the circulation of blood being poor. At this stage trench foot is crippling. It's possible some chaps tie their puttees too tight, ignoring advice. Despite orders to regularly apply whale grease and give their feet a good rubbing, foolish chaps ignore the condition. They think it manly to carry on, girly to complain. A few suffered to the stage where gangrene set in! Amputations resulted. It was believed some men deliberately allowed their feet to deteriorate in the hope it would become a Blighty condition. It was hard if not impossible to tell the genuine sufferer from the shirker. Some chaps seemed more susceptible to trench foot than others, particularly those with pale skin or who had desk jobs before Army life. Away from the front, to the disapproval of one of my senior officers, for he thought I was being too familiar with the men, I occasionally demonstrated the procedure to help prevent trench foot to new chaps. I'd remove my boots, dry and rub my feet, apply foot grease or Vaseline, sometimes powder, and order the men to do likewise. I wanted to show there was no shame in looking after your feet. Feet are, I always said, an infantryman's first weapon: you can't march without 'em!

Many men carried the Bible, a New Testament at least. It's said they've saved lives by stopping shrapnel or bullets entering the body. Increasing numbers have however abandoned their belief in God because, they say, God's abandoned them. Or joined the Germans. Prayers for the rain to stop remained unheard, certainly unheeded.

The rain dragged us all down at some point. Seeking to lighten the mood in the officers' bunker, a friendly Canadian lieutenant talked about the Cree, native Indians who dance around something called a totem pole to make the rain fall. He jigged and hopped demonstrating their dance. But he couldn't say if they had a dance to make the sun shine, and continued larking around. We laughed at the Canadian's antics until abruptly interrupted. 'So what the hell was the point of saying that?' a major snarled. 'Pointless. Totally bloody pointless. Who cares what those savages do?'

The Canadian was taken aback, as were we all, including a French priest visiting the front. Wisely, I thought, the young lieutenant, extremely tall and thin, ignored our officer's rudeness to avoid any argument. By so doing he maintained a certain dignity. He simply gathered his things, donned his helmet, and spoke quietly saying he must get back to Brigade HQ before dawn. He received apologetic smiles from the rest of us as he left the dugout. The priest had a short conversation in French with the Canadian. As the officer departed the priest, I was later told, wished him 'God's speed and blessing'. No sooner had the lieutenant left when a shell exploded outside the dugout. Two of us rushed to check on the men. We found the Canadian's arm, severed completely from his body, smouldering. His shattered torso rested twenty feet away in the shell's crater. There was nothing to do or could be done, except call for a stretcher bearer. I carried the man's severed arm and placed it across his chest. Even after the many times I've carried them, I'm always surprised how heavy human parts are. Heads seem as weighty as iron.

The ill-tempered major telephoned Battalion HQ to inform them of the Canadian officer's death. 'A fine young officer,' he was heard to say, causing eyebrows to be raised. Fatefully, it was the first shell to fall nearby for several hours, and the last until late afternoon. If the lieutenant had left our bunker just ten seconds earlier, or ten seconds later, he would still be alive. If the priest had not delayed him in conversation, he would still be alive. If the major had not shown his short temper, the young lieutenant would have stayed with us a little longer. If, if, if.... It was not to be. In all those hours of peace, before and after, he chose those seconds to step outside into mortal danger. One random bomb. One random moment. Damn bad luck or similar words echoed around the bunker until I fell asleep. When chaps say a bomb or bullet had his name on it, it's easy to dismiss the idea as nonsense. But it makes you think...

Mid-September I received an order to attend Brigade HQ. Previous experience had taught me not to ask the reason; I wouldn't get an answer. The Battalion Adjutant's face gave nothing away handing me the chit, neither smiling nor frowning. I suspected a transfer, probably to a training unit. I had apparently an aptitude for instructing, and several officers reported this up the command. I hoped however to stay on the Western Front. Unlike many, I did not wish for a transfer to Britain. I hadn't done my bit until Fritz was beaten. I started in the war here and I wished to end it here. After three years and one month, apart from a few minor injuries, I remained unscathed. I still dismissed luck as the reason although, thinking of the Canadian, I wonder if a bullet or shell waits out there with my name on in it.

After completing the morning's inspection of my platoon and changing into my 'Sunday best' (but still well-worn) uniform and new pattern cap, I realised I was running late. No motor transport was available and it would take too long to walk the five miles to Brigade HQ. I went to the stock lines and the corporal selected a handsome gelding. I'm not a good horseman, having mostly ridden farm ponies, nags and cart horses. The raven-black cavalry mount was far superior to anything I'd handled. I should have confessed that a pack pony would have been more akin to my riding ability. But I stayed silent, and I had told the corporal I was in a hurry. I would have to keep this frisky lad on a tight rein otherwise I'd be falling off. Nine-year-old Lucius sensed my insecurity, but also my respect for him as a fine beast. He delivered a smooth ride over very rough terrain and I gave him much praise and thorough pat on his neck. I was sorely tempted to ask if I could keep him. His cavalry officer had been sniped off his back. But I'd managed thus far without a horse and the temptation passed.

Brigade HQ was housed in a badly damaged chateau. Repairs made it reasonably habitable for officers and staff. Planks covered broken windows and shell holes had been filled with rubble and sealed with mortar. Canvas stretched across the roof where slate tiles had not yet been replaced. To one side of the small mansion an area the size of a rugby pitch had been levelled. Royal Engineers had dug a deep drainage ditch around the perimeter and installed pumps. It signalled a clear intent to keep at least one area of ground in Flanders free of mud.

Two full companies, about two hundred men and several officers, were assembling for a parade, a ceremony of some kind. A podium, large enough to accommodate a dozen officers, had been erected with three steps at either end. Tall freshly painted white poles stood immediately behind the plinth. The Union Flag and various Regimental Colours fluttered when the breeze caught them. I reckoned Divisional or even Corps commanders were about to visit, such was the bustle to get the ranks right and every soldier shipshape.

I dismounted Lucius and he was led away by a young private. The sergeant in charge of the greeting party, standing behind a trestle table, asked my name. When he found it on the list I was directed to a stone staircase at the side of the chateau. I couldn't read the sign in French, but I suspect it meant the same as Tradesmen's Entrance. Looks can deceive, for the door at the top opened to a large hallway, still elegant despite bomb damage. A Regimental Sergeant Major greeted me warmly, even though I was late. But, to my relief, I was not the last. Six chaps were expected shortly by motor bus, he said. The RSM ticked my name on his attendees' list and he pointed to a waiting room. Forty or so chaps, officers and other ranks, stood in groups drinking tea. And there was cake! What occasion was this? It looked peculiar: tea was served from a battered army urn into the most delicate ornate cups I'd ever set eyes on. A lieutenant asked what I was 'up for'. I must have looked blank-faced because he went on: 'What have you been recommended for, you know, a ribbon, a DCM? What, not a DSO or VC?' Everything fell into place. I'd forgotten about my promised award, which turned out not to be the Distinguished Service Medal nor the Distinguished Service Order, nor the Victoria Cross. My medal wasn't however the biggest surprise of the day.

The RSM interrupted the gathering and called out our names and a number, the order in which we were to receive our awards. A

Royal Fusilier asked were we not to wait for a few more chaps. 'I'm afraid not, Sir, they've been delayed,' the RSM reported. 'I've orders to crack on, gentlemen, if you don't mind. We're already fifteen minutes late and we can't keep the generals waiting.' Several asked their names and who exactly was presenting the awards. Most of us assumed it would be the Brigade or, time allowing, perhaps the Division commander. 'Oh, gentlemen, hadn't you heard?' The RSM knew perfectly well we remained in the dark. He smiled teasingly, paused, and spilt the beans. 'Your much-deserved awards, gentlemen, will be presented by no less a personage than the General Officer Commanding, Second Army, General Sir Herbert Plumer.'

Surprised, gasps of 'good grief' and 'well I never' and 'by George', the traditional battle-cry of English soldiers, could be heard. Many, unthinkingly, hand-brushed and straightened their tunics, tightened ties, adjusted cap badges and rid boots of unwanted blemishes. The RSM escorted us to the parade ground and sat us, in the allotted number sequence, at the side of the podium. The two Battalion companies provided a splendid parade and guard of honour. A decent sized band had been assembled which played very well, including the Duke of Wellington's regimental march, *Wellesley*, and the King's Own Yorkshire Light Infantry's *Jockey to the Fair*. In the middle of the senior officers on the podium stood Sir Herbert. He looked older and shorter than I imagined, with a flushed complexion sporting a very bushy white moustache. His face looked stern, his blue eyes icy. You would not wish to be on the receiving end of his tongue-lashing. So, when he smiled, his warmth and friendliness came as a great relief.

Names were called, citations read, ribbons, bars and medals presented. My heart pounded waiting for my name to ring across the parade ground. I would have been less agitated leading an enterprise on a German trench! The silliest thought came to me: will he notice my unpolished buttons? (Deliberate, for I didn't want them to catch the light at night. But Generals probably wouldn't know shiny buttons can give a man's position away to a sniper.)

Officers on the podium welcomed each of us. Sir Herbert shook our hands and exchanged a few words of congratulations. He was a soldier's soldier. I admit, I felt proud, but tempered by remembering again pride leads to a fall. The warm mid-morning sun, the parade ground, flags, Army comrades, tea in fancy cups, cake, a band playing lively tunes, a handshake from my GOC and several generals and colonels, wine, whisky, brandy - and a Military Cross. Why not be proud? At least for today, for tomorrow that bullet with my name on it may well leave Fritz the sniper's *gewehr*.

If my MC was a surprise, my promotion to Captain was a shock! I couldn't believe it, however many times I whispered to myself, 'Captain, I'm a Captain'. Furthermore, I was returning to the front commanding not one platoon but four: a *Company* Commander. Equally hard to believe. Surprises this day were not yet over. A tap on my shoulder and I turned to find a face that looked familiar, but could not immediately attach a name. The brigadier-general saved my embarrassment.

'You'll remember me on the road to St Quentin in '14, Ogden, when you had that wounded chap in the cart: Allen, then Captain Allen of the Royal Irish Rifles. I believe we've both aged a bit since then.'

'Yes, Sir, I remember you very well indeed. But how did you....?' I couldn't believe this officer, now a general for heaven's sake, remembered me.

'I recall your goat,' he laughed, reading my mind and shaking my hand. 'By the way, jolly well done for your MC. From what I've heard you deserve about ten VCs, but you know how it is.'

'Yes, Sir, I think almost every man deserves a medal.'

'You're not wrong there, Ogden.'

Noticing my empty glass, the general beckoned a private with a tray of drinks. Somehow the young soldier tripped over. He and several glasses of wine went crashing to the ground. Everyone in the room stopped talking and all eyes fell on the private. I felt very embarrassed for the lad. His corporal supervising the catering stormed towards the private clearly intending to tear him off a strip, but General Allen intervened and helped the private to his feet. The lad was red-faced on the verge of tears. General Allen told him, in a voice loud enough to make sure the whole room heard, that accidents happen and not to worry. A quick brush, mop and pan would have the whole thing sorted in a jiffy, he added. With the look of relief and

305

admiration on the private's face, I honestly believe if the general would have told the lad to charge a German pillbox armed with a twig, he would have gone gladly. A minute later the private was back with a tray, this time with only two tall glasses.

'Sir, General, Sir,' the waiter said nervously. 'Corporal says to give you these an' tell you it's all that's left in the whole bleedin', er, the whole mansion, Sir, beg your pardon.'

'Thank you, Private, and thank your corporal,' Gen Allen said. 'It's obvious the Top Brass have drunk most of the *bleedin'* champagne.' The lad would now attack that pillbox stark naked!

'Sir, may I ask, you were a friend of Captain Harcourt, have you managed to keep in touch and is he…is he all right?'

'We hope so. He was definitely among most of a platoon taken prisoner last September in the Somme sector, near Thiepval in fact.'

'I wasn't far away, Sir, in Albert, and then round to Flers through Longueval.'

'I know, Ogden. I've kept on the trail of several chaps from the start. Half, I'm afraid, have copped it, more than half in the infantry.'

'They said you'd put in a good word to get me into officer training, Sir.'

'And look how splendid you've turned out, Ogden. Although the top man noticed your buttons were dull when he presented your MC.'

My breath was taken away.

'Don't worry, Ogden,' Gen Allen said. 'That old bird Plumer doesn't miss a trick. He knows a proper fighting soldier keeps his buttons dull.'

I remained speechless.

'Your leather kit seems in remarkably good order, though, considering what you've been through.'

'It came as a mystery gift, Sir. I felt it only right to care for it. It gets a lot of dubbin. But the gun that came with the Sam Brown got shot clean out of my hand and lost in mud during a close-quarter scrap. Its lanyard had been cut earlier by a German's bayonet. I spent time looking for it, but it was hopeless.'

'Good to see you've updated it though,' General Allen said. 'The Mark VI is a much better revolver all round. Longer barrel. Bigger man-stopping bullets, eh?'

And then I realised. How slow I'd been!

'It was you, Sir, wasn't it? Otherwise you...you couldn't have known about the newer model. You sent the kit.'

The Brigadier-General pursed his lips. 'I stand accused, Ogden, and I must confess...'

Forgetting myself I dared to interrupt a senior officer. 'Why, Sir, I don't understand?'

'Your determination to rescue your friend, what was his name?'

'Dale.'

'That's right, Dale, and your amazing shot disposing of the sniper saved me and all those chaps from certain capture, or worse. Oh, I've entertained many a chap about your goat and cart and instant sniping of the sniper ever since.'

'It wasn't that difficult a shot.'

'And, Ogden, please don't take offence, an officer's kit on a sergeant's pay costs an arm and a leg. So, as I was partly responsible for your becoming an officer, I felt duty bound to make sure you got off to a damn good start. Some new officers get themselves into debt buying specialist kit and uniforms and the like, half of which is not necessary. Some chaps even buy pedigree horses!'

***

Lucius, a pedigree whose owner had been shot off her back, remembered the return route. I was grateful for her intelligence. My head spun at the day's surprises. Champagne. Wine. Shaking the hands of generals. A Military Cross. Meeting Captain Allen again, now a General. His secret support. Mysteries solved. And me, a Captain. A Captain, me.

Across open fields and tracks on the way back to camp, Lucius galloped at the full as if on a cushion of cloud, not hard earth.

I didn't care. I didn't fall off. I wasn't sniped.

CHAPTER 34

September 1917
III BATTLE OF YPRES - PASSCHENDAELE

Perhaps the trouble inside Russia forced our Commander in Chief's hand. It appears with Russians now more interested in fighting themselves than the Germans, General Sir Douglas Haig realises the Hun could soon replenish the Western Front with men and weaponry no longer required on the Eastern. We need to act, and act now - with the biggest big push yet undertaken.

When Czar Nicholas abdicated last March following years of internal strife, the provisional government vowed to stick with us fighting the Germans. But the Russian government isn't really governing. Nobody appears in charge. The whole country is in revolt. Chaos rules. We're told of mass starvation and fuel shortages. Fights are breaking out everywhere over the smallest scrap: a potato, turnip, piece of coal, a shard of firewood. Russian losses in the war are even worse than ours. In 1915 alone they suffered over two million casualties. Many officers and men simply abandoned their posts and returned home having had enough. Should the Russians agree a truce with the Germans, it spells more danger for us. I doubt the Germans would completely trust the Russians to stay at peace. They will doubtless leave some troops to keep an eye on them. But with no fighting on the Eastern Front, countless thousands of German troops will be heading towards us.

In April the Germans returned to Russia a chap called Vladimir Lenin. He and seventeen other revolutionary Bolsheviks were shipped in a special sealed train from Zurich, where they had been in exile for several years. The Czar's fall and political mess made the coast clear for them to return home. The Germans know the returnees will pour fuel on the flames of trouble inside Russia. Perhaps they pay these Bolsheviks to whip up disorder hoping Russia will give up on the fight with Germany. Russian guns will then turn onto fellow citizens in a struggle for power. The Bolsheviks want control. But they are not the only ones grabbing at power. Tsarist generals and a group called Mensheviks also wish to rule. Mr Lenin is already singing the German's tune, calling for Russians to end the war and seek peace with the Kaiser.

There is another pressing reason why we must get a rush on to end this damnable war. The Royal Navy, under the First Sea Lord, Admiral Sir John Jellicoe, needs to clear the Belgium coast of Germans and destroy their anchorage and shipyards at Ostend and Zeebrugge. To reach these ports we need to move northwards breaking the German line beyond the Ypres salient. Since 1st February, when Germany declared a restart of unrestricted U-boat attacks, their submarines have caused havoc to Allied shipping. Last year, 1916, over one thousand one hundred Allied and neutral ships, including nearly four hundred British vessels, were holed by the Germans, nine hundred and sixty-four of them by U-boats. Countless tons of food and other essential supplies have sunk to the seabed. Should these assaults go on against merchant fleets, we and the French could be starved of food and munitions.

It came as no surprise when, on 2nd May, King George issued a royal proclamation from Buckingham Palace for a nationwide cutback on bread consumption. It was read out in churches for several weeks in the hope people would heed the call. The royal household had been rationing bread by a quarter since early in the year.

Military Intelligence believes the German Navy has nearly one hundred and sixty U-boats. And it's likely, judging by their success, their shipyards are building more at a rate of knots. Like aeroplanes and weaponry, these underwater assassins, with their torpedoes and deck guns, have developed rapidly since the outbreak of war. War makes mankind make many new things - and existing things bigger, better, deadlier. The German submarine fleet has extended its reach, speed and firepower. U-boats are carrying more torpedoes with greater explosive force, and they can set more mines. Their deck guns sink ships as well as torpedoes. U-boats not only sail around Britain but also range across the Mediterranean and even further afield. One submarine, *Deutschland*, last year on 9th July arrived off the east coast of the United States, in Baltimore. Its captain claimed to be unarmed and simply acting as a cargo vessel. America was then still neutral. Even so, as the *Lusitania* was sunk by a German submarine just fourteen months earlier with many Americans on board, I would have been sorely tempted to blow the *Deutschland* to smithereens. President Wilson must have thought about it, especially as several close friends were on board *Lusitania*, including the millionaire yachtsman Alfred Vanderbilt. Since then dozens of American cargo ships have been attacked by German U-boats, one of which would have been a fully-armed *Deutschland*. Perhaps the President regrets not ordering its destruction or capture.

***

At the end of September 1917 we Dukes with 4th Division moved from the Arras line towards the Ypres salient. We entrained first at Baumetz, journeyed to Peselhoek, detrained, and marched to our billets. Like most camps this was a mixture of buildings, hutments and, because of the large number of troops coming and going, hundreds of tents. A week later we entrained again, this time to Elverdinghe, three miles north-west of Ypres and our gateway to the front. The very next night, October 8th, at 11 pm, our time came to march up the line towards Passchendaele. We had to be ready at 4 am on the 9th for our first engagement in what we called the Third Battle of Ypres, later named the First Battle of Passchendaele. The men called it Wipers Three.

It rained. Again. And lots of it. Sometimes we think the weather has caused the death of as many men as bullets and shrapnel. The weather weapons of rain and snow have certainly accounted for many. If it wasn't raining, it was drizzling. If it wasn't drizzling, we suffered what many called Scotch mist. Even the youngest in my Company, lads not old enough to shave - although some pretended - knew the conditions would quickly deteriorate. This low-lying land had always been a mud-bath after the slightest rain, but now it was a quagmire, an ocean of mud.

The men serving here since August looked as miserable as I'd ever seen the British Tommy. Most chaps as always put on a brave face trying to be cheery for themselves and their comrades. But thin smiles can't hide deep sadness. Father said he would always choose to fight with ten cheery chaps than twenty disheartened men, happy fellows being twice the fighters of the down-hearted. Fed-up soldiers throw away their rifles and put up their hands readily, Father added. He was right. Lads that laugh together fight better, especially in tight corners. This gloominess, then, worried me. Our vigour, certainly our cheerfulness, seemed stolen, as if the mud had sucked up our spirit.

Our Commanding Officer, Lieutenant-Colonel Horsfall, at zero time 5.20 am, took it upon himself to lead us, The Duke of Wellington's Regiment, 2nd Battalion, into the front line. To see him with us gave a brave heart to all and lifted the gloom. Our first objective, a farm and its outhouses between Langermarck and Poelcappelle, was taken easily. The Boche resisted for a few minutes, but once one chap came out waving a white handkerchief, the remaining thirty or so followed. We proceeded cautiously in case this was one of those German ruses: some walk out in surrender, then suddenly drop to ground as we become exposed to their machine gun ambush. I always advised my men that, anywhere near the front, always move as if you're under fire, even when all seems safe. On this occasion the Germans' surrender was genuine. They tried no tricks.

Moving beyond the farm eastwards towards Poelcappelle we faced heavier fire. Our next objective, a badly damaged farmstead, stood five hundred yards away. It was going to be a far harder target to take. Lt Turner took a shot. He urged his Platoon on and not to bother about his injury. Slipping and sliding from one shell hole to another was the only way forward. We needed to edge forward in numbers before launching our final all-out attack. Every pit we jumped into had at least a knee-deep sump of sticky strength-sapping mud. And most had bodies, British, Indian, Australian, German. Corpses came as no surprise. But to find chaps who had stayed injured in these holes for days certainly was. I slid into one pit with some of my Company to find two men from the 2nd Manchester Regiment. They said it was their fifth day stuck in the hole! One had broken his back and could feel nothing from the waist down. The other soldier's legs looked mangled and one arm was broken. Whatever way employed, they had been unable to crawl out of the pit. They had received no medical attention. Nor had any attempts to rescue them been made. They'd exhausted their rations two days earlier and survived drinking rain or mud-water. Our troops had been in and out of the hole, they said, some stepping on them not realising they were alive. But the Manchesters accepted that 'advance' not rescue stood as the overriding order.

Chaps advancing were naturally more concerned with bullets hissing over their heads than bodies - dead or alive - under their boots. Three privates who had followed me into the pit offered the Manchesters their field rations. All their supplies! Their generosity made me proud of them. But I ordered them to give only part of their rations, explaining they themselves will need this food over the coming days. As we prepared to make our next rush, I gave the Manchesters my packet of Rowntree's Fruit Pastilles. Everyone laughed when I suggested to the two Lancashire lads that, as the sweets were made in Yorkshire, they might turn down my offer, the rivalry between the two counties as strong as ever! Quick as a flash, one of them replied: 'Not on your Nellie, Sir, however bitter they taste!' It was time to go. We bolted from the pit into a fusillade of bullets. One of my lads instantly took a shot to the head at the rim of the pit. He slithered down over one of the injured Manchesters, his blood pouring over the pastilles.

Lt White was the next to fall. Seconds later, Lt Harrison. Both scrambled for cover, always a good sign they're likely to survive. Many shell holes contained bodies, recent kills and some bloated and decomposing. The firing, like the rain, was incessant. If anything, getting heavier. My Company, while attempting to maintain the correct method of open attack, had divided into pockets of men moving forward when best they could. Some of us found cover behind a low wall. Chips were being shot out of it at all angles. If a machine gunner concentrated his fire on the spot, or a high calibre rifle sniper got us in his cross-hairs, bullets would penetrate through to us. To my left I could see Lt-Col Horsfall giving orders to his runner. With firing now so heavy, progress unlikely and men falling all around, I assumed he was recommending withdrawal to consolidate our position: a decision I would endorse.

From my vantage point I could see the CO was increasingly vulnerable to sniper fire. As in many battles, I wanted to shout, 'Get Down!' to someone I could tell was exposed. Not that he would have heard sixty yards away through the noise. At that precise moment at least one bullet struck him in the chest. I knew immediately he'd be dead after a few gasps when his body emptied of blood. Nobody survives a shot through the heart. Lt-Col Horsfall's orderly, Pte Ramsden, caught his body as it crumpled. But he could do no more than lay the officer's body neatly on the ground and wash away the blood around his neck. Faithfully serving to the end, Pte Ramsden stayed with him the rest of the day until taken for burial. He made sure the stretcher bearers treated the former CO's body with the respect it deserved. Captain Browning, the most senior Battalion officer present, immediately assumed command.

Those of us in the field went no further forward that day, so intense the firing. And the Germans, much to our relief, did not launch a counter-attack. I doubt we had the numbers to mount an effective defence and we would have perished or been taken prisoner, the former more likely. I knew in those circumstances 'killing and leaving' is far easier than capturing and conveying captives back down the line. Now, as a captain, it is more likely my life might be spared if taken prisoner - and if the attacking soldiers would be sharp enough to recognise my rank. The Germans believe, as we do, officers have more information than Other Ranks about the state of the war, troop movements, weaponry, reserves, plans and so on. Truth is, I didn't know much more than one of my privates, although that would not have prevented German intelligence trying to beat information out of me.

We received orders to withdraw under cover of darkness. On the way, still troubled by random bursts from machine guns, I took a squad of eight and went to find the two Manchesters. Having survived that hell hole and shown the will to live, the least they deserved was to be rescued. The shape of land changes between darkness and daylight, and when artillery shells constantly churn the ground, orientation is even harder. There was no feature to indicate their location: no tree stump, no abandoned field gun, no barn, nothing except a mire of shell holes, the dead and dying. We were certainly in the vicinity, but we could not find the two chaps. I came to fear their pit had taken a direct hit and their bodies blown to pieces or buried in the earth. After thirty minutes of hole-hopping, as the corporal put it, and not wishing to place my chaps in any more danger, I abandoned the search.

The following day, after hardly any sleep but joined by fresh reserves, we attacked again. Major Officer and Captain Coke suffered wounds in the first rush and, near me, Lt Horsley took shrapnel in the shoulder. We quickly became pinned down as tightly as the previous day. When night fell we received orders to withdraw. In the debrief we discovered Lt Johnson was missing and, after enquiries, not one chap in his platoon or the neighbouring one could account for his disappearance. Over those two days, the loss to the Dukes stood at twenty-two killed, ninety-nine wounded and forty-nine missing, presumed dead, as no-one observed prisoners being taken. A total of one hundred and seventy 2nd Battalion men, plus eight officers, had become casualties. Not an inch of ground had been taken beyond our first objective, the farmhouse where the Germans couldn't wait to raise their hands.

***

We Dukes came off the front arriving tired and dishevelled in Arras on 22nd October at the most unusual barracks we had ever experienced: a huge underground series of tunnels and caves beneath the centre of the city. Several passageways ended in galleries with tiled floors, ornate pillars, stairways to other chambers. Schramm Barracks, compared to what we had been used to, offered luxury accommodation. We could enjoy a good wash, shave and brush up, out of the rain and mud. The caverns provided space to house thousands of men, and a hospital. But our wonderful billet didn't last for long. The end of October found us east of Wancourt in trenches.

A few days earlier, 26th October, the Second Battle of Passchendaele commenced as part of the Third Ypres Offensive. By now the whole front had concentrated on the Canadian Corps' attempts to gain Passchendaele village itself. Because of the all-but collapse of the Italian Army facing the Austrian Army two days

314

earlier at Caporetto in the Julian Alps, General Sir Douglas Haig felt compelled to dispatch two divisions to bolster the Italians. It wasn't until 6th November when the Canadian Corps resumed the fight that Passchendaele village was seized. But the Boche continued launching damaging counter-attacks. It took another Canadian effort on 10th November to effectively secure the area around the village and the ridge it stood upon. What good soldiers and loyal supporters of the British and the Empire the Canadians proved to be.

Our Battalion settled into the routine of trench life over the winter of 1917-18. Depending on enemy activity and our own troop movements, we usually spent five days in the front line and five days in reserve. We also enjoyed periods of rest in rear areas, although I can't recall more than two days when working parties were not required for some task. Much of my time was spent running training exercises across the whole Battalion. The artillery, on both sides, rarely ceased their shelling. Even well back from the front the odd stray bomb fell amongst us, as if to keep us on our toes - lest we forget there's a war on.

Both sides continued to mount occasional raids. B Company made one very successful trench-to-trench attack at night in late November. They captured sixteen Germans and killed about the same number. The rest bolted like rabbits with a ferret snapping at their tails, the Company Sergeant gleefully reported. But the captured trench was isolated, a hundred and fifty yards forward from our main line. Conditions made it impossible to construct communication trenches to it. It was just too wet, even for Flanders, and we didn't have materials to keep the slopes from collapsing. Our newly appointed Battalion Commander, Major R J A Henniker, after discussing the matter with key officers, decided to abandon the position the following evening. When he asked my opinion, I agreed that it was right to pull out, and fast. With all their reserves and supplies to hand, I said, Fritz will not hesitate to launch a swift powerful counter-offensive and slaughter B Company at the first opportunity. And any support we could offer would mean going over the top. Fritz will have mounted extra machine guns and mortars to catch us. A bloodbath will result for no advantage.

As darkness fell the following afternoon, B Company, platoon by platoon, made their way quickly and quietly back to our main line. Within minutes of the Company Commander reaching us, having been at the rear to make sure all his men were accounted for, the Germans attacked the now abandoned trench in considerable numbers. Hundreds of grenades and mortars were lobbed into it. A dozen machine guns at least fired at the parapet to catch anyone attempting to escape. Fifteen minutes the onslaught went on without respite. When the German infantry finally attacked with bayonets fixed, we imagined with delight their disappointment at discovering the vacant pit. Thousands of bullets, hundreds of grenades and mortars, and not one dead British soldier in sight. But, having prepared our sights and mortar angles on the trench during daylight, we accounted for plenty of them!

This winter turned out less gruelling than the previous three I'd endured in the trenches. Everyone was issued with extra clothing of fur waistcoats or leather jerkins, woollen underclothing, gloves and waterproof cap and helmet covers. Although small items, together they made a big difference to our warmth and comfort. A waterproof cap serves, after all, like the roof on a house. At the other end of the body, I continued to insist that all my lieutenants and NCOs instruct the men on caring for their feet to avoid trench foot. For the few of us remaining in the Battalion who survived the first winter in France, the new attire was a big improvement on the khaki greatcoat.

As 1917 came to its end, victory looked as far away as ever. Heartened by the USA's entry into the war in early April, our joy soured when only one Division of the American Expeditionary Force reached the Western Front by the end of June. Then we discovered they lacked training with no idea about modern warfare or trench fighting. The Americans I met had an eagerness to 'get to the action', although not everyone appreciated this childlike enthusiasm. Our senior officers criticised the lack of discipline American soldiers displayed. 'Some of their chaps behave as if they're here for a picnic,' one said. 'They seem to believe they can walk up to the Germans, go "boo", and have them run back to Berlin,' said another.

To further annoy our generals, the American troops, under the command of Major General Pershing, wanted to fight independently from the rest of us, particularly the French. Cooperation and coordination, however difficult that can be, is the only way we will win this war. Eventually the Yanks swallowed their pride and accepted training from us and the French. Until now it seemed the Americans had no idea the Germans posed a formidable foe. Nor had they grasped the sheer scale of the fighting. 'Black Jack' Pershing had only fought native tribes, tropical island tribesmen, and a few skirmishes with Mexicans. The American troops called themselves 'doughboys'. When asked why, we got different answers. No-one seemed to know how the nickname came about. A lot of their lads also called Germans 'Heinie' instead of Fritz, Boche, Hun or Jerry, apparently because Heinze and Heinrich are popular names in Germany.

The Italian front collapsed at the end of October. The Austrians killed over ten thousand Italians, wounded far more, and took nearly three hundred thousand soldiers prisoner. More alarming are reports that around half a million Italian soldiers simply flung down their weapons without a fight and bolted. Military police tried stopping deserters, but we hear the payment of a bribe allows a fugitive to slip the net.

More significantly, Russian Bolsheviks in early November overthrew the Provisional Government in Petrograd. The second revolution in eight months. It has brought Vladimir Lenin and a chap called Leon Trotsky to power. Bolsheviks have the slogan: 'Peace, land, bread, and all power to the Soviets.' It also appears the Russians have all but given up the fight with Germany and are having meetings to 're-establish a state of peace and friendship'.

The only good news of late is that we beat the Turks after four years fighting in Sinai and Palestine. The Armistice was signed on 30th October, although Turkish troops in Jerusalem held out until surrendering to General Edmund Allenby on 9th December. Arthur Balfour, our Foreign Secretary and former Prime Minister, declared in November that Jews should have a permanent national homeland in Palestine. This victory will go some way to fulfilling that aim for the fifty thousand Jews in the Holy Land wanting a separate state from the half a million Arabs in the area.

My fourth Christmas of the war was far more enjoyable than any of the previous three. On Christmas Day morning we returned to the Schramm Barracks in Arras by motor bus. As we entered the caverns and chambers our stomachs started to rumble at the delicious smells of roast meat. We all thought this food was being prepared for some other lucky devils, French troops perhaps, or senior officers. But it turned out to our delight that we were 'the guests of honour' and sat at tables decorated with sprigs of holly and served a magnificent meal. It was by far the best meal I'd experienced since Christmas 1913 at home. The feast was fit for our King, and we toasted him, the Country, the Empire.

Since the Third Battle of Ypres began at the end of July, we British have suffered over a quarter of million casualties. (Some officers whisper the figure could be much higher.) The Germans almost certainly suffered far fewer, tucked away in their deep defences. In addition to our Regiment's action at Poelcappelle and the Canadians at Passchendaele, British forces launched attacks at Becelaere, Gheluvelt, Houthulst Forest and Zandvoorde. If these had broken, the path to the ports of Ostend and Zeebrugge would have been open and the submarine menace severely curtailed. But with the enemy's ever-deeper trenches and improved defences, it is fair to say we failed to achieve our objectives, perhaps apart from at Passchendaele. Yards rather than miles have been taken.

As news of our efforts filtered through, the mutterings I overheard made it clear many - from generals to privates - felt deeply upset at the great loss of life in this mud-bath for such little success. The Germans, under their commander Ludendorff, had built many machine gun positions in concrete pillboxes that even direct artillery hits usually failed to penetrate. What hope then does the infantryman have with his .303 calibre rifle and his one-pound six-ounce Mills grenade?

Men scrambled over the top to be shot. Too many. The relentless rain continued to kill too. So slippery were the duckboards, like ice on glass, that men who slid off drowned in the sea of mud unless they grabbed immediate hold of the boards, a ladder, pole or rope. Making our way back one day, about fifty yards in front of my Company, a length of duckboard tipped up and about a dozen artillery men tumbled into the quagmire. Eight drowned, some clinging to each other, despite desperate efforts to haul them out of the bog. So deep and greedy the mud, some sank within seconds. One chap, eager to rescue his friend, jumped in trying to save him. He failed, of course, and one man more than necessary died. No-one admired his bravery; everyone condemned his stupidity.

Despite the tremendous loss of life and limb, most chaps here, even many reluctant conscripts, continue to believe the war to be a just war. The Kaiser and his cronies need beating. We're doing the right thing but some question, quietly, if we're doing it the right way. Surely so many lives can't be lost for so little territory? Surely we can't fight all the way to Berlin one trench at a time? But France cannot become part of the German Empire because, it she fell, Britain would be next. Fritz would use France's northern coastline to launch an invasion on our shores, perhaps within weeks of their occupation. German aeroplanes will fly much further over England. Aeroplanes, on both sides, are getting faster and extending their reach. Like the improvements engineers have achieved with submarines and motor vehicles, it won't be long before enemy aircraft extend flights to Wales, Ireland and Scotland. German Gotha G-IV three-man bombers already range about three hundred miles. If France fell the Boche would also build more U-boats in French shipyards. They in turn will sink more ships and cut supplies of food and other necessities. Britain would be under siege, many of our own Empire's trade routes severed.

Make no mistake, be in no doubt, Flanders and France are Britain's front lines. Despite the losses, perhaps *because* of the losses, this is the place to stand and fight. To leave now would be to let down everyone who has laid down his or her life to stop the Hun. Millions have suffered and continue to suffer because of the Kaiser's evil greed and mad mind.

Chaps new to the Battalion, who faced their first fight around Poelcappelle, took time coming to terms with what they witnessed. They are striving to erase images of death, struggling to banish memories of horror, fighting to clear their heads. The task is as hard as whitewashing a barrel of tar. They'll fail. No normal person will dispel such memories, no sane person can. Somehow each man must find a distant corner of his mind to lock these horrors away like diamonds in a safe. If he fails, he will go mad. He will live amongst us in body, but alone in his own mind. Gruesome pictures will plague every moment of his life - when awake, when asleep. He will re-live the death of others and his own near-death. He will constantly see the carnage, smell burning flesh, taste blood, breathe noxious gas, hear bullets and blasts. He will feel his own fear. The terror will be as real in his daydreams and nightmares as it was in the field.

***

Officers and men are increasingly worried about the safety of their families at home, more so than their own necks, even with enemy trenches fifty yards away. We expect bullets and bombs here. In battle areas among fighting men, it's fair enough. We now accept gas and flame-throwers and the killing of animals as a means of victory. But attacking innocent people at home, children at school, is beyond contempt. I've never seen officers and men angrier than about the airship and aeroplane raids over England. For those whose families are within striking distance of Hun aircraft, particularly chaps from London, Essex and Kent, their blood boils with fear and frustration. Such despicable deeds make men here determined to fight with even more vigour. Many Londoners, perhaps up to three hundred thousand, now sleep in underground stations to shelter from the aerial bombing.

At home people are 'doing their bit' to win the war. Women especially continue to support us in many ways, such as making munitions and clothing in factories up and down the land. After a hard day's labour, many return home to make the most for their families out of ever-dwindling rations, especially on meatless days. There's also a shortage of potatoes at home, although we have plenty. A few chaps still talk down the ladies' hard work, claiming they're not up to the job. But as the war drags on they're being proved wrong. Men in their heart of hearts know the true value of women-folk. Some just don't like to admit it. Others objected to the recent granting of the vote to married women aged over thirty. Chaps generally, especially younger ones, think it a good decision, although the odd stick-in-the-mud objects. 'Women voting! What is the world was coming to?' one chap whined and shaking his head. I couldn't resist replying that it couldn't be any worse than this mess men got us in to.

It's clear the rallies and protests of suffragettes, and the vital war work of women, gained the right to vote. For men returning home after this war, victors or vanquished, there will be major changes in society. The world cannot stay the same, nor should it.

CHAPTER 35

January - June 1918

New Year, but nothing seemed new. Everything I could see was bombed, worn, tired and torn. Land, buildings, locals. The war grows older, and so too young men before their time. As one year merges into the next, it was time for reflection. Quietly, in his own way, every man considered the past year of life, the changes it had brought. For those who fought, especially in close-up combat, they'll be considering the miracle of their survival and the tragedy of their pals' deaths. They'll quiz their future. No answers will arrive. They'll worry about whether they'll live or die. For some, hope will outweigh despair. For others, fear will grip their guts.

Young lads may feel home-sick, even miss their mothers, although none would admit so. Married men may yearn for the warmth of their woman, the joy of watching their children play and grow. We all miss our homeland, the soil of Scotland, Ireland, Wales and England. Most wish to return to the routine of daily life and Civvy Street job. Who can blame them? Only a madman would swap a cosy fireside for a freezing trench, a safe street for no-man's-land, a pen for a grenade.

Always I try - and always fail - to look neither back a year nor forward. Both are bleak times. The past is where pain has been, the future is where pain will be. Only now, being alive and well at this moment, can bring comfort. I've learnt to measure my life at the front by the minute, by the next advance, from one shell hole to another. Perhaps I'm too gloomy, weigh bad in favour of good. Yet I'm alive, a Captain, a Military Cross holder. I should be grateful. But I'm not.

Neither did the New Year change the old routine. The 2nd Battalion of the Duke of Wellington's Regiment remained stationed north of Arras in January and February manning and maintaining trenches in the Roeux sector. Our time was as before divided between the frontline, in reserve, or back from the lines in training or resting. Every night we undertook working parties, fetching, carrying, building or repairing trenches. Six new lieutenants and two hundred and fifty other ranks joined the Regiment during these two months. A captain, eight more lieutenants and one hundred and fifty-eight men from the Regiment's 8th Battalion boosted our numbers too. Some of the chaps from the 8th had been in the Gallipoli Peninsula at Suvla and Scimitar Hill during 1915. Three lieutenants and many of the chaps had also served in Egypt during 1916. What a change for them: from the scorching sand of the Sinai Desert to the cold mud of Flanders.

Many believe 1918 will see the end of this war. But we remember generals and politicians claiming the war would be over by Christmas 1914. Silly optimism over sensible reality, we now know. I also remember voices in January of 1915, 1916 and 1917 predicting this was 'definitely' the year when the war would close. Nobody can possibly know apart from the Kaiser, and he's sixpence short of a shilling. He could end the war today with three words: 'Germany declares peace.' Millions of lives would be spared death, pain and sorrow. We could build instead of destroy, walk instead of hobble, live instead of die.

Changes are afoot, however. Among the many uncertainties, one thing is sure: the Germans are transferring divisions from the Eastern Front to the Western, relieved by the armistice with Russia. The Hun are without doubt planning a new offensive on a scale we haven't experienced before. Senior officers say the Germans want to win the war before the Americans start to fight in earnest. That will mean another German push to Paris, which will involve pushing us aside, or crushing us. The British Expeditionary Force is holding a front of approximately one hundred and forty miles. The Germans will see their best chance of victory through the weakest spot on our line. They will want to rid the French of their British ally before sweeping through the rest of France. If they can do so quickly before the Americans get into their stride, the Yanks might turn their ships and sail back to the United States. German U-boats will sink east-bound ships and ignore those west-bound. Even if American troops station themselves in England to stop any immediate German invasion, Fritz will play a patient game. Once they rule mainland Europe, they can wait, perhaps for years. They have no need to hurry. They will rebuild their war machinery knowing that at some time American patience will run out and the Yanks will sail home. With unlimited production of German submarines and aeroplanes, within weeks everyone in Britain will be eating less while being bombed more.

It seems however Lloyd George doesn't share the view of our senior generals. The Prime Minister wants to *reduce* the number of soldiers joining the Western Front, or at least starve us of fresh men. He's embarrassed at the high number of casualties, some say. But what does he expect in war? And to starve the front of more soldiers will lead to yet more casualties overall - and the prospect of German troops marching down Whitehall into Downing Street. To say we are aghast would be an understatement. Rumour has it that the PM dislikes our Commander in Chief, General Sir Douglas Haig, and wants to clip his wings. But to risk thousands of lives - even lose the war - to make a political point, or because of a personal disagreement, is madness.

The Prime Minister's other idea is to stretch our front to help the French. If true, I would say our leader is as crazy as the Kaiser. Although the French hold a front around three times longer than ours, much of it is quiet. Our fronts around Arras, Somme and Ypres are far from peaceful. Because of Lloyd George's reluctance to release more men from Britain, we in France and Flanders are in, as our commanding officer said, 'a bugger's muddle' reformulating our divisions. Divisions have been reduced from twelve battalions to nine. This explains why, in the second week of February, our Dukes Battalion was switched from 12th Infantry Brigade to join 10th Brigade, although still within 4th Division. Our Brigade was made up of ourselves, 1st Royal Warwickshires and the 2nd Seaforth Highlanders. Officers at all levels are criss-crossing regiments, divisions and battalions. Second-line territorial and New Army divisions especially are being scattered around like balls on a billiard table struck by drunks. One captain told me he'd been switched from one post to another three times in two weeks. 'We're playing musical chairs while the Germans are seriously gathering their forces over there,' he said, pointing eastwards. 'And I'm sure German spies will have taken delight in telling the German High Command of our shindigs.'

During the third week of February the fragile armistice between Russia and Germany ended. One of the Bolshevik leaders, Trotsky, stormed out of a conference with German leaders. The breakdown between them was music to our ears. It meant the Germans would have to retain their Army on the Eastern Front and stop transferring troops westwards to fight us. Better still, they might have to send divisions back to fight a resurgent Russia. On 18th February German troops, although reduced in numbers, immediately attacked the rag-bag Russian Army, now called the Red Army. Trotsky's bad temper played into German hands allowing them to snatch yet more territory. Indeed, they marched almost unopposed into Estonia. In five days they covered around two hundred miles and were threatening the Russian capital, Petrograd, hardly a hundred miles further on. Trotsky had told the Germans: 'We are not signing the peace of landlords and capitalists.' But the very next day Lenin managed to have Trotsky outvoted and declared that Russia would accept Germany's peace terms. On 3rd March Lenin and his Bolsheviks signed the Brest-Litovsk treaty on tougher terms than the ones they had earlier rejected. This means unfortunately that German troops will not be sent back to fight Russia. Worse, with a permanent peace treaty in place, more German divisions will be heading our way.

Russia's peace treaty with the Central Powers amounts to a surrender. Under the terms of this Brest-Litovsk agreement, the new Bolshevik government promised three thousand million roubles in reparation to its former enemies. Those who understand such money matters said this would bankrupt Russia, although they doubted it would or could ever be paid. Russia also accepted the independence of Ukraine under so-called German protection. Mr Lenin and Mr Trotsky surrendered Courland, Lithuania, Poland, a chunk of Belorussia, and the Baltic Sea port of Riga to Germany. Those lands contain most of Russia's coal mines, half its industries, and the great wheat-growing bread belts of Ukraine and Poland. In the Caucasus they've given territory to Turkey.

There is a civil war raging across Russia. Instead of killing German, Austro-Hungarian and Turkish forces, Russians have switched to fighting amongst themselves and killing their own people, besides giving away their land rather than protecting it. The 'bolshies' in their revolution have also upset their former friends: ourselves, the French and the United States. Perhaps ordinary Russians would prefer the certainty of the Romanov's three-hundred-year-old dynasty - however bad - than the uncertainty of these revolutionary Bolsheviks.

February ended with more bad news from home. In addition to the rationing already announced, butter and margarine were added to the list. Meat too has been reduced further to 20oz a week per adult. And despite being clearly marked with three huge red crosses on its port and starboard sides, a despicable German submarine without warning torpedoed *HMHS Glenart Castle*, a hospital ship in the Bristol Channel, with the loss of ninety-five lives. Some people have no shame.

*** *

It was the day of the Grand National, 21st March, when Germany launched the largest offensive of the war. Three million men would be involved in the clash. Lt Jones, who six months earlier had been teaching history, said it would be the biggest movement of men the world had ever seen. In the north, the Seventeenth Army had General Otto van Below at its helm; to the south, the Eighteenth Army under General Oskar von Hutier; between them the Second Army commanded by General Georg von der Marwitz. All three reported to German supremo General Erich von Ludendorff.

At 4.40 am the German artillery opened fire along a fifty-mile front. Over six thousand six hundred artillery guns - and more than three thousand five hundred heavy trench mortars - launched a storm of shells of all kinds towards us. High explosives scattered shrapnel everywhere killing and maiming. Green Cross shells spread lethal phosgene. Blue Cross shells released chlorine to melt lungs within seconds. Yellow Cross shells fell full of mustard gas to cause internal bleeding and vomiting of bile and blood. The weather again favoured the Germans, certainly in our sector. A spring mist severely restricted our view and we couldn't see German activity. To make matters worse their bombardment severed our telephone cables. We didn't know at certain periods what was happening along our line. With few or no communications from Division or Brigade HQs, battalions and even companies acted as they saw fit. Should we hold our position and defend? Should we retreat to regroup and ensure we don't become isolated? Should we attack - the action our enemy would least expect - in the hope of nipping their infantry assault in the bud? And, if that met with success, should we keep moving forward to close down their artillery?

Shortly after 9.30 am our choice was taken away: German *stoss-truppen*, storm-troopers, appeared through the mist. Every square yard of no-man's-land filled with gas-masked men committed to kill. Each attack battalion had four hundred infantry troops, one machine gun company with six machine guns, a bombing company armed to the teeth with stick grenades, a flame-throwing company, and one battery of assault artillery. Within moments men were shooting each other at close range, stabbing with bayonets, lashing with knives and beating with clubs. If bombs, bullets, gas, flames, bayonets, knives and clubs failed to kill, men grappled on the ground trying to throttle one another with bare hands.

When the Germans launched their Spring Offensive, we Dukes remained entrenched north of Arras at Roeux. We were a mere mile from the battle raging across the River Scarpe. So close, how long would it be before we engaged? Expecting an attack any minute, every man remained on tenterhooks. As the day progressed it seemed the Germans had set their main sights south of our position. But tension and vigilance remained high. Flank attacks can happen hours after the first thrust - and often when you think the threat is over. When messages from the line got through, it was worrying to learn our forward zone had been over-run by the *stoss-truppen* and occupied by general infantry and field artillery. Hun howitzers had destroyed our wire and most of our forward trenches. All we Dukes could do was wait, watch and hope our men in the thick of battle could repel the onslaught. I knew the terror those men felt and the horrors they faced, but I could do nothing.

One man in war can feel like no man at all.

Although our 10th Brigade remained alert, I encouraged my Company to take as much rest as possible when not required in working parties. Expecting this German onslaught, we had throughout the winter been building our new three-zone 'defence in depth' system, although much work was still required on the redoubts in the rear zone. There's been a lot of digging and construction, with more to do. But nothing saps strength and courage as much as waiting in fear with nothing to do.

The Hun bowled everything at us. And, it must be admitted, if the attack itself was not a surprise, its scale and ferocity shocked us. The German thrust was concentrated between Croiselles, eight miles south-east of Arras, southwards to La Fère, a town twelve miles south of St Quentin. Our Fifth and Third armies struggled under the enemy's cosh. Divisions from our own First and Second armies were eventually sent to the front, their departure delayed in case the initial German attack was a diversionary ploy. With so many communication lines down, it was hard to grasp exactly what was happening in the fighting zone. Some messages got through, others didn't, the messengers being killed, injured or delayed. By the time a communication arrived the situation had usually changed. French forces nearby that could have helped were held back too. Their Commander-in-Chief, General Philippe Pétain, believed his own positions, also under bombardment, could be the real target for the Germans, especially if they turned south towards Paris.

The German plan became harder to understand. We believed General Ludendorff's aim was to break through our lines and swing north to seize the French ports through which our supplies came. Major W G Officer, appointed as our new Battalion Commander, asked for the thoughts of Company Commanders about what the Germans were up to. I expressed the view that, if Paris was the goal, it would have made sense to start the attack further south. Why go the long way around and engage at least two British armies and give French forces time to prepare? Alternatively, if Ludendorff really wanted to defeat the British and take control of the English Channel ports - as intelligence reports predicted - we in Arras would now be in the middle or at the southern end of his attack, not on its northern margin. I could only conclude that Ludendorff's main aim was to divide British and French forces - before the US Army became engaged.

The day ended with our spirits down. If the news reaching Brigade HQ of casualties and prisoners is only half true, we British have suffered a very bad day. Nearly forty thousand men have been killed or injured, reports say, and about twenty-one thousand taken prisoner. Hundreds of artillery guns have been lost too. Our grim news was only slightly eased by hearing of the Hun's misfortunes. For once, because they fought in the open instead of being tucked away in their deep trenches, they suffered even greater losses. Wanting to maintain their morale, Major Officer asked Company Commanders to keep the British casualty figures from the men. As a former private I would bet the chaps had heard the news already: the grapevine often works better than the telephone, and bad rumour travels faster than good gossip. No-one, of course, says a word. News seeps through gaps under doors!

Heavy mist the next morning again helped hide the *stoss-truppen* attack following a downpour of artillery fire. All along our line we perished. So swift the storm-troopers' advance we had no time to dig in or find defensive positions in the ruined villages. The Fifth Army withdrew several miles west towards the River Somme. Further north our Third Army was also on the back foot, leaving V Corps extremely vulnerable to being isolated in the Flesquières Salient. At almost every crossroad as we retreated convoys of traffic converged in chaos. Junior officers and NCOs tried to direct troops and traffic in an orderly fashion. But every senior officer claimed their brigade, battalion or company had 'priority' over everyone else! In the end it became a free-for-all. To make matters worse Hun aircraft busied themselves strafing and bombing convoys. Men scattered to find what little cover they could. Horses bolted and artillery guns became stranded in the middle of the road, adding to the log-jams until pushed aside. When enemy aeroplanes swooped low several officers stood firm firing their revolvers and men their rifles. Some received a body full of bullets for their bravery. Not one aeroplane fell from the sky. A machine gun crew, speedily set up on a lorry, fired at three aircraft as they descended one after the other. Despite riddling the aircraft with bullets, they somehow managed to fly on.

By 24th March, after advancing over twenty miles, the Germans broke our line along the Somme. General Sir Hubert Gough's Fifth

Army, with exhausted men and a few reinforcements, proved no match in men or weaponry for the Germans. This presented General Sir Julian Byng with a huge dilemma: should his Third Army, covering the area approximately from Albert to Arras, drop back to maintain a British line side-by-side with the Fifth, or try and hold his position leaving a vacuum behind that the enemy might fill? His decision, without exaggeration, could determine the outcome of the war. Would a German military wedge be driven not only between the British but also between the British Fifth and the French? Furthest north was General Plumer's Second Army and, to their south, General Horne's First Army, responsible for protecting the advantageous Lorette and Vimy ridges. These positions could face a further onslaught from the east through Belgium. Ludendorff had plenty of men to mount such an attack. Since early November German troop trains had conveyed nearly fifty additional divisions from the Eastern Front following Russia's capitulation and, since the Brest-Litovsk Treaty, even more would become available.

The Germans continued to win their way west towards Amiens. They crossed the River Somme. The outlook for us was bleak. In the five days since the start of their Spring Offensive, which the Germans called the *Kaiserschlacht*, the Kaiser's Battle, our casualty toll had risen to around seventy-five thousand. Worse was to come, and the 2nd Battalion of the Duke of Wellington's Regiment was in the thick of it. Just as some officers and men thought the Germans had forgotten us, we received a thunderous reminder they hadn't. On 28th March, a week since the so-called Kaiser's Battle began, their Seventeenth Army launched a ferocious attack on both sides of the River Scarpe near Arras. Our vigilance, maintenance of and improvement to our defences stood us in good stead when, at 3 am, a deafening storm of shells landed all about us. For three hours, hardly a second elapsed without a shell of one kind or another crashing on our doorstep. It was as if all the bombardments I'd survived since Mons had been put together as one. Even with gas masks donned, I could sense the terror on every man's face. But the men maintained sharp eyes, pursed lips and firm jaws in readiness for the fight. Every man understood that many men would die this day; even more would suffer horrendous wounds. On the dot at 6 am came a pause in the barrage, a silence of seconds as cannon barrels angled upwards and before shells fell behind us. This meant one thing only: storm-troopers heading our way.

My men fought magnificently. The training, discipline and camaraderie paid off. New drafts particularly now realised all their battle drill, field exercises, digging new and improving existing trenches had been worthwhile. Even in the height of battle chaps found it amusing that I took a rifle and joined them shooting at advancing Germans. But a revolver's no use until the enemy is upon you! When I mounted one ramp to find a loophole a young private, so surprised to see his Captain with a rifle to hand, stood to salute. I immediately pulled the silly ass down just before bullets hissed overhead. As the *stoss-truppen* advanced, I was pleased to see the lad had a good eye and matched me for finding Boche bodies. There was no spring mist that beset our colleagues on the 21st, so we could supply plenty of gunfire at distance. We killed many and, as far as I could tell, without loss. It seems our redoubts proved to be in better shape too than our unfortunate colleagues further south, for today they held up well against the shelling. But by mid-afternoon, overwhelmed by the vastly superior numbers of Germans, we had to fall back. No good soldier likes going backwards, losing ground, withdrawing, retreating - whatever word you use makes it no less painful. But falling back is often the sensible action to take. You can take stock, reorganise, retaliate more effectively. And that's precisely what we did.

Not to be outdone and regain some pride, three Companies of the Dukes, including mine, the West Yorkshires and the King's Own Scottish Borderers, retook part of the lost ground the very next day. The dogged British defence and constant counter-attacks around the River Scarpe eventually paid dividends. Within a few days the German Seventeenth Army's advance came to a halt. It was as if General von Below decided the large loss of his men was not worth the small gain of land. I reminded my men, however, an injured Fritz is not a dead Fritz: if he still holds a gun, he can still shoot you! The Germans haven't gone away.

Regaining many of our former positions was not without loss. German machine guns wounded 2nd Lt McDowall and forty-seven others. Nine died. Despite prompt attention at the casualty clearing station for gas poisoning, Capt Newroth and 2nd Lt Banham required admission to hospital. It's reported they sacrificed their own safety by removing their masks to assist others. Commendable perhaps, but doing so inevitably makes two casualties instead of one. Eight men couldn't be found. It's impossible to say whether they were captured or their bodies buried under bomb debris. In the uncertainty, families will live with the hope that when the war is over, their son, husband, father or brother will return. They'll believe the next knock on the door will be their loved one, even after a thousand callers. They'll imagine Tommy standing at the threshold with his familiar cheeky smile as large as life. A few families have however told me they would prefer the certainty of 'killed' rather than the uncertainty of 'missing, presumed dead'. To my letter, one father replied: 'We can't mourn Bernard's death because we don't know he's dead. With no body, no witness to his demise, we cling to the smallest hope he's alive. Not knowing if he is alive is as painful as knowing for certain he is dead. Bernard promised Mother he would return home safely. And she reminds me daily that Bernard always kept his promises.'

Every soldier going to war promises they'll return home.

Further south, along the Somme valley, the Germans continued to press towards Amiens. But they became victims of their own success. So fast and furious their advance that communications, artillery and supplies lagged behind. On swampy shell-holed terrain light-footed infantry move faster than heavy cannon on wheels, so the storm-troopers forged ahead with little or no artillery support. For us, defending a line is much easier without artillery shells landing all around. There was also a noticeable reduction in the use of stick-grenades, mortars and flame throwers - a clue of supply lines breaking down. At the same time as the Germans being stretched, our reserves started to arrive, infantry and artillery. At last the politicians in London, particularly Lloyd George, realised the gravity of the situation in France. It was believed the Prime Minister deliberately withheld reinforcements. He feared General Haig would squander soldiers' lives after last year's four hundred thousand British casualties at Passchendaele.

Troops that had been held back in Britain arrived in France - just in time. Hot on their heels came divisions that had been fighting in Egypt, Italy and Palestine. Officers on the Western Front often described these as 'minor campaigns'. A few went further calling these ventures 'distracting side-shows'. From the start of the war, many thought we should beat the Germans here first before tackling other trouble-spots. If the troops that went to Gallipoli in 1915 had been fighting on the Western Front the Germans, they argue, would have been beaten by 1916. Right or wrong, I can't say. What I know is these new reinforcements are welcome and needed. Once the reinforced Royal Field Artillery got to work, the Germans started sustaining heavier losses. General Ludendorff and his German High Command, the *Oberste Heeresleitung*, had clearly accepted there would be a high price in human life to pay for this Spring Offensive. Was it 'all or nothing' for him, the 'last throw of the dice'? We had heard there was mass starvation in Germany and a growing resentment against the war. True or not, it is a fact that martial law was imposed at the end of January following mass strikes whipped up by socialists calling themselves Spartacists.

Amiens, which had become my private city of refuge, leisure and learning - thanks to Mr Unia and the library at the Hôtel de la Paix - remained in Ludendorff's sights, like a pike eyes a minnow. Day by day the German Army edged to within striking distance of the city, primarily to seize its vital railway junction. I hoped the staff at the hotel would have the sense to move away before the place is bombed to pieces. Mr Unia, as a reporter, would be certain to stay if he was in the area. He liked to be at the 'epicentre' of the action. (Another fine word he taught me.) There was little doubt the Germans would flatten the city. Defending the Somme region was far from easy for our Fifth Army, which suffered tremendous losses. But it did become easier thanks to the arrival of French troops.

Field Marshal Ferdinand Foch, recently appointed as the Supreme Commander of the Allied Armies on the Western Front, declared Amiens had to be protected 'at all costs'. There was hope for it yet. Foch ordered the French First and Third armies to fight alongside our ailing Fifth, the new formation to be called the Group of Armies of Reserve. A Frenchman, General Émile Fayolle, was put in charge.

333

Our General Gough was relieved of his command and replaced by Sir Henry Rawlinson.

We Dukes and other regiments in 4th Division continued to defend our line on the north side of the River Scarpe near Arras. The order was simple: stand firm. We should not withdraw, unless the situation was hopeless. Nor, for now, should we attempt to recapture our lost territory. After five days of continuous fighting the enemy eased off. It was 1st April, but we were not fooled into thinking Fritz had gone home to Berlin. The lull did allow us to sleep and rest for longer, wash and shave. Most chaps had not taken their boots and socks off for a week. We also managed to heat food again and brew plenty of tea - the greatest pick-me-up known to Tommy Atkins!

Artillery shells fell occasionally, but nothing like the round-the-clock service of previous days. The odd bomb is a useful reminder we're still at war, I told my chaps, smiling, knowing after the last few days not one of them would ever forget. But to prevent anyone forgetting snipers are still looking for a head, I conducted my favourite demonstration to each of the four platoons in my Company along the fire line. I take a tin hat 'and remove the head'. Then I mount it on a stick and raise it just inches above the parapet. To keep everyone's interest, I always offer double rum rations should my 'experiment' fail to attract a bullet inside one minute. Within ten seconds the first helmet took a heavy calibre rifle round. Further down the trench with the next platoon the second 'test helmet' attracted a machine gunner within fifteen seconds. (I'd carried out this demonstration about fifty times and only once did I have to authorise extra rum: damn Fritz snipers that day must have fallen asleep on the job!) The chaps were obviously disappointed not to receive extra rum. But the demonstration might have saved a life or two.

Forty-five miles to the south of us, the Boche unfortunately enjoyed greater success. By 27th March they had cut off a key railway route to Paris at Montdidier. They'd advanced almost forty miles since their starting line on the 21st. It did indeed seem like the Germans viewed the Spring Offensive as a race - a race against growing dissatisfaction with the war at home, amongst the troops themselves, and before the US Army got into its stride. President

Wilson had wasted little time introducing conscription. He said around twenty-four million men would be eligible for registration and, from that number, nearly three million would be called up for service. The US planned to send around three hundred thousand men every month from May onwards to join us. Once the doughboys are trained and ready for the front, probably about six weeks after landing in Europe, they are bound to make a significant difference. There is one worry: captured Germans say their submarines will sink many of the ships transporting the troops across the Atlantic. Our intelligence officer says this is bravado speaking, although German U-boats continue to sink ships at an alarming rate.

On land, too, German success seems unstoppable. By 30th March, eleven days after their Spring Offensive commenced, they reached the outskirts of Amiens. On the way, they captured around eighty thousand British and French prisoners and nearly one thousand artillery pieces. Not to mention the damage to our morale. Casualties are thought to be over a quarter of a million men. And this was supposed to be the year when we beat the Boche back to Berlin: misplaced optimism if not misjudgement. Nothing it seems can halt their westward march. At this pace of progress the enemy will be in Abbeville or even Dieppe looking at the Atlantic Ocean within the week. The Germans could divide the Allies as surely as a heavy axe splits a log. Those of us north of the Somme will then face two fronts, south as well as east.

At our darkest hour of the war, a ray of light. The Germans came to a halt. Infantry legs stopped walking, artillery wheels ceased turning. Had supply convoys broken down leaving the front short of bullets and cannon shells? Could it be that German troops, after ten round-the-clock days of fighting, were as exhausted as ours? Whatever their reason, the mighty German war machine ceased rolling forward. We suspected the pause was simply to take in supplies before a head of steam was rebuilt. But the four-day lull provided enough time for the French, and what was left of our Fifth Army, to build a defensive line ten miles to the east of Amiens. A corps of fresh and eager Australians also joined to boost our battered British and French force. But German legs and wheels started to move again on 4th April. Had they brought up even heavier artillery and reinforcements to replace their heavy losses? Would this be the all-out push to the Atlantic Ocean?

The Hun moved towards Villers-Bretonneux and clashed with the Allies just outside the town. The fighting was fierce. It always is now. Certainly in this war, with ever-heavier guns, stronger shells, fire and gas, tanks and aircraft, the days of gentle battles with small arms are over. But as if stiffness had set in, like cold old bones in the morning, the German thrust was not what it had been. Their drive lacked the will to win hitherto demonstrated since the start of the Spring Offensive. It seemed the soldiers' support for the *Kaiserschlacht* had waned. Knowing of the huge death toll of their comrades in their Kaiser's Battle, the suffering at home, the growing number of anti-war demonstrations, it felt like each trooper had lost his hunger to kill, his thirst for a fight. In his heart of hearts did he want the war to end, and end now? Battles, obviously, need at least two sides to clash, and nothing should be taken away from the organisation, discipline and courage of the Allies outside Amiens to repel the Boche. Our determination to stop their advance was greater than theirs to pursue it.

We crippled the German war machine on the Somme, at least for now. Whatever Ludendorff's military objective - to turn north and send us into the English Channel, to go west until reaching the Atlantic, or curve south to topple Paris - it had failed. If he measured success by the damage he caused the Allies, however, then he would be content, if not overjoyed. Nearly three hundred thousand French and British casualties had been sustained in his Spring Offensive. Over three thousand artillery pieces and machine guns destroyed or seized. Around two hundred tanks damaged or became stranded behind their lines. (Within days some tanks will have been repaired, repainted with the Iron Cross, and used against us.) Our aeroplanes too, perhaps two hundred, damaged or destroyed. The enemy had successfully penetrated forty miles further into France along the Somme. But they hadn't scored their goal. Their success could be their undoing. The new German salient, an isolated limb of ruined land, would now have to be defended.

***

Mid-April my Regiment moved ten miles north from Arras to the La Bassée Canal. The next day we Dukes joined the Warwicks to attack an unknown number of Germans inside dense woodland, Pacaut Wood. The patch extended about one mile by half a mile and was surrounded by ruined farms, shell-holed fields and orchards. The area had suffered regular shelling since the Germans first invaded in '14. Despite being victims of war, the ash, sweet chestnut, hazel and oak showed their resilience with this year's fresh green growth. Even crippled apple, plumb and pear trees, not to be outshone by their uncultivated cousins, produced pink and white blossom, as if to tell mankind life must go on. Since we regained the ground north of the River Scarpe, British action in the area had been confined to artillery shelling. The Germans likewise stuck to their big guns. German infantry attempted no advancement, not even small night raids. It was thus decided we should take the initiative and rid the wood of enemy. We believed tanks and ammunition were stored there alongside numerous artillery cannons. It was into the new spring-green foliage we crawled. Brambles, nature's barbed wire, became our first foe.

Two companies with just over four hundred men approached the wood from the west. The Warwicks, also with two companies, came from the south-east. Within five minutes of our final dash we had destroyed six machine guns and four light cannons and disposed of between fifty and sixty Germans. They appeared surprised by our raid in broad daylight. The ones who got away fled into dense cover. Within my hearing a lad asked his corporal if he should shoot men running away in the back. The corporal, correctly, told him a soldier fleeing is not a soldier surrendering. Momentarily distracted by the boy, Cpl Tillotson took a bullet to the arm. The lad was less fortunate. Attending to his corporal, bending over him instead of keeping low, a bullet ripped through his throat. A round I suspect from a Fritz who had legged it, stopped, turned and fired. With only a flesh wound and no major bleeding, Cpl Tillotson courageously continued with one good arm. He was pleased I offered my revolver in exchange for his rifle, although he said he'd never shot a handgun. Don't try hitting Fritz unless you see the whites of his eyes, I advised, otherwise you'll miss. As we chased the Huns a line of well-hidden machine guns stopped us in our tracks. We tried to destroy them, but we became hopelessly outgunned and our casualties mounted. We withdrew taking six prisoners. One of them, a young officer, spoke very good English. I asked him how long he had been speaking English. My guess would have been since childhood, so good was he.

'Oh, Captain, Sir,' he said, 'I just started learning the English last year only.'

'It's very good,' I said, amazed he could speak my language so well after such a short time. 'It would take me twenty years to learn German as good as you speak English already.'

The German added, casually but modestly, 'I also learnt Russian quite well and improved my French in this time. I think my English will much improve now I'm prisoner.'

Our venture into *Bois de Pacaut* turned out expensive for the Dukes: thirty-two men died, one hundred and seventy-nine injured, seven missing. Of our officers, two 2nd lieutenants died in action, a third, J Stocks, died later of his wounds. Captain Browning and four 2nd lieutenants took injuries and Lt Walker was missing. The Warwicks suffered even greater losses, largely at the hands of machine gun teams who spied them approaching and waited until many chaps became exposed in open ground. That evening the Germans launched a heavy bombardment from inside and beyond the woods. My men believed it to be a revenge attack. They were right.

***

Distracted by the German's Spring Offensive, the news eventually reached us that on 1st April the Royal Flying Corps and the Royal Naval Air Service had merged into one Royal Air Force. These fellows still use an assortment of aircraft, although most of them here fly the Sopwith F-1 Camel or the SE-5. The War Office and General Headquarters believe one RAF will be more effective. An inquiry by a General Smuts found that between the RFC and RNAS there had been too much rivalry, waste and a lack of coordination.

A few days following our raid in Pacaut Wood, the Dukes moved to trenches on the canal bank near Hinges. Our Battalion Commander, recently promoted to Lieutenant-Colonel, was wounded in one of the daily shelling attacks. After the first injury Lt-Col Officer struggled on. But a second chunk of hot shrapnel got the better of him and he required a long period of hospital treatment. Lt-Col Officer's last task in the line was to read a 'personal message' to all the Regiment's officers. This, in turn, would be read out to all the men. The statement came from our Commander in Chief, Field Marshal Sir Douglas Haig:

Many amongst us now are tired. To those I would say that victory will belong to the side which holds out the longest. The French Army is moving rapidly and in great force to our support. There is no other course open to us but to fight it out. Every position must be held to the last man. There must be no retirement. With our backs to the wall and believing in the justice of our cause each one of us must fight on to the end. The safety of our homes and the freedom of mankind alike depend upon the conduct of each one of us at this critical moment.

With no space at the front where I could easily and safely assemble all my Company of over two hundred, I had to read our leader's statement four times, to each platoon in turn. By the last time I had learnt it by heart. I could see it affected every man. Most reacted with resolve, determined to dig in and do their best. Fear crossed the faces of a few, and not necessarily the younger chaps. They worried about what 'no retirement' and every position 'held to the last man' would mean in battle.

Our life in trenches next to the Aire-la Bassee Canal took on a familiar routine. We were in and out of the forward trenches and suffered daily shelling. Fritz, or Jerry as most new chaps now call the Germans, have started raiding again. At any time, day or night, we can expect a visit. We then retaliate with raids of our own, as tradition dictates, our Commanding Officer often added. Every attack results in casualties on both side. But as usual the attacking side exposed crossing no-man's-land suffered the greater loss.

I've found night raids with just five or six eager volunteers or hand-picked men are the most effective. A specific objective must be set. Each man must know his duty to the finest detail. We would typically hit an enemy listening post on no-man's-land, attack a specific part of the enemy trench, or take out a machine gun placement. After dark, keeping low, going slow, in silence, we'd make our way to the target using every available hole, gully, tree stump, hedge or broken wall. Always know your next step, I stressed. Expect an enemy flare to reveal your position at any moment. We often got to within a few feet of our prey undetected. On one occasion five of us crawled to a trench parapet and looked down on about a twenty Germans. Their heads were not a yard beneath us, close enough to hear their breathing! They ate and talked quietly. Sentries were in post, but too wide apart to detect our approach - one advantage of a small band of top men. My well-drilled team knew exactly what to do next without any order. As slow as a fox stalking a grazing rabbit, we each took a grenade. Simultaneously we eased out the pin - all had been primed with a little gun oil or Vaseline - to free the lever. On my nod our palms opened. We counted 'one and two' in our heads and lobbed the bombs into the trench. Each man assessed the best spacing to gain the maximum kill. Two seconds later, as we rolled away, the explosions rocked the ground. Dust and debris fell everywhere through the smoke. The sentries foolishly rushed in the smoke-filled trench and we took care of them both with a bullet. As expected a blind outburst of machine gun fire followed into the trouble spot. But we had already withdrawn several yards into pre-determined hiding holes. Flares went up and we stayed down to remain hidden. After a minute of continuous gunfire, the machine gunners paused. My chaps knew what to do: do nothing. Stay hidden. Patience can be a life-saving virtue in combat. More flares were launched, but the Germans could not see a Tommy anywhere. A popular word in Yorkshire best described the enemy's mind at this stage: flummoxed. They were bewildered and confused as to what happened. Lance-Corporal Dewhurst, who spoke some German taught by his Swiss mother, said a Fritz shouted the attack must have been carried out by 'ghosts', a 'spirit' of some kind! I'm sure that's what *geist* means, he said later.

***

Outside the officers' dug-out near Hinges there was much excitement. It was packed with happy chaps and I couldn't get near the entrance. Had the war ended? No. That wasn't it. Someone had died, apparently. Everyone was delighted, so was it the Kaiser? Ludendorff? Hindenburg? 'Shot down in flames, he was,' I heard someone say. Eventually the victim was revealed: Rittmeister Captain Manfred von Richthofen, the Red Baron flying ace. His Fokker triplane had been shot from the skies over the Somme. A Canadian pilot, Captain Roy Brown, was on his tail at the time. And as Richthofen was so low, machine gunners and riflemen also had a go. One or more bullets brought him down to ground. Having destroyed at least eighty Allied aeroplanes and raided many convoys on the ground, his death was a cause for celebration. 'I hope he roasted all the way down to the ground,' one chap said, 'and burns forever in hell.'

Germans don't quit easily. It would take more than the loss of their top airman to curb their ambitions. We should have realised that if Amiens was their target at the beginning of April, and they had not taken it nor gone away, they would have another crack. And on 24th April they moved in again. But this time, refreshed, reinforced, resupplied, they broke through our 8th Division at the town of Villers-Bretonneux to set their sights on Amiens, just ten miles further on. But that night the Australian Corps launched a forceful counter-attack. It was vicious and bloody with much close-quarter fighting. The Australians showed no mercy. Any German who hadn't escaped was shot or stabbed. Surrender was not accepted. It was said that men could not be spared to escort prisoners to the rear.

Although German infantry failed to set foot inside Amiens, their bombs landed everywhere in the city. Throughout April and May Amiens was levelled. Few buildings, if any, escaped damage. Thousands of soldiers and civilians died as bombs fell in batches day and night. Many French had hoped beyond hope that something of their lives could be salvaged among the ruins. Its buildings were broken, but its citizens' spirit survived. Just. They wished to stay in the city they loved. It was time, they said, to stop running, dig their heels in, stay put. Many did. Many died. Shrapnel scattered at every

341

angle when bombs fell. For some of those who found shelter from the shrapnel, Fritz sent clouds of mustard gas to swirl, curl, twist and turn into every crevice. Children, women and men, sometimes whole families huddled together, inhaled gas as men in the front line.

US troops, not unlike the Australians, settled speedily into their stride on the Western Front. Since April around three hundred thousand US troops arrived in Europe every month, ten thousand a day. The enemy, with spies at every port and major railway junction, knew it. Pressure mounted day by day on the German High Command, who desperately needed a swift victory.

On 9thJune the Germans attempted to rip out the heart of France, Paris. They advanced a few miles south along a twenty-two-mile front between Montdidier and Noyon. Thanks to the US 2nd and 3rd Divisions at Château-Thierry on the River Marne, alongside French forces, Ludendorff's push to Paris was thwarted. Not only that, the Americans went on to sweep away the enemy from Belleau Woods in nearly three weeks of intense fighting. The Yanks suffered tremendous losses, far too many, several French and British officers said. They claimed that with better battle tactics, discipline, more experience - and much more patience - many of the US troop casualties could have been avoided. When I heard such talk, remembering how many lives I had seen squandered, I kept my views to myself. We British had learned the hard way, perhaps the Americans had to too. Whatever the criticism, the courage and determination of the doughboys could not be questioned. One story doing the rounds serves as an example. It tells of when a French commander advised a colonel of the US Marine Corps Brigade that a tactical retreat might be wise, the officer retorted, 'Retreat? You gotta be joking, right? We only just got here!'

Paris has already suffered an invasion of one kind, not from German troops, but from shells fired from up to seventy-five miles away. Since March as many as twenty shells a day have dropped on the capital causing hundreds of deaths and injuries. On the 29th of that month a shell hit an ancient church during the Good Friday service. Eighty-eight worshippers died and sixty-eight were injured at St-Gervais-et-St-Protais when the roof collapsed. The giant shells are estimated to weigh around two hundred and thirty-four pounds,

342

nearly seventeen stone, about the same as a very big man! The bullet-shaped shells are over a yard long and about nine inches wide. Our artillery chaps say that, like a bullet, the shells are 'rifled' - grooves in the howitzer's barrel spin the shell making its flight more stable and accurate. Some call any howitzer 'Big Bertha', named after the wife of one of Germany's main manufacturers, Gustav Krupp. But this new gigantic weapon has become known as the Paris Gun, as it seems the capital is its only target. For now. We worry that soon German engineers will have a howitzer powerful enough to send a shell-storm of ever-bigger bombs to London, perhaps anywhere in Britain, bringing yet more misery to our folks at home.

We know our people in Blighty are suffering increasing hardship. On top of general rationing being introduced, we heard of an explosion only a few days ago at an armaments factory in the Midlands. Over one hundred died and even more injured. It's not the first time. And I dare say it won't be the last. When there is such an urgent need for so much heavy machinery, including weapons, I'm sure corners are cut putting people at greater risk of injury in the dash to complete a task. Factories, foundries, mills, quaysides and workshops may not be the front line, but war poses a greater danger for everyone. Some men say their wives and older daughters are working so hard making articles for the war they are falling asleep on their feet or at their benches. Many women are - discreetly, quietly, without complaint - volunteering to eat less so their children, elderly relatives and those over here can have more.

Every man here, without exception, would prefer that sacrifice the other way around. The greatest pain for any man to endure at war is the pain of his family, whatever his own agony, whatever torture inflicted upon him.

The unanswerable question is again being increasingly asked: when will this war end? It plays constantly in the minds of men, like a popular tune you can't clear from your head. For me, the question seems pointless. When asked, I tell the truth: I don't know. I think of today, not tomorrow. Consider the battle, not the war. Apply tactics, not strategy. That's the generals' job. Focus only on the man in your gunsights, not the man to his side. Know the next hole to hide in, think not of any distant ridge - until there are no more holes.

Success or failure in battle will determine when the war will end. And the destiny of war can change on the smallest detail. When training to become an officer, we heard how, at Crécy in 1346, Genoese crossbowmen in the service of the French were outshot by English archers because of one simple fact: rain had softened the enemy's crossbow strings. English longbow strings made of hemp could be removed in a few seconds and kept dry until needed. Rain helped our victory!

At Verneuil, Normandy, in 1424, French and Milanese cavalry overran a flank of English archers because of the hot dry August weather. The hard-baked ground stopped our archers driving in their stakes to protect them from the charge. The sun helped our demise!

Whatever the weather, it plays a role in the fortunes of war. Somewhere, somehow, sometime, this war will end. The tide will turn. In whose favour, I know not. But the suffering will continue for many years after the guns are silent. This war has slashed such deep scars on so many families that it will take generations to heal. Children not yet born will feel the pain, perhaps for a hundred years or more.

CHAPTER 36

July 1918

It is tempting to claim the balmy days of mid-June to mid-July in France and Flanders made us sluggish. Observers might surmise long days of summer stillness and short nights reduced our desire to fight. It would be easy to say the sun, hot and high in a cloudless sky, sapped our will to kill. But they'd be wrong. And, for once, we can't blame the weather, or I don't think we can. The reason for the month-long reduction in hostilities was more mundane: influenza. The epidemic, which afflicted both sides, achieved what armies and armaments had failed to do; bring peace, at least temporarily and only partially. Snipers still sniped and shells still fell, but somehow in a lethargic way, as if reflecting the illness many men suffered. Old folk usually blame winter draughts for chills, but this crippling 'flu struck at the height of summer. Our Medical Officer offered the opinion that the disease had been brought in by the Americans, although doughboys appeared less affected than us and the Germans.

Disease or no disease the Germans, ever more desperate, planned another bold attack, this time from east of Reims along the River Marne in the Champagne region. On 15th July Ludendorff's First, Third and Seventh armies rolled south and west with Paris again in their sights. Fortunately, days earlier, the French had learnt from German prisoners the exact time of the assault. Only a fool would believe the word of a captive, of course. That doesn't mean you disregard completely what they say. Indeed, many may tell the truth believing it will help bring the war to a speedier end so they'll be released and returned home. You seek corroboration of prisoners' stories. Air reconnaissance confirmed the build-up of troops and ammunition dumps under camouflage in the areas captives had said. Acting on this intelligence, General Pétain cleared his front lines to reduce casualties and opened fire first. Pétain's early strike caught the Germans off guard and caused chaos and confusion in some German sectors. Further along the Marne, particularly the twenty miles between Château Thierry and Epenay, the Germans managed to ferry many men across the river under cover of night and by deploying smoke screens. Enemy engineers also speedily constructed several bridges. To span the Marne, eighty yards wide in parts, was an admirable feat under any circumstances, but especially so under fire.

To our amusement, we learnt from captured Germans they had called this latest incursion the *Friedensturm*, 'Peace Offensive'. We could only assume from this title Ludendorff, and probably his Kaiser, still believed that if Paris fell the war would be won and Europe would be at peace. I can't imagine what kind of peace that would be. The hatred and resentment will linger for a very long time, forever in the hearts of many. Since Mr Unia introduced me to the wonderful game of chess, and several fellow officers have been good enough to hone my skills, it's as if Paris is the king on the board, more symbolic than useful. But should Paris fall, will France capitulate? The Germans think so. I'm not so sure. With America's invaluable help, and troops from around the Empire, I believe and hope that we British will stick to the task of beating Germany even if Paris fell. We might soon discover the city's fate. The Germans have advanced to within forty-five miles of the capital, the closest to Paris since September '14. Even if hostilities in the city cease following an invasion of Paris, much fighting will be fought afterwards across the country. France is far bigger than Paris. And the French are nothing if not stubborn.

The night of 17th July stood eerily quiet throughout Picardy along the River Marne. Not a shot or shell fired. After their advance south over the past three days, up to eight miles forward in some areas, it appeared the Germans wanted or needed to rest. The break was equally welcome on our side. We too could catch breath and fortify positions.

But peaceful nights often foretell violent days. The lull before the storm. Silence and stillness in war can be as worrying as noise and movement, perhaps more so. When nothing is happening, all you can do is prepare for what might happen; once fighting starts, all you can do is face what is happening.

French soldiers call him 'the butcher'. And when their General Charles Mangin's Tenth Army struck at 4.35 am through the dawn

346

mist on the 18th, you can see why. His attack fell as firmly as a cleaver removing a sheep's head. Earlier, in the dark, behind the lines, nearly three hundred and fifty tanks coughed and spluttered into life. The French used their three main types of tank to spearhead the easterly attack between the rivers Aisne and Marne. The cumbersome St Chamand tank was useless except on smooth terrain. All but the narrowest trench would stop it in its tracks. And nearly half of the Schneider tanks broke down because of their unreliable engines. Fortunately the small, light and reliable Renault FT-17, which made up the bulk of France's tank force, rolled forward crushing the German barbed wire entanglements to the delight of all infantrymen. Each FT-17 was equipped with a revolving turret with a .315 machine gun which made a significant difference to our progress. 'Butcher' Mangin also dispensed with any preliminary shelling and commenced a creeping barrage with around fifteen hundred artillery guns. French infantry regiments, accompanied by troops from the American 1st and 2nd Divisions, advanced as a shell storm flew overhead towards the Germans. (Our 15th and 34th Divisions stood in reserve.) To Mangin's right and south, the French Sixth Army, alongside two American divisions, the 4th and 26th, also advanced eastwards between the rivers Ourcq and Marne.

General Mangin's first objective was to take the important rail junction town of Soissons on the River Aisne, approximately seven miles behind the German front line. After two days and nights the Allies had advanced about five miles. It hadn't been easy. It never would be fighting Germans. At times there was confusion between the French, their colonial troops from various African countries, and the American Expeditionary Force. Groups of doughboys narrowly escaped being crushed by French tanks driving through wheat fields in which the Americans hid. African troops failed to take cover when German machine guns opened fire, and they suffered tremendous losses. People watching said it was as if many of them relied on fate rather than their own skill to keep alive. Partly because of this lack of coordination and experience, Mangin's Tenth Army fell short of taking Soissons. Nevertheless, by early August the Germans had lost almost all the territory they had gained since Ludendorff's May offensive. This Second Battle of the Marne, although the French preferred to call it the Battle of Soissonnais and Ourcq, resulted in ninety-five thousand French, thirteen thousand British and twelve thousand American casualties. Intelligence believes the Germans suffered nearly one hundred and seventy thousand casualties, and we know twenty-five thousand German prisoners were taken. Despite this setback, Ludendorff ordered fresh attacks - and we Dukes stood in the middle of the action.

***

June and July 1918 turned out to be the quietest months I'd experienced in the war, except for my time as an officer cadet during spring '16. The Duke of Wellington's Regiment continued to help hold the front at La Bassée, sixteen miles north of Arras, where several lieutenants received injuries during this time, including Lomax, Morgan and McFarlane. McCulloch was knocked out by shell fire and Wildbourne killed. I'm sorry to say that three men suffered at the trigger-fingers of snipers owing to their own carelessness rather than any forward infiltration by a devious rifleman. No-one in my Company, thankfully, caught a sniper's bullet. Sergeant Foster said this was 'down to your nagging, Sir'. I remained unsure whether this was a compliment or criticism. But several men across the Regiment, two from my Company, died in random shell-falls. 'Wrong place, wrong time,' was all one could say.

During these two 'quiet' months for the Dukes, we carried out small raids to obtain enemy identification and, hopefully, gain information about any German plans. In the early hours one morning C Company moved forward on such a mission. Corporal Padley and six men made a dash and came across a post occupied by three Boçhe. One ran off. He gambled on not receiving a bullet in the back - and won. Our chaps sensibly refrained from firing to avoid provoking a burst of retaliatory fire. But they collared the remaining two, an elderly corporal and a young rifleman, a scrag of a lad, from the 5th Reserve Infantry Regiment. It seems the Germans, like us, had resorted to recruiting younger lads and older men, neither the best physique or age for soldiering. It was also clear from their poor condition that Germans troops no longer received the generous rations they once enjoyed.

In July five officers and two hundred other ranks received instruction to leave the line and prepare for a week for another raid on Pacaut Wood. Our attempt in April alongside the Warwicks had failed, despite destroying several machine gun redoubts and killing quite a few Fritz. But the main objective had been to clear *Bois de Pacaut* of German men, machinery and stores. I remember that raid clearly because of the young German officer we captured who spoke almost perfect English after just a few months of learning. We believed *Bois de Pacaut*, north of the Aire-La Bassee canal, held at least two companies of enemy with machine gun posts and light artillery. Captain Hill was to command the new move, with 2nd lieutenants Banham, Craven, Huffam and Little. Accompanying the party were three sappers from 526 (Durham) Field Company Royal Engineers. The four companies of fifty men would each have three Lewis guns and eight stretcher bearers. Our orders read:

A detachment of the Battalion will carry out a raid on 18th July 1918. Intention: to clear a sector of Pacaut Wood in two phases, and capture the garrison, thus obtaining identifications and causing casualties. Phase One: Penetrating and clearing houses, orchards, and enemy positions immediately outside the north-east edge of Pacaut Wood. Phase Two: To penetrate and clear from north to south-west so much of Pacaut Wood as lies with the limits named. No titles, regimental patches, or other articles which might cause identification are to be worn by any of the party. Special raid identity discs are being issued. White bands will be worn on the left arm.

Our attack commenced at 2.30 pm. The artillery barrage gave cover as each of our four platoons mounted the parapet one after another at twenty-five yard intervals. Within minutes an enemy machine gun post was taken and already several Boche had raised their arms. The second phase through the woods was harder work, particular because of the brambles. Nature's entanglements had trebled in length, complexity and barbed-ferocity since April! Every man suffered scratches and cuts and torn puttees and uniforms from the thorns. Despite the dense shrubs and enemy fire, in twenty minutes we had swept back to our Battalion's line and it was time to count the cost: five Dukes killed, twenty-five wounded, two missing. It was the price we paid for killing many more enemy, at least eighty. Our Stokes mortar barrage on their main line of resistance in the wood caused many enemy to perish. Dug-outs had been blown in and the occupants killed. Some Boche failed to surrender and had to be shot or taken out with grenades. Further on, at the edge of the wood in a shallow trench, a crew of four machine gunners we encountered foolishly refused to lift their arms. Fearing they would make a sudden dash to discharge their *maschinegewehr* I disposed of them with a grenade. Many Boche ran from the woods and some of these would have suffered under our main artillery barrage. Twenty-nine prisoners were taken.

Later in the afternoon we received messages of congratulation on the successful raid from Army Corps, Division and Brigade Commanders. The men showed great delight at hearing these communiques. I suggested to the junior officer supervising the rum ration that evening to make sure the sergeant gave 'an extra nudge' of the jar to the men involved in the raid. 'Is that…' the young officer started to question, before realising I was really issuing an order.

Talk in the Battalion Officers' dug-out that night was not only about the day's action. There was much speculation that Germany may have to again mobilise against Russia following the assassination of the German ambassador in Moscow on July 6th. Socialist revolutionaries, opposed to the communists and the Brest-Litovsk peace treaty, were named as the guilty party. And just two days ago, July 16th, it was reported that Russia's Bolshevik rulers had massacred Czar Nicholas II and his family. If true, the Romanov dynasty was shot and bayoneted in a cellar in Ekaterinburg, a pro-Bolshevik town in the Urals. Some reports added the family's doctor, valet, cook, maid and dog were murdered too. But I suspect no one person can possibly know what is happening across such a vast country with so many factions fighting each other. Perhaps we will learn the truth one day. Maybe not. Russia sounds like a country of rumour, speculation, half-truths and half-lies - and no-one can tell the difference.

CHAPTER 37

August 1918
BATTLE OF AMIENS

While we Dukes helped hold the line in northern France and Flanders, our comrades to the south achieved several significant gains. They started reversing the German advances made from late May towards the River Marne through Soissons to Château Thierry. We had not won the war. Far from it. But it looked less likely that we would lose.

A few months ago, following the enemy's rapid advance east on Amiens and south across the Marne towards Paris, many of us feared - for the first time - that we could be defeated. No-one voiced his feeling within my hearing. But there was no longer confident talk of our victory and increasing discussion about a 'negotiated settlement' between the Allies and Germany. Our hearts resisted what our heads told us. Facts didn't lie: the Germans had broken through our lines again, and again, and again.

Now, in August, it looks as if the very speed and depth of their advance left the Germans vulnerable to counter-attack. Be it supplies unable to keep up with the fighting front, exhausted soldiers, less capable conscripts or high casualty figures, Ludendorff's push to Paris and to the Atlantic coast had failed. Whatever the reasons, it seems the Germans are no longer the formidable force they once were. The Kaiser's mighty military machine looks as if it is breaking down, at least running out of fuel. It is being forced to backtrack towards the River Aisne, occupying roughly the same territory as before their spring 'Peace Offensive'. French forces spearhead the pushback with vital assistance from the American Expeditionary Force and, to a lesser extent, we British, called in as reserves and helping with supplies.

Call me a stick-in-the-mud, but I urged caution. The Germans could be playing a trick, a large-scale ruse. They could be feigning injury and catching breath before springing back and hitting us hard when our defences are down. I will not rest easy until all German

351

troops are back in Germany without a gun or grenade. Those of us at the front hope our leaders share that caution and are not lulled into a false sense of security. We mustn't buy German bluff.

For those of us entrenched, not pushing forward or being forced back, recent months have been frustrating. The Dukes haven't however been idle. We made raids on the Germans and always caused more casualties than we suffered. We captured more prisoners than we lost. Danger remained and remains a constant companion. Our vigilance has been maintained throughout. We always expect the unexpected attack, day and night, from either a shower of shells or infantry with bayonets fixed. A cloud of gas could drift over us at any time or a handful of stick grenades land at our feet. They did. They do.

Away from the front we trained many new chaps released from home service. Most of the fresh drafts needed to get fit for fighting. All the men have regular drill and exercise and, in the rest camps, they've enjoyed a full programme of sport: boxing, soccer, cricket and hockey. The Duke of Wellington's Regiment prides itself especially on our prowess in rugby-football. The Army's very own Calcutta Cup, Rugby League's premier trophy competition, was won by the 2nd Battalion in 1903 and 1905. (The King's Own Regiment beat us in the semi-final in 1904.) Our India-stationed 1st Battalion's record in the Calcutta tournament is outstanding. Between 1906 and 1913 it did not lose a single match. It also won the cup at Bombay on six occasions and at Madras seven times, before this wretched war stopped play. It is said that our Regiment's namesake, the 1st Duke of Wellington, once remarked, 'The Battle of Waterloo was won on the playing-fields of Eton'. We understand what he meant by this.

I've again been given the responsibility to give further instruction to new drafts of officers and men on frontline warfare. This includes the gruesome but essential skill of hand-to-hand combat. Chaps need the whole truth about what happens when a man is fighting for his life. The first fact to remember: killing is not sport. It's no game. Battle grounds are not playing fields, at Eton or anywhere else. Fighting to survive is not even like a Saturday night brawl on the street after a beer too many. It's not football or rugby or boxing. There is no referee. It's not a contest with rules. But if there is one rule, there are no rules. It is a dirty fight to the death. You're not fighting to disarm or disable like a policeman making an arrest. Mercy, pity or sympathy must not be in your mind or deeds. If you're squeamish, you'll perish. You do what you need to do to kill your opponent quickly. You 'cheat', although there is no cheating. You shoot, stab, slash, stamp, kick, scrape, scratch, throw, shout, spit, squeeze, bite, poke eyes, kick testicles - anything with one intention and one intention only. Kill. It's the only idea in your head. Kill. Think of anything else and you're dead. Kill. If you delay, you'll die. Kill. A Fritz will pretend to surrender. Kill. Unless you have a gun on him and you're sure he's unarmed, ignore him. Kill. He might have a knife down his boot or up his sleeve. Don't believe his plea. Kill him. He'll slaughter you the second you show leniency. When he's dead, think no more of him. Find another enemy to slay until there are no more.

German snipers still oblige me when I'm demonstrating to the new chaps the need to keep one's head below the parapet. Sometimes I suspect the sniper knows it's just a helmet on a stick, but appreciates the target practice! Our occasional raids have taught us that Fritz is no longer the fighting force he once was. Germans give themselves up more quickly than before, officers as well as men. They seem pleased to become prisoners. Many are hungry and dirty, as if they have lost all pride in their appearance. Even in the most dreadful trench conditions men can, and should, take the best possible care of themselves, their clothes and kit. Men who have lost pride in their appearance are usually the chaps who fall first to illness and injury.

Throughout August our scouting patrols found larger gaps between German sentries, a sign their lines are thinner. One patrol of four men, under 2nd Lt Morris, located an enemy listening post. They took one prisoner and disposed of the rest. The prisoner, a corporal, freely confessed that some soldiers had abandoned their posts and, if our translation was right, 'disappeared into the night'. Whole platoons had vanished, he reported. So more of our patrols went forward with greater confidence, but maintained caution. As no enemy was located we advanced to the village of Quentin, a mile north of Pacaut Wood and nearly two miles from our forward entrenchments on the Aire-Le Bassée Canal. Here we faced resistance and had to fight. After further reconnaissance and discussing our plan of attack, a company from the Dukes under Captain Hoole, with the 1st Royal Warwicks and 2nd Seaforths, captured the village magnificently. The bill to pay was seven killed and twenty-seven wounded, chiefly from machine guns. We could accept this toll knowing of many more enemy casualties. In keeping with the captured corporal's comments, it was noticed that many Germans slipped away from the village once they realised resistance was futile.

The weakening of the German front in our sector at Le Bassée indicated it was happening elsewhere, although not everywhere along the enemy's front. But wherever the allies now conducted a concentrated attack, territory was gained. This crucial fact was not lost on our leaders. The time had arrived when we could beat the Germans, or at least push them back to the lines held at the beginning of the year. This shift in the balance of fortunes probably explains why our top brass have been shuffling divisions around during the past two months. General Sir Henry Rawlinson has simplified the Fourth Army's structure on the Somme, particularly around Amiens. General Sir Julian Byng has repositioned some of his thirteen divisions of the Third Army north of the Somme between the rivers Ancre and Scarpe. In our Arras sector, north of the River Scarpe to Armentières, Ypres and beyond, General Sir Henry Horne has arranged divisions in such a way it makes me believe we're in for another big push. Secrecy, surprise and subterfuge are important weapons of war, I therefore kept my notions to myself.

***

Early morning on Thursday, 8th August 1918, fog enveloped much of northern France. In the Somme valley visibility was confined to fifteen yards at most. A French officer from nearby Lens, on attachment to our Battalion, said thick fog was most unexpected this time of year. 'September, perhaps,' he shrugged. 'October or November, definitely. But early August? *Brouillard? Non, non, non. Impossible!* God must have changed sides today. *Dieu merci!*' At last, with or without holy intervention, weather conditions played in our favour. Its timing could not have been better: the day of our biggest big push of the war.

Along a fourteen-mile front east of Amiens, Royal Air Force reconnaissance, helped by ground 'flash spotters' and scouts, had over the previous week identified the precise position of over five hundred enemy artillery pieces. They could not locate all the guns from the flashes when fired, or from aerial observation, but most of them. To counter them we sited over one thousand three hundred and eighty field guns plus nearly seven hundred heavy guns. They had been set with the utmost stealth over several nights and carefully concealed. Each gun aimed at a specific German target, and every gun team trained and eager to launch a colossal barrage of high explosives and gas. This onslaught would nullify much of the opposition's violence on our infantry as we ventured onto no-man's-land. And because we had already calibrated the range, the fog did not thwart our artillery attack. Indeed, the fog curtain would hide our infantry movement until within grenade-throwing distance.

Secrecy played a vital part in bringing thousands of troops and supplies to the front. Nearly three hundred trains conveyed the men and materials, quite an achievement with only two railway lines available. Deception helped too. Our generals cleverly provided the Germans with the impression our attack would be about seventy miles further north. Two Canadian battalions, casualty clearing stations and a wireless detachment had been moved to Kemmel in Flanders. The Canadians 'kicked up dust' to make sure German aircraft and spies observed their deployment. We also 'forgot' to cover up some of our tracks to provide a false trail. Finally, if these measures failed to fool the Germans into thinking Flanders was the site of our big push, the construction of new aerodromes in the area certainly convinced them. The ploy worked.

At zero hour, 4.20 am, sixty minutes before the summer sun would rise and burn off the mist, our Fourth Army commenced the Amiens Offensive. Fritz received a surprise. German General von der Marwitz and his Second Army had no time to enjoy breakfast. (We heard later from a Canadian officer who interrupted a group of German officers enjoying breakfast.) Our deception had been so effective the Germans could not believe they came under attack and some commanders failed to deploy their units.

The vanguard, a swarm of over three hundred heavy tanks, crushed the wire entanglements allowing our infantry to advance eastwards. The bomb-pounded land wasn't easy to cross, but far easier and quicker without barbed wire to cut through. Following the 'heavies', ninety-six new fourteen-ton 'lightweight' tanks quickly penetrated German lines and caused chaos with their four .303 Hotchkiss turreted machine guns. We first saw these tanks earlier in the year. Because of their small size and fast speed - compared with heavy tanks - we nicknamed them 'whippets'. They were of course nowhere near as fast as a real whippet! A brisk walker could keep up with them. But they are effective killing machines. At Cachy, near Villers Brettonneux, a company of seven whippets killed over four hundred enemy infantrymen caught on open ground.

Seven divisions opened our attack: British III Corps' 18th and 58th, Australian Corps' 2nd and 3rd; and Canadian Corps' 1st, 2nd and 3rd. A contingent of the American 33rd Division also fought alongside our chaps north of the Somme. Showing great courage and enthusiasm, the Australians and Canadians surged towards Marwitz's six divisions, believed to contain around eighteen thousand fighting men. Our enterprising scouts had again successfully laid down ribbon, rope and string to guide men forward in the dark. These guidelines are such a simple but highly effective device. They've concentrated our attacks and saved lives by preventing men straying in the wrong direction, especially when wearing gas masks. With the unexpected overnight fog-fall, the strings proved doubly helpful.

After advancing a few hundred yards, blurred, ghost-like figures slowly emerged through the faint light. Mist swirled around each indistinct shape stood as still as a statue. Huns, alone and in huddles, gradually appeared with their hands high in surrender. They were naturally fearful about their fate, worried we might shoot or stab them. Surrendering was a chance soldiers on both sides took, especially if the fighting is furious. When fear flows fast through your veins, men often shoot without thinking. Most Fritzes appeared happy to give up the fight, and we refrained from firing. As one prisoner told me, 'I better alive prisoner than soldier *kaput, tot'*. His finger tracked the line of a bayonet slitting his throat.

Until it lifted, the fog absorbed the metallic noises of battle. The sound of war seemed soft. Even death appeared mellow, injury gentle, the cry of pain calm. Shells still streaked overhead, guns fired and grenades exploded. Yet under the muffling cloak of mist, war's sharp edges became dull. The strident din of war however soon returned with the rising sun. No softness, dull edges or muffled cries remained in Picardy east of Amiens. Fog's damper had lifted. The full war orchestra again played its piercing tune of booms and blasts, screeches and screams, whistles and wails.

We watched in clear sky RAF aeroplanes in the distance strafing German infantry and artillery lines. Many pilots ventured further to attack airfields, railway junctions, major supply roads and bridges. With around eight hundred aircraft we outnumbered German aeroplanes by three if not four to one. The French used over a thousand aircraft for the offensive. Twenty-six tons of bombs dropped on enemy lines that day plus forty-three tons earmarked for railway junctions.

We again used the creeping barrage method with infantry advancing alongside heavy tanks and whippets. Yet more Germans surrendered, no longer in dribs and drabs but whole platoons, even companies. Hundreds of men stood waiting for capture. Officers appeared to order their men to surrender. We noticed one officer force his men at gunpoint to throw their weapons down before he himself dropped his and raised his arms. The fleeing Germans looked in a tizzy, throwing all manner of items onto wagons and trains in a rush to get away. Suddenly, as tanks are prone to do, a whippet went zigzag and our chaps had to jump out of its way. One lad, slow to escape harm's way, was completely crushed. Moments later an older fellow was caught under a heavy tank's tracks as it lurched into him. Both legs were pressed flat against the hard ground by the 29-ton machine, his cry catching everyone's ear even through the perpetual din of shell fire. The Mark V tank driver, from the 14th Battalion, was most distraught to learn of the accident, of which he knew nothing at the time. You can't hear a damn thing inside a tank except the roaring engines, he said. You can hardly see to drive. Steering a tank was like threading a needle wearing boxing gloves, a tank crew member told me. But it wasn't long into the offensive before many tanks broke down owing to mechanical failure, although they had contributed greatly to the attack.

The major sticking point on day two of our offensive proved to be the north bank of the Somme. The Germans held a commanding position on a high spur outside the village of Chipilly. It delayed our III Corps' progress at the bottom of our sector and the Australians at the top of theirs, the river our dividing line. With the Germans well dug in on high ground it was difficult to dislodge them, especially with few infantry pieces to hand. After a frustrating day, at dusk an enterprising platoon of Australians slipped across the river from the town of Cerisy and captured Chipilly village. We British simultaneously renewed our attack from the west and, as darkness arrived, our joint pincer movement captured the spur. Knowing the game was up, many Germans again called it a day. We disposed of the forty or so foolish chaps who resisted.

The Battle of Amiens ended after three triumphant days, gaining around fifteen miles of territory. Every step forward now feels like a small victory, a step closer to Germany. But the big push eastward has only just begun.

The Germans still offer stiff opposition in Albert, although we have moved to within a mile. With constant shelling, if not a miracle, it is certainly miraculous that the gilded statue of the Virgin remained dangling from Albert's basilica. When even much of the rubble surrounding the church is bombed to dust, like grains of wheat pounded to flour, Mary maintains her defiance.

CHAPTER 38

DECLARED DEAD

Behind our frontline, in the wasteland of war, German prisoners collect their dead and bury them in long trench graves. No-one can say if these trough-tombs will be their final resting place, a mass of dead men and remains, some known, others unrecognisable, never to be identified. They fought and died together. Perhaps their bodies should rot together, merge as one into the earth. But, in some far-off future peace, I suppose each family will want its own body to bury, a grave to catch tears, a headstone with a name, even if it's Unknown Soldier.

Our stretcher bearers continue to collect corpses too. Meanwhile, most of the seriously injured, having gone through a casualty clearing station, will be at Stationary Hospital No 42 in Amiens, or SH No 5 (B Sector) in Abbeville. Many of the seriously injured Australians have been taken by train to Stationary Hospital No 5 (A Sector) in Dieppe, staffed largely by Australian nurses and doctors.

To August 15th we continued our fight eastwards, seizing a further ten miles in some parts. But hundreds died every mile, such is the way of war. It was also sad to see war-torn villages, ruined farms, ravished fields and woods full of broken trees, scorched and stripped of summer leaves. When attacking across new and unknown ground, every step is fraught with danger. Just when you think the Germans are down, up they spring like a jack-in-a-box. We faced many ambushes, most ending in close-quarter fighting. I hoped my pupils remembered there were no rules and to think only of killing. But even the best fighters die. When struggling with a man in front, you can't in open ground prevent another stabbing you in the back. That's why, when you can, you fight with your back against a wall, trench slope, even a thick tree stump.

A German garrison stuck in Albert like an irritating sharp stone in a shoe. Their stubborn resistance held back our progress along the whole front. It was time to retake the town, if ruins and rubble can be described as such. The Germans would take some shifting. We believe they had been ordered to fight to the death. Any man falling back would be shot and, if they attempted to surrender to us, they'd be shot in the back. This would be the third time since 1914 we have fought over Albert. And could we oust the Germans without bringing the basilica's Virgin crashing to the ground? Would we incur the curse if she fell and lose the war? A silly superstition, of course, but some people believe such nonsense.

On Wednesday August 21st thirteen divisions of General Julian Byng's Third Army attacked Albert and its surrounds. Although resistance at first was fierce, by Thursday evening we had overwhelmed the enemy. Germany's well-trained disciplined troops of 1914 would have held out a good week, even against our superior numbers and weaponry. Quick-trained conscripts cannot match well-prepared full-time regulars. Once the door of Albert opened, it unleashed our wider assault across the Somme. This involved not only Byng's Third, but also Rawlinson's Fourth Army and much of the Australian Corps. The German 2nd Army was pushed back along a fifty-mile front as Allied troops, now including American and New Zealand forces, advanced towards Arras. In keeping with a new order from Field Marshal Sir Douglas Haig, we no longer stopped to consolidate positions taken, but carry on. His command read:

To turn the present situation to account, the most resolute offensive is everywhere desirable. Risk, which a month ago would have been criminal to incur, ought now to be incurred as a duty. It is no longer necessary to advance in regular lines and step by step. On the contrary, each division should be given a distant objective which must be reached independently of its neighbour, and even if one's flank is thereby exposed for the time being. Reinforcements must be directed on the points where our troops are gaining ground, not where they are checked. A vigorous offensive against the sectors where the enemy is weak will cause hostile strongpoints to fall, and in due course our whole army will be able to continue its advance. The situation is most favourable. Let each one of us act energetically and without hesitation push forward to our objective.

***

I remember the blinding flash. Then nothing. Everything looked blurred when I finally recovered from the knock-out blow. They told me I was lucky. Two men at my side died from shrapnel. The sergeant lost an arm and, unless it begins to heal, his leg will be sawn off. Since the war began field medics and doctors at Casualty Clearing Stations and hospitals have greatly improved the way they treat injuries. They now save limbs that in the early days would have been lopped off without hesitation. They are making repairs to broken and burnt bodies with surgical procedures unknown before the war. War not only brings progress in weaponry, such as we've seen in bomb-making, tanks and aircraft engineering, but also in medicine. Today's victims help tomorrow's. The Royal Army Medical Corps have built on an enormous amount of experience saving life and limb since Mons. The surgeon's hopeful the sergeant's leg can be saved.

'If we can keep infection away,' he added. 'And that's largely down to the nurses. But they are very good here, the best I've ever seen, even when Matron's not keeping an eye on them!'

The shell rendered me unconscious, they said for about half an hour. One orderly declared I was a goner. The other didn't, otherwise I'd have been carted away with the truly dead. That was five days ago and, apart from a throbbing head now and then, I'm well. The gash in my leg and a few bruises will soon heal. My uniform was in tatters and yesterday I ordered a replacement. Thankfully my faithful Sam Browne belt that General Allan surreptitiously bought for me survived. The leather has a few more scars and wrinkles, like my skin. The belt is my constant companion. Alongside Father's lighter, it's the only item I've retained in the past two and a half years, with one exception, my trusted vernier compass. Its simple magnetic needle has directed me and my men in and out of places hundreds of times, day and night, in all weathers. Finding the way home over no-man's-land in darkness, in fog, or through a flat featureless land of cavities and corpses, the compass becomes the most important piece of kit. It is truly a life-saver. I'm almost embarrassed to admit it, but I want to carry this compass with me for ever. It's as if without it I would be lost in life. Perhaps Father's lighter and my compass have been my lucky charms, even though I still don't believe in luck, and the war's far from over. Things just happen, good and bad. In life, as I've found in war, control what you can and don't worry about the things you can't.

Discharged from hospital, I returned to my beloved Dukes on Saturday August 24th at St Catherine on the western edge of Arras. A few days earlier my Battalion had been taken out of the line on the Aire-La Bassèe Canal to be repositioned. Many changes along the Western Front took place as our attacks gathered pace. We Dukes, as part of General Henry Horne's First Army, were poised to be in the thick of the next phase of fighting. From Arras we marched several miles south-east along the Cambrai road to an assembly point at Feuchy Chapel. We heard the fighting ahead as we set out, and it grew louder each step of the way. My Company of nearly two hundred and fifty men, indeed our whole Battalion, had been heartened by the success north of the Somme in Amiens and Albert. The French Tenth Army too were enjoying progress south of the Somme, an action which commenced on August 20th. My men, ready for the fight like thoroughbreds before a steeplechase, chewed at the bit. As always before engagement fear fused with excitement and the self-questioning: this time tomorrow will I be alive, dead, injured or prisoner?

The 4th Canadian Division carried out good work pushing the Germans back to Monchy le-Preux, two miles west of us. We Dukes alongside several thousand others were required to rest for the night. Sometime tomorrow, probably at first light, we'd be moving to the front. I ordered my platoon commanders to ensure the men had as much rest as possible immediately after supper. Chaps found sleeping spaces in the fields and settled down. It was a warm evening and, better still, it wasn't raining. Meanwhile I attended the officers' briefing at Brigade HQ, a bombed barn with canvas for a makeshift roof draped over its cracked walls. As darkness fell the main fighting died down. Skirmishes continued spasmodically however as company commanders took it upon themselves to go for a raid. In keeping with Field Marshall Haig's order, if an opportunity of advancement presented itself, it should be taken. Any sleep was thus constantly interrupted by outbursts of mortars or field gun shelling. One stray crump landed in the middle of an adjoining field to us.

Fortunately, because men prefer to sleep as close as possible to hedges and walls, nobody had bivouacked where the shell fell. We also suffered two gas alerts throughout the night, although no gas floated our way; they turned out to be false alarms.

At first light on Sunday August 25th men from all over Britain and the Empire moved into the front line alongside the Canadians. We Dukes covered the crossroads just short of a hamlet of flattened cottages called Vis-en-Artois. Our first objective was to reach the River Sensée, four hundred yards beyond the ruins. All day and into the night we attacked and suffered counter-attacks. We secured the lane running south-west to the villages of Cherisy and Wancourt, but failed to reach the river. Every yard of the hundred yards we gained had been hard won. I lost three privates: Robertson, aged 21, Phoenix, 19, and Beech, whose date of birth was obscured by blood in his Service and Pay Book. His friend, 17, believed him to be the same. The Regiment also lost Lance-Sergeant Atkinson, 23, and Sergeant Alfred Tetley. The next day, Monday August 26th, our First Army launched a huge attack across the whole Arras sector. Hopes were high that we would at last have the Hun on the run! By Tuesday, in our small sector of this huge war, we had gradually worked our way down the fields to the river bank. My Company lost privates Atkins, Ripper and Whitehead, aged 37.

Wednesday August 29th proved an outstanding day. Having crossed the River Sensée - a much smaller river than the Somme - and secured both banks, we pushed north-east and captured the village of Haucourt. We occupied a line immediately east of the village, yet another sad heap of ruins. We heard of even greater success that evening: New Zealanders had captured the major town of Bapaume, half way between Albert and Cambrai, twelve miles to the south of us.

The next two days we faced fanatical close-quarter fighting before we paused to gather breath and regroup. It was time, too, to count the cost to the Battalion. Two second lieutenants, Ward and Little, were killed. Lieutenants Banham, Hebblethwaite, Morris and Tunstall sustained injuries. Thirty-six other ranks died and one hundred and sixty-two wounded. Seven men were missing; two of these possibly drowned crossing the river. On August 31st we attacked a small area of woodland called Stipe Copse to seize and hold the position. We achieved our objective without any supporting artillery barrage. But we couldn't maintain our stance for more than a few minutes. We just didn't have enough men to resist the heavy counter-attack following a violent bombardment. We Dukes, perhaps because of the well-known stubbornness of Yorkshiremen, hate giving up hard-earned possessions. But common sense prevailed over pride, and we retreated. If we hadn't, I believe up to three hundred men would have perished for not the slightest advantage.

As night approached, however, the urge to reverse the morning's failure overcame us. Courageously, cleverly, quickly, we recaptured Stipe Copse and more beyond, including a position known as St Servin's Farm. Regimental pride was restored - with interest! We took forty-five prisoners, including two officers. The Battalion lost 2nd lieutenants Anson and Watmough and, a fine man in my Company, Sydney Johnson. 2nd Lt Blackburn was gassed and Lt Skelton taken to hospital. Fourteen men died, thirty-six wounded, seventeen missing. Most of the missing came from one platoon on the extreme right flank. We're hoping they are holding out somewhere, caught behind enemy lines. One young soldier 'thinks' he saw them captured. When quizzed, he told his sergeant it was quite dark and he couldn't swear to it. I wrote 'missing, possibly captured' in my report. During the attack on St Servin's Farm we captured nine machine guns and the field gun.

Men demonstrated incredible courage over recent days. I can honestly say not one man in my Company that I observed shirked his duty. Not all acts of bravery are seen, and because there are so many, few are considered out of the ordinary. During heavy fighting it is almost impossible to choose the bravest of the brave. And an act of bravery to one is viewed by another as reckless. If a mission succeeds it is courageous; failure makes it foolhardy.

I must cite the magnificent actions of 2nd Lt James Huffam. With three men, he rushed an enemy machine gun post and put it out of action. This gun had already killed several and kept my Company pinned down. Huffam then came under fierce fire from German riflemen and another machine gun crew. One of his men was shot. The situation looked hopeless for all of them, unless they took a chance and made it back quickly. Nobody would have criticised the lieutenant had he retired to save his own skin. But no. He lifted his injured man across his shoulders and zigzagged back with bullets whizzing within an inch of his life. If that wasn't enough action for any man in a day - if not a lifetime - that evening 2nd Lt Huffam, a softly-spoken Scot from Dunblane, set out with two men to St Servin's Farm. They rushed *another* enemy machine gun! And this time the intrepid three enjoyed a bonus of capturing eight prisoners. This enemy position had also pinned us down, so Huffam's action again allowed our advance to continue.

The following day, September 1st, the Dukes alongside the 1st Royal Warwickshires - an excellent Regiment we had grown to respect during the many battles we had fought together - attacked and captured what was known as Pear Trench. This was our last action before being relieved and placed in Divisional Reserve. Back encamped in the fields at Feuchy Chapel on September 2nd, I was pleased to read the following message to my Company. It had come through in orders from 4th Division, 10th Brigade, the previous evening:

The General Officer Commanding wishes to convey to Lieutenant-Colonel Pawlett and ALL ranks of the 2nd Duke of Wellington's Regiment his great appreciation of the magnificent way in which this Battalion has fought during the past days' heavy fighting east of Monchy. The Battalion has shown fighting spirit worthy of the best traditions. Signed, Lawrence Carr, Lt-Col, General Staff, 4th Division.'

I also took the opportunity to share additional news with the men that officers had heard during our briefing. In the Somme sector, I announced, the Germans appear to be retreating. The men cheered. Yesterday, I continued, a key battle took place at Mont St Quentin, just north of Peronne. The Australians crossed the river and took a key hill only to be beaten back. Men groaned. But, like us a few days ago at Stipe Copse, they bounced back to give the Germans a thorough beating. More cheers and smiles. We're also hearing the Canadian Corp are, as I speak, attacking the Drocourt-Quéant Switch Line, an extension to the Hindenburg Line. At last it looks as if we're batting on the front foot, as all of us who enjoy cricket say. Chaps threw their caps in the air. I worried I'd painted too rosy a picture.

'However, chaps,' I said, hoping to balance expectations, 'Fritz is not out of the race. He *will* fight back. The war goes on. I doubt he'll roll over and let us tickle his tummy without trying to bite our hand. Like animals, our enemy is most dangerous and cunning when cornered. There is still fighting to do. The job's not over.

'Each one of you has been magnificent over the past week. I could not be prouder of you. So, chaps, rest while you can. Clean your kit and rifles - oh, and yourselves.'

I pinched my nose and looked offended. They laughed. Men smell. And when confined together in fear and fighting, unable to wash or change clothes, we smell even 'higher'. We learn to live with it, because we can't avoid it.

Following the Allies recent success, the atmosphere at Battalion HQ that evening was full of jovial confidence. Supplies and a kitchen had caught up with us to provide plenty of hot food. One generous officer supplied several bottles of wine and brandy for those wishing to imbibe. I had grown to like wine over the last two years, although I never over-indulged. I failed to develop the taste for brandy and, frankly, some of the French spirits I found revolting. Whisky, with a dash of soda or water, I could tolerate. I still suffered occasional headaches following my run-in with the whizz-bang two weeks earlier, so I politely declined Lt-Col Pawlett's offer of a drink with that reason. My cup of tea sufficed.

***

When all the officers expected arrived at HQ, around twenty of us, the Colonel stepped onto an old apple box. The adjutant called for our attention and the room fell silent. The Colonel announced he had three interesting developments to share with us. First, intelligence reports revealed that rioters in Berlin had recently destroyed pictures of the Kaiser. Clearly this indicates growing resentment against the war which puts additional pressure on him to seek a settlement. Second, on August 30th, an attempt was made on the life of Vladimir Lenin in Russia. The country is in turmoil. There are so many revolutionaries my head is spinning, he said. (It was the closest the Colonel ever came to humour, and we obliged with polite laughter.) But, the Colonel continued, before we become complacent, all is not well in Britain. A week after London's underground workers went on strike for equal 'war wages' for women doing men's jobs, London's policemen decided to strike too. Over two thousand policemen marched from Scotland Yard to Tower Hill demanding more pay. The Colonel made his views on the matter clear: they should be locked in the Tower of London to remind the blighters we are at war! No-one asked what everyone was thinking: who would arrest them?

The Germans by the end of August had been pushed back to the Canal du Nord and Hindenburg Line. All their gains - and more - since Ludendorff's surge in May had been reversed. Also, in Flanders, particularly the Lys region, Fritz had been ousted from his holdings occupied since 1914. But it was rumoured that in London, the new Chief of Imperial General Staff, General Sir Henry Wilson, was thinking of delaying any further big pushes until 1919, even 1920. Perhaps he didn't wish to stretch our success too far and, as the Germans had done, run out of fighting power as we reached Germany. If the rumours turn into reality, all hopes of an end to trench warfare will be dashed. Yet again we'll dig in. Life with rats and chats will return alongside routine raids and counter-attacks over no-man's-land. Having experienced the freedom of open warfare over the past three months, the prospect of returning to tunnels and trenches is unwelcome. But, if we must, we will.

I was reassured to hear however that Field-Marshal Haig was of a different opinion to that of General Wilson, and to that of the Prime Minister, Lloyd George. Did the Ministry of Defence and Downing Street not realise the Germans were on the run? Or did our leaders in London know something that we at the front didn't? Fortunately, Field-Marshal Ferdinand Foch, Chief of General Staff, agreed with Haig: with Fritz falling back, we should keep moving forward.

If politicians can't win peace through politics, fighting should be left to fighters.

CHAPTER 39

September & October 1918

Thousands of letters written on Wednesday September 11th went in the post to the United States of America. From Washington to Florida, California to Maine, the missives arrived. David Moser promised his Ma and Pa he'd make it home 'for sure' in one piece. Alben C Barkley thanked his wife for the lovely photograph of their new-born son. I can't wait to hold him, he wrote, and promised that one day he would. Earl White told his betrothed he loved her more than she would ever know. He ended with the words, 'don't you worry about me now, I'll be just fine'. The letters arrived home, the men didn't. Sentimentality doesn't protect a man on the battlefield. Words are no armour against weapons, and bullets and bombs kill promises as easily as bodies.

Around four thousand five hundred doughboys died during the next four days. On Thursday September 12th the US Army launched its first major offensive of the war in the region of Lorraine. The Germans had extended their occupation of this area between the rivers Moselle and Meuse. General Pershing had wanted his American forces to fight in this area almost from the start of their arrival in 1917. Supplies could be brought up easily from ports used by the Americans in the Bay of Biscay, particularly St Nazaire, where the US Army had developed the harbour, including a refrigeration terminal for fresh meat, fish and citrus fruit. Doughboys, we British noticed with more than a little envy, enjoyed their food even more than the French. They certainly ate more of it.

The Americans had trained hard for many months and now felt ready for the fray and to run their own show. Once Field-Marshal Foch gave permission to Pershing, the General moved his First Army HQ to the St Mihiel area on August 11th to finalise his attack plan. Over the next four weeks over half a million US troops in fourteen divisions moved to the zone. Such a massive movement of men and machines, which included over four hundred tanks and nearly three thousand artillery pieces, largely French, could not be kept secret.

Indeed, the impending attack on the German line in Lorraine was reported in a Swiss newspaper. It went so far as to publish the date, time and duration of the preliminary barrage.

Pershing's plan required two attacks in a pincer movement. Three divisions in his Fourth Army, the 1st, 42nd and 89th, would advance north spanning around seven miles, with its left flank advancing to the village of Vigneulles. Here it was hoped the 1st Division would meet with French forces attacking from the west. The US First Army had deployed four divisions, the 2nd, 5th, 90th and 82nd. They too moved north and planned to spread about eight miles wide with its left flanking division, the 2nd, aiming to secure the village of Thiaucourt.

As if Lorraine wished to create the same conditions as Picardy and Flanders, heavy rain fell a few days before the scheduled assault. Roads became muddy, fields muddier, trenches swamps. But Pershing was not to be deterred by the weather, not after all the preparation and with so many troops at the ready. On September 12th at the allotted time - exactly as the Swiss newspaper had reported - nearly three thousand artillery guns commenced the barrage. For most of the Americans it was the first time they had experienced so many artillery guns fire so many shells simultaneously and continually. Like all of us undergoing this frightful pounding for the first time, the troops became excited, encouraged and afraid in equal measure. The ground under your feet shakes. Air is sucked from your lungs. Your brain seems to swell in your skull by the sheer din. Every instrument in the orchestra of war plays at maximum volume with the minimum of melody in a hundred rhythms. You become aware of everything and of nothing and of something. Sometimes the smallest detail, such as a beautiful butterfly amid war's ugliness, or a loose button hanging by a thread on your tunic, occupies your mind.

Most of the artillery gunners were experienced Frenchmen and therefore spot-on their targets. But very little return fire came from the Germans. This puzzled frontline commanders. Perhaps the Germans had planned some surprise counter-attack. But the reason for this lack of resistance soon became clear. Allied aircraft, including nine bomber squadrons of the Royal Air Force, reported the Germans had already started retreating. Thousands of Allied shells had been sent to empty enemy trenches. We'd been fighting phantoms! However, as the gun barrels raised and shells projected further, many Germans suffered as they retired along roads, across fields and through woodland. French, American and British aeroplanes - around one thousand five hundred - caused additional havoc shooting and bombing the fleeing Germans. Allied pilots sent streams of machine gun bullets onto the retreating columns. Men, horses and vehicles scattered in every direction trying to avoid the onslaught. On some roads hiding places could not be found. No trees, walls, hedges or buildings. Even drainage ditches couldn't provide cover from swooping aircraft following the line of the road. Shelter under abandoned vehicles provided fleeting hope for some. But many cars and wagons burst into flames as hot bullets ignited petrol tanks or struck explosive ordnance. Men and horses in their hundreds lay dead and injured, abandoned amongst the wrecked vehicles.

Despite the artillery barrage, infantry advance and aerial attacks, most Germans escaped unscathed - apart from a big dent in their pride - before both sides of the pincer movement met. Most of the Germans, around forty-five thousand, belonged to the Army's C Detachment. They were hopelessly out-numbered by the Americans, at least eight to one, not to mention the French forces on their right flank. It came as no surprise then that the US First and Fourth armies reached their objectives ahead of schedule. Frontline commanders, brimming with confidence and eager to push home their advantage, wanted to pursue their prey and asked permission to do so. But General Pershing curbed their enthusiasm. He worried that, by allowing the US attack to advance, he would break the agreed plan with the Supreme Commander, Field-Marshal Foch. Although German resistance wasn't as tough as expected, it was sufficient to cause around four thousand five hundred American deaths, and around two thousand five hundred severe injuries. Together with the French, the Americans captured around fifteen thousand Germans and four hundred and forty-three artillery guns. Approximately two thousand Germans were killed alongside five thousand five hundred casualties. By the day's end on September 15th the new Allied front, called the Michel Line, had moved at least five miles forward and, in places, twenty miles into long-held German territory. Compared with the going nowhere years of trench warfare, this was wonderful progress in four days of fighting. The doughboys raised our spirits, and I'm sure they crushed Fritz's.

With this victory fresh under their belt, the eager Americans wanted more. Pershing had wished to advance another ten miles north along the River Moselle and take the city of Metz. But the Germans regrouped and showed their resilience. They formed a defensive line putting a stop to any swift Allied advance. US Army supply lines had also been stretched and severed, so rapid their progress. The front would have to delay further movement until food and materials caught up. Pershing would have to wait. So too the French. They were particularly desperate to regain Metz, 'stolen' by the German Empire following its defeat in the Franco-Prussian War. France had been compelled by the 1871 Treaty of Frankfurt to hand over Metz to the German Imperial Territory of Alsace-Lorraine. For the French, Metz was more than a dot on the map: the city was a symbol of patriotic pride.

Within a day of Americans at home hearing of their Army's action in France, the number of men registering for conscription across the United States rose to fourteen million.

***

Since we last faced the foe, at Pear Trench on September 1st, we Dukes have enjoyed a well-deserved and much-needed rest in Divisional Reserve at Averdoignt, five miles east of St Pol. Fresh details of eight 2nd lieutenants and one hundred and eighty other ranks joined us, replacing the officers and men lost to death, injury or transfer. Most of the new chaps seem up to the job, if a little wet-behind-the-ears, which is to be expected even after basic training. No instruction, no exercise, no practice, no lecture can adequately prepare a person for the reality of war, the experience of battle. I always try my best to make men ready for the fight. But the scenes of slaughter, screams of pain, the sights and smells of shot and burning bodies cannot be demonstrated in advance. Even if these realities could be presented, perhaps they shouldn't. Come the combat, each man must fight his own fight, face his fears, find his strengths, confront - or cover up - his weaknesses.

Soldiers say if politicians and desk-bound generals in Blighty witnessed the fighting first hand, the war would stop instantly. If they only realised the true extent of the suffering and waste, men in power would end the carnage. But these thoughts are unfair, and probably wrong. I'm sure the Kaiser knows the pain and damage he's caused. He just doesn't care. Or he's willing to tolerate it. Many of our generals in their younger days engaged in combat, be it in Africa, Afghanistan or India. Yes, sideshows compared with this slaughter, but men still died and suffered terrible injuries. But it would of course be as silly as impractical for old generals and politicians to fight at the front. They would be a liability. Fighting is not for old men. And if brawling for your life in a small hole in Flanders, you can't see the big picture of what's happening in the whole war.

Many of the generals have visited the front and seen the aftermath of battle. They have viewed rows of corpses. They've watched stretchers pass by carrying blooded, broken men. They've talked with the injured, doctors and nurses. Politicians and generals have lost sons, brothers and nephews. They have walked through flattened towns, villages, the scarred countryside, and witnessed civilians fleeing for their lives. Their families and friends at home will have shared tales of loss and hardship. I can't speak for politicians, but to say our generals don't know or understand the effects of this war is mistaken, even offensive. Our generals, certainly all of them here in France and Flanders, know first-hand the devastating impact of this war. And they are willing to fight on facing Fritz to maintain our freedom, just as most officers and men.

Twenty miles away from the nearest front, calm and rest prevailed during our two weeks in reserve at Averdoignt. The occasional rumble could be heard from howitzers, especially when the wind carried artillery sounds eastwards, although most breezes came off the Atlantic to the west. Time itself, peace and quiet, and the occasional day of fly fishing finally cured my whizz-bang headaches. I could think clearly and see straight once again. In the officers' mess, a discussion about equal pay for women was in full swing, distracting me from reading *The Times*. The debate followed an announcement that the government had established a commission to consider the matter. Some chaps got hot under the collar about it, while others believed women should be paid the same, provided they are doing to same work. The argument was interrupted by Lt-Col Pawlett. We stood smartly as he entered. The Colonel's resolute expression indicated he brought important news: orders returning the Dukes to the front had arrived. He announced that we were to take over the L'Eclase sector from the 8th Middlesex of the 56th Division.

Within days we found ourselves again near St Servin's Farm. All was quiet, except for the occasional light shelling and bursts of machine guns when crews believed they spied suspicious movement. We, the Allies, had no desire to disturb the peace. Experienced chaps suspected this indicated another push was planned: small skirmishes spoil big plans. The Germans too seemed content to keep clashes to a minimum. Perhaps they also had some scheme up their sleeve. Whatever the reason, not one raid took place from either side. Some chaps believed the Hun had lost the will to fight, the stuffing knocked out of them by the defeat at St Mihiel. But, as always, I counselled against complacency. I had seen too many men die of that disease.

***

Our instincts were right. Today's calm signalled tomorrow's storm. A big push was being planned by our leaders. Yet this was to be a drive like no other. Supreme Commander Ferdinand Foch, Field Marshal Douglas Haig, US General John Pershing and all our leaders prepared an offensive of a new kind. Instead of attacking in one zone, we would advance against the German Army along the whole Hindenburg Line. It would not be another big push, but a Grand Offensive. From Ypres in the north to the Argonne Forest in the south, the Allies will attack as one. (Officially, the USA was an Associate Power, not one of the Allies.) The combined forces of France, America, Belgium, Britain and its armies from the Empire, mainly Australia, Canada, India and New Zealand, will take on Germany.

Our leaders discussed delaying the Grand Offensive until next spring. In London, the Chief of Imperial General Staff, General Sir Henry Wilson, had already urged caution. Would it not be wise to wait? Build a bigger Army? Make more armaments, especially tanks and aircraft? After all, the Germans are going nowhere and, according to intelligence reports, they're running short of supplies, including food. German U-boats had lost much of their devastating bite and most supplies now reached Britain and France. At least wait until spring 1919 so as not to get bogged down or snowed in by winter weather. Remember what happened to Napoléon Bonaparte, those who urged caution cried, as if French winters were comparable with the Russian snows of 1812 which destroyed Bonaparte's army near Moscow. Despite arguments against the timing of a Grand Offensive, the assault went ahead.

Tenacious Foch, determined Haig and impatient Pershing made a formidable team for any doubter to resist, especially if that sceptic was safely tucked behind a desk in Paris, London or Washington DC.

When most people in normal circumstances would be drifting into their dreams, half an hour before midnight, the Grand Offensive began. Calm ended. The storm started. The date I'll never forget is Wednesday 25th September 1918. For the next six hours without a minute's break - in fact without a second's respite - artillery shells of every type drenched the Germans. Countless thousands of high-explosive, shrapnel, incendiary and gas shells flew through the sky to cause casualties and confusion. The earth trembled. And so did many men, with just cause. At dawn boots, filled by Frenchmen and Americans, stepped into battle. It was precisely 5.30 am when the French Fourth and American First armies launched their assault northwards along a forty-four-mile front between the River Meuse and Reims, including the tough terrain of the Argonne Forest. The Americans, heading towards Sedan, at first made excellent progress and quickly gained seven miles of ground. But high casualties resulted. Very high, and much higher than they needed to be. French officers reported many Americans demonstrated tactical '*naiveté*'. They are as brave as lions, one said, but their discipline under fire is poor. Some of the men seemed to ignore instructions from their company commanders. Others forgot basic battle-craft in which they had trained so very hard over many months, as if they lost their heads.

The next day, Friday, witnessed our British First and Third armies and the Canadian Corps strike the exceptionally well-fortified Hindenburg Line east of Cambrai. Many troops had to cross the half-built half-empty Canal du Nord under considerable enemy fire. The mud-soaked channel itself did not pose a substantial feature to surmount. But it became a real stumbling block, a death-trap for too many, because behind the canal the Germans had three well-armed defensive lines. The Canadians again fought magnificently and, along with the British, eventually pushed back the enemy.

If the Germans were surprised by two consecutive days of attack, then Saturday's attack of the Grand Offensive must have rocked them to the core. Our third frontal assault was launched in the Ypres Salient, familiar ground to some old hands. Royalty, a King no less, spearheaded the Allied troops in an operation to oust the Germans from his country. Albert I of Belgium was in charge of the army which, of course, included Belgian troops, the British Second Army, under General Plumer, and the French Sixth, commanded by General Degoutte. King Albert wisely took advice from the two highly experienced generals about their approach. The Belgians heading home were naturally keen to oust the invaders from their land. Perhaps too eager. The attack initially made good progress but supplies could not keep pace with forward troops. The Germans too, as so often before, rallied quickly and resisted strongly. But for all the enemy's defiance, by the day's end the Allies had breached Passchendaele Ridge. For the British, sweeping through the battlegrounds of the Ypres Salient reminded men of those mud-soaked corpse-filled fields of the previous year, especially Passchendaele, a name that will forever send a shiver down the spine of every British soldier.

Day four of the Grand Offensive fell on Sunday. Even after over four years of fighting, I could not rid myself of the feeling that Sunday was the day of chapel and church, rest and 'Sunday best' clothes. It was the day of the week more than any other I thought of home in Haworth. Sunday was when the front room became open in the afternoon, especially when visitors called, and, if chilly, the coal fire lit. Commercial activity in the village ceased for the day and all shops closed. People walked to their place of worship, some with Bibles and song books, talking politely and wishing each other well. The Salvation Army band, songsters and 'God's soldiers' marched to the top of Main Street for an 'open air' service. Salvationists, in dark uniforms with caps and bonnets, formed a circle between The Black Bull and the Post Office, run by Alice's parents. They sang hymns, prayed, collected coppers from passers-by. From those who could afford such generosity, the collectors hoped silver sixpences and shillings would drop into the collection box.

Even your farthing can help God's work on earth, the lady told me when I was a little lad. It was the only coin in my pocket, but I felt obliged to help God's work on earth. I resented not having my liquorice sticks for a whole week and vowed never to stand and listen to the band again - certainly not with money in my pocket.

Work on the farm, milking, egg collection, feeding stock, lambing and birthing cattle continued of course. But some Bible bashers disapproved if crop work took place on Sunday, even during harvest when they could see clouds amassing. If gathering crops on Sunday was sinful, I wondered how they might describe the slaughter of thousands of men on God's 'day of rest'.

On Sunday 29th September we attacked eastwards through Picardy's Somme region to the middle of the Hindenburg Line. The target extended from Vendhuile village twelve miles south along a canal to St Quentin. Both the St Quentin Canal and the city itself had become part of the German's defensive barrier since their incursion in September 1914. By March 1916 the invaders had ousted any remaining French citizens and looted every home, church, public building, office and factory. Whispers told of almost every woman in the area, even young girls and grandmothers, had been violated by the Hun, although French folk refused to acknowledge such rumours. Perhaps this explains why French soldiers fight with fury in their hearts: their people as well as their land had been abused. Eight out of ten buildings in St Quentin had been almost or completely destroyed. Not one building stood without bullet holes or shrapnel scars.

Over three miles of the canal ran through an arrow-straight tunnel between Vendhuile and the village of Bellicourt. It was here that General John Monash, in overall command of the operation, decided to attack by going over the top of the tunnel. His Australian Corps, tired and depleted by a series of engagements since August 8th, used reinforcements from the US Army, the 27th and 30th Divisions. The Americans provided plenty of much-needed muscle, but their inexperience caused problems.

Two days earlier, in advance of the main attack, the US troops had been required to rid Germans from their forward dugouts and trenches. But they failed to clear these outposts and several of the twelve companies went missing, their forward positions unknown. Some said this failure was owing to a shortage of American officers, eighteen only in the twelve companies. On the day of attack these missing troops restricted our preliminary barrage for fear of killing and injuring hundreds of the Yanks lying low somewhere in no-man's-land. As the US 27th advanced in the main attack, the same errors of inexperience repeated themselves. Pockets of Germans were bypassed, particularly machine gun nests, and these were left to cause many casualties as they ambushed the next wave of men moving forward. The 3rd Australian Division, which was supposed to leapfrog the Americans, had to divert their attention to help mop up the enemy. A great deal of bloody close-quarter fighting took place before the Australians and what remained of the US 27th could advance. The US 30th, covering the southern half over the tunnel, managed to achieve their objective and allowed the Australian 5th Division to capture Bellicourt. But the hand-to-hand fighting to the north delayed their further progress for a while.

In the southern sector, the British Fourth Army, under the command of General Sir Henry Rawlinson, commenced their early morning attack through rain and mist. Knowing no US troops were 'lost' ahead, this advance could proceed with the benefit of a preliminary bombardment to soften up the enemy. The Germans responded with equal ferocity. The intensity of the shelling meant a man could not hear the man next to him unless he shouted directly into his ear, and sometimes not even then. In battle with well-trained men, each knowing his job and duty, there isn't much need for talk anyway.

Men of our Fourth Army's IX Corps battled their way to the St Quentin Canal where it emerged from the tunnel half a mile south of Bellicourt. In front of the canal, the enemy's outer defences had survived our artillery pounding. But they were soon overrun, and many Germans started surrendering. By now, the fourth day of our Grand Offensive, most Fritz at the front knew the game was up, even if military bosses Ludendorff, Hindenburg, Marwitz, Groener and the Kaiser himself didn't. Having reached the canal, a far bigger challenge confronted our chaps, particularly those from the 46th Division. As the canal emerged from the tunnel, the land rose steeply and the water channelled through a ravine. Where the British planned to cross, the gorge was the equivalent of four storeys deep. It would have been so easy to stop and fire from the ridge. But experienced men knew this would never shift the dug-in Germans on the other side. The order was thus to cross the canal 'at all costs'. Without a moment's hesitation, the men stepped forth and did not consider the price they would pay.

The steep slope posed a serious hazard, in places almost a vertical drop into the ravine. But a greater danger revealed itself: German machine gun crews, burrowed into the ravine's opposite bank like badger setts, kicked away scrub that had been hiding their positions. When our chaps started descending the slippery slope, the guns, five of them, opened their endless rattle of fire. Many, many died, for an easier target you couldn't find. The dead and injured plunged and slithered into the cold water. Some injured chaps drowned if help wasn't to hand quickly. Those miraculously dodging bullets slid or stumbled into the canal. Up to their armpits in filthy water, chaps carried rifles above their heads wading to the far bank. Two of the machine guns had angles deep enough to shoot at men as they crossed. The brown water turned red with British blood. Our machine gunners then got busy and knocked out some of the enemy's nests. And once agile chaps climbed high enough on the enemy's bank, they lobbed grenades into their gun tunnels. The enemy machine-gunners killed, the canal was crossed.

Not far away a battalion of the North Staffordshire Regiment, under Captain Charlton, seized the Riqueval Bridge over the canal - minutes before the Germans planned to set off their explosive charges to bring it down. Along with other captured bridges, their enterprise made a huge difference to the reinforcements and supplies following on behind in support of the advance parties.

Despite setbacks and many casualties, the Grand Offensive struck a significant blow to the enemy's body. On 2nd October, our 46th and 32nd Divisions, ably supported by the Australian 2nd Division, had split open a gap in the German defences of nearly eleven miles. By 5th October the Allies had breached the entire depth of a nineteen-mile front. By 8th October the British First and Third Armies cracked the German fortifications at Cambrai. French, Belgian, American and British Empire forces had, at last, penetrated most of the long-established Western Front, the Hindenburg Line. Almost every captured German said their country was finished, '*Deutsch Kaput*'! Surely the German High Command must realise that too. Prisoners say the politicians at home are making promises to help the people and a new Chancellor has been appointed, Prince Max von Baden. But politicians are not believed, the prisoners add, and princes don't help ordinary people.

***

Since the start of the Grand Offensive the Dukes have been out of the main 'show', as some called it. Most officers and men felt frustrated that we stayed stuck in the L'Eclase sector, east of Arras. Germans occupied trenches not three hundred yards away, and we suffered intermittent shell blasts and machine gun bursts, but we remained trench-bound in a what was considered a quiet zone.

If our idleness wasn't irritating enough, the first ten days of October were spent away from the front line altogether, back at St Catherine, west of Arras. The band of our 4th Battalion played for us on our return to camp. But the medley of joyful tunes, including our Regimental March, *The Wellesley*, didn't appease the frustration. It seemed as if the whole Allied Army marched towards Germany - and we Dukes strolled in the opposite direction from the action! The men didn't hold back their feelings. They expressed their annoyance, almost anger at being in the peace instead of in the war. Many had done much hard fighting and now, as the bell rings for what seems the final knock-out round of the contest, they've been told to withdraw to the dressing room. Germans have their backs on the ropes and our prize fighters have been ordered to take off their boxing gloves!

It was necessary to tell my men that our Regiment, any regiment, can't always be in the thick of the action. War, soldiering, is about teamwork. Not everyone can run with the baton. Only one person can score a goal at a time. We deserve and need rest. The Dukes have played a vital role in this war. We're one cog in the military machine, but without each cog, the machine would break down.... my guff went on. Such sentiments didn't, of course, reduce the sense of disappointment. But what else could I say? It's an officer's responsibility to keep the men's morale as high as possible. In truth, having been in this war from the start at Mons, I was angrier than any man in my Company at missing the Grand Offensive. This war had become my life; I believed it would cause my death. Indeed, it was crucial to remind the men - and myself - the war was not over. Predictions of its end have been wrong before and the war could drag on into next year or even 1920.

Bulgaria surrendered on September 30th. Compared with the Western Front, this fight seemed a side-show. It was not that however for the men advancing through northern Greece to beat the Bulgarians. Once the push started, our forces succeeded in Bulgaria in less than a fortnight, even against German reinforcements drafted in at the last-minute. The crucial breakthrough came mid-September from French and Serbian forces in Macedonia. They breached a line held by the enemy since November 1916. The Allies surged northwards into Albania and Serbia, reaching the city of Skopje on the River Vardar, and the vital Balkan route between Belgrade and Athens. The Allies also crossed into south-western Bulgaria, and that breach was enough for the Bulgarians to throw in the towel. We're told the surrender came in the traditional way: a Bulgarian officer walked towards our line holding aloft a white flag. An armistice was duly signed at Salonika at 11 pm on September 29th. If only

Ludendorff or the Kaiser would do the same. But I suspect aristocratic German pride in Berlin will hold out longer than a sensible Bulgarian officer facing the British Army.

The war in Palestine also came to an end. Major T E Lawrence, having fought the Turks all the way through Arabia, arrived in Damascus on October 1st to a warm welcome from the Syrians. They rejoiced at their freedom from the Ottoman Empire's cruel yoke. Many of the three thousand Arab horsemen, who had supported Major Lawrence for over two years, also rode into the city in celebration. A few Turkish soldiers remained in Damascus, too ill or injured to run. Many suffered ill-treatment or were finished off by locals in retaliation for the Turks' treatment of them over many years. Trouble also arose between various Arab groups. The Australian Mounted Division fortunately arrived in Damascus on the same day to bring a semblance of order. The Allied Commander of the campaign, General Edmund Allenby, with around fifty-seven thousand troops at his disposal, will soon impose a military government to keep order. It has been agreed the French will eventually take control of Syria and Britain will hold Palestine.

Meanwhile, General Allenby's forces continue northwards to meet the French in Beirut and Aleppo to make sure all the Turks are cleared from the region and securely back in Turkey. At some point, when considered no longer a threat, most of the seventy-five thousand Turk prisoners will be released. The campaign in Palestine against the Ottoman Empire has employed nearly one million two hundred thousand men from Britain and the Empire. The British alone suffered over fifty thousand casualties in the fighting. But disease claimed over half a million.

Disease is also rife in Britain. Everyone calls it Spanish 'flu, although no-one really knows where it originated. Thousands of people are off work and some folk have already died from the infection. Several thousand soldiers are suffering too. Everything is being disrupted, especially our supplies, telecommunications and post. Doctors claim that more people could die from this disease than killed in the war! That's hard to believe. It's also humbling to think that some little invisible thing can be mightier than men and deadlier than bombs and bullets. Like potato blight, it seems once this 'flu takes hold, nothing can stop it until it has no more crop to kill. We hear millions have already died in India and China. The doughboys tell us it's spreading across America too. The Federal Bureau of Health already reports more American servicemen have died of this 'flu than in the war.

Yorkshire people, and doubtless others across Britain, will have already started smearing goose fat on their chests hoping to keep the infection away. Farmer Booth will have gone one better: he shot badgers to render their fat for his own and his family's use. He'd sell any surplus pots of the smelly grease too. He claimed badger fat was a stronger medicine than goose grease at keeping chills off the chest. When I was a boy, it was said that Miss Toothill, who lived alone at Rough Nook Cottage on the edge of the village, swallowed a live frog in spring and a live spider in autumn to fend off 'flu. She was very old, but is still alive, as far as I know. Perhaps everyone will resort to such measures if this seemingly unstoppable contagion continues.

***

Orders arrived directing us towards the front on October 11th. It was time to get back to the fight. Waiting had tested our patience. The Dukes didn't want to miss their part on stage in the Grand Offensive, although every man harboured worries about moving into the danger zone. And he should, if he has any sense. Buses transported us the twenty-three miles from Arras to the outskirts of Cambrai. The road was so straight someone said it must have been built by the Romans. 'On their way to invade England,' another quipped. Only the day before had the Germans been completely cleared from Cambrai after four years' occupation. Before they fled, spiteful Fritz officers ordered the torching of the old city hall and many buildings in the centre, adding to the city's woes. Cambrai held a special place in the heart of the Duke of Wellington's Regiment. It was here between 1815 and 1818, during the British Army of Occupation, where the Iron Duke based his headquarters. It's strange to think that exactly one hundred years ago our Regiment's namesake was in this place, perhaps on this very street.

From Cambrai we marched six miles to billets and encampments in the small town of Naves. Most officers took transport or rode their horses. But I had no concerns about leading my Company on foot. I welcomed the open air and exercise. And, by dropping back now and then mingling with the men, it was a way of keeping up with soldiers' tales, worries and gossip. I remember as a private that when marching, with eyes fixed on the road ahead, chaps say things they wouldn't normally talk about if you were looking directly at each other. Perhaps that's why, in the confessional box, a screen separates the face of the priest from the sinner. Guilt is shared, shame confined. And it's just the same now between the young raw recruit and his Captain.

On arrival at Naves we learnt that two of the Battalion's four companies would be accommodated in tents owing to a lack of space inside the few buildings the Germans had left standing. Captain Hill and I drew the short straws. Together we looked despondently at the field, already a mud-bath, as our sergeants marched the men to the tents, some little better than temporary bivouacs. Hill, like me, believed the men and junior officers should take the best tents. I slept happily enough in a one-man bivouac stretched over a wall in the corner of the field. I was, as the saying goes, as snug as a bug in a rug. The nights were drawing in and becoming chilly but, nevertheless, I prefer life under canvas than in a bunker. We remained for a week in immediate reserve, our time occupied with routine drills and training, consolidating our work on open warfare.

Late on Thursday October 17th I heard the name of another place that rocked my whole body as surely as a bomb exploding at my side. Simply hearing Le Cateau hurt as much as hot shrapnel. It stirred memories as bright as the midday sun instantly replacing the moon at midnight. Divisions of our Fourth Army had just captured the town. Over four years ago, on a mill rooftop outside Le Cateau, my closest friends died, apart from Bertie Dale. We had escaped Mons with German bullets whizzing over our heads. But my one and only true Platoon was destroyed at Le Cateau when Meadows, Bottomley, Thwaites and Smith fell. Those friends were irreplaceable. I've served with hundreds of men since, most fine fellows, but none valued as highly in my heart. How can your village schoolmates and workmates be replaced by new drafts you've never met before? Without doubt, despite all the destruction and devastation of people, places and things I've experienced, that day at Le Cateau was the worst of my life. When my friends were lost, part of me was taken away with them as sure as I'd lost a limb, although it was really part of my heart.

On October 18th we moved forward to relieve one of our sister battalions, the 1/6th, in the small village of Villers-en-Cauchies, four miles north-west of Solesmes. On all fronts the Allies had advanced at a rate which even a few weeks back would have been impossible. The capture of Cambrai itself was achieved much faster than expected and with reasonably low casualties. After scurrying east, the Germans decided the River Selle would become their new line of resistance in this sector. Flowing almost directly north through Le Cateau, ten or so miles south of Solesmes, the river formed a natural barrier. And, after they'd crossed it, the enemy blasted all the bridges. At night on the 19th it was required the Dukes move forward two miles and take the village of Saulzour, through which the river flowed. The enemy had cunningly sited four machine gun nests in the village on 'our side' of the River Selle. The crews, as well as their officers who positioned them, will have known they stood no chance of survival, their retreat cut off by the river. I was delighted that not only my Company but all the Battalion made their approach into Saulzour with great skill. Our open warfare drills had paid dividends. The first two enemy machine gun crews fought bravely. It was unfortunate that we had to dispose of them with mortars. The remaining two crews then quickly and sensibly surrendered, keeping their hopes alive they would see their loved ones again.

The river presented the next barrier to our advance, as well as the waiting German guns on the opposite bank. I ordered two of my Company's scouts to slip southwards upriver to see if an easier crossing point could be found. Within thirty minutes they returned with helpful intelligence. Four hundred yards upstream of the village they discovered a stretch of water shallow enough to wade across. I didn't need to ask Private Woodcock how exactly he had gathered that fact: he was dripping wet! He added that most of the enemy had 'set up shop' on the railway line, which ran parallel to the river. I immediately informed Battalion HQ of this intelligence, who then informed Brigade. I was surprised to receive an order to attend Brigade HQ soonest alongside my Lieutenant-Colonel.

On arrival, the Brigade Commander asked for opinions as to the best way to proceed. Everyone chipped in. On turning to me, I suggested to the General that, while it was still dark, a company wades across the river at the point the scouts identified and create as much noise as possible feigning an attack. Let off mortars, grenades and gunfire even if enemy positions can't be seen, I said. Perhaps our artillery could shell beyond the Germans to add to their confusion and tempt them out of their holes. The Boche would believe they were being attacked from behind and on one flank. The diversion would then allow the main 10th and 11th Brigades to cross the river on rafts as planned and, at narrower but deeper points across the river, use the planks already prepared for the task. A second or even third company could also be ready to cross at the wading point, identified by Pte Woodcock, and take up the attack for real alongside the 'diversion' company. After the senior officers discussed the various proposals, it was agreed to adopt the plan. I realised of course I'd be required to implement the diversionary attack. When informed of their task, my chaps cheerily accepted they faced a cold soaking. Well, I heard no grousing.

Within the hour, at 2 am, the plan commenced. Slow, silent, careful movement was required by every man crossing the river and climbing the bank into position. I made sure every chap smeared mud on his face to blend into the dark. Our scout, Pte Woodcock, volunteered to go first to show the way. (He'd only just dried out from his previous crossing, poor chap.) I ordered that he carried rope to secure on the opposite bank to provide a guide and support for each man crossing subsequently. (I made a mental note to ensure Woodcock received promotion to corporal. He commanded natural authority as well as demonstrating initiative.) At the agreed time, 2.30 am, when my Company of two hundred had successfully negotiated the river, we caused a great commotion. I ordered a bugler to sound the attack and the men to scream and shout and shoot and send mortars and grenades flying - but stay in position. We made sufficient racket for Fritz to believe a thousand-man battalion was attacking him. One of my sergeants said it was the first battle he'd enjoyed in two years of fighting. As a bonus, many of our bullets, mortars and grenades were not wasted: we knocked out three machine guns and a light field gun, killed about thirty and sent dozens on the run. The fighting was thankfully far lighter than expected and we reached our objective. The following day, October 20th, the 2nd Seaforths passed through us to take up the fight and they soon captured the high ground overlooking the Selle valley.

Over the next few days we gradually gained ground, a further six miles since crossing the River Selle. The Boche had dug trenches and laid wire entanglements and fought better than of late. But we surmounted the obstacles, especially with the help of a shrapnel barrage from six brigades of Field Artillery. By October 25th our Battalion had taken over three hundred and fifty prisoners, captured thirty-one machine guns and two 38mm calibre heavy mine launchers with their stacks of ammonium nitrate-carbon explosive shells. That morning our patrols discovered the enemy had withdrawn further, and we occupied the vacated space without a shot fired. Later in the morning we Dukes received orders to return to billets in Verchain, a village we had taken two days earlier. At parade, the Commanding Officer rightly told the men they could be proud of their achievements and deserved a rest.

But when you rest, you reflect, and it was time to think of those gaps in the Battalion's ranks caused by the recent fighting. 2nd Lt Wolfenden had been killed. I didn't know him, but my platoon commanders said he was exceptionally clever and very committed to his men. He died crossing the river with a group of them caught by two machine gun crews. Lieutenants McHugh, Jackson, Livsey, Shearme and 2nd Lieutenants McHugh and Blackburn, and Captain Hill, suffered injury. Forty-six men died, one hundred and sixty-three wounded, most from machine gun fire. A doctor at Casualty Clearing Station No 30 in Cambrai reported that a little over half the officers and men would be incapable of returning to active service. Those who could be moved without causing too much pain or further damage had already departed for Blighty.

The CO's promise of 'rest' lasted for the remainder of the day: early next morning we were training hard. With new draft replacements joining us at Verchain, it was important for the whole Battalion to get the green chaps shipshape. Most had gone through two weeks at the 'bull ring', the popular name for our training grounds at Etaples, but they were still not up to scratch for the Dukes. It was our Regiment's tradition to believe you were only as strong as your weakest man. Even our weakest therefore had to be strong. Our reputation for fighting, drill and sport was of the highest, and we intended to keep it. Instruction in warfare will not, of course, stop death and injury. But training will reduce deaths and injuries. If every man knows his duty and sticks to it under fire, the better it will be for all. Few platoons nowadays composed of conscripts can match the regular soldiers from the original British Expeditionary Force. Former full-time regulars in my 'old' platoon would knock spots off any of today's platoons. They would outmarch, outrun, outgun and out-manoeuvre any platoon I've seen since. Not because they were better men, but because they were better trained for months and years, and had much more experience working together. Most of all, they were better because they *wanted* to be soldiers. It was their job. They hadn't been pulled out of Civvy Street and pressed into khaki.

However, Hebden Iveson, a fent dealer from my village and a familiar face to me, said although he resented being called up, especially at the 'ripe' age of 39, once in uniform he enjoyed soldiering.

'Instead of going from rags to riches, I've gone from rags to Regiment,' he joked. 'And, young Ogden, I never thought I'd be calling you "Sir". I remember you as a little snotty-nosed scamp and ragamuffin!'

My sergeant, overhearing the comment, whispered to me that he would put Iveson on sanitary duties to 'teach him a bit of respect'. I told the sergeant it would be wrong to punish a man for telling the truth!

Towards the end of October rumours spread as fast as fire consuming dry heather that German politicians looked to broker a peace deal. The flames became fanned when we heard Germany's senior general, Ludendorff, had resigned. The Austrian army had also evacuated Italy. Even better, Turkey surrendered, the six-hundred-year-old Ottoman Empire all but crushed. The Dardanelles, the scene of our Gallipoli disaster, had again opened to Allied ships. We hoped peace was on its way. Some prayed to help its journey. My Regiment and I wanted to fight on to secure the peace. Too many times I had seen Fritz rise and return to battle after appearing defeated. The Boche had the ability of Phoenix, the legendary bird that killed itself in a raging pyre but was reborn from the ashes. It would be a major mistake to stop pressing forward until the Kaiser's Army was destroyed. Wounded men can rise and kill again. Dead men, in bits or six feet under, can't.

Despite these significant events affecting the fate of millions worldwide, that evening, on the last day of October, we felt most sorry for just one man. Sergeant-Major Secombe was handed the telegram amid many officers and fellow non-commissioned officers following a briefing from Division HQ. With an ear-piercing scream, he fell to his knees in a crumbled heap and wept inconsolably: a bold man, broken. The telegram told, in stark bold capitals, that his wife, son and daughter had died of influenza. In London alone over two thousand two hundred deaths had occurred in the past week, despite the closure of many schools thereby hoping to contain the infection. It was so sad to see this tall tough man crying like a child, and we all felt helpless. There was no gaping hole in his guts to plug, no bleeding artery to stem the flow, no broken leg to splint, nowhere to carry a disabled man. We could do nothing, say nothing. Secombe's pain was greater than if a limb had been blown away, deeper than any penetration of shrapnel. He would have gladly given his life to save that of his family, as would every decent man here.

Everyone, apart from a fellow sergeant and the Commanding Officer, quietly walked away to allow the man privacy in his grief. Secombe was granted immediate compassionate leave to attend to his domestic affairs. He would need time to console his two surviving children, and arrange for their care. Alas, perhaps stupidly - certainly frustratingly - the telegram's author omitted to name the two deceased children. The desolate widower and father did not know which two of his four had perished. This uncertainty doubled Secombe's misery. Not knowing made him imagine *all* his offspring pale, cold, dead. After several attempts to have telephone lines connected, and chase health officials to check their records in

Secombe's home town of Bradford, our Commanding Officer eventually learnt the names of the deceased children.

Ernest and Jane had died, the two youngest, just hours before their mother; Amos and Sarah had survived. Secombe had hoped to know which of his children had survived would somehow ease the pain. It didn't, not one jot. But, having regained his composure, Secombe thanked the CO for his trouble and was relieved to hear that Amos and Sarah had been taken in by Secombe's sister, Mavis, who, it transpired, had sent the telegram.

Secombe was offered a travelling companion, several chaps being due home leave, but he said he'd prefer to travel alone. He also refused transport to the railway at Cambrai, saying he'd cadge a lift along the road. It was nearly midnight when some of us watched the Sergeant-Major stride out along the road to Saulzoir at the start of his long lonely journey home. He marched, head held high, jaw to the fore, arms swung to the full, just as Standing Orders stipulate.

A broken man, maybe, but not a broken soldier.

CHAPTER 40

November 1918

Three days later we Dukes followed the Sergeant-Major's footsteps and marched along the road to Saulzoir. We covered the two miles in exactly thirty minutes. In camp that evening on November 3rd we received wonderful news: the Austro-Hungarians had accepted an armistice on the Italian Front. Germany had no more allies. The German High Command, and Hindenburg's replacement, General Wilhelm Groener, cannot deny the game is up. For the first time in over four years I allowed myself to think the Boche might be beaten. Perhaps, after all, I did not have to fear the Phoenix. Germany would not - could not - rise from the ashes of defeat. Germany had fallen to its knees, if not flat on its face.

But dangerous days remained. And, fighting in war, you keep kicking a man when he's down until you know he's out. We British alone had suffered over three hundred and sixty thousand casualties since August, nearly one in three of these dead or rendered unable to fight. Our allies suffered similar losses. Open warfare is far more dangerous than fighting from trenches. This was not, though, the time to dig in again to reduce our casualties. This was the time to move in for the kill.

Our next offensive began on November 4th. On cue, as if we couldn't manage without it, like oil in an engine, the rain fell! Field Marshall Haig ordered our First, Third and Fourth Armies to attack on a front of thirty miles from Valenciennes south to Oisy. Further down the French and Americans advanced. We Dukes moved forward to Préseau, a village almost at the Belgian border. Despite shells and gunfire from retreating Germans, townsfolk and villagers welcomed us to their war-torn streets with hugs and kisses. Some of the younger chaps became quite red-faced at such female attention! *'Vive la France!'* and *'Vive l' Angleterre!'* folk cried through tears of joy and relief. 'Viva la Yorkshire!' and 'Viva la Dukes!' some of our comedians retorted. French flags, squirrelled away for over four years of German occupation, became unfurled and hung from windows and lamp posts. One Tricolour had been half-eaten by moths. German moths, the old man claimed sourly.

The Germans may be on the run, but they still fought. Retreating, they blasted bridges and set booby traps, including delayed-action mines. They felled trees across roads and tracks to obstruct our way, or left damaged vehicles in our path. Buildings were also blown up and the rubble used to curb our progress. But some homes and buildings seemed destroyed for no reason other than spite. Retreating Germans murdered innocent citizens and plundered homes, shops, churches and other buildings. Rumours again spread that women and girls had been molested by the rampaging enemy, despite many locals hiding or fleeing to the countryside to avoid the marauders. One old Frenchwoman said these victims stayed indoors 'to hide their shame', although she nor any British soldier blamed them for the despicable behaviour of the Boche. Indeed, it stiffened the men's resolve to hunt the enemy and inflict death or pain as punishment.

The troops, officers and men alike, took on a strange mood. We felt victors, but not victorious. The war ending, but not ended. The game won, but the referee had not blown the final whistle. And what if...what if? Did the Hun have a final trick, one sneaky bullet left in its barrel? Shells still fell, bullets flew, men died. Nests of enemy machine-gunners continued to ambush us as we advanced cross-country or along roads and pathways. Why, we all asked, couldn't the Germans just clear off? Why go through this farce of defiance? Why add to the pain and suffering on your retreat? Why not simply return to Germany with whatever dignity you can muster? But our questions didn't stop their abominable actions, including booby-trapping the corpses of their own men with grenades.

None of us want to cop it at any time, but especially now when the war's end is in sight. For those of us who have fought throughout the full four years and three months, the thought of dying or being injured now, at the very last hurdle, seeped into our heads. I'm sure we tried to dispel the notion, to carry on as normal. But we failed. Niggling doubts remained. Men are dying. Men are being severely injured, burnt, gassed, losing limbs - and their sanity. From just my Company I lost seven chaps on November 4th: Privates Blackburn, Bower, Patchett, Riley, Trussell and Wardle. I was very upset at the loss of Pte Harold Woodcock. He was our exceptionally brave scout who discovered the wading route across the River Selle two weeks' ago, which undoubtedly saved many lives and enhanced our attack. I deeply regretted his promotion to corporal had not been ratified. At the earliest opportunity I wrote to his family and told them of Harold's exceptional skill and courage. People say kind words bring great comfort to the bereaved, perhaps not at first when the pain is raw, but hopefully over time.

Woodcock was one of countless thousands who did far more than 'their bit' without any official recognition: no medal, no mention in despatches, sometimes not even a word of praise from his commanding officer or a pat on the back from his pals. To me, every officer and man who took one step forward into enemy fire is a hero. And sometimes more the hero for not seeking recognition, or even thinking their act of courage was courageous. To them, facing fire, rescuing a fellow soldier, running across no-man's-land to throw a grenade into an enemy position, was just part of the soldier's duty. I was reminded of the inscription in gold leaf in the chapel of our barracks in Yorkshire: *'Duty, duty, must be done; this rule applies to everyone.'* Even most of the conscripts of recent years - reluctant recruits to us old-time regulars - quickly adopted the call of duty once they donned khaki. Whatever their Civvy Street name, they all became Tommy Atkins.

The road looked familiar, so too the gentle curves of the countryside to either side. There was something about the pattern of the hedgerows and walls between the fields that made it recognisable. Even the shape of the hillside woodland seemed to stir a distant memory. It was like knowing the face, but unable to put a name to its owner. Unexpectedly, a fear overcame me. I needed to escape to avoid being trapped. I turned quickly to seek a hiding place and my head spun as if tumbling under water. There was no obvious threat. But I felt threatened. I knew my feelings were foolish, fear without foundation, groundless, senseless. Nevertheless, an alarm rang loud in my head. I acted to avoid harm, although I'm not sure what I did. I don't know and I didn't ask if a few seconds or minutes had passed before the lieutenant's voice returned me to my senses. I didn't hear his exact words at first. They were hazy and muddled as if recovering from a fainting spell. Gradually they became clearer. 'Are you all right, Sir?' he asked. 'Would a drink of water help?' He was kneeling over me, for I found that I'd thrown myself into the roadside ditch, cowering, expecting a shell or a fusillade of bullets. And then I recalled all. I could name the face, so to speak. I was on the same stretch of road that we used on our escape from Mons. My first true terror of the war had returned, brought on by the surroundings, as if this stretch of road had held the memory of my dread. The landscape had locked-in my feelings and released them on my return. Like first love, first fear stays in your soul.

My distress departed as quickly as it arrived. I tried to reassure my lieutenant and the men around me that I was perfectly all right. I'd suffered a momentary loss of mind owing, I claimed, to a sharp headache caused by an old shrapnel wound. Animal instinct and four years of trench life had made me drop into the nearest hole. There was really nothing to worry about. Despite telling them I felt fine, I had every confidence they'd be keeping a wary eye on me for the next few days. We continued, cautiously and in battle formation, along the road to the small town of Bavai, fifteen miles south of Mons. I was indeed almost within touching distance of where my war began, where I faced my first German. It felt strange, uncomfortably so. Would this be where it would end? And how?

Fleeing Germans continued to abandon equipment, including vehicles that had ran out of fuel. They found time nevertheless to set barriers and traps and loot on their exit from France. We regularly encountered resistance, although this appeared to be weakening. But I made sure everyone remained vigilant. I suggested the Germans might even mount a counter-attack. The expression on some of the junior officers' faces indicated they thought I was suffering another bout of the vapours! Surely they're done for, Sir, one ventured to say. I agreed it was extremely unlikely we'd face a charge from their cavalry or an artillery barrage. But I could not guarantee that over the next hill retreating forces hadn't gathered for one last stubborn stance. I hadn't come this far in war to let my guard down now.

Approaching Bavai about twenty Boche stood across the road with their arms raised. But I was immediately suspicious because their rifles rested at their feet, too close for comfort. And some of the

Germans left their guns across a boot - a ruse that allowed them to quickly kick up their weapons to hand and fire. At forty yards, I instructed my men to spread out and keep their rifles aimed at the Boche. Shoot without hesitation if I give the order, I said. I asked 2nd Lt Corley, who spoke good German, to order the line of would-be prisoners to move away from their weapons. They looked at each other as if they couldn't understand his clear directive. He repeated the order, louder. The Germans hesitated. Some fell to their rifles, others kicked them to hand. Several raised their arms higher in surrender. But it was too late. I had already ordered 'Fire'! My men, rightly, released several shots into each Fritz to ensure he posed no further threat. Nineteen Germans died needlessly. Not one of my men was harmed. A two-second delay in the order would have resulted in British casualties.

The war has changed the whole world, and it has changed the whole of me. I was at the start Private Samuel Ogden, aged twenty. Now I'm a Captain, one hundred and twenty-four! Boy to man, no-one to someone, at least to a few men. At the beginning, I took all military orders, now I give more than I take. My first platoon, some of them childhood friends, lived larger than life. Now they are dead, apart from Bertie Dale. Perhaps. Having not heard, he too might have passed away. Bertie would not succumb to his physical wounds, but rather from the sadness they wrought, his mind weaker than his body. I've changed from never reading a book to devouring pages as a cold starving man would sup hot soup. Mr Unia, my friend from India, thanks to our chance meeting in Amiens, had introduced me to a world far beyond the one I knew.

Opening a book opens the mind, takes you places beyond any destination on earth. There are no boundaries other than your imagination, and that's infinite. A simple sentence may summarise complex thoughts. Clear words of others expressed what my own muddled mind couldn't. Concise words of poets tell detailed tales. Books of fact and fiction transport us back in time and provide ideas about the future. Great engineers, historians, philosophers, writers and scientists have shared their knowledge with folk like me, exposing the limitations of my meagre education. And it is so true that the more you learn, the more you need to learn. The further you sail into the sea, the deeper its water.

But even a ragamuffin, a simple soldier, a former farmhand, can see that knowledge and words can be used for good and evil, for truth and deception, to cause war and, hopefully, bring peace.

***

Amid the oak, beech and hornbeam of Picardy's Forest of Compiègne, Marshal Ferdinand Foch's private train came smoothly to a halt at the small village of Rethondes. Steam hissed away from the bowels of the mighty engine as the driver released the pressure, force no longer needed to drive pistons. A column of smoke shot skywards sending the industrial tang of coal-dust through the clean countryside air. The fireman would occasionally shovel coal into the firebox while the train remained stationary, but using only sufficient fuel to maintain warmth throughout the railway cars.

Before stepping down from his carriage for a short stroll through the woods before dark, Foch took slow deep breaths of the musty autumn air. He scanned the forest and admired the vibrant reds, bright yellows and dull browns of the leaves as they fluttered through the still air to carpet the forest floor. Deep in his heart, he felt that every leaf represented a Frenchman who had fallen for his country. Although not fighting with weapons at the front, Foch could not forget that many women - mothers, sisters, daughters, wives and sweethearts - had also sacrificed their lives and loved ones for France, for freedom, *liberté*. And just as each fallen leaf eventually turns into earth, the bodies of his fellow citizens - over one million three hundred thousand - will become one with the soil of France, Flanders, and other countries far from home. The dead will truly become the land on which future generations stand.

Despite his contemplation, the sharp-eyed soldier noted a troop of pale yellow chanterelle. Foch told his entourage that he was surprised they were still growing so late in the season. But the weather, like life, had been abnormal for over four years. He suggested *chef de cuisine* might use them in an omelette with garlic, parsley, and, of course, a dribble of lemon juice. A young aide eagerly made a note of every word. Perhaps he harboured the ridiculous notion that Foch's personal chef would not know the recipe for his commander's favourite breakfast. Foch was an impatient man, often quick-tempered, especially after the knock to his head in a car accident earlier in the year. But this evening he was content to bide his time and enjoy the peaceful woodland in the company of his senior staff. The enemy would arrive in the morning, Friday, November 8th. Foch was looking forward with relish to greeting them. He was most insistent, however, that he would take breakfast alone before the Germans arrived. And chanterelle must be savoured slowly.

First light saw the enemy's train stop at the edge of the clearing. After a few minutes several Germans detrained and were escorted towards Foch's carriage. Instead of brandishing rifles and grenades, the delegates carried briefcases and documents: appropriate accessories for a peace agreement. After diplomatic courtesies observed with handshakes and pleasantries, the delegates climbed into Foch's carriage, assigned the number 2419 by the French railway.

Space was at a premium, but the nine senior delegates sat at the simple wooden table, hardly bigger than a house door. Foch suspected the Germans found the venue disagreeable, almost insulting. With so many spacious elegant buildings in France, it seemed demeaning to be crammed into the confines of a railway carriage for such an important meeting. But Marshal Foch was still at war, they still the enemy. He didn't care one jot for their thoughts or feelings. Nor did he consider this gathering a forum for discussion. Carriage 2419 was to be the site of abject surrender by Germany. Talks would naturally take place. But Foch had a list of demands the Germans would meet, with or without debate. He personally would take little part in the discussion. Foch introduced the meeting and, surprising the Germans, announced he would return for the final signing ceremony. Detailed discussions would be left in the capable hands of First Sea Lord Admiral Rosslyn Wemyss, the British representative, General Maxime Weygand, Foch's Chief of Staff, alongside Rear-Admiral George Hope and assistant Captain Jack Marriott.

In four and a quarter years of war, Foch had learnt to leave nothing to chance. Just in case of a double-cross, or the Germans became obstinate, Foch wanted time to finalise his plans for a new offensive, scheduled for November 14th. If necessary, he would be ready to push the Hun back to Berlin if they failed to sign the armistice within the next day or two, or reneged on its conditions after signing.

Later that day Foch heard that our *HMS Britannia* had been torpedoed at the western entrance to the Straits of Gibraltar. The ship listed to one side for over two hours before sinking. This mercifully allowed most of the seven hundred and sixty-two crew to be rescued. But fifty men lost their lives below decks, mainly due to toxic cordite fumes following the torpedo's strike. The sinking justified Foch's suspicion that not all Germans genuinely wanted peace.

Meanwhile, in the railway carriage, the terms of the armistice were presented. Matthias Erzberger, the politician sent by Germany to conduct the agreement, was accompanied by Count Alfred von Oberndorff, from the Foreign Ministry, Major General Detlof von Winterfeldt, representing the Army, and, for the Navy, Captain Ernst Vanselow. They didn't like the terms. They believed them to be too harsh, unfair and unjustified. With the German army in retreat, their options became limited by the hour. If these terms were not accepted, they ran the risk the conditions next presented would be worse.

Germany was defeated. Delegates on both sides knew it. Demonstrators flooded the streets of Berlin and many cities and towns across the land. The war must stop, change had to start. Army discipline almost collapsed. Many soldiers started making their own way home. Officers who threatened deserters with punishment found themselves ignored, beaten, or even killed by their own men. The German High Seas Fleet had already mutinied at the end of October. Despite this, their U-boats continued to pose danger for Allied shipping, as the sinking of *HMS Britannia* confirmed.

German politicians experienced as much disarray as the military. As the peace talks started Germany's Chancellor, Prince Max von Baden, the man who two days earlier had sent Erzberger and his team to France, resigned. He was immediately replaced by the socialist parliamentary leader, Friedrich Ebert. At a stroke, the

German Empire became a German Republic. And after much 'encouragement', Kaiser Wilhelm II finally came to his senses and abdicated. Many, especially Germans, expressed outraged when they discovered the Kaiser had sneaked into exile in The Netherlands. They believed he should be caught and face a firing squad. Busy and isolated in the railway carriage, guarded by hundreds of France's best troops, none of the German delegation heard of the Kaiser's abdication until the morning of Sunday November 10th. Foch took great delight in having the newspapers from Paris sent into them headlining the Kaiser's departure.

Discipline had been maintained in the German Seventeenth Army, and it decided to make a last-ditch stand on November 10th. Of all places, it chose Mons for the fight. The site where the British Expeditionary Force began fighting the war became the place where it ended, although the Canadians delivered the final blow to the obstinate Germans in the town. At 4.30 am on Monday November 11th the British and the Canadians took control of Mons. Precisely forty-five minutes later, at 5.15 am, in Foch's railway carriage in the forest, the German delegation signed the Armistice.

The Germans face tough terms. In short, Germany is forced to de-militarise and provide reparations for the immense damage they have caused. Included in the thirty-five conditions are that, within six hours of the Armistice's signing, all hostilities on land and in the air must cease. Within fourteen days all German troops must be out of France, Belgium, Luxembourg and Alsace-Lorraine. Likewise on the Eastern Front across Turkey, Austria-Hungary and Romania. The Brest-Litovsk Treaty with Russia, and the Treaty of Bucharest with Romania, must be renounced. Germany to hand over, in good condition, five thousand artillery guns, thirty thousand machine guns, two thousand war planes, and all her U-boats. The surface fleet will be interned in British waters, with only caretaker crews. Furthermore, the Germans are to deliver five thousand locomotives, one hundred and fifty thousand railway cars and five thousand lorries to the Allies. After the Germans quit the countries they invaded, they are subsequently to remove all their forces from territory on the left bank of the Rhine, with additional nineteen-mile bridgeheads to the right bank of the Rhine at Mainz, Koblenz and Cologne. These areas will be occupied by Allied and US troops, paid for by Germany.

For many, soldiers and civilians alike, the most important demand in the Armistice was the immediate release of all French, Belgian, British and Italian prisoners of war. Millions are living with the agony of not knowing whether family or friends have died or are being held captive. Even though relatives heard their loved ones had perished in battle, thousands still hoped a mistake of identity or observation of events had been made. Many relatives will not accept anything but the most certain of reports of a loved one's demise, hope outliving despair. For the Germans, until the full peace treaty is signed, their POWs will remain interned, the sea blockade against them continued.

The Armistice was signed, but The Great War carried on. Senseless though it seems, although news of the peace agreement spread rapidly along the Western Front, fighting continued to the very second the Armistice came into force: the eleventh hour of the eleventh day of the eleventh month. Whether it was pride, habit, revenge or a rigid adherence to the agreement, maintaining the symmetry of the elevens cost lives. At 10.59 am shells fired and fell and killed and maimed. At 11.00 am the shelling stopped. War to peace in the blink of an eye.

We Dukes lost several Havercake Lads in those final days, including privates Albert Barlow and Reuben Bennett. Pte Joss Hey died on the last day of the war and, from injuries, James Foster on the 13th and David Tunmore on the 17th.

The Prime Minister, David Lloyd George, told Parliament: 'At eleven o'clock this morning came to an end the cruellest and most terrible war that has ever scourged mankind. I hope we may say that thus, this fateful morning, came to an end all wars.'

***

The war is over. Its legacy remains. Its history to be told, its secrets unfold. Great joy and deep sadness, relief and regret, live side by side. Everyone knows someone the war has killed or crippled or returned in one piece, although not always in sound mind. For chaps in the depths of despondency, everything is too dark to see light. This vile but necessary war has left rivers of blood, fields of bones, seas of tears, hearts of sorrow. Grief has no time limit. Sadness will haunt millions until their dying day.

Despite our huge losses more airmen, sailors and soldiers survived than died. We struggle as individuals and as a nation to find the right balance between happiness and sadness; getting on with life while respecting the dead. Guilt hurts people when they laugh, as if it's sinful to smile after all the suffering. Others seem overly cheerful, perhaps trying too hard to hide their sadness. A few chaps are unduly downcast, wallowing in self-pity, and often those who avoided the thick of it. They need to pull up their socks, look forward, not back.

We may never know the exact numbers of deaths and injuries caused by this war, military or civilian. The sheer scale and nature of warfare makes it impossible to deal in precise numbers. As summary casualty reports come in, it looks as if the total number of military killed in the war is between eight and ten million. More than twenty-one million wounded, nearly eight million taken prisoner or missing. At least a quarter of a million British men suffered amputations. Over sixty-five million men had been mobilised in military forces around the globe. Civilians, the innocent victims of war, suffered enormously too. Nearly seven million perished, perhaps a million as a direct result of military action, the remainder lost through famine and disease. Such figures would have been unimaginable before the war. They are barely believable now.

***

A week after the war ended, we Dukes marched back to Valenciennes and into billets. It wasn't long before routine Army life returned with ceremonial drills, route marches, exercises and rifle-range shooting. Boxing, football and tug-of-war competitions started again to help keep the ranks fit and busy. On December 4th the Battalion paraded before His Majesty the King, where he presented medals.

Demobilising commenced and chaps set off home, keen to return to their families and Civvy Street. A few reluctant conscripts admitted they had grown to quite like the Army and would have happily remained in the ranks. Others homebound realised they faced a different kind of Blighty. Britain has changed, the world has changed, although it is hard to say how. The war turned the lives of so many upside down, inside out. Men, and women especially, moved into jobs and roles they might not have gained in peacetime. Demobbed men will not face anything as frightening as Fritz with a flamethrower, grenade or bayonet. They won't any longer suffer endless days in trenches as shells fall as freely as hailstones. But, like Britain itself, they will face an uncertain future in a changed and changing world.

***

Christmas Day 1918 was very special for our small cadre of pre-war regulars remaining in the 2nd Battalion. Everyone was cheery, and deservedly so. But each one of us also found quiet moments to spare thoughts for our families, friends and comrades, alive and lost. Christmas dinner in the church hall was a splendid affair with plenty to eat and drink. Officers and men mingled heartily. High jinks tomfoolery was the 'order of the day', especially when, as tradition dictates, officers serve the men pudding. Cheeky chaps gave us trivial tasks to complete, such as clearing crumbs off the table, or ordering us to fetch clean spoons after 'accidentally' dropping them on the floor. One brazen fellow dared to point out a gravy stain on his Captain's tunic and asked the Sergeant to 'take his name'. Laughter erupted. Stealing the phrase our local newspaper always writes about happy social events, 'a good time was had by all'.

Before the jollity started, in sombre mood, the Commanding Officer read a passage from the Bible telling the nativity story and the visit of the three wise men bearing gifts of gold, frankincense and myrrh. The Reverend prayed before we honoured our fallen comrades with two minutes of silence. Tears rolled down the rigid faces of many men. Others held tears back by swallowing hard or clenching teeth. During that silence, a gallery of faces of the many men I'd fought alongside rolled across my mind's eye. Alas, most dead, many injured, and some somewhere, destination unknown.

Returning to a lighter mood, one of the men read to the assembly what had become known as the Regiment's poem, *Life at Lebong*, by Thomas Atkins. It tells a soldier's story of life at the West Bengal hill station in India where our 1st Battalion is regularly based.

They say in an Indian 'ill station
You all 'ave a clinkin' good time
But I don't think Darjeeling's so cushy
I'll try an' describe it in rhyme

In the first place we're not in Darjeeling
But way down t'Khad at Lebong
It's only a thousand feet climb up
But it seems about twenty miles long

You're sweatin' and puffin' and blowin'
Before you've got 'alf way there
And you 'ave to unbutton your tunic
And wipe the muck sweat off your 'air

There ain't much to do up there neither
There isn't a pub anywhere
And as for the nursemaids, lor' love me
They drives you to utter despair

I read a short passage from the end of *A Christmas Carol* by Charles Dickens. The room cheered when I quoted Scrooge saying he would raise Bob Cratchit's salary. But chaps jeered when I said Scrooge adhered to his Total Abstinence Principle! When I finished with Tiny Tim's words 'God bless us, every one', applause rang out. I felt happy, a feeling I'd forgotten.

New Year, like standing on the crest of a hill, always provides a point to look back at the path you've travelled and forward to where you may tread. I had survived the war, my limbs intact, my mind clear, although it often replayed images I'd rather forget. Time may heal; scars will remain. Seven months earlier it looked as if we could lose the war. But we triumphed. After Mons, Le Cateau and Néry in 1914 I genuinely believed the next battle - always the next battle - would be my last. It's good to be wrong, it helps teach you what's right.

Death now holds no fear. There is nothing after death for the dead. But the will to live is stronger, because those who died fighting sacrificed themselves for those who remain. Survivors of war have a duty to thrive, as those who died had a duty to fight. Your life, my life, our living, our freedom provides proof the fallen found victory in death. Soldiers die so citizens can live. Death, for life. War, for peace.

Early in 1919 the 2nd Battalion of The Duke of Wellington's Regiment moved to Binche, west Belgium. Demobilisation had severely reduced our numbers and we reorganised within two Companies. We may have been depleted in quantity, but not in quality. Representing XXII Corps, our chaps won the First Army Championship in cross-country running. Five of the Battalion team finished in the first ten. Sergeant Garside came first, Private Bastow second. The will to win, to be the best, still the soul of Havercake Lads.

On 8th June 1919 the last of the 2nd Battalion returned to Britain. Five officers and sixty other ranks sailed from Antwerp and landed at Tilbury. The next day I travelled home via London's King's Cross. At the station's entrance, from a dark recess, a woman asked if I wanted 'company'. I couldn't reply, for I didn't know what I wanted, and walked on. 'Bugger off then, you toffee-nosed snob,' she shouted.

Eight hours later, stepping off the train at Haworth, I stood still on the platform taking a deep breath of familiar air, the air of my childhood, of happy times. I viewed the surrounding hills, 'Wuthering Heights', although now, after the flat land of Flanders, they seemed as high as the Himalayas. Among passengers arriving and departing I was the only soldier, alone, out of place at home. The station master's whistle made me to flinch. But there was no ladder to climb, parapet to clear, gunfire to face. Through its swirling clouds of smoke and hissing steam, the train chugged away. I watched it disappear, swallowed by the cutting. Up steep Bridgehouse Lane I walked, slowly, resisting the urge to march. Old Hall, the Chapel and burial ground at the bottom of Main Street looked unchanged, untouched by the war's brutality.

When the war started, Sir Edward Grey, the Foreign Secretary, declared: 'The lamps are going out all over Europe; we shall not see them lit again in our lifetime.'

Approaching home on Sun Street as darkness fell, neighbours started lighting lamps. A baby cried. I wept too - for the life in the light, and the dead in the dark.

Although tears are always for oneself.

THE END

ACKNOWLEDGEMENTS

In 2013 my wife, Kathy, alongside her day job as Advanced Nurse Practitioner, undertook a part-time PhD at King's College, London. It became clear that many hours of doctorate work would consume our otherwise shared leisure time. I'd better find something to occupy *my* evenings and weekends, while she conducted her study into insulin treated Type 2 diabetes. Write a novel, my second, seemed a good idea. She could tap on her keyboard, and I mine. Little did I realise my research would become an obsession, and the writing over three years to complete. This novel is therefore really thanks to Kathy's long-held belief in and pursuit of lifelong learning.

If Kathy laid the kindling, author and journalist Max Hastings generated the spark with his 2013 *Catastrophe: Europe Goes to War 1914*. This marvellous work investigating 'what happened to Europe in 1914?' prompted me to ask how would I have coped with military life, the conditions, the horrors? What was it *really* like to be in the thick of it? What did the men know, think, feel and do as the war dragged on?

Havercake Lad answers some of these questions, but not all. That would take 65 million books, for each fighting man had his story to tell, his own self to find.

Thanks also must go to my wonderful family for being my wonderful family, especially Jemma, Eva and Aaron, Lesley and James, Rosemary and Adrian. You can't of course choose your family, only friends, but I'd have chosen you given that choice.

Thanks to several friends too, particularly Peter, Malcolm and Vadim, who suffered endless hours of my Yorkshire 'yammer' about this book. I trust they will enjoy reading the final product more than listening to the process of its production.

Special thanks to:

Bankfield Museum, Halifax, Yorkshire: www.museums.calderdale.gov.uk
Bronte Parsonage and Bronte Society: www.bronte.org.uk
Commonwealth War Graves Commission: www.cwgc.org
Duke of Wellington's (West Riding) Regiment – Regimental Association: www.dwr.org.uk
Haworth Band: www.thehaworthband.co.uk
Imperial War Museum: www.iwm.org.uk
Tank Museum, Bovington: www.tankmuseum.org
Bill Harriman, British Association of Shooting and Conservation: www.basc.org.uk
Glyn Freeman: www.cumbriaflyfishing.co.uk
Michael Louca: www.watsonbrosgunmakers.com

BIBLIOGRAPHY

Books

Adams, Simon *Eyewitness: World War I* Dorling Kindersley in association with The Imperial War Museum 2014

Baden-Powell, Robert *Quick Training for War* Conway 2011 (First published 1914)

Bales, P *History of the 1/4th Battalion, Duke of Wellington's (West Riding) Regiment 1914 – 1919* 1920 (Available via www.naval-military-press.com)

Banks, Arthur *A Military Atlas of the First World War* Pen & Sword Books 2013 (First published 1975 by Heinemann Educational Books Ltd)

Barker, Juliet *The Brontës* Weidenfeld and Nicolson 1994

Brittain, Vera *Testament of Youth* Virago Press 1978 (First published 1933 by Victor Gollancz)

Bruce, C *History of The Duke of Wellington's Regiment [1st & 2nd Battalions]* 1927 (Available via www.naval-military-press.com)

Burgess, Christopher *The Diary & Letters of a World War I Fighter Pilot* Pen & Sword 2008

Cowper, Marcus and Pannell, Christopher *Tank Spotter's Guide* Osprey 2011

Dalrymple, William *Return of a King* Bloomsbury 2013

Doherty, Simon and Donovan, Tom *The India Corps on the Western Front* Tom Donovan Editions Ltd 2014

Doyle, Peter *The British Soldier of the First World War* Shire Publications 2008

Doyle, Peter and Walker, Julian *Trench Talk* History Press 2012

Doyle, Peter and Foster, Chris *What Tommy Took to War 1914 – 1918* Shire Publications 2014

Ferguson, Niall *Empire* Allen Lane 2003

Hastings, Max *Catastrophe: Europe Goes to War 1914* William Collins 2013

Hart, Peter *The Great War* Profile Books 2013

Holmes, Richard *Wellington: The Iron Duke* Harper Perennial 2003

Ingleton, Roy *Fortress Kent* Pen & Sword Military 2012

James, Lawrence *The Rise and Fall of the British Empire*, Little, Brown and Company 1994

Kershaw, Ian *To Hell and Back: Europe 1914 – 1949* Allan Lane 2015

La Motte, Ellen *The Backwash of War* Conway Publishing 2014 (First published 1916)

Lawrence, T E *Seven Pillars of Wisdom* Doubleday 1926

Liddell Hart, B *A History of the First World War* Pan Books 2014 (First published 1930 as *The Real War, 1914 – 1918* Faber and Faber Ltd)

MacGregor, Neil *Germany: Memories of a Nation* Allan Lane 2014

Putkowski, Julian and Dunning, Mark *Murderous Tommies* Pen & Sword Military 2012

Sargeant, Graham *The Death of the 'Dukes'* Valence House Publications 2017

Solzhenitsyn, Alexander *August 1914* Bodley Head 1971

Strachan, Hew *The First World War* Simon & Schuster 2003

Thayer, Alexander *Life of Beethoven* The Folio Society 2001 (First published 1964 Princetown University Press)

Tomalin, Claire *Charles Dickens: A Life* Viking 2011

Tomalin, Claire *Thomas Hardy: The Time-Torn Man* Viking 2006

Tombs, Robert *The English and Their History* Allen Lane 2014

Watson, Alexander *Ring of Steel* Penguin Books 2014

Westwell, Ian *Weapons of World War One* Anness Publishing 2011

Whitworth, Alan *Yorkshire VCs* Pen & Sword Military 2012

Additional sources:

Great Battles Parragon Books 2010

His Majesty's Stationery Office *Field Service Pocket Book, Infantry Training 1914, Cavalry Training, Field Service Regulations, Trench Standing Orders 1915-16, Notes on the Tactical Employment of Machine Guns and Lewis Guns, Notes on Minor Enterprises 1916, Military Law, Instructions for the Training of Platoons for Offensive Action 1917, Trench Orders, 4th Division, Instructions Regarding Recommendations for Honours and Awards 1918*

Location of Hospitals and Casualty Clearing Stations, British Expeditionary Force, 1914 – 1919 Ministry of Pensions (Reprinted by Imperial War Museum)

Up the Line to Death: The War Poets 1914 – 1918 Metheun 1964

Ordnance Survey Office, *Haworth & Lees cum Cross Roads* 1906

Illustrated London News Archive (plus Illustrated War News, The Graphic, The Tatler) 1914 - 1918

The Wipers Times Conway Publishing 2013 (First published 1916 – 1918)

#0066 - 040618 - C0 - 210/148/22 - PB - DID2212765